United Sta

The Sanitary Commission of The United States Army

SALZWASSER
VERLAG

United States Sanitary Commission

The Sanitary Commission of The United States Army

Reprint of the original, first published in 1864.

1st Edition 2022 | ISBN: 978-3-75259-164-4

Verlag (Publisher): Salzwasser Verlag GmbH, Zeilweg 44, 60439 Frankfurt, Deutschland
Vertretungsberechtigt (Authorized to represent): E. Roepke, Zeilweg 44, 60439 Frankfurt, Deutschland
Druck (Print): Books on Demand GmbH, In de Tarpen 42, 22848 Norderstedt, Deutschland

THE SANITARY COMMISSION OF THE UNITED STATES ARMY:

A SUCCINCT NARRATIVE OF ITS WORKS AND PURPOSES.

NEW YORK:
PUBLISHED FOR THE BENEFIT OF THE UNITED STATES SANITARY COMMISSION.

1864.

INTRODUCTION.

The United States Sanitary Commission may safely leave its history to be written in the Annals of the War. In that history, however, the public has an interest which calls for the occasional publication of such records of the work in progress, and such a description of its methods, purposes, and results, as shall correctly set forth the practical features of this great system of supplementary aid.

This volume has been prepared with the design of meeting the demand for a succinct narrative of the origin, purposes, progress, and present condition of the Commission's methods and departments of labor. Connected outlines, together with reviews and condensed abstracts of current reports, are made to bring forward a concise record of the work, from the period of its inception to the present time. The faithfulness of the narrative has been verified at every step, by one who has attentively observed the Commission's plans and labors from the beginning, and his object will be fully attained if the book conveys to the reader's mind a truthful and connected view of the whole scheme—past and present—of the objects, spirit, and practical operations of the Commission.

A French military writer has recently said, "It is one of the greatest characteristics of the present age, that *the cause of humanity has become identified with the strength of armies*" And, in this view, with a knowledge of our campaigns and battles, and with the records of the Sanitary Commission before us, it would be difficult to say whether this grand system of sanitary care and succor in the Federal army is more important as a work of humane benificence than as a patriotic scheme of aid to the effective strength of our military forces. In this mixed work of humanity and patriotism, the records of the Commission show that there has been untiring and generous effort to enlarge and strengthen all the regular official methods of Sanitary care and timely succor, while, by all available means of supplementary aid, a special work of *prevention* and *relief* has been successfully pursued in all the divisions of the army. The various questions that have most concerned the Sanitary Commission and the public in this supplementary work are so clearly presented in a few paragraphs of a recent article in the *North American Review*, that we can best conclude this introductory by quoting them.

"The Government is, or ought to be, the soldier's best friend, being the only friend in a situation to give him constant and efficient protection. Whatever struggles with the Medical Department the Sanitary Commission has at any time had, have always been, not in the way of obtaining rights, privileges, or opportunities for itself, of making itself more active, important and influential; but, on the contrary, always in the way of stirring up the Department to a larger sense of its own duty, a more complete occupation of its own sphere, and such a successful administration of its affairs as would tend to render the Sanitary Commission, and all other outside organizations of benificence to the army, unnecessary.

"The principle was seen from the first, and has been resolutely maintained under all circumstances, that the people's care for the soldiers, if permitted a free and spontaneous course, might become a main dependence of the army, and thus weaken the sense of responsibility and the zeal and efficiency of the official sources of supply and protection. This would be so unmeasured an evil, that, rather than incur the risk of it, it was a serious question, during the first year at least, nor has it ever since ceased to come up as a doubt, whether the regular service of the Government, left wholly to itself, would not more rapidly and thoroughly cure its own defects than when placed under any system of bolstering and supplementing which humanity and outside sympathy could invent or apply. How long and how far, it was continually asked from the very first, is it safe and wise for the nation, in its home character, to undertake to do what the Government can do, and ought to do?

* * * * * * *

"The answer to this most urgent and pertinent question is, that in a national life like our own, a democracy, where the people take a universal part in political affairs, the Government has no option in the case. The popular affections and sympathies will force themselves into the administration of army and all other affairs in times of deep national awakening. The practical question was not, is it best to allow the army to depend in any degree upon the care of the people, as distinguished from the Government? Considered on administrative grounds alone, that question, we have no doubt, shonld be answered negatively. But no such question existed in a pure and simple form. It was this question rather: How shall this rising tide of popular sympathy, expressed in the form of sanitary supplies, and offers of personal service and advice, be rendered least hurtful to the army system, and most useful to the soldiers themselves? How shall it be kept from injuring the order, efficiency, and zeal of the regular bureau, and at the same time be left to do its intended work of succor and sympathy; to act as a steady expression of the people's watchful care of their army, and as a true helper and supplementer of what the Government may find it possible or convenient to do from its own resources? It was this mixed question the Sanitary Commission found itself called to answer; and its whole plan and working has been one steady reply to it. It could not be deemed wise, much less was it possible, to discourage and deaden the active sympathies of the people. * * * * *

"The Commission knew that the average annual death-rate in armies in our former wars had been exceedingly high, and that an army of *volunteer* forces is most liable to fatal diseases. * * * * In our vast armies of volunteers, the problems of sanitary science were to be wrought out as a national and patriotic work. The death-rates of the Mexican campaign would imperil the national cause, and bring sorrow to every home in the land. Can the average sickness-rate be kept at a minimum point? Can the average death-rate from disease be reduced to a fraction of that which was registered in the Mexican war? This result the Commission believed possible. It was to be accomplished by *prevention* and by *succor*.

"The Commission was strongly impressed with the facts that the destroying angel who follows in the trail of armies 'exacts from every man to the full whatever penalties follow on the infraction of natural law;' that 'the waste of human life and the destruction of human health and happiness [in time of war] have been in all ages many times greater from disease than from actual encounter in the field, and that the faithful records of all wars are records of preventible suffering, disease, and death.' In view of these facts, and considering also that the sick and wounded must sometimes be sacrificed to unavoidable military necessity, the Commission claimed that 'all the more should they be supplied with whatever mitigation of suffering military necessities leave possible.

"Unity of plan, earnestness, patriotism, and a broad *nationality of sentiment and influence*, are inscribed upon all the methods, counsels, publications, and labors of the Sanitary Commission. The very conception and birth of its plan were shaped and quickened by this spirit of Federal loyalty. Every woman and child in our Northern homes has insensibly caught the spirit of the Commission's work while contributing their handiwork for succor through the branches of the Relief department, and the soldier himself is made happily conscious of this spirit of national unity whenever he receives sanitary relief.

"The great range and magnitude of the Sanitary Commission's work have been inevitable results of the vast increase of our forces, and of the original and fixed policy of the Commission, 'to secure for the men who have enlisted in this war that care which it is the will and the duty of the nation to give them.'

"This work has been, and must continue to be, rendered practicable by the hearty support and sympathy of our free and loyal people. It is a necessity which an advancing civilization has laid upon their hearts and their hands. And while in our peaceful homes and in our popular armies it is joyfully accepted as a work equally of patriotism and of love, the influence of this great scheme of beneficent labor has gone out to all other civilized nations as an impressive illustration of the progress of that humane Christian spirit which is augmenting the popular appreciation of the sacredness of human life and human sympathies, and which shall yet elevate the brotherhood of states and nations above the very causes of war."

THE

WORKS AND PURPOSES

OF THE

SANITARY COMMISSION.

THE UNITED STATES SANITARY COMMISSION has a history and a record which belong to the times, and in the faithfulness and success of the work which it has been commissioned to perform, every loyal heart is justly concerned.

Stirring events of the War are still so closely crowding that opportunity is not given for compiling a perfect history of the Sanitary Commission's work; but in the following pages we propose, from materials at hand, to give a faithful sketch of the progress and methods of its several departments.

Origin and Organization of the Sanitary Commission.—In an official communication addressed to the Secretary of War by the acting Surgeon-General of the Army, dated May 22d, 1861, it is stated that—

"The pressure upon the Medical Bureau has been very great and urgent; and though all the means at its disposal have been industriously used, much remains to be accomplished by directing the intelligent mind of the country to practical results connected with the comforts of the soldier by preventive and sanitary means.

"The Medical Bureau would, in my judgment, derive important and useful aid from the counsels and well-directed efforts of an intelligent and scientific commission, to be styled 'A Commission of Inquiry and Advice in respect of the Sanitary Interests of the United States Forces,' and acting in co-operation with the Bureau, in elaborating and applying such facts as might be elicited from the experience and more extended observation of those connected with armies, with reference to the diet and hygiene of troops, and the organization of Military Hospitals, etc.

"This Commission is not intended to interfere with, but to strengthen the present organization, introducing and elaborating such improvements as the advanced stage of Medical Science might suggest."

Thus early in the war, did the acting Chief of the Medical Bureau, Dr. R. C. Wood, officially and generously open the way for the beginning of a great and humane work.

Acting in concert with the Medical Bureau, a joint committee of delegates from a number of the earlier voluntary aid associations visited the National Capital soon after our forces had begun to gather there, and a few days previously to the letter above cited from the Surgeon-General, [May 18th,] that committee addressed the Secretary of War upon the subject of special measures for the sanitary protection of the rapidly gathering volunteer army, and also in reference to the utilization of voluntary contributions from the people, for the soldiers' welfare. In their preliminary address to the Secretary of War, subsequently published, that committee said:

"The present is essentially a people's war. The hearts and minds, the bodies and souls, of the whole people, and of both sexes, throughout the loyal States, are in it. * * *

"Convinced by inquiries made here of the practical difficulty of reconciling the aims of their own and numerous similar associations in other cities with the regular workings of the Commissariat and the Medical Bureau, and yet fully persuaded of the importance to the country, and the success of the war, of bringing such an arrangement about, the undersigned respectfully ask that a mixed Commission of civilians, distinguished for their philanthropic experience and acquaintance with sanitary matters, of medical men, and of military officers, be appointed by the Government, who shall be charged with the duty of investigating the best means of methodising and reducing to practical service the already active but undirected benevolence of the people towards the Army; who shall consider the general subject of the prevention of sickness and suffering among the troops, and suggest the wisest methods, which the people at large can use to manifest their good-will towards the comfort, security, and health of the Army.

"It must be well known to the Department of War that several such commissions *followed* the Crimean and Indian wars. The civilization and humanity of the age, and of the American people, demand that such a commission should *precede* our second war of independence—more sacred than the first. We wish to prevent the evils that England and France could only investigate and deplore. This war ought to be waged in a spirit of the highest intelligence, humanity, and tenderness, for the health, comfort, and safety of our brave troops; and every measure of the Government that shows its sense of this will be eminently popular, strengthen its hands, and redound to its glory at home and abroad."

In a document printed May 23d, the day subsequent to the Surgeon-General's letter, quoted above, this Committee communicated to the Secretary of War a statement in outline of the plan and powers they would recommend in the organization of the proposed Commission. In that statement the Committee suggest that—

"1. The Commission being organized for the purposes only of inquiry and advice, asks for no legal powers, but only the official recognition and moral countenance of the Government, which will be secured by its public appointment. It asks for a recommendatory order, addressed in its favor to all officers of the Government, to further its inquiries; for permission to correspond and confer, on a confidential footing, with the Medical Bureau and the War Department, proffering such suggestions and counsel as its investigations and studies may from time to time prompt and enable it to offer. * * *

"The general object of the Commission is, through suggestions reported from time to time to the Medical Bureau and the War Department, to bring to bear upon the health, comfort, and *morale* of our troops, the fullest and ripest teachings of Sanitary Science in its application to military life." * * *

"As the Government may select its own Commissioners, it is hoped that the character of the Commission will be the best warrant the Government can have that the inquiries of the Commission, both as to their nature and the manner of conducting them, will be pursued with discretion, and a careful eye to avoiding impertinent and offensive interference with the legal authority and official rights of any of the Bureaus with which it may be brought in contract."

Such, then, were the *objects* of the proposed "Commission of Inquiry and Advice in respect of the Sanitary Interests of the United States Forces": and in the specifications that follow in the statement by the Committee, to the War Department, we find the projected scheme of Inquiry and Advice presented under the heads of—1*st. Materiel of the Volunteers; 2d. Prevention; 3d. Relief.*

How the work was to be executed may be inferred from the following remarks, which we find in that document, under the head of *Prevention*:

"The Commission would inquire with scientific thoroughness into the subjects of Diet, Cooking, Cooks, Clothing, Tents, Camping Grounds, Transports, Transitory Depots, with their exposures, Camp Police, with reference to settling the question, How far the regulations of the Army proper are or can be practically carried out among the Volunteer Regiments, and what changes or modifications are desirable from their peculiar character and circumstances? Everything appertaining to outfit, cleanliness, precautions against damp, cold, heat, malaria, infection; crude, unvaried, or ill-cooked food, and an irregular or careless regimental commissariat, would fall under this head."

These printed statements, addressed to the War Department, preliminary to the institution of Sanitary Commission, bear the signatures of HENRY W. BELLOWS, D. D., W. H. VAN BUREN, M. D., J. HARSEN, M. D., and ELISHA HARRIS, M. D.

The official warrant or order for the organization of the Sanitary Commission appears to have issued from the War Office June 9th, and to have received the President's signature four days subsequently.

In that document it is ordered that "*A Commission of Enquiry and Advice, in respect of the Sanitary Interests of the United States Forces*," be organized, and that the Commission "direct its inquiries to the principles and practices connected with the inspection of recruits and enlisted men; the sanitary condition of the volunteers; to the means of preserving and restoring the health, and of securing the general comfort and efficiency of troops; to the proper provision of cooks, nurses, and hospitals; and to other objects of like nature."

That official paper proceeds to state that—

"The Commission will frame such rules and regulations, in respect of the objects and modes of its inquiry, as may seem best adapted to the purpose of its constitution, which, when approved by the Secretary, will be established as general guides of its investigation and action.

"A room with necessary conveniences will be provided in the city of Washington for the use of the Commission, and the members will meet when and at such places as may be convenient to them for consultation, and for the determination of such questions as may come properly before the Commission.

"In the progress of its inquiries, the Commission will correspond freely with the Department, and with the Medical Bureau, and will communicate to each, from time to time, such observations and results as it may deem expedient and important."

Without delay the greater number of the gentlemen named by the Surgeon-General and the Secretary of War convened at Washington, and adopted the Plan of Organization, which still remains as the broad basis and outline-scheme of its widely extended operations. This scheme, which we find republished in No. 25 of the Commission's Documents, appears to have been entirely harmonious with the views set forth by the Special Committee that had originally suggested the institution of the Commission.

The organic structure of the Commission was, from the first, and still continues to be, exceedingly simple and effective. With its President—always actively on duty—with its General Secretary, a Treasurer, and one or two Committees, its wheels have ever moved forward vigorously and unclogged. In session with but brief interruptions the first three or four months of its existence, the Commission then not only laid broad foundations for its operations, but entered upon a great variety of special inquiries and labors for the hygienic welfare of the rapidly-gathering national forces.* Immediately after its organization its President and an Associate Secretary hastened upon a visit of observation and inquiry among the gathering troops upon the Ohio and the Mississippi; while other Commissioners visited the forces at the East. Even before the first battle of the Army of the Potomac, the business of *systematic* sanitary inspection

---

* *Organization and membership of the United States Sanitary Commission.*—The present organization of the Commission is as follows:

H. W. Bellows, D.D., President, New York; A. D. Bache, LL.D., Vice-President, Washington, D. C.; George T. Strong, Esq., Treasurer, 68 Wall street, New York; W. H. Van Buren, M. D., New York; Gen. G. W. Cullum, U. S. A.; Col. A. E. Shiras, U. S. A.; Elisha Harris, M. D., New York; R. C. Wood, M. D., Assistant Surgeon Gen'l U. S. A.; Wolcott Gibbs, M. D., Cambridge, Mass.; S. G. Howe, M. D., Boston, Mass.; C. R. Agnew, M. D., New York; J. S. Newberry, M. D., Cleveland, Ohio; Rt. Rev. T. M. Clarke, Providence, R. I.; Hon. R. W. Burnett, Cincinnati, Ohio; Hon. Mark Skinner, Chicago, Ill.; Hon. Joseph Holt, Washington, D. C.; Horace Binney, Jr., Philadelphia, Penn.; Rev. J. H. Heywood, Louisville, Ky.; J. Huntington Wolcott, Boston, Mass.; Prof. Fairman Rogers, and C. J. Stillé, Philadelphia, Penn.; Fred'k. Law Olmsted, Cal.

In the earlier history of the Commission its membership was mentioned as follows: "Its presiding officer, a man of learning and a divine, was able to speak with authority of the demands of the philanthropy of the country. Of the military members, one was chief of the staff of Lieutenant-General Scott, another the active head of the Medical Bureau, another the active head of the Commissary Department; two others had previously been in the service of the War Department; and one other had been in foreign military service; one was a man of distinguished reputation in science; another was a man of science, and of medical skill and experience of a special character, and who was, at the time, also in the service of the War Department. Another had the same professional recommendation, and had also been a medical military officer; another was a physician who had been in charge of the most important Government hospital in the country; the fourth was a member of the directory of several important corporations, commercial and benevolent, and was immediately elected Treasurer of the Commission; and another

was well commenced, and the General Secretary at the Central Office had collected and made use of a large number of reports of such inspection; so that when the first startling collisions in arms occurred, at Blackburn's Ford and Bull Run, the Sanitary Commission was ready to enter upon its great field without delay.

In the published proceedings of the Commission, as early as July 9th, we find the Secretary making an extended report upon present and prospective sanitary wants of the volunteer regiments, based upon facts already observed. Encampments and camp drainage, malaria, water, tents, sun-stroke, personal cleanliness, latrines, camp police, clothing, food, and cooks, are among the subjects discussed in that report. Of the systematic sanitary inspection in camps, which had then been commenced, that report contains the following suggestive remark:

"The Secretary is inclined to believe that the greatest value will soon consist, if it does not already, in the fact, that while aiding the inspector, the attention of the regimental officers is for the first time gravely and specifically called to the sources of danger which they have allowed to be established in their camps, and which they cannot account for without acknowledging a neglect of their own, and to the information and suggestions for improvement which they will incidentally receive from the inspector." * * * * * *
* * * * * * *

---

was the chief executive officer of a public work employing more than three thousand men, and was immediately elected chief executive officer of the Commission."
* * * * * * * * *
Every member of the Commission could lay claim to a standing and reputation as an expert of some one or other of the special functions assigned by the President to the Commission as a body.

"Of the members since added, one is the Judge Advocate General of the United States, a second is a bishop of the Protestant Episcopal Church, and the three others are men of high professional standing, each holding positions of unusual trust in their respective communities."

There are now twenty-two Commissioners, and they respectively represent the several departments of learning, public experience, and humane effort with which the Sanitary Commission is legitimately concerned.

"Thus presenting themselves to make official inquiry only, they will, without special effort or intention, really be the best possible missionaries of sanitary science to the army."*

In a letter to an auxiliary committee of finance, that had been organized at New York, in aid of the Commission, published early in July, immediately after his preliminary tour through the Western encampments, Rev. Dr. Bellows, President of the Commission, makes the following graphic statements:

"Consider the prospects of 250,000 troops, chiefly volunteers, gathered not only from the out-door, but still more from the in-door occupations of life; farmers, clerks, students, mechanics, lawyers, doctors, accustomed, for the most part, to regularity of life, and those comforts of home which, above any recorded experience, bless our own prosperous land and benignant institutions; consider these men, used to the tender providence of mothers, wives, and sisters, to varied and well prepared food, separate and commodious homes, moderate toil, to careful medical supervision in all their ailments—consider these men, many of them not yet hardened into the bone of rugged manhood, suddenly precipitated by unexpected events into the field of war, at the very season of the greatest heat, transferred to climates to which they are unwonted, driven to the use of food and water to which they are not accustomed, living in crowded barracks and tents, sleeping on the bare earth, broken of rest, called on to bear arms six and eight hours a day, to make rapid marches over rough roads in July and August, wearing their thick uniforms and carrying heavy knapsacks on their backs—and what can be looked for, but men falling by the dozen in the ranks from sheer exhaustion, hundreds prostrated with relaxing disorders, and, finally, thousands suddenly swept off by camp diseases, the result of irregularity of life, exposure, filth, heat, and inability to take care of themselves under such novel conditions."

* * * * * * *

"I went in some little anxiety as to the welcome I might receive as the envoy of that mixed body, scientific, medical, military, and civil, the Sanitary Commission. But I found my way prepared before me. Tidings of the appointment of the Commission had already spread far and wide. Orders for our cordial reception had providently gone forth from the War Department.

---

* See note on page 20.

From the highest to the lowest officials the most generous courtesy, the most willing coöperation, the most grateful sympathy, flowed without any interruption from a jealous etiquette or an imperilled dignity. The officers of the Regular Army were just as kind and cordial as those of the Volunteers, and I am now sure that none of the difficulties anticipated from a conflict of powers, are at all likely to arise with a reasonable discretion on our part."

* * * * * * *

"A nobler, manlier, a more intelligent, earnest, and valuable body of troops was never gathered on the earth's surface, than the 20,000 men I saw in these camps! They are fully equal to the best of our Eastern troops in clothing and equipments, and, better than that, their equals in moral force, and directness and seriousness of purpose."

* * * * * * *

"The perils of the actual battle-field are nothing to such men; the injury their open enemies can do them, almost not worth thinking of; but will malaria, fever, pestilence—irrational and viewless enemies—be as little dangerous? No! It is before these inglorious but deadly foes that our brave boys will flinch; before their unseen weapons that they will fall! Their generous and self-devoted officers are likely to be the first to suffer. They share the hardships, they more than share the labor and exposure of their commands. They have the best purposes. But they know not yet how to control the diet, the personal habits, the ventilation, and police of their quarters and camps. They are studying war *tactics*, intent on making *soldiers;* they rashly assume that intelligent men know how to take care of themselves; and they are already finding camp dysentery seizing their regiments with a most threatening grasp. The most striking difference is already apparent in camps and troops, according as attention is given or denied to the character of the water used, the situation of the camp with reference to the prevailing winds, and to the regulation of sinks and the cleansing of tents and quarters. Two regiments, separated by a quarter of a mile only, contained, in one camp not a dozen sick men; in the other, two hundred and fifty men more or less ill with dysenteric diarrhœa, and all because one was on a plain with decent well-water at hand, the other in a wood, with a wretched puddle of black ditch-water as the only resource for drinking and cooking!"

The disasters at Bull Run, on the 18th and 21st July, called forth sympathies and offerings from every northern home, and aroused the Government and the people to a just conception of the enemy's vigor, and to the peril of delaying a day in the organization of an army adequate to the struggle for National life. And while the loyal people offered and urged larger forces of volunteers than could possibly be supplied with arms, they looked to the People's Commission of Sanitary Inquiry and Advice for the measures and the means by which the sanitary welfare of their soldier-sons in Camp and in Hospital, should be secured. Thoughtful and patriotic citizens sent timely material aid with words of encouragement and promise, while the loyal women sent such offerings as mothers, sisters, and wives could best prepare for the benefit of soldiers in hospital, so that with these offerings from women, a large store-room in the Treasury Building was crowded in a single day, even before the first flag of truce by General Wadsworth had brought back information of the enemy's denial of the request for our wounded and dead. It was this spontaneous opening of the never failing fountains of woman's sympathy and aid for the sick and wounded, that fully inaugurated the Sanitary Commission's department of *Relief.*

What was done in council by the Sanitary Commission during its protracted night-and-day sittings, at its Central Office in the Treasury Building, Washington, while the national forces were being organized, cannot here be fully stated; but the scheme of Sanitary Inspection in Camps and Hospitals was immediately and vigorously extended throughout the lines of the gathering armies, East and West; a Bureau of Sanitary and Vital Statistics was established at the Central Office; the publication of an extended and most valuable series of monographs in medicine, surgery, and hygiene, for the use of Military Surgeons, was commenced; and a great variety of practical and vitally important suggestions for improvements in hospitals, camps, recruiting and inspections, were presented to the attention of the Military authorities. The practical importance of military discipline and order, and of military education, as means of promoting the sanitary welfare and martial effectiveness of the forces, appears to have received merited attention; for we find a special committee composed of Gen. George W. Cullum, and Prof. A. D. Bache, members of the Commission, reporting by appointment a list of the resigned graduates of West Point that were presumed to be available for military service, to be officially addressed by circular. And upon the subject of military discipline and official faithfulness and authority, we find the following Resolutions published in the proceedings of the Commission, July 29th, one week subsequently to the disasters of Bull Run:

"*Resolved*, That the Sanitary Commission, in their endeavors to promote temperance, cleanliness, and comfort among the troops, have become convinced that the first sanitary law in camp and among soldiers is *military* discipline; and that unless this is vigorously asserted and enforced, it is useless to attempt and impossible to effect, by any secondary means, the great end they propose—which is the health and happiness of the army."

"*Resolved*, That looking only to the health and comfort of the troops, it is our profound conviction that any special relaxation of military discipline in favor of volunteer troops, based either upon their supposed unwillingness or inability to endure it, or upon the alleged expectation of the public, is a fallacious policy, and fraught with peril to the lives of the men and the success of the national cause; and that, speaking in the name of the families and the communities from which the volunteers come, and in the name of humanity and religion, we implore that the most thorough system of military discipline be carried out with the officers and men of the volunteer force, as the first and essential condition of their health, comfort, and morality."

"*Resolved*, That the health and comfort and efficiency of the men is mainly dependent on the uninterrupted presence, the personal watchfulness, and the rigid authority of the regimental and company officers; and that all the great defects, whether in the commissariat or in the police of camps, are radically due to the absence of officers from their posts and to the laxity of the discipline to which they are themselves accustomed—a laxity which would never be tolerated among regulars, and which, while tolerated among our soldiers, will make a mob of armed men rather than an army."

"*Resolved*, That it is the public conviction of this Commission, that the soldiers themselves, *in their painful experience of want of leaders and and protectors*, would heartily welcome a rigid discipline exerted over their officers and themselves; that the public would hail with joy the inaguration of a decisive, prompt, and rigid rule, extending alike to officers and men; and that any despondency or doubt connected with our military and national prospects, or with the health and security of our troops, would disappear with the first indications of rigid order enforced with impartial authority throughout the whole army."

"*Resolved*, That the Sanitary Commission assure Major-General McClellan in advance, of all the moral support and sympathy of their numerous constituents, and beg him to believe that the humane, the intelligent, the religious, the patriotic, will uphold his hands in every endeavor to communicate a spirit of subordination, fidelity, and obedience to the troops, even by resort, if found necessary, to the utmost rigor of military law, believing that the health, comfort, and efficiency of the army are all united in their dependence on a strict, uniform, and all-pervading military discipline."

What was being done by the Sanitary Commission in camps and in hospitals during the two or three months succeeding the first battles, would best be told by the Actuary of its Statistical Bureau, and by the journals and balance sheets of its Relief Department, or by the hundreds of hospital and regimental surgeons, with whose daily service and wants the Sanitary Inspectors had made themselves familiar. From the day contributions commenced flowing to its treasury, the Commission began to supplement special wants in the military hospitals; and there is an impressive significance in those orders and receipts for such supplementary relief to the sick and wounded. The first we find on record is an order for water-beds, and then, for the first hospitals, at Alexandria and Washington; it was—

"*Resolved*, That the following articles be procured for immediate use in the general hospitals: 100 small tables for writing in bed, 100 iron wire cradles for protecting wounded limbs, 30 boxes of dominoes, 30 checker-boards, 5 lbs. of Delphinum."

And not only did the Commission express concern for the comfort and welfare of the individual patients, by thus tenderly remembering their wounds, their social wants, and bodily discomforts, but it specially investigated the hygienic condition and medical wants of the hospitals,* reporting to the proper authorities their structural and administrative defects, and preparing plans and details for the required improvements; while its treasury paid the wages of Cadet surgical-dressers, until they

---

* In the Report of the Hospital Committee, adopted by the Commission, July 31st, 1861, (*Document No.* 23,) we find the following statement:—

"But the principal want experienced by the sick, was found by your Committee to be clean and appropriate Hospital clothing. But for the liberal forethought of the benevolent women of the nation, our soldiers would have been compelled to lie sick and wounded in the clothes in which they entered the Hospital wards, and which, in many cases, had not been changed or even washed for weeks before. Many had been already supplied, and your Committee had the satisfaction of seeing that every sick man in Hospital was fully provided with a proper suit of clothing, by the authority of the Commission."

"No available provision being made by Government for the washing of the clothing worn by volunteers on their entering Hospital, the Committee secured the authority of the Commission for employment of laundresses for this purpose; so that when the soldier is ready to leave the Hospital and resume his duties, his clothing will be clean and fit for use."

"The services of a barber were also procured for the sick, and your Committee can bear witness that he contributed not a little to their cleanliness and comfort. Wire frames for the protection of wounded limbs from pressure of bedclothes, were found to be wanted, and they were supplied."

* * * * * * * *

"Another subject was recognized by your Committee as possessing much interest and importance, viz.: the provision of systematic and reliable means of identifying the remains of soldiers dying in the General Hospitals, and of properly marking the graves in which they are interred, so that the reasonable inquiries of friends and relations may be properly answered. This matter was brought before the Commission, and referred to a Special Committee, for immediate action."

"Your Committee venture to embody their conclusions in the form of suggestions, and would submit to the Commission (2dly) the propriety of recommending to Government that hereafter instead of hiring old buildings for General Hospitals they should order the erection of a sufficient number of wooden shanties or pavilions of appropriate construction, and fully provided with water for bathing, washing, and water-closets, and ample arrangements for ventilation and for securing warmth in winter, to accommodate from thirty to sixty each, and to be sufficiently distant not to poison each other. This suggestion embodies the latest and best views as to the construction of hospitals, and its adoption would save both lives and money."

"If the present hospitals are to be occupied during the fall and winter months, some plan should be at once adopted and applied, by the competent authorities, to correct their architectural defects, to provide facilities for bathing and water-closets, to introduce water on each floor, and to separate the dead-houses from the wards occupied by the sick. Measures should also be taken to improve their ventilation, and for their thorough warming in winter."

could be recognized by law and the regulations; and its Sanitary Inspectors furnished to the surgeons of regiments and hospitals in the malarious districts the necessary prophylactics. The work of sanitary inspection was vigorously pushed forward, and the train of evils that imperilled the health of recruits, was measurably controlled, and the more important causes of special suffering, discomfort, and dissatisfaction among the volunteers were pointed out and remedied. By the Commission's agency a receiving station and a Soldiers' Rest, were established at Washington, with special means of providing suitable care for the sick or specially needy, as well as for supplying the means for cleansing, rest, and refreshment to the multitudes of weary, unwashed, and hungry soldiers that daily crowded in the vicinity of the Washington railroad depot, impatiently waiting assignment and rations, or transportation. Similar "Rests" and "Homes," for way-worn volunteers were soon established at the West, and elsewhere; while to the proper departments of Government, at Washington, the officers of the Commission faithfully presented the special wants and perils of the regiments, in regard to malaria, to special causes of home-sickness and of insubordination, to camp vices, and suggestions in respect of rations, camp cooking, &c. And in the printed catalogue of the topics of specific inquiry for the guidance of the Camp Inspectors, judicious direction was given to the investigation, in every regiment, of some two hundred practical questions relating to the hygienic welfare of the men in the field.

The Sanitary Commission's work in camp and hospitals had, at this early day, manifestly secured for it, in a remarkable degree, the hearty confidence and support of the people and the Government. And it certainly was no trivial task adequately to meet or anticipate the rapidly augmenting demands of the accumulating forces. Yet this appears to have been well accomplished, for we find the General Secretary early in December, 1861, reporting the reception at the central office of more than four hundred full returns of the stated schedules of inquiry from regimental camp inspections, and at the same time presenting his own careful deductions from such returns of two hundred regiments whose sanitary history and wants had been specially studied and reported by the Sanitary Inspectors during the months of September and October.

To obtain a just conception of the magnitude of the work thrown upon the Commission during the first six months of its operations, the reader has but to recall the rapidly crowding events of those first months of our national struggle.

The 75,000 volunteers and State troops, under the President's call of April 15th, did not complete their three months' service without sharing in the earlier benefits of the Sanitary Commission's labors; and of the seventy-five regiments, under the levy of May 3d, of soldiers for the war, scarcely a battalion failed to be reached by the Sanitary Inspectors and the Commission's benefactions either before or soon after the first series of conflicts into which they were led. And we think it may be asserted, that some of these hastily recruited regiments early became so effectually indoctrinated in the practical teachings of the Commission that they vied, and have continued to vie with regulars and veterans in camp police, good discipline, high health, and military effectiveness. We can never forget the impression left upon our mind as a civilian, visiting a regiment of this class of those early volunteers, upon the Chickahominy, during the severest of the Peninsula Campaign; a full regiment having but *four* men *sick* in general and regimental hospitals—and this was a regiment that never neglected its *camp police* and its *camp cooking*, even when bivouacking. To this regiment, during its first fortnight in camp, in July, 1861, the Sanitary Commission had assigned Mr. Sanderson and a skilled assistant to teach two men in every company the art of preparing the army rations, and those men and their companies were apt pupils. Among the seventy-five regiments of that first levy for the war were many excellent examples of the influences of the hygienic teachings of the Sanitary Commission, and, as in the remarkable instance mentioned by Baron Steuben* among the volunteers of the Revolution, these good examples were widely contagious. But before these seventy-five regiments had all been reached by the Commission, Congress, being aroused by the early disasters, in July, had authorized the organization of an army of 500,000 men, and quickly the President's call was issued for 300,000 volunteers, and with it came the demands of the people and the petition of the Sanitary Commission for the greatest military vigor and good discipline, to render the national forces in the highest degree effective, reliable, and physically and morally strong.

To authorize and call forth such an enlargement of the army, and to accumulate the necessary equipage and materiel for such an army, was a business scarcely more important or difficult than

---

* Baron Steuben's efforts, under WASHINGTON's direction, for the improvement of the untrained and freshly recruited forces of the Revolution, happily illustrate what may be accomplished by skillfully preparing and presenting *perfect examples*. Of his first labors as military instructor, with the title of "Inspector-General," of the volunteers then gathering for the war of the Revolution, Steuben writes:—

"I commenced operations by drafting one hundred and twenty men from the line, whom I formed into a guard," &c. I made this guard my military school. I drilled them myself twice a day......I often took the musket myself to show the men, &c.. ..All my Inspectors were-present at each drill." [A Colonel from each Division, and a Major from each Brigade.] "We marched together, wheeled, &c., &c., and in a fortnight my company knew perfectly well how to bear arms, had a military bearing, knew how to march, &c., &c."......"I had my company of guards exactly as I wished them to be. They were well dressed, their arms clean and in good order, and their general appearance quite respectable."

* * * * * * * *

"Having gained my point, and dispersed my apostles, *the Inspectors*, my new doctrine was eagerly embraced. I lost no time......I applied my system to battalions, afterwards to brigades, and in less than three weeks I executed manœuvres with an entire division."—*Kapp's Life of Steuben. Chapter* VI.

the adjustment of the means and agencies that should insure a high health-rate in all those untrained and unacclimated forces; yet this was the problem which the Government had committed to the Sanitary Commission as the accredited aid and co-worker of the War Department and the Medical Bureau. How the Sanitary Commission attempted the solution of this problem, and how it discharged the duties germain to it, in council, in communications with the War Office, and with military commandants in the camps and in hospitals, will certainly fill an instructive page in the history of this great war against the rebellion. The following quotations from the Commission's Report to the Secretary of War, December, 1861, set forth very interesting facts respecting certain results and plans of operation up to that period:—

"Fourteen well qualified physicians are now employed by the Commission, each having a defined portion of the army under his observation. Six other gentlemen, each possessed of special acquirements, are engaged on special duties. A list of their names and of the posts to which they are respectively assigned, is appended. It is proper to record the fact that they have in several cases withdrawn from positions far more remunerative than that now occupied by them, and have undertaken their present duty from motives of the highest benevolence and patriotism."

* * * * * * *

"The influence, however, which officers unconsciously receive through the mere direction of their attention to neglected duties, by the inquiries which the Inspectors have need to address to them, constitutes the chief part of the value of the services of the Commission. This, of course, cannot be specified and recorded. But the effect of the advice given by the Inspectors of the Commission is found not to be confined to the particular camp visited, or to the officers with whom they converse. The example of one regiment in reforming abuses and enforcing sanitary laws is very generally followed by others near it, and an emulation is excited among company and regimental officers, the beneficial effects of which have been noticed in many cases where an ill-regulated regiment has been transferred to the neighborhood of a cleanly, well-policed, thoroughly drained, and salubrious camp."

* * * * * * *

"There is no doubt that systematic attention to sanitary laws is becoming more generally understood to be a part of the duty of a military officer; and it is satisfactory to observe that the more recently enlisted regiments begin better than those enlisted at the opening of the campaign, and improve faster. This, in part, may be fairly attributed to the publications of the Commission, which, to the number of more than one hundred and fifty thousand, have been scattered through the country and largely reprinted in the newspapers."

* * * * * * *

"The Commission has distributed gratuitously to the surgeons and officers of the volunteers, three thousand each, on an average, of five concise treatises on the best means of preserving health in camps, and on the treatment of the sick and wounded in camp and the battle-field. As the surgeons of the volunteer army are almost altogether drawn from civil practice, and as no books, or even circulars of instruction in regard to their novel responsibilities, have yet been supplied them by Government, these modest works have been found of considerable value.

"*Camp Police, in general.*—Of the camps inspected, five (5) per cent. were in admirable order, forty-five per cent. fairly clean and well policed. The condition of twenty-six (26) per cent. was negligent and slovenly, and that of twenty-four (24) per cent. decidedly bad, filthy, and dangerous.

"In those camps which are referred to as in a neglected and positively bad condition, some or all of the following sources of danger to the health of the men were found to exist, viz: drains wanting or clogged up, and retentive of stagnant water; the camp streets and spaces between the tents littered with refuse food and other rubbish, sometimes in an offensive state of decomposition; slops deposited in pits within the camp limits, or thrown out broadcast; heaps of manure and offal close to the camp, and the privies neglected.

"In about two-thirds of the camps, the streets were found fairly clean, but in only about one-third were the edges of tents, the spaces between them, and the camp drains, entirely free from litter and rubbish. On the whole, a very marked and gratifying improvement in the custom of the volunteer regiments in respect of camp police has occurred during the summer. Faults in this respect, which were at one time generally regarded as unworthy of the attention of regimental officers, are now considered disgraceful, and the number of camps in which officers and men take pride in maintaining an exact and severe camp police, is rapidly increasing."

* * * * * * *

"*Military Hospitals.*—At the close of the October session of the Commission it was understood that Government would at once commence the erection of two cheap temporary model hospitals at Washington, in conformity with plans carefully prepared by a committee of the medical members of the Commission, and approved by it as embodying the latest results of sanitary science. These plans have been formally approved by the Quartermaster-General, the Commander-in-Chief, and the Medical Director of the Army of the Potomac, and the ground for the example buildings has been staked out."

* * * * * * *

"*Volunteer Hospital, and other Supplies.*—The Commission did not, at first, contemplate furnishing hospital and other supplies to the army on any large scale, but confined itself mainly to the duties of 'inquiry and advice' assigned it by the Secretary of War. It could not refrain, however, without doing violence to the human sympathies of its members, from supplying some few of the more pressing wants which they saw existing in the military hospitals of Washington and elsewhere. The absence of any hospital fund, already referred to, made these wants remediless, except by the Commission, or more properly, by the generous and patriotic people of the loyal States, whom the Commission represents as their agent and almoner."

* * * * * * *

"*Amount of Supplies Distributed.*—The demand for articles of clothing and protection for the sick has naturally increased during the past month, but the means placed by the community at the disposal of the Commission has enabled its Inspectors to keep pace with this increase. Thirty-four thousand four hundred and eighty-one articles of hospital clothing were distributed from the Washington depot alone during the month of November, besides a large bulk of unclassified articles.

"The supplies thus distributed from the Washington depot have been issued to one hundred and thirty-six hospitals; twenty of which were general, and one hundred and sixteen regimental. The average number of articles supplied to each was a little more than two hundred. About one thousand are now daily distributed from the same depot, and their value in money is not less than five hundred dollars.

"At the Cleveland depot sixty-nine thousand articles have been received since its organization; and fifty-one thousand, besides several tons of articles of hospital diet, have been already issued from it to the army of the West, at various points.

"From the Wheeling depot, four thousand eight hundred and fourteen articles of bedding and clothing, alone, have been distributed."*

Of the work of Special Relief—then designated Irregular Relief, one of the most systematic and interesting department of labor under the Sanitary Commission, we must speak in a subsequent page; and so of the Statistical Bureau; the system of Mortuary and Burial Records, the Publication Department, etc., all of which were in complete operation before the close of the year 1861. The Report, No. 40 of the Commission's current documents, from which we have just been quoting, contains in its hundred pages a very condensed statement of the first six months' work of the Commission, in its several departments.

To every unbiassed and discerning mind, whether in the medical profession, or the army, the Sanitary Commission has manifestly been, from its organization until now, the most unfaltering and faithful friend and ally of the Medical Department, and of all that is good and faithful in it. And we believe it may safely be stated, that the British Sanitary Commission in the Crimea excited far greater animosity and as-

---

* The *financial basis* of the Sanitary Commission seems to have been simply faith in the intelligent sympathy and co-operation of the people. In this Report to the Secretary of War, dated December, 1861, the Commission makes the following statement respecting finances:—

"As the Commission was to receive no pecuniary support from Government, it was under the necessity of calling on private liberality for the fund it required to sustain it. Its appeal for this purpose was responded to with promptitude and liberality, and the Commission was thus enabled to go into operation without delay. The Life Insurance Companies of Massachusetts, New York and New Jersey, were most generous in their contributions—one of the number (the New York Life Insurance Company of N. Y.,) having given five thousand dollars to the objects of the Commission. It has received in money from all sources, up to the 25th of November last, twenty-eight thousand one hundred and seven dollars, ($28,107,) the larger portion of which has been contributed by citizons and institutions of New York. Whether public liberality can be depended on as a permanent source of supply is uncertain. Should it fail, the Commission will be under the necessity of terminating its labors, unless Government should see fit to assume its support."

perity of feeling in army and bureau circles than have ever yet been called forth in our army by the U. S. Sanitary Commission. Not that this Commission has been less faithful and bold in its inquisitions, and in efforts for reform and improvement, than the Crimean Commission, but the contrary rather. Indeed, it should be stated, to the credit of the Medical Staff and Military Commandants of our armies, as well as the honor of the Commission, that its enlightened and well-directed zeal in specific efforts, its fearlessness and candor, and its broad and forecasting plans and practical undertakings, have, from the first, commanded for it and its officers the fraternal sentiments, the profound respect, and the gratitude of all our best Generals and Surgeons in the field.

The Sanitary Commission has not been silent when important principles or facts were to be asserted, nor have its counsels been timid, indefinite, or hesitating, when its advice or leadership in specific reforms and innovations have been necessary. It fearlessly attacked the policy of *perpetual succession by seniority alone* in the medical service of the army, and as boldly grappled with the radical vices and defects of *usages and regulations* that not only permitted but compelled delay and insufficiency in the care and provision for sick and wounded soldiers, in field and in hospital. The Commission was in duty bound to discover, and expose the causes of such faults, and it heartily accepted and discharged the onerous duty.

The following paragraphs, which we extract from the Report to the Secretary of War, in December, 1861, indicate the spirit and objects of the Sanitary Commission in dealing with questions liable to excite controversy and opposition where radical reforms were demanded;

"The object had in view by the Commission can be effectually accomplished only by the direct action of Government, through officers who can order, where the Commission can only advise. The cause our armies have to defend is alone dearer to the people than are those who have to suffer in its defence. The strength and mobility of the army cannot be sacrificed to the care of its sick and wounded. The sick and wounded should be sacrificed unflinchingly, to every unavoidable military necessity; but all the more should they be supplied with whatever mitigation of suffering military necessities leave possible. And these should be furnished them, not as if a hard master were driving a bargain with them—as in the commutation of a board contract—but as if the love and pity of mothers, wives, sweethearts, and sisters, were exercised with the far-seeing providence, boldness, ingenuity, tact and industry of true military generalship—Surgeon-Generalship.

"The duty of guarding against the defeat of our armies by disease, needs to be undertaken as earnestly, as vigilantly, with as liberal a policy, and with as resolute a determination, as any other military duty.

"To secure this result, the Commission is convinced that a higher place needs to be accorded the medical staff in the organization of the army. Its relations with all departments and all ranks, as well as with the Government itself, needs to be more intimate, confidential, and influential.

"Whatever and whoever stands in the way of this, the Commission wants put out of the way. But if an impression prevails in any quarter that the members of the Commission, in their devotion to this purpose, have been over-zealous, or sought, individually or collectively, to bring it about by action not absolutely within their assigned duty, or that they have used any indirect or unworthy means therefor, that impression is without the smallest foundation in truth."

* * * * * * *

"The one point which controls the Commission is just this: a simple desire and resolute determination to secure for the men who have enlisted in this war that care which it is the will and the duty of the nation to give them. That care is their right, and, in the Government or out of it, it must be given them, let who will stand in the way."

Early in its session, during the winter of 1861–2, Congress revived its discussions upon the medical and sanitary care of the army. The occasion for enlarging and radically improving the organization of the army medical service had arrived; a variety of new or revised acts were being presented—each based upon views and purposes more or less limited by personal interests—and all of the bills too incomplete and inadequate for the emergency. Enjoying the confidence and counsels of the chief military authorities of the army, and being in a position to confer advisedly with the Military Committees of Congress, the Sanitary Commission was freely consulted in reference to the hygienic and medical wants of the volunteer forces, and it accepted the responsible duty of aiding in the preparation and advocacy of the New Medical Act which was finally agreed upon by both Houses of Congress. By that Act a special Corps of Sanitary Inspectors was ordered to be appointed from the staff of regular and volunteer surgeons; the number of regular Surgeons and Assistant Surgeons was ordered to be increased; the Corps of Medical Cadets was enlarged, and needless restrictions upon the employment of hospital assistants were removed, and the hands of medical purveyors were so unloosed as to enable surgeons instantly to meet the wants of their patients. And, lastly, that Act provided for the appointment, by the President and Senate, of a Surgeon-General, upon the ground of merit and fitness.

The Sanitary Commission had clearly won the right to a preponderating opinion in the choice of candidates, and when consulted, it unhesitatingly expressed its preference, and gave good reasons for such choice. Dr. WILLIAM A. HAMMOND, an Assistant Surgeon of the regular army, was duly nominated and confirmed as Surgeon-General. In the army he was known as a medical officer of rare ability and great strength of character, whose patriotism and *esprit de corps* had, at the very opening of the war, impelled him to relinquish a Professorship and the tempting professional relations of civic life, to resume his former rank and service in the Medical Staff: to the scientific world he was favorably known as a distinguished physiologist, and as an assiduous student of medical science in its conservative and higher applications; and his researches and publications had won for him a high position as a physician and scholar of advanced and definite views; while, in the estimation of the Sanitary Commission, his claims to pre-eminent qualification and fitness for the immense responsibilities of the Medical Bureau rested scarcely less upon proved ability in service than upon his eminent attainments;—for Dr. HAMMOND, in his published official Reports of Inspection in Hospitals and Camps, had displayed a capacity to grasp with peculiar power all those practical questions of military hygiene with which the Medical Department is concerned, and upon which the problem of needed reforms mainly depended.

In the prime of life, and with endowments—physical and mental—adequate to the vast responsibilities of the Medical Bureau of the Army, SURGEON-GENERAL HAMMOND entered upon his labors at the critical period when the largest resources of his department of the service were overdrawn, and when the greatest promptitude, foresight, and expansion, were demanded alike by humanity and the exigencies of the military service. Five hundred thousand troops were in the field, and all the armies were moving rapidly. The military hospitals contained a crowded population of sick and wounded men, and that vast population of needy sufferers was daily augmenting with great rapidity. The national victories at Mill Spring, Fort Donelson, Pittsburg-landing, Island No. 10, Hilton Head, Fort Pulaski, Roanoke Island, Newbern, and New Orleans, had not only overwhelmed the means and capacity of the military hospitals, but had increased greatly the causes of disease. The Army of the Potomac, in its Sisyphus-like movements upon Manassas and back to the Potomac and the Peninsula, after its protracted hybernation, had left many thousands, or *nearly six per cent.* of its force, in the general hospitals about Washington; and, with insufficient medical and hospital supplies, that model army had plunged into the swamps and impracticable mud-fields between the York and James rivers. Over mud-roads, and in the storms of early spring, that noble army toiled on,—marching and trenching, on picket, and in camps more perilous to health than any duty,—until many more, or *nearly ten per cent.* of the soldiers that moved upon Yorktown and Williamsburg had succumbed to disease and exhaustion before the beginning of June; and upon the day we occupied the former town the Sanitary Commission, by authority of General McClellan, undertook the responsible and very necessary duty of immediately transporting to Northern hospitals the many thousands of sick and disabled soldiers that were left in peril and want, as the army moved up the Peninsula. How the Commission did this and many other things of the kind, and what occurred to mark its spirit and test its means and their adaptability, during that memorable campaign, we shall presently mention.

For a moment, in this place, reverting to the relations of the Sanitary Commission to the Medical Department, it should be particularly noted that, while persistently praying and laboring for such reforms and new regulations in the Medical and Sanitary administration as would effectually unfetter its staff of surgeons and purveyors, and promptly provide ample life-saving means and measures, the Commission undoubtedly hoped for an opportunity to withdraw some of its more expensive and extraordinary agencies from the field. The new corps of Sanitary Inspectors, as well as all the other enlargements and reforms ordered in the New Medical Act, tended somewhat to relieve the Commission from responsibility and expense. But the improved regulations and appointments under that Act were not confirmed until upon the Peninsula, and upon the Cumberland and the Tennessee, the Mississippi and the Atlantic coast, the progress of our arms, and the vast increase of wounds and sickness, had more than quadrupled the demands upon the Medical Bureau, as well as upon the Sanitary Commission. The month of May, 1862, had opened with the progress of our forces through Yorktown and Williamsburg and up the Pamunkey, the occupation of New Orleans, and the rapid progress and enlargement of the armies that had simultaneously and successfully pressed forward upon the rebel territory, throughout its extended coastwise and river-flanked borders. At this period, the *constant sickness-rate* of the Federal army had reached about one-seventh the total force,—the permanent and regimental hospitals together containing more than 100,000 sick and wounded,—and the ratio of this sickness-rate was rapidly increasing in the army of the Potomac, having been more than doubled in two months.

For the Sanitary Commission to withdraw any of its agencies, or retrench in its offerings of supplementary aid and supplies, both for the work of preventing disease and for mitigating the sufferngs of the sick and wounded, was manifestly impossible at such a period. Its work went on. The public demanded it; the new Surgeon-General required and appreciated its presence everywhere in the Army; and everywhere the soldier, and every right-minded officer, alike desired and sought the aid of the Commission.

We had begun to mention the new demands upon the Sanitary Commission in General McClellan's campaign upon the Peninsula, but there was nothing to distinguish its work in that march of the Potomac Army, and its heroic struggles, more than has characterized the Commission's ordinary work in the other grand armies at other periods,—except it be that the events of that campaign were so condensed and so great, the necessities and care of sick and wounded soldiers so urgent, and the Commission's work, in its surprising and rapid expansion so near and so impressive, that what the Commission did in that eventful campaign, and why it did it, furnish to the world an epitome of its purposes, its methods, its means, and its beneficent power. Yet, the record of the Sanitary Commission's work during the Peninsula Campaign is mainly a record of its single "Department of Relief,"—a department that must necessarily be kept subordinated to that of Sanitary Inquiry and Advice. And so pregnant with interest is the record of that department of the work during the Peninsula campaign, that a history of the Commission's usefulness would be incomplete without a special notice of it. Let the "*Hospital Transports*"* tell, imperfectly it must be confessed, what that work was. We extract only the following paragraphs:

"A sudden transfer of the scene of active war from the high banks of the Potomac to a low and swampy region, intersected with a net-work of rivers and creeks, early in the summer of 1862, required appliances for the proper care of the sick and wounded, which did not appear to have been contemplated in the Government arrangements." * * * *

HOSPITAL TRANSPORT "DANIEL WEBSTER,"
CHEESEMAN'S CREEK, April 30, 1862.

"I received General Meigs' order under which this ship came into our hands on Friday. She was then at Alexandria, and could not be got over the shoals to Washington. It was not till near night that I was able to get a lighter, and this, after one trip, was taken off to carry reinforcements to McDowell at Fredericksburg. I succeeded before daylight of Saturday in getting a tug at work, and by the next morning (Sunday) had her hold full. At eleven o'clock got the hospital company on board." * * * * * *
* * * * * * * * *

"*May 1st.*— * * * * * * The Commission has here at present, besides the *Daniel Webster*, one or two storeships, and the *Wilson Small*, a boat of light draught, fitted up as a little hospital, to run up creeks, and bring down sick and wounded to the transports. She is under the care of Dr. C., and has her little supply of hospital clothing,

---

* HOSPITAL TRANSPORTS: *A Memoir, etc.* Boston: 1863.

beds, food, &c., always ready for chance service. There is also a well-supplied storehouse ashore. * * * *

* * * * * * * *

Furnished wine, tea, and bread, to a surgeon who had been told that the Commission's flag was flying here, and had come seven miles across the swamps, and rowed out to us in a small boat to try for these things."

* * * * * * * *

"*May 5th.*—On Sunday, the *Ocean Queen*, coming up from Old Point, grounded about five miles off the harbor, and I went down, and put a few beds and men on board." * *

* * * * * * * *

"I had sent the *Webster* to sea, and with Mrs. ——— and sister, B., and some two or three others, started in the *Small* to go to the telegraph and mail, and to bury the body of a patient who had died in the night. It was raining hard. When we reached the shore, there was no post-office, no telegraph,—nothing of the military station left, except some wagons and transports. Our storehouse was a mile back. I left a portion of our party to move the goods from it on board the barge, and started in the *Small* for Yorktown, to which I presumed head-quarters would have been moved." * 1 * *

* * * * * * * * *

"As I pulled out through the vessels at the wharf, I saw to my surprise two small "stern-wheel" steamboats coming alongside the *Queen*, one on each side. Hastening on board, I found that these boats were loaded with sick men, whom an officer in charge was about to throw off upon the *Queen*. They were the sick of regiments which had been ordered suddenly forward last night, and which were at this very moment engaged in the battle of Williamsburg; we could hear the roar of artillery. They had been sent during the night by ambulances to the shore of Wormley's Creek, where a large number had been left, the officer assured me, lying on the ground in the rain, without food or attendance." * * * * *

* * * * * * * * *

"The boat from Baltimore brought six excellent New York surgeons, twenty-six nurses, and ten surgical dressers (medical students). I got them all on the *Small*, and, having succeeded in obtaining the more important supplies in limited quantities, at noon left for Yorktown. On reaching here we found the "stern-wheelers" again alongside, and over three hundred patients on board; many very sick indeed, some delirious, some comatose, some fairly *in articulo*. The assistant-surgeons, left behind at the abandoned camps, are too anxious to be rid of them, so as to move with their regiments, and have surgery of war. And as their orders authorize it, they hurry them off to us in this style, after a day's ride in army wagons, without springs, over such a country, without roads, as I described last week. They were horribly filthy, and there was no time to clean them, often not to undress them, as, sick and fainting, they were lifted on board." * * * * * *

* * * * * * * * *

"Here were one hundred miserably sick and dying men, forced upon us before we had been an hour on board; and tug after tug swarming round the great ship, before we had a nail out of a box, and when there were but ten pounds of Indian meal and two spoons to feed them with. No account could do justice to the faithful industry of the medical students and young men."

* * * * * * *

"Sick men were at this time being carted into Yorktown from the various abandoned camps in the vicinity, and the Sanitary party going on shore after the departure of the *Queen*, these were found lying in tiers in the muddy streets, while tents were being pitched and houses cleared for their accommodation. Several wagon-loads of hospital supplies were sent to them from the store-boats of the Commission; twenty-five dollars were given to the surgeon in charge, to be used to stimulate the exertions of his limited force of attendants, and for the purchase of odds and ends, and he was informed that, if more should be required, it would be provided by the Commission, and then the company started on their little boat for West Point, where a battle was reported in progress."

A month later, we find this thrilling record continuing as follows—narrating events in the Commission's work, after the battle of Fair Oaks:

"The Commission boats were all here, and ready to remove the wounded of the battle of the 1st and 2d of June. They filled and left with their accustomed order and promptitude."

* * * * * * *

"*June 5th.*—"We had been helping the ladies on the *Elm City* all night, had returned to our quarters, and just washed and dressed, when Captain —— came on board, to say that several hundred men were lying at the landing—that the *Daniel Webster* No. 2 had been filled, and the surplus was being sent on board the *Vanderbilt*—that the confusion was terrible; there were no stores on board either vessel. Of course the best in our power had to be done. Our supply-boat *Elizabeth* came up."

* * * * * * *

"The *Knickerbocker* had, by estimate, three hundred and fifty on board. The night being fine, many were disposed of on the outer decks, and before I left, at eleven o'clock, nearly all had been washed, dressed, and put to bed decently, and were as comfortable as circumstances would admit of our making them. All had received needed nourishment, and such surgical and medical attention as was immediately demanded. Leaving the *Knickerbocker* in this satisfactory condition, I came back in a small boat, at midnight, to the landing, where I found that the *Elm City* already had five hundred wounded on board. I ordered her to run down and anchor near the *Knickerbocker*. There had been a special order in her case from the Medical Director to go to Washington. (I judge that this was given under the misapprehension that she had failed to go to Yorktown, and had her sick still on board.) She was unable to go at once for want of coal, which could not be furnished her till the evening of the next day (Monday). This finished the Commission's boats for the present. The *State of Maine* had been ordered to the landing by the Harbor-master, and the wounded remaining on shore, excluded from the *Elm City*, were flocking on board of her. Our ladies on the *Elm City* sent them some food, and we put on board from our supply-boat bedding and various stores."*

* * * * * * *

---

* The following beautiful tribute to the Commission's Transport work and its women helpers, we extract from an article in the *Atlantic Monthly*:—

"Amidst all the heroism of daring and enduring which this war has developed, amidst all the magnanimity of which it has shown the race capable, the daring the endurance, the greatness of soul which have been discovered among the men and women who have given their lives to this work, shine as brightly as any on the battle field—in some respects even more brightly.

* * * * * * *

"Theirs is the dark and painful side, the menial and hidden side, but made light and lovely by the spirit that shines in and through it all. Glimpses of this agency," (the Sanitary Commission,) "are familiar to our people; but not till the history of its inception, progress and results is calmly and adequately written out and spread before the public, will any idea be formed of the magnitude and importance of the work which it has done. Nor even then. Never, till every soldier whose lost moments it has soothed, till every soldier whose flickering life it has gently steadied into continuance, whose waning reason it has softly lulled into quiet, whose chilled blood it has warmed into healthful play, whose failing frame it has nourished into strength, whose fainting heart it has comforted with sympathy—never, until every full soul has poured out its story of gratitude and thanksgiving, will the record be complete; but long before that time, ever since

"At the time of which I am now writing (Monday afternoon), wounded men were arriving by every train, entirely unattended, or with at most a detail of two soldiers, two hundred or more of them in a train. They were packed as closely as they could be stowed in the common freight-cars, without beds, without straw, at most with a wisp of hay under their heads. Many of the lighter cases came on the roof of the cars. They arrived dead and living together, in the same close box, many with awful wounds festering and swarming with maggots. Recollect it was midsummer in Virginia, clear and calm. The stench was such as to produce vomiting with some of our strong men, habituated to the duty of attending the sick."

Such were some of the labors undertaken by the Sanitary Commission in a single Department of the Union Army during the months of May and June, 1862; and in the other and more distant fields its labors were constantly increasing step by step with the progress and conflicts of our forces. But we can never forget that other most important work which the Commission is ever doing among the camps of our armies, and which was not neglected in the forces of the Potomac when before Richmond; for with that army, when within sight of the Confederate capital were found the Commission's Sanitary Inspectors, and all the tributary agencies of supplementary aid; and there, near the field-terminus of the Richmond and York

---

the moment that its helping hand was first held forth, comes the Blessed Voice, 'Inasmuch as ye have done it unto one of the least of these my brethren, ye have done it unto me.'"

The following schedule and classification of the Hospital Transports which were under the care of the Sanitary Commission, give us some idea of the extent of that work of mercy, and of the business-like management of it:

Sea Steamers, fitted for passages outside.—S. R. Spaulding, Daniel Webster No. 1.

Coast-Steamers, which must make a harbor on the approach of bad weather, and which should not be sent beyond Philadelphia, unless the necessity is urgent.—Elm City, State of Maine, John Brooks, Commodore, Kennebeck, Daniel Webster No 2.

Coast-Steamers which should not be run outside.—Vanderbilt, Whilldin, Louisiana, Knickerbocker.

Sailing vessels adapted to be used as Stationary Hospitals, or to be towed outside.—St. Mark, Euterpe.

The aggregate capacity of these vessels is equal to the accommodation of four thousand (4,000) patients, and may be increased to five thousand (5,000) if necessity is urgent.

From the time a boat leaves, until she can be prepared to leave again, will be, if she runs to New York, 7 days; to Philadelphia, 6 days; to Washington, 4 days; to Annapolis 4 days; to Baltimore 4 days; to Old Point, 3 days.—(*Hospital Transports, p. 156*)

river railway, the writer of these pages found the Commission's relief and stores, and their merciful tents for the personal shelter, and humane agents for the provisional succor of the sick and wounded as they were brought in from the lines. And these, like the Commission's labors in transports and ashore, at the Pamunkey base of the Peninsula field, were directed in person by the General Secretary, Mr. Olmsted, whose remarkable genius had helped to give shape and system to the work in every department of the Commission's service.

How the same kind of special labor was at that period progressing in the Western field may be judged, from the fact that the Sanitary Commission's agents, and its supplementary supplies for the sick and wounded, were everywhere welcomed, and everywhere sought in that field. The following paragraphs from a letter of the Western Secretary of the Commission, dated May 16th, 1862, and addressed to an auxiliary branch of the Supply Department, presents the same evidences of promptness and thoughtful preparation and sufficiency, as were witnessed then in the Eastern field:

"On my arrival at Cincinnati, I found the 251 boxes and barrels sent May 1st to my address. * * *

"These stores were on board the *Lancaster* No. 4—the steamer we had chartered—without delay or accident.

"The 251 packages to which I have referred, contained, according to the accompanying invoices, 317 bed-ticks, 275 comfortables, 1,223 towels, 15 mattresses, 546 sheets, 191 pairs socks, 874 pillows, 2,010 pillow-cases, 800 shirts, 889 handkerchiefs, 641 cushions, 98 pairs drawers, 7 vests, 2 pairs pants, 15 coats, 98 pairs crutches, 8 blankets, 452 sheets, 24 bed-gowns, 37 pairs slippers, 270 pin-cushions, eye-shades, &c., 988 lbs. dried beef, 384 lbs. groceries, 6 boxes dried fruit, 15 lbs. dried apples, 961 cans and jars of fruit, 5 kegs pickles, 1866 dozen eggs, 1 box apple butter, 519 lbs. butter, 124 lbs. bread, 985 lbs. cheese, 1,462 lbs. dried fruit, 7 bottles lemon syrup, 360 bottles wine, 2 boxes lemons, 11 bottles horse radish, 21 bottles catsup, 9 lbs. soap, 10 gals. maple syrup, 632 lbs. sugar, 29 spittoons, 28 basins, 310 vols. books, 3 boxes magazines, 130 lbs. linen list.

"I also, in accordance with your instructions, and with the money furnished by your Society for that purpose, purchased in Cincinnati nearly 200 packages of such articles as could be best procured there, and such as seemed necessary for the comfort and well-being of the sick among our soldiers in Tennessee."

* * * * * * *

"Most of the sick are greatly debilitated, and are much more in want of stimulants and nourishing, appetizing food, than any kind of medication. Most diseases here assume a typhoid type, and more than half of the severely sick have typhoid fever. Scurvy is beginning to make its appearance among our troops, and the health of all is impaired by their long-continued deprivation of fresh meats, fruits, and vegetables. I cannot describe, nor can you fully imagine, how great blessings the eggs, the butter, the oranges, the lemons, the thousand cans of fruit, the sauer kraut, the pickles, the ice, the potatoes, the ale, the wine, and other articles of equal value, which composed your generous gift, will be to these poor, feeble, feverish, and almost famished fellows, now lying in in the hospitals at Hamburgh Landing."

* * * * * * *

"On receiving the sick on board our steamer, the most seriously ill were placed on cots in the cabin and on the guards. Each cot was spread with quilts, comfortables, clean white sheets, and pillows; as inviting a bed as a sick man could ask. It would have done your heart good if you could have heard the expressions of satisfaction which fell from the lips of these poor fellows when their soiled camp-stained garments were taken off, each washed throughout, and clad in clean under-clothes, then laid between the sheets to which they had so long been strangers."

* * * * * * *

"Those who were less sick were provided with comfortable beds spread on the boiler deck, mattresses filled with straw, quilts and comfortables in abundance, from the boxes which you sent.

"The food furnished to the sick was abundant, varied, and excellent. Fresh bread, butter, eggs, fresh beef in the form of soup, tea and coffee, boiled rice, stewed apples, canned fruits, with wine and ale to those requiring them."

* * * * * * *

"I may perhaps weary you with an enumeration of these details, but you must remember that not an article of food or clothing was dispensed on our boat which was not your gift.

"On Sunday religious services were performed by Mr. Merwin, and as cleanliness is next to godliness, our convalescents were tempted to self-purification by the offer of a pair of socks to every one who would wash his feet, to those who would perform a general ablution, clean shirts and drawers. In this way, with little trouble to ourselves, we soon brought our whole cargo of living freight into a more comfortable and presentable condition." * * *

The records of this humane service of the Western river Hospital Transports have not yet been given to the public, but the statistics and results are said to exceed those of the same kind of service in the Eastern field. At the same time the Commission's Camp Inspectors were laboring in every *corps d'armée* in the Southwest; yet, we believe, that in that field, more than in the East, the duties pertaining to Supplementary Supplies of "sanitary stores" have considerably and continually overshadowed those of the sanitary inspection of camps. But it would appear from the publications of the Commission, and from the statements made by all army correspondents, as well as by the medical officers of the forces there, that aside from improvement of sanitary police in the camps, the supplying of anti-scorbutics—fresh vegetables, fruits, &c.—has been the first, greatest, and most constant hygienic necessity among these forces,* and that the Sanitary Commission has fully appreciated that necessity, and has munificently provided for it these two past years.

Upon a preceding page we have alluded to the New Medical Act, with the enlargements, reforms, and new life, it promised

---

* That this view of the importance of the anti scorbutic "sanitary stores" is not an over-estimate, will appear in a subsequent section of this narrative: But the writer will here quote a remark that has, on the day of this writing, been made in his presence by a distinguished Medical Director in our Southern army:—

"No other official duty," said this Medical Director, "during all my service last year, seemed so important, or actually did so much for the health and military effectiveness of our forces, as the aid I rendered the Sanitary Commission and the Commissariat in supplying the men with vegetables and fruit. The demon of Scurvy was lurking in all our camps and hospitals, and with potatoes, onions, and other anti-scorbutic stores, we hunted him thence."

to the medical service of the army, and the relief it would afford to the Sanitary Commission. The hope of such results from that Act and the influence and labors of the new Surgeon-General and the Corps of Inspectors, was not disappointed; although the failure of the Senate to confirm a competent Inspector-General, as provided by that Act, greatly diminished the effectiveness of that Corps. But we find in the "*Hospital Transports*" the fact emphatically stated by Mr. Olmsted, the Commission's Secretary, that the new statute, and the chief officer under it, did immediately inaugurate improvements vitally important to the forces in the field. Mr. Olmsted, in his note, says:—

"Shortly after the battle of Fair Oaks, the new and vastly more provident, liberal, and wisely economical policy introduced into the medical service, with the appointment of Dr. Hammond as Surgeon-General, and of the new corps of Medical Inspectors, began to be felt in the Army of the Potomac,—and although many of the agents necessary to the perfect success of that policy were unable at once to accommodate their habits to the required change, the Commission, scrupulously adhering to its purpose to do nothing which the properly responsible officials in any department evinced any readiness to do without its assistance, had the satisfaction of seeing the necessity for its special service, in connection with the hospital transports, grow gradually smaller and smaller."

And in another note Mr. Olmsted quotes from one of his letters to the Surgeon-General, as follows:—

"Steamboat 'Wilson Small,'
Off White House, Va., June 17, 1862.

"My dear General,—Your very prompt action, of which I am notified by your telegram of this date, in securing the shipment of large supplies of anti-scorbutics to the Army of the Potomac, without waiting for the Medical Director to assume the responsibility of ordering them, leads me to hope that you may think it right in like manner to interpose for the protection of the army from other evils, for which the remedies are equally obvious, and more readily attainable.

"I therefore urge that tarpaulings, old sails, felt, or canvas in bolts, with means of putting it together, be sent here immediately, in quantities sufficient to form a shelter for ten thousand wounded men." * * *

In another note in the "*Hospital Transports*," it is stated that, "During the month after the army reached and intrenched itself on the James River, the vessels managed by the Commission probably did a better service in what they brought to the army, than in the comfort they secured to the sick who were sent away upon them." And yet we find that the demands for both these kinds of service from the Commission, and for the continuance of its co-operation with the medical department, continually kept pace with each other, for a letter from an hospital transport at Harrison's Landing, says:

"The promptness with which the cargo—nearly a thousand barrels—would have been discharged, will be somewhat affected by the inability of some of the regiments of Heintzelman's corps to send transportation, on account of a movement for which they are ordered to stand in readiness to-day...... The sudden orders given yesterday for the immediate transportation of several thousand sick, have caused an influx of sick to the landing, overrunning all that the exertions of the Medical Director could do to provide for them.......

* * * * * * *

"As the poor fellows, many of them just getting up from fever, had been, in most cases, finding their way from the camps to the landing on foot, during the night, their want was urgent. Fortunately, we had a good supply of the concentrated beef of the Maison Dorée, New York, Martinez's preparation [beef-juice], and were not long in getting ready an excellent breakfast for them. It is in just such cases as this, where misery is massed, and where what is done tells not only for the relief of misery, but for the strength of the army, and the putting down of the rebellion, that we find the greatest satisfaction in stepping in with the gifts of the people. Many of these men were in just the condition in which a set-back would be likely to lead to a relapse and lingering disease, and in which again, if they were well cared for, they might be built up rapidly, and soon be sent back to their muskets."........

While the Sanitary Commission was thus held to its life-saving and humane work in the Peninsula campaign, even to the last, the national forces that had so triumphantly conquered firm footholds upon the coasts of the Carolinas, Georgia, and Florida, and upon the Mississippi, as well as within the scathed and desolated inland borders of the rebel territory, were at every point experiencing necessities that created demands upon its resources which were even more urgent than at earlier periods of the war; and in endeavoring to meet such wide-extended requirements, the Commission was impelled to throw in its agencies and its means of supply, to the utmost limit of its exchequer. The demands were immense, and there is incidental evidence that the bottom of its treasury was for months very suggestively and painfully visible to its finance committee. But the Commission's policy would not permit it to hold the hand in doing and disbursing so long as it had a dollar to sustain its operations. In a letter, which we find in one of the Commission's published documents, the earnest purpose and determination in regard to the work and the means for accomplishing it, are thus expressed by the General Secretary to his Associate Secretary, Dr. Newberry, at the West:—"*The* "*governing purpose of the organization is to avoid delay and* "*circumlocution to the end of accomplishing efficiency and direct-*"*ness of action. All practicable checks and methods consistent* "*with and subsidiary to this are to be observed. None are to be* "*cared for which assuredly interfere with it.* * * * *

"*What one man cannot do, two must. It is immaterial whether* "*the work is done here or there. The question is one of time,* "*not of trouble. When the money gives out, we are to scuttle* "*and go down—till then, do our work thoroughly.*"

While working in this spirit, and always most gratefully withdrawing from any responsibility or burden which the

Medical Department would fully assume, the extent and terrible energy of the National struggle, and the corresponding enlargement of the forces by new levies, served to augment the inevitable demands upon the Sanitary Commission. General McClellan's Army, reinforced by General Burnside's, had united with General Pope's forces, received terrible shocks from Lee and Jackson's combined attacks, and thus required the Sanitary Commission to send forward with our pursuing troops such means of supplementary aid as its Central Office could then command.

The Commission was in session in Washington at the time of the great battle at Antietam, and, with confidential advices concerning the urgent necessities of the occasion, its orders and arrangements for answering those wants were not restricted or delayed a moment in view of the impending exhaustion of means. The following extracts from published Minutes and Documents show what the Commission did, and something of the way of its doing:

"The Secretary reported that since the commencement of active operations in Maryland, and previous to yesterday, five wagons and one railroad car, loaded with supplies, had been sent, by the Commission to and beyond Frederick; that six Surgeons and Inspectors of the Commission, with a car-load of supplies, were sent on yesterday afternoon; that three wagons left Washington for the front of the army on the Upper Potomac at 12 o'clock last night, with a party of eight, in charge of Drs. Agnew and Harris; that a train of army wagons are now loading with supplies, to be despatched immediately for the battle-field, also by way of Frederick; that Dr. Crane had been previously stationed at Chambersburg or Hagarstown, with large discretionary powers to act for the Commission; and that despatches had been sent to Philadelphia, ordering the purchase of large supplies at that point; that these, with stores forwarded to Hagarstown in charge of special agents." * *

* * * * * * * * * *

"The battle of Antietam was in progress, and during the session several wagon trains, one of them accompanied by a member of the Commission, departed for the battle-field from before the door of the building in which the session was held. More than 30,000 articles of clothing, with several tons of articles of nourishment, stimulants, &c., were sent during the week from the Washington depot, for distribution to the wounded by the method of the Commission."

The battles at Corinth, Iuka, and Perryville, followed closely upon the bloody engagements of our forces in Virginia and Maryland, and though remote from the base of supply, those fields were likewise witness to the timely aid of the Sanitary Commission. In a report of the relief work at Perryville, Dr. Reed, the Sanitary Commission's agent there, says:

"On our arrival we learned that we were the first to bring relief where help was needed more than tongue can tell. Instead of 700, as first reported, at least 2,500 Union and rebel soldiers were at that time lying in great suffering and destitution about Perrysville and Harrodsburg.

"In addition to these, many had already been removed, and we had met numbers of those whose wounds were less severe, walking and begging their way to Louisville, 85 miles distant. To these we frequently gave help and comfort by sharing with them the slender stock of food and spirits we had taken with us."

"There had been almost no preparation for the care of the wounded at Perryville, and as a consequence the suffering from want of help of all kinds, as well as proper accommodations, food, medicines and hospital stores, was excessive. For this state of things, however, the surgeons are not to blame. Both those in authority and those in attendance had done, and were doing, all in their power to prevent and mitigate the suffering to which I have alluded. The fault lies higher than they—with the superior military authorities, who withheld from the surgeon the information, and denied them the resources, which alone would have enabled them to meet the emergencies of the case.

* * * * * * * * *

"Surgeons were then notified that stores could be had, and they were rapidly given out. There were, at this time, some 1,800 wounded in and about Perryville. They were all very dirty; few had straw or other bedding; some were without blankets, others had no shirts; and even now, five days after the battle, some were being brought in from temporary places of shelter, whose wounds had not yet been dressed. Every house was a hospital, all crowded, and with very little to eat."

At Corinth and Iuka, the Inspector, Dr. Warriner, reports that the Commission had prepared itself beforehand, by massing its supplies at Bolivar and Columbus. And it is a fact full of significance that, although the regular Medical authorities made every exertion to meet the wants of the armies in the Southwest, and to liberally anticipate the demands of battle-fields, we should find the following special order, promulgated by Major-General Rosecrans:—

"Head-Quarters 14th Army Corps,
"Department of the Cumberland,
"Nashville, Dec. 11th, 1862.

"The General Commanding, appreciating the vast amount of good which the soldiers of this Army are deriving from the Sanitary stores distributed among them by the United States Sanitary Commission, directs:

"That all officers in this department render any aid consistent with their duties, to the agents of this society—and afford them every facility for the execution of their charitable work.

"By order of
"Maj. Gen. W. S. Rosecrans."

While from the Medical Director of the Dansville District, then populous with military patients in hastily extemporized Hospitals, the following hearty and grateful acknowledgments were made to the Commission's Western Secretary. We extract them from a letter in Document No. 64, of the Commission's publications:—

"When the hospitals were first established in this district we were almost entirely destitute of hospital and medical supplies, including almost every article necessary for the comfort of the sick. With an unusually large number of sick and wounded on our hands, we were compelled to see them suffer without the proper means of affording them relief.

"The condition of things was immediately telegraphed to the Medical Purveyor in Louisville, and that officer with his usual promptness at once furnished everything necessary to render our sick comfortable, but from some cause the supplies were detained several weeks on the road, and were not received until long after those arrived that were sent by the Sanitary Commission.

"Considering the large number of sick and wounded in the District, (between six and seven thousand,) and the almost total absence of everything necessary to render them comfortable,* I have no doubt that the timely aid afforded by the Commission in this single instance has been the means of preventing much suffering as well as of saving many valuable lives."

At the period of which we now write, nearly a million soldiers were enrolled in the national army, and the Military Hospitals, though they had rapidly increased their capacity, and immensely extended and improved their facilities and their hygienic appliances, were already overcrowded, so that at the end of October the Medical Department had upon its hands the care of more than a hundred thousand sick and wounded men in organized hospitals, in addition to the daily medical and sanitary wants of the vast armies in the field. At that period the several corps of medical officers consisted of—

Regimental Surgeons	about	1,000.
Do. Assistant do.	"	1,200.
Surgeons of *Regular* staff (old corps.)		50.
Assistant Surgeons do. do.		125.
Surgeons of Volunteers (Regulars for the war.)		140.
Assistant do. do. do.		50.
Medical Cadets (undergraduates, dressers.)		50.
Civilian Surgeons, under contract by the month		1,250.

These, under the Surgeon-General, with his special corps of eight Medical and Sanitary Inspectors, as provided by the New

---

* In a special report of the battle-field work of the Commission at Perryville, Dr. Newberry, the Western Secretary, after designating the official heads upon whom rested the responsibility for the needless suffering upon that field, remarks that, "from a combination of causes, the condition of the wounded in this fight was peculiarly distressing. No adequate provision had been made for their care. The stock of medicines and hospital stores in the hands of the surgeons was insignificant. They had almost no ambulances, no tents, no hospital furniture, and no proper food." * * * * * * * * * * *

Dr. Newberry reiterates, as every member of the Sanitary Commission has done again and again, that the first remedy to be applied is, "*the addition to the medical corps of a body of trained assistants, whose duty it shall be to gather up and remove the wounded from the battle field, and perform for them the first necessary offices of relief; and entrusting to that department independent means of transportation and subsistence for the sick, much will be done to economise life, prevent suffering, and improve the health of the army.*"—(See Document 64.

Medical Act, were charged with the medical and surgical care and all the administrative service of the General and Field Hospitals; and with the sanitary and medical service of nearly eight hundred thousand men in the field.

With such overwhelming responsibilities, and in times so momentous, the Medical Department could not dispense with that systematic and well considered aid which the Sanitary Commission was promptly rendering in every field; nor did the Commission find opportunity to withdraw itself from the responsibilities which it had found augmenting in an even ratio with the extraordinary efforts that had been put forth to meet the demands that human life and our national life were presenting, and which most urgently, throughout the long lines of our armies, and in the wards of the ever-enlarging military hospitals, commanded its attention. And though the Commission did endeavor gradually to diminish its work of *camp inspection*, and its daily reports of such inquiry, the time never arrived when it could entirely throw off its responsibility and its interest in that most important department, nor is it probable it ever can relinquish such duty while the war lasts. It is as essential to the military effectiveness of the forces in the field as it is important to the Commission, as the best source of definite knowledge of the causes and the preventive agencies with which the Commission is concerned.

In the city and immediate vicinity of Washington alone there were, in October of that year, between sixty and seventy large edifices occupied as General Hospitals, and, with the Field Hospital at Harewood, containing at one time nearly 30,000 sick and wounded men. At Frederick were 5,000 wounded men from the battle-fields of Northern Maryland, filling the churches and other public buildings; and at Louisville, Nashville, St. Louis, and various other points, vast numbers of sick and wounded were likewise accumulated from the greatly imperilled armies of the

Southwest. Only a year previously to this period the Sanitary Commission had furnished plans and earnestly recommended the construction of the first pavilion hospitals, and urged the entire abandonment of old hotels and other unsuitable structures that were at that time being leased and occupied as hospitals. In the autumn of 1862, a large number of extensive pavilion hospitals had been completed; yet the exigencies of the summer and autumn campaigns had filled a vast number of churches and other public buildings with the sick and wounded. And in view of the vital importance of knowing and anticipating the perils and hygienic wants of such crowded hospitals, the Sanitary Commission undertook a special inspection of all the General Hospitals, the enlightened Surgeon-General having authorized such inspection, with advisory powers.

Under the guidance of a committee, composed of Drs. Wm. H. Van Buren, Wolcott Gibbs and C. R. Agnew, a suitable number of distinguished members of the medical profession were selected and invited to accept temporary appointments, for pursuing these inspections. This important work was commenced immediately after the battles in Northern Maryland, and, under the special superintendence of Dr. Henry G. Clark, of Boston, it was continued until May last. These hospital inspections had commanded the highest talent of the profession, and in the more permanent duties connected with this work, a distinguished expert and special inspector engaged upon practical improvements in ventilation, Dr. David Boswell Reid, died while on active duty.

The beneficial results of this temporary undertaking can only be estimated by the hospital statistics of death-rates and convalescent-time-rates, in the hospitals,—improved and unimproved. The reports of the Inspectors, of course, are unpublished; but in his first published statement respecting the progress and results of the work, as seen in the month of November, 1862, we find its Superintendent, Dr. Clark, saying that—

"The suggestions, contained in the reports, with regard to defects and evils found to be existing in any of the Hospitals, have, when transmitted by me, as they are frequently, by extracts, synopses, or verbally, to the surgeon, invariably received his immediate and effective attention.

"An inspection of the reports of the different Inspectors, at different and consecutive dates, will also show, in many instances, a very marked and progressive improvement in the condition of the Hospitals inspected.

"This improvement has, no doubt, been partly owing to the natural effects of time, and the better experience and opportunities of the officers in charge, but partly, also, I am assured by the surgeons themselves, to the friendly influence of the Inspectors, and of the establishment, in this way, of a sort of standard of excellence. In fact, it is impossible but that the opinions of men of standing and knowledge in the profession should have its proper weight upon a class of earnest, hard-working, and many of them capable men, upon whom the accidents of war have unexpectedly and suddenly cast the gravest labors and responsibilities."

In the Documents from which we have just quoted, we find that an Inspector reports as follows: "The most urgent and "instant want, not only of the places I have officially visited, "but of every military station in the West where I have been, "is—Hospitals." But, to the honor of the Medical Bureau, it must be stated, that every effort was being made to provide appropriate and well supplied hospitals, and that before the Sanitary Commission's special inspection of the hospitals had terminated, the West as well as the East had ample and excellent General Hospitals. In Document 56, of the Commission's publications, Dr. Clark, the Inspector-in-Chief, remarks:

"I feel bound to say in relation to them, that, in so large a field, it would be wonderful not to find some weeds; to start and put into working order the ponderous machinery of Hospitals which contain, in the mass, more than 70,000 beds, without any friction, would be a miracle. Let us, then, instead of criticising too sharply, rather admire the energy, the skill, the administrative capacity, shown in extemporizing and systematizing an agency so beneficent and so grand."

The history of Military Hospitals in all wars of modern times fully justified the liberal plans of the Surgeon-General's new pavilions, and abundantly warranted the practical concern that the Sanitary Commission manifested for the improvement of all the Hospitals,* and for their adequate supply of sanitary appli-

---

* It was said by Sir John Pringle, the distinguished Army Surgeon of the Walcheren Campaigns, that "Hospitals are among the chief causes of mortality in armies;" and an eminent French surgeon of the same period, asserted that "Hospitals are a curse to civilization." And such strong terms of denunciation were justified by the high death-rate that prevailed in military hospitals in former times. Even in the recent Crimean campaign, Miss Nightingale and the Sanitary Commission found a frightful rate of mortality in the hospitals; the percentage of deaths (46.7 *per cent.* in the hospitals of Scutari and Koulali, in February, 1855), was nearly as great as the percentage of recoveries. But that alarming mortality was speedily checked by specific sanitary works, so that the death-rate fell to two or three per cent. (2.2 *per cent.* in the same hospitals) of cases treated. Miss Nightingale states, that there was "in the first seven months of the Crimean campaign, a mortality among the troops at the rate of 60 per cent. per annum from disease alone." . . . . . And that during the last five months of that campaign—after the sanitary improvements came into operation—"The mortality among the troops in the Crimea did not exceed 11.5 per 1,000 (or 1.1 *per cent.*) per annum.

Justly does that devoted lady exclaim: "Is not this the most complete experiment in army hygiene! We cannot try the experiment over again for the benefit of inquirers at home, like a chemical experiment. It must be brought forward as *a historical example.*"

The United States Sanitary Commission having sprung into existence under the light and impulse of such examples, had early occasion to give warning against the perils of which our national forces and their hospitals were exposed from the class of causes to which Miss Nightingale alludes.

In Document. No. 42 of the Commission's publications, we find quoted a Report upon the "*Condition of Military Hospitals in Grafton and Cumberland, by Dr. Wm. A. Hammond,* Assistant Surgeon U. S. Army;" in which that intelligent officer describes 21 hospitals where fevers and a threatening mortality were prevailing; and the following opinion, which Surgeon Hammond expresses concerning one of the largest of those fever-nests, shows what perilous evils existed in many of our military hospitals during the first year of the war: "I do not hesitate to say, that such a condition of affairs *does not exist in any other hospital in the civilized world;* and that this hospital is altogether worse than any which were such *opprobria* to the allies in the Crimean war."

ances and "sanitary stores." We have already referred to the practical efforts of the Commission in that direction during the first months of the war. And it is a fact worthy of note in this place, that some of the ablest Reports that have yet been made upon the subject of our Military Hospitals, were hastily prepared in the regular course of his official duty, by Assistant-Surgeon Hammond, now the Surgeon-General.

In its earliest labors, at the opening of the war, the Sanitary Commission had expressed its intelligent concern for the institution of an adequate and most improved system of military hospitals, and of hospital administration, nursing, and supplies; and in its later efforts for improvements in this department of the medical service, it enjoyed the heartiest and most enlightened co-operation of the Surgeon-General. And in this, as in other fields of its labors, the Commission possessed an independent and very reliable means for guiding and determining in advance the measures, or at least the special functions, that from time to time have been required at its hands by the sanitary interests of the army and the army hospitals. Its scheme of systematic statistical inquiries and records which was instituted prior to the first battles, and which had analytically registered the vital and sanitary statistics of the first engagement of our forces at Bull Run was more complete than any attempted in previous wars, soon had grown into a well-ordered Bureau of Sanitary and Vital Statistics. Under the guidance of the General Secretary of the Commission, the skillful Actuary of that Bureau was charged with the duty of applying the most exacting analysis to the voluminous reports that daily reached the Commission's central office from its inspectors and agents throughout the Union lines. By this means the Sanitary Commission has always enjoyed peculiar advantages. Through this class of labors it has been able to indicate with comparative certainty the Sanitary perils, weakness, or wants of the National forces.

Whoever will look into Mr. Elliott's Bureau of figures and facts at the Commission's central office will be able to understand something of the work of that Bureau and what are the practical and verifying values of its *anticipating* estimations as well as of its *ex post facto* registries. Impossible as it is to quote any abstract of statistics in this place, the reader may obtain, from the following extracts, some idea of the nature and practical relations of deductions that are daily attained by that department of the Commission's labor. We quote from Document No. 46 of the Commission's publications:

"It will be remarked that the mortality of the armies recruited at the West (and which as a rule operate at the West) is almost three times (3.01) that of the troops recruited in the Middle and New England States (and which as a rule serve with the armies of the East), the Western rate from wounds received in action being five (4.9) times, and that from disease and accident, a little less than three (2.8) times as great as the corresponding Eastern rates."

* * * * * * *

"A like contrast is observed in the *sickness-rates* of the troops East and West, the rate of the latter (one hundred and sixty-one per 1,000) being more than twice (more exactly 2.1 times) that of the former (namely, seventy-six per 1,000): the average constant sickness rate for the *entire* army, so far as returned, being one hundred and four (104.4) per 1,000 strength."

* * * * * * *

"There is reason for the belief that the excess of the rates of sickness and mortality in our Western armies over those in the East, is due in no small degree, not merely to the greater activity of the former in the field, to over-exertion and exposure, as the results of severe and long-continued marches, and to stubborn and deadly encounters with the enemy in arms; but also, to badly chosen camp sites, to imperfect and neglected drainage, (the nature of the surface and soil not unfrequently being such that suitable camp sites, free from malaria, and affording ample facilities for drainage could not be found, if sought); to the too crowded condition of hospitals; to less of variety in food (soft bread and dessicated vegetables in very many Western regiments being seldom or never had,) and to less of skill and care in its preparation; to water of impure quality and sometimes of insufficient quantity; to the greater disposition on the part of the soldiers to negleci appliances for personal comfort; and to the greater neglect of, or a lack of means for enforcing cleanliness of person and camp." * * *

It pertains no less to the history of the Sanitary Commission's labors than to that of the Medical Department's progress that, so far as has seemed practicable, the Department has manifestly endeavored to extend its official methods or its official sanction to all the plans and appliances of the Commission; and that the Commission has from the beginning studiously adapted all its special methods and labors, whether temporary or permanent, to work in harmony with the regulations and official necessities of the medical service. The statistical inquiries of the Commission, and the Surgeon-General's "Medical History of the War," illustrate this fact. In that class of labors the Commission first opened the way, and has popularized and can well defend the work;* and we doubt if it has yet suggested any scheme of reform affecting the medical or sanitary service of the army, which has not directly or indirectly been affirmed and practically sustained by some definite action of Government. This tendency, which is really inevitable, has been very strikingly

---

* Says an eminent journalist:—"How much life and vital force does the great "War for the Republic necessarily and inevitably require, and how much does it "needlessly waste, are questions that not only concern every citizen and every "home in the land, but profoundly concern the State and the great interests of "humanity."

* * * * * * * * *

"It is a fact well known to the profession that, in the earlier period of the war "it was regarded as doubtful whether the suddenly gathered medical staff of the "volunteer army could or would be brought into the habit and duty of faithfully "reporting statistics, and practically enforcing systematic sanitary regulations, and "exact hygienic observations." * * * *

In a recent "*Report of the Committee on the Preparation of Army Medical Statistics*," *&c.*, for the British Government, and of which Lord Herbert was Chairman, the practical importance of such statistical records is thus alluded

illustrated by the sequence of events in those measures which from time to time have been instituted against scurvy and other camp diseases in our armies. The Statistical Bureau of the Medical Department to-day is organized, and its returns are being analyzed, and the practical conclusions are being published for the benefit of the army; pavilion hospitals are substituted for old-style structures; camp-cooking receives increased attention, and the Commission's Department of Relief responds to the requisitions of the Sanitary Inspectors, and instantly forwards to designated camps and hospitals such anti-scorbutics and special supplies as are demanded; and, subsequently, the regular Commissariat and Quartermaster's Departments find it practicable and expedient to procure and bring forward similar and abundant supplies, as advised by the medical staff; and then, again, the Sanitary Commission's functions in that line will cease until like necessities recur. In various other ways, and continually, does this principle hold true, and it should be mentioned, to the infinite credit of the Medical Department, that, under all the temptations and official difficulties of their mutual relations, it maintains with the Commission such an *entente cordiale* as makes its constituted agents and supplementary appliances welcome in every camp and hospital, and upon every battle-field.

---

to:—"Reports exhibiting the results of extensive observations over a wide field "will serve to measure the influences of each known cause of health; and will "probably lead to the discovery of new causes, both of impaired and of vigorous "life. They will contain new contributions to the science of health, in which "the whole nation is concerned."

"The reports will be the means of improving the health of the army. They "will contribute to diminish the army's sickness, which is attended with expense "as well as suffering. For a sick army is the worst extravagance in which a nation "can indulge......At the same time they will effect a still more important saving; "for they will save the lives of our soldiers......If soldiers die in battle by "hundreds, they die of disease in hospitals by thousands......The economy of "life resulting directly from the information which statistical returns supply, has "been already strikingly exemplified," &c.

In the history of the Sanitary Commission's relations to the medical and other departments of the army service, and in its best labors for the conservation of life and effectiveness in the forces, there must be many passages that cannot properly be made public during the progress of the war. In searching out official delinquencies and defects that imperil the health of the troops, and in reporting facts and opinions to the higher military authorities, and in the greater part of its intercourse and correspondeuce with Heads of Departments, Bureaus, or military organizations, and likewise, in nearly all efforts to procure reform of abuses, as well as in most of its duties of Inquiry and Advice, the Sanitary Commission's work is, and must continue to be, unpublished, and to the public unknown. But there is abundant evidence that this class of duties is discharged most fearlessly and faithfully, and that it has constituted the burden of the Commission's work, from the day of its organization to the present time.

It suffices that the people know the fact that the Sanitary Commission faithfully performs its duty to the army and the Government in such matters as in war-times must be as confidential as they are searching and fearless. But there is a department of the Commission's work most interesting and humane, and which unreservedly invites the popular attention and concern, and it is the duty of the public to know all about it, for it is *the people's share* in, and contribution to, the Sanitary Commission's great work of life-saving and humane ministry in the war.

The Department of Relief.—In every town and hamlet, and probably in every household in the loyal States, it is known that the United States Sanitary Commission provides and distributes material aid to the sick and wounded in the camps and hospitals. This knowledge of a particular function of the Commission not only was the first, but continues to be almost the only information that has generally gained access to the people respecting its character and purposes as an institution of the Government; and this has led to some curious results, for example, by a singular but significant metonymy, a single branch of this incidental function of special relief, in the matter of hospital garments, delicacies, concentrated articles of diet, and the means of cleanliness, etc., soon became known and designated as "*sanitary stores;*" and, innocent of philological definations or technical distinctions, multitudes of Soldiers' Aid Societies and Village Sewing Circles at once assumed the title of "Sanitary Commission;" or, often, more modestly and properly, "Branch of the U. S. Sanitary Commission."* But the U. S. Sanitary Commission can afford to regard such innocent misnomers only with gratitude, so long as it maintains a special Department of Relief, which, among other duties, receives, classifies, and disburses the people's offerings to the sick and wounded. Indeed, the Aid Societies are true Branches.

The department of Relief and Supplementauy Supplies is nearly a complete institution of itself, and although it has been elaborated and organized within the Sanitary Commission—constituting what was expressly designated in the Commission's original Scheme of Organization, the third *stem* of the *branch* of "Advice;" [there being two branches of duty assigned to the Commission—1. Inquiry; 2. Advice]—it has a history and a purpose peculiarly its own. In its organization, however, the framers of the Commission manifestly had a purpose every way worthy the grand results that have flowed from it; for, in their

---

* "*Branch of the United States Sanitary Commission*" is now a fully authorized title for the Central Auxiliaries of the Commission's Supply Department, and well is that title honored by such tributary Associations as those whose good works we shall presently mention.

Scheme of Organization, as approved by the President and the Secretary of War, we find the following among other statements forecasting upon this subject, when arranging for duties pertaining to the third *stem*, as just mentioned:—

"3. A sub-committee in direct relation with the State governments, and with the public associations of benevolence. First, to secure uniformity of plans and then proportion and harmony of action; and, finally, abundance of supplies in moneys and goods, for such extra purposes as the laws do not and cannot provide for."

* * * * * * *

. . . . . . "Thus the organizing, methodizing, and reducing to serviceableness, the vague, disproportioned, and hap-hazard benevolence of the public, might be successfully accomplished." . . . .

We have already mentioned that at the beginning of the war the Commission had instituted methods of systematic relief in military hospitals, and that it also undertook what it then termed "*irregular*" relief for the benefit of the sick, the way-worn and hungry, and the disabled or destitute soldiers found about all the great military depots. How exceedingly regular and well organized this branch of the Relief service became we shall presently see. But the other and main branch of Relief, for the sick and wounded in camps and hospitals, was, from the beginning, a systematic business.

The whole work of Sanitary Relief, whether under circumstances that were *regular*, or under those that were *irregular*, soon became strictly systematic; and although sufficiently expansible and independent in its several branches and methods to meet the greatest variety and urgency of exigencies, all this business has been studiously harmonized in a central plan. It may be classified as follows:

General Relief to	*Hospital Supplies and "Sanitary Stores" to General Hospitals;* *Hospital Supplies and "Sanitary Stores" to Battle-fields and Field Hospitals;* *"Sanitary Stores" to the Regimental Hospitals and Armies in the Field.*
Special Relief to	*Needy or Sick soldiers in the vicinity of Military Depots;* *Needy or Sick soldiers accepting furlough or discharge from service;* *Prisoners and paroled men, and individual cases of special suffering wherever found among soldiers, for which the Army Regulations fail to provide;* *The Sick and Wounded and their Friends, by the Hospital Directory and other means.*

The Relief Department of the Commission's work has, from the beginning, received the most intelligent and painstaking care from the whole body of the Commission and from the best men that could be commanded for its service. And to the branch of "Special Relief" work not only did the President and General Secretary bring all the power of their earnest minds, but Providence brought a Superintendent and Chief Aid who, from the scenes of the first Bull Run, to the presecut hour, has given to this work for the soldier and the people such zealous, discreet, and beneficent services as few men could give, and such as probably no man ever before rendered in such work.*

* "During the dark days immediately succeeding the first battle of Bull Run, a clergyman from Massachusetts was among the foremost in administering to the wants and alleviating the distresses of our troops at the national capital. His means at first were simple enough. A pail full of coffee and a basket full of bread

Studiously consulting the necessities of the army and hospitals, and after advising with military and medical officials, the Commission early succeeded in bringing forward supplementary supplies and in offering special relief in a great variety of ways and by methods so appropriate, effectual, and acceptable, as to commend this work to all classes of Government authorities. Of this there is good evidence from the fact that, early in the autumn of 1861, when the Commission issued a circular inviting general contributions of special supplies for the sick and wounded, that appeal was endorsed by an emphatic note of approval from PRESIDENT LINCOLN and GENERAL SCOTT.*

Through its Sanitary Inspectors, and by other means of information from the camps and hospitals, the Commission's advices respecting their deficiences and special wants, and re-

---

constituted the material, and a few tin cups the appliances, at his control. The necessities of the case were numerous, urgent—really appalling. Almost instantly there grew up, with this same large-hearted Rev. Frederick N. Knapp at its head, the Special Relief Department of the Sanitary Commission. Its beginnings were small enough. 'The most we could do,' says he, in his first report, 'was to have a place assigned us—part of the smaller building, the "Cane Factory"—where we put the sick as they came in, separate from the crowd of the other building, and here we had a pile of blankets, from which we made such beds as we could, and then brought tea and coffee and supplies for the men from the restaurant in the station house, or, more often, from a boarding house on Pennsylvania avenue.' First in the crowded streets, then in a dingy workshop, and *thence* came the Soldiers' Homes of the Sanitary Commission. Since then these beneficent institutions have been multiplied until there is now no important place of military transfer in which one may not be found."—*Sanitary Reporter.*

* When the Postmaster-General had sent 80,000 of those circulars freely throughout the land, he followed it by posters for every Post Office in the States, and the following note to the Postmasters:—

"POST OFFICE DEPARTMENT, WASHINGTON, *October* 15, 1861

"*To the Postmaster at*

"SIR,—You are requested to take measures to effect an organization, if none exists, among the women of your district to respond to the accompanying appeal of the Sanitary Commission.

"The Executive Government here very much desires to obtain the active cooperation of the women of America for the holy cause of the Union in this appropriate mode, and relies upon you to make known this wish to them, and aid as far as possible in securing its accomplishment.

"Yours, respectfully,

"M. BLAIR,
"*Postmaster-General.*"

specting exigencies occurring or anticipated in the movements or the engagements of the troops, have always been immediate and definite. In that first circular, which we have mentioned as indorsed by President Lincoln and General Scott, we find the following statement respecting the special relief administered in hospitals and camps:—

"Under its present organization, every camp and military hospital, from the Atlantic to the Plains, is regularly and frequently visited, its wants ascertained, anticipated as far as possible, and whenever it is right, proper, and broadly merciful, supplied directly by the Commission to the extent of its ability. For the means of maintaining this organization, and of exercising through it a direct influence upon the officers and men favorably to a prudent guard against the dangers of disease to which they are subject, which is its first and principal object, the Commission is wholly dependent upon voluntary contributions to its treasury. For the means of administering to the needs of the sick and wounded, the Commission relies upon gift offerings of their own handiwork from the loyal women of the land. It receives not one dollar from Government.

"A large proportion of the gifts of the people to the army hitherto have been wasted, or worse than wasted, because directed without knowledge or discrimination. It is only through the Commission that such gifts can reach the army with a reasonable assurance that they will be received where they will do the most good and the least harm."

* * * * * * *

"Some special defect, error, or negligence, endangering health, has not been pointed out by its agents, and its removal or abatement effected. There has not been a single instance in which its services or advice, offered through all its various agencies have been repulsed; not a single complaint has been received of its embarrassing any officer in his duty, or of its interfering with discipline in the slightest degree. Its labors have, to this time, been chiefly directed to induce precautions against a certain class of diseases which have scourged almost every modern European army, which decimated our army in Mexico, and which, at one time, rendered nearly half of one of our armies in the war of 1812 unfit for service. That there are grander causes for this than the labors of the Commission cannot be doubted, but that, among human agencies, a larger share of credit for it should be given to those labors, it is neither arrogant nor unreasonable to assert. In this assurance, what contribution that has hitherto been made to the treasury or the store of the Commission is not received back tenfold in value?

"More than sixty thousand articles have been received by the Commission from their patriotic countrywomen. It is not known that one sent to them has failed to reach its destination, nor has one been received that cannot be accounted for. It is confidently believed that there has not been of late a single case of serious illness in the Army of the Potomac, nor wherever the organization of the Commission has been completely extended, in which some of these articles have not administered to the relief of suffering."

This statement was made in September, 1861, and we quote it here as a key to the whole theory and *modus operandi* of this business of Systematic Relief. How this branch of service increased in importance, and why the Sanitary Commission has given such special attention to it, the history of our armies will best tell. The people seem well to understand that the best and surest channels through which their affectionate and homely gifts for special relief can flow directly to their sons and brothers in the army, are those which the Government has especially authorized, and the Sanitary Commission laboriously and skilfully prepared.

Fortunately for suffering men in hospitals and upon battle-fields, the leading Societies of Aid for soldiers not only became tributary to the Relief Department of the Sanitary Commission, but they quickly learned, how to labor and contribute systematically and most effectively. And this success in learning how to do such work and how to gather and transmit supplementary supplies, thus systematically, was brought about by earnest purposes and deliberations in which women as well as the Government Commissioners shared. In the First Report of the "Woman's Central Association of Relief, at New York," we find the following sensible remarks upon this subject in a call for the public meeting that organized that model Society of

Aid. That call bears date April 25th, 1861, and thus it introduces its object, and seems to foreshadow the work of the Sanitary Commission itself:*

---

* The following additional passages from that Circular present the objects which were then definitely had in view :—

"*To the Women of New York, and especially to those already engaged in preparing against the time of Wounds and Sickness in the Army.*—The importance of systematizing and concentrating the spontaneous and earnest efforts now making by the women of New York, for the supply of extra medical aid to our Army through its present campaign, must be obvious to all reflecting persons. Numerous societies, working without concert, organization, or head,—without any direct understanding with the official authorities,—without any positive instructions as to the immediate or future wants of the army,—are liable to waste their enthusiasm in disproportionate efforts, to overlook some claims and overdo others, while they give unnecessary trouble in official quarters, by the variety and irregularity of their proffers of help or their inquiries for guidance.

* * * * * *

"To make the meeting practical and effective, it seems proper here to set forth briefly the objects that should be kept in view. The form which woman's benevolence has already taken, and is likely to take, in the present crisis, is, first, the contribution of labor, skill, and money in the preparation of lint, bandages, and other stores, in aid of the wants of the Medical Staff; second, the offer of personal services as nurses.

"In regard to the first, it is important to obtain and disseminate exact official information as to the nature and variety of the wants of the army; to give proper direction and proportion to the labor expended, so as to avoid superfluity in some things and deficiency in others; and to this end, to come to a careful and thorough understanding with the official head of the Medical Staff, through a committee having this department in hand. To this committee should be assigned the duty of conferring with other associations in other parts of the country, and especially through the press, to keep the women of the loyal States everywhere informed how their efforts may be most wisely and economically employed, and their contributions of all kinds most directly concentrated at New York, and put at the service of the Medical Staff. A central depot would, of course, be the first thing to be desired.

"In regard to the second form of benevolence—the offer of personal services as nurses—it is felt that the public mind needs much enlightenment, and the overflowing zeal and sympathy of the women of the nation, a careful channel, not only to prevent waste of time and effort, but to save embarrassment to the official staff, and to secure real efficiency in the service. Should our unhappy war be continued, the army is certain to want the services of extra nurses, not merely on account of casualities of the field, but of the camp diseases, originating in the exposure of soldiery to a strange climate and to unaccustomed hardships. The result of all the experience of the Crimean war has been to prove the *total uselessness of any but picked and skilled women in this department of duty.*

* * * * * *

"To consider this matter deliberately, and to take such common action as may then appear wise, we earnestly invite the women of New York, and the pastors of churches, with such medical advisers as may be specially invited, to assemble for counsel and action, at the Cooper Institute, on Monday morning next, (April 29th,) at eleven o'clock."

"The importance of systematizing and concentrating the spontaneous and earnest efforts now making by the women of New York, for the supply of extra medical aid to our army through its present campaigns, must be obvious to all reflecting persons. Numerous societies, working without concert, organization, or head, without any direct understanding with the official authorities, without any positive instructions as to the immediate or future wants of the army, are liable to waste their enthusiasm in disproportionate efforts, to overlook some claims and overdo others, while they give unnecessary trouble in official quarters, by the variety and irregularity of their proffers of help or their inquiries for guidance."

In the first report of the "Soldiers' Aid Society of Northern Ohio," an association of remarkable efficiency, organized a week previous to the one in New York, we find another suggestive remark concerning the best method of reaching the sick soldiers' wants. That report says:

"The officers of the Society deeply felt the burden and responsibility of dispensing with prudence, impartiality, and wisdom, the precious fruits of so much patient and loving toil, and on October 9th, 1861, application was made for permission to act as auxiliary to the U. S. Sanitary Commission."

There is reason to believe that the Sanitary Commission assumed the care and distribution of hospital supplies with some misgivings and only after careful inquiry, while the far-seeing General Secretary, and the excellent subordinates to whom he committed the work of "inspection" and aid, appear to have given their best energies to the duty of thoroughly systematizing the whole work of Relief. In the Autumn of 1861, Mr. Olmsted reports to the Commission that,—

"The principal depots of stores for the Commission are in New York, (under charge of the "Women's Central Relief Association" of New York); at Boston; at Providence, R. I.; at Philadelphia; at Cincinnati, Cleveland, and Columbus, Ohio; at Wheeling, Va.; at Louisville; at Chicago; at Cairo; at St. Louis, and at Washington."

The same report also states, that nearly 100,000 articles had then been received at those depots, and that from the Washington depot alone one hundred and twenty-six hospitals had received such supplies as that depot could furnish. As the principles and methods of distribution, which at that period had been adopted, remain essentially the same at the present time, we will here refer to them by quoting a concise statement that appears in the above-mentioned report:

"*System of Distribution.*—It is the duty of the Commission to prevent, as far as possible, the sacrifice of human life to matters of form and considerations of accuracy of accounts. Its method of distribution is as thorough and exact as can be maintained consistently with this duty."

* * * * * * *

"Vouchers signed by the surgeon, or his assistant, of every regiment or hospital aided, and countersigned by an inspector of the Commission, who has ascertained that the articles supplied are actually needed, have been obtained, however, for every dollar's worth issued at all the depots directly controlled by the Commission."

"Caution is exercised in the distribution of the gifts of the people, chiefly in the following particulars:

"1. That they should be as fairly divided as is practicable—those most needy being most liberally dealt with;

"2. That no officer shall be unnecessarily relieved from an existing responsibility to secure for all dependent on him all the supplies which it is his right and duty to demand directly of Government."

The nature and extent, the business-like system, and the well-organized methods of the Commission's Department of General Relief and Supplementary Supply may best be appreciated by inspecting the daily operations of that Department at one of its principal depots, like that at Washington or Louisville, or by witnessing the rapid accumulation, and equally rapid disbursement and forwarding of "sanitary stores" at temporary depots in the immediate vicinity of armies in the field, as at Chattanooga or Morris Island. The system and methods of this work may briefly be described as follows:—At Washington, Louisville, and New York, the Commission has established Central Depots of supply where the "sanitary stores" are systematically accumulated from the countless and unfailing tributaries of voluntary aid, —the Associations of Relief and the Soldiers' Aid Societies,—that have been organized by the people everywhere in in the loyal states, and which, in Boston, Buffalo, Cleveland, Philadelphia, Pittsburg, Cincinnati, Detroit, Chicago, and some other great commercial centres, have been fully systematised in grand branches that serve as permanent auxiliaries to the Central Depots here mentioned.

Properly classified, packed, and made ready for shipment on instant orders, the "sanitary stores," thus accumulated in the Central Depots and Branches, are subject to such assignment and distribution as the movements and exigencies of the armies and wants of the hospitals may demand. And wherever the exigencies and whatever the demand arising from wants of the sick and wounded or needy, it is the first duty of the Commission's Sanitary Inspectors to direct the Relief Agents to bring forward the requisite supply of the needed "sanitary stores," and distribute them to the very places where they are required. For the facility and promptitude of such distribution and direct application of these supplies there is a moveable or temporary depot and distributing office maintained in every Department and in almost every Corps of the Army.

Though the greater proportion of such supplementary supplies come directly from the hands of the loyal and humane women of the States, there is a large and important class of stores that can only be procured by purchase at wholesale, and in such purchases,—mostly for "battle-field relief,"—the Sanitary Commission has expended the golden gifts of California.

But the gifts and handiwork of women are far more valuable and important, though not more indispensible, than the contributions of money. The "sanitary stores" that have been sent to the Commission's Depots by the women, already amount to an aggregate of several millions of articles,* possessing a cash value that has been estimated at more than SEVEN MILLIONS OF DOLLARS.

---

* The following passage from Miss NIGHTINGALE's replies to the Questions (put by the Royal Commission):—"*Were any difficulties experienced in obtaining food, clothing, bedding, and medical comforts?*" "*What appears to be the cause of such difficulties?*" and "*How were theg overcome?*" strikingly illustrates the similarity of the wants which she met upon the Bosphorus, and which the U. S. Sanitary Commission meets in our much larger hospitals and more hastily gathered army: We here give the abstract of the replies of that remarkable woman, whom a distinguished surgeon in the hospitals at Scutari, has aptly termed the "Good Providence of the Barrack Hospitals:"—

"Difficulties were experienced in obtaining some articles of extra diet, shirts, clean linen, and bedding, ward-furniture, and utensils."

*   *   *   *   *   *   *

"With regard to stores, I can best answer * * * by putting in an abstract of some of the principal articles supplied from private sources to the hospitals, &c,, at Scutari, on requisition from medical officers, as well as those in the Crimea, and only after ascertaining, in most instances, that the articles did not exist in the purveyor's store, or were not to be issued thence: (1.)

"Shirts (flannel and cotton)	50,008	Drinking Cups		5,477
Pairs of Drawers	6.848	India Rubber Sheeting (yds.)		825
Socks and Stockings	28,743	Baths,	Brooms,	Flannel,
Slippers	8,626	Soap,	Bed-pans,	Gloves and Mits,
Dressing-gowns	1,004	Games,	Combs,	Thread and Tape,
Handkerchiefs	10,000	Table,	Brooms,	Boilers,
Air-beds and Pillows	232	Lanterns,	Lamps,	Camp Kitchens,
Towels	5,826		Cooking Stoves, &c., &c."	
Preserved Meats (cases)	258			

* * * "The purveyor purveys according to his 'warrants,'—but the soldier, wants according to his circumstances. The absurdity lies in attempting to provide for war, an abnormal state of society, by normal rules,—non-expensive."

*   *   *   *   *   *   *

"A far more serious question, however, than the want of stores, which, with the Anglo-Saxon race, will always be supplied, in such cases, by private interposition, is the non-organizatiou of a system of general hospital government. For the clash of departments which now constitntes that system cannot bc called a hospital government at all. * * *

It is a lamentable fact that the same clash of departments is still permitted by our Federal authorities to interfere with the proper administration of the army Medical Bureau, and with the government of our general hospitals.

(1.) We quote from Miss Nightingale's abstract only the more important items, and by referring to subsequent pages the reader will be able to compare the above table with similar abstracts of the "Woman's Central Relief Association," the Cleveland, the Boston, and other Relief tributaries of the Sanitary Commission.

In order justly to estimate the nature and the ever-recurring necessity of the supplementary aid that is afforded by the Sanitary Commission's Relief Department, the fact must be borne in mind that the Army Regulations are not as expansible and as facile in their applications to special and unusual emergencies as the necessities of war—especially of such a terrible contest as ours—and the sudden wants of the sick and wounded, often demand. And it is just here that the Sanitary Commission steps in and quickly bridges the chasms of want, while at the same time it throws its most friendly influence in favor of the regular supplies through regular military channels. But, as MISS NIGHTINGALE has graphically said, "the soldier wants according to his circumstances, but the purveyor purveys according to his warrants" (regulations). And it is because the Sanitary Commission has the power and the earnest purpose to come to the aid of the Medical Department and the needy soldier, just when its more expansible and multiform appliances are desired and indispensible, that the people of the loyal States have so generously elected its channels for the transmission of their contributions of material aid for the sick and wounded, or for the soldier wherever and whenever his need is most urgent. Its agencies and appliances of relief follow the soldier through all the encampments, bivouacks, and toilsome marches, until he reaches the battlefields, and to those fields, as closely as non-combatants can approach, it gathers its best supplies for wounded and field-worn men. Then, in the ambulance, and to the general hospital, its "sanitary stores" are always at hand, and to the invalid, the convalescent, and the discharged soldier leaving the hospitals, or wherever he may be found in need of sanitary and friendly aid, the Commission is ever at hand with its well-organized methods of immediate relief, and the advice that such persons require. The peculiarity of the Commission's methods of working in each of these special fields of Relief, require separate consideration in this narrative.

Supplementary Supplies and Special Relief upon Battle-fields.—The experience gained at Ball's Bluff, Pittsburg Landing, Corinth, and upon the bloody fields of the Peninsula, the Rappahannock, the Antietam, and Manassas, as well as in the later great conflicts, as at Gettysburg, Vicksburg, and Chattanooga, have impelled the Sanitary Commission to impart such shape and resources to this department of Supplementary Supplies, as should render it adequate to the exigencies which invariably follow upon the sanguinary conflicts of our forces in the field.

We have already seen how the Commission administered its material and personal agencies of *relief* and aid during the Peninsula campaign, and upon the earlier battle-fields, but those aspects of this subject which most concern the people and the soldiers we will now present somewhat more fully in detail; for the people have a right to know precisely how directly and certainly their gifts go to mitigate the woes of the brave men who fall in battle.

Solferino and Magenta had some of their horrors mitigated by corps of *Infirmiers Volontaires*, and until the new Medical Act and the new Surgeon-General had breathed new life and enlargement into the medical service, our Army Sanitary Commission seemed likely to be burdened with the duty of providing such corps of nurses and field-hospital attendants; and we believe that hitherto nearly every great battle-ground of our forces has borne witness to the readiness of the Commission to assume such service when necessary. But on battle-fields and in the field-hospitals, as well as in the general hospitals, the Commission has mainly endeavored to aid the regular methods of service, co-operating with its officers, and supplementing deficiencies as far as practicable.*

With independent means of transportation and disbursement, and regardless of risks which the military bureaus are slow to incur, the Sanitary Commission's supplies are expeditiously thrown forward towards points where great engagements are impending; and the records of the timely service thus rendered our brave men in their time of greatest need, will live with the history of the war.

This is the method of the Sanitary Commission's work in the vicinity of battle-fields. The Relief Department, as advised by the Sanitary Inspectors in the field, and as directed from the Central offices, sends forward with the moving columns of the army, and also, when practicable, to designated convenient points in the vicinity of the army's line of movement, such well packed trains of selected supplies as for the time are deemed necessary to provide for probable necessities of wounded and exhausted men in the ambulance dépôts and field-hospitals. In most of our armies, whether encamped or moving, the Commission maintains a "flying depot," or special wagon-train of "sanitary stores," under the supervision of the Inspectors and

---

*In support of the policy and the measures adopted by the *U. S. Sanitary Commission*, in its plan of "*Battle-field Relief*," we quote the following emphatic statement, which was made by the representative of the King of Prussia, Dr. Löffler, Physician-in-Chief of the 4th corps in the Prussian army, at the *International Sanitary Conference*, *at Geneva*, Oct. 1863:

"It would not be consistent with the principle of wise State economy to give, in times of peace, and in a continued manner, to the sanitary service of armies, that measure of attention and that great development which it claims in times of war. Moreover, the history of the great contests in our times has demonstrated that when war is about to break out it is impossible for the official authorities to provide the means of succor with sufficient rapidity, and even in a sufficient degree for all possible exigencies. It is to the charitable support and co-operation of the public that we must address ourselves to surround the victims of the contest with all the care to which they have a well-deserved right, and which the heart of the true philanthropist must demand for unfortunate fellow-beings."

Relief Agents, as was first ordered and brought into full operation by a member of the Commission during the march of the Potomac Army through Maryland in the autumn of 1862.*

At certain points designated by military advice, and convenient to the protected flank of the moving columns, and sometimes much nearer the points of anticipated combat than the regular Medical trains are permitted to approach,† the Sani-

---

* In a communication dated September 11th, 1862, that Commissioner made the following statement respecting the organization of "flying depots" of "sanitary stores," to move with the columns of the army:

"I went to the front to organize a more perfect system of supply and distribution of Sanitary Commission Stores, and have succeeded, I think, in doing so. We have now two two-horse wagons with supplies, moving with the advance column of the army, with orders to keep close up with the line of battle. Dr. Chamberlain is with one of these, and Dr. Andrews with the other. Smith is to relieve Chamberlain. I have also sent out some four-horse army wagons, laden with supplies from our Washington depot, under charge of Mr. Mitchell, with orders to move a mile or two in the rear of the line of battle. I say "line of battle," because the army is now moving and camping always in line of battle. Our Inspectors in the advance are instructed to go through the divisions and brigades, and distribute their stores on the requisition of the army medical officers, not only to sick men but to the feeble and weary. Some of the regiments have lived so long on hard bread, coffee, &c., that they are asthenic. Our Inspectors in the advance draw on Mitchell's army wagons, and thus keep their two-horse wagons constantly full. As soon as the army wagons are exhausted, others will be in place, with stores from our Washington depot, and I think our resources will thus be effectively applied. * * * * * * * *

"I wish we could afford to keep such an organization moving with every army corps—a *depot on wheels*, fed from stationary depots." * * *

† * * * "After the battle of Gettysburg, when Meade was pursuing Lee's flying army, and another general battle was hourly expected near the old field of Antietam, the General would not, and could not allow the vast medical stores required in case of a battle to be brought over South Mountain, because Boonsboro, beyond which his own headquarters lay, and where the Sanitary Commission had opened its store-houses, was liable any day to be attacked and ransacked by the enemy's cavalry. This was prudent and humane; and yet in case of a great battle it must have caused enormous suffering. Now, for this very reason that it was not safe for the Government stores, the Sanitary Commission determined to run the risk of its own stores, that if a battle did occur, it might alleviate the wants of the battle-field, till the regular medical stores could be brought up. Thus the Medical Department followed its legitimate and bounden course of duty in obedience to judicious orders from headquarters. The Sanitary Commission, with its independent transportation, and independent movements in general, followed also its legitimate and necessary duty, and stood ready to prevent the evils which must otherwise flow from the best and wisest course left open to the Medical Department."—*North American Review, January*, 1864.

tary Relief trains rendezvous, and establish dispensing depots. In all cases the Inspectors and Relief Agents endeavor, under military advice, to keep the Sanitary train sufficiently in advance with the moving columns of the forces to be prepared for the oxigencies of battle.

The moment a general engagement of the forces is announced, the Inspector who for the occasion is in charge of the Commission's work, directs the necessary regulations for the distribution of "Sanitary stores" for the succor of wounded men, and, at the same time, he and his aids undertake to ascertain by personal inquiry what may be the extent and nature of wants to be supplied by such supplementary means. Then by couriers and by telegraph, requisitions are made upon the Commission's nearest depots for such supplies, while from the Central Depots still larger invoices of assorted supplies for battle-field relief are hastened forward to the field or to the temporary depots, as occasion may require; and being continually informed respecting the actual and prospective wants of the wounded, the Central and the Branch offices promptly respond to special requests from the field and to orders from the Commission. By all practicable means, and usually by several routes, the supplies are pushed forward towards the field hospitals, and along the lines where the means of succor are most required.

Each battle-field of course presents its peculiarities, and a distinct history of woes, and of insufficiency in the means of relief of the wounded, and it must be confessed that upon all great battle-fields there has been a vast amount of unrelieved suffering from causes that ought never to exist in well organized forces; and it must also be stated that in every great battle that is fought in open fields, or under ordinary conditions, a certain amount of unrelieved suffering, from want or tardiness of succor to the wounded, is inevitable. The former occurs in consequence of defects of the ambulance system, and the great difficulty in providing adequate medical aid; the latter, or inevitable wants, are supposed to result from the military necessities that are inevitable in war; the choice of evils must be made, and if wounded men cannot safely be conveyed to the rear, or if they fall into the enemy's hands, their suffering is accepted as the "fate of war." But the Sanitary Commission has earnestly endeavored to diminish, and by every possible means to prevent this want of timely succor, and upon some of the later battle-fields, as at the second great battle before Chattanooga, the sufferings of the wounded for needed relief have, by the prompt and abundant aid of the Sanitary Commission, co-operating with the surgeons, been reduced to a minimum never before equalled in such conflicts.

The extent and urgency of wants which the wounded are liable to suffer from lack of timely succor, also depends largely upon the haste and magnitude of the movement of the forces and their supplies, the difficulties of transportation, and the severity of the combat; therefore, the difficulties that lie in the way of the Commission's work of battle-field relief correspond to these various circumstances, but as that work is now organized, these circumstances are met by corresponding efforts and resources in the relief work, and notwithstanding the difficulties and perils that surround such work, the duties it imposes are never shirked by the Inspectors and Relief Agents who engage in it, and vast as the demands for aid may be, the resources and methods of the Commission are rendered so expansible, that they promptly apply all the means of relief which the munificent contributions from the people enable them to offer. In the earlier period of the war, it sometimes occurred that the Commission's resources were inadequate from lack of funds in the Sanitary Treasury, and exhaustion of reserved supplies in the Commission's depots. But as the business and methods of battle-field relief became systematized and well understoood, the liability to insufficiency and delay steadily diminished.

Upon occasion of great battles, when the National cause and the sympathies of the people are put to severe trials, neither the treasury nor the storehouses of the Commission hold from responding to the largest requisitions that can be made available for the relief of the wounded. We have already alluded to the present methods of "battle-field relief" during General McClellan's campaign in northern Maryland, and we will, from this point of the narrative, recount some incidents from the published records of the Commission's work in this branch of relief.

The memorable battle-field of Antietam will ever be remembered in the history of the Commission, as the field and the occasion upon which the providence of California's golden gifts confirmed the humane purposes of Sanitary relief, and first ministered to the wounded. Previous to that period the system and means for such aid were insufficient, yet the subject had received much attention from various members of the Commission, particularly from Dr. Newberry and Mr. Olmsted, and under the direction of those two officers, and in the abundant experience they had in the working of that system experimentally during spring campaigns of 1862, the methods of supplementary field work which had proved both practicable and necessary, were always too limited in means. The people, through their societies of voluntary aid, and the great branches of supply that had allied themselves to the Commission, had liberally contributed materials for succor; they had also supported the Sanitary Treasury to such a degree as to keep those early methods of labor in operation. But the vastly increased magnitude of the demands for the succor of the wounded, as the campaigns of 1862 progressed, and the unobstructed opportunity which was officially granted for such work, threw upon the Commission a responsibility that required a vast increase of its financial resources. The fact is now known, that in its endeavors to bridge the chasms of want and terrible necessities upon the numerous battle-fields of the summer of 1862, the Commission was impelled by urgent considerations of duty to the wounded and to the country to put its hand to the very bottom of its Treasury, and to the last packages in its Central Depots. In a statement then published [Document No. 48] the following facts are mentioned by a member of the Commission writing from the field, on the fourth day subsequent to the battle of Antietam:

"It should be remembered, that so rapid was the movement of the army through Washington, after the disaster and losses of the Virginia campaign, that the regimental, and brigade, and division medical officers could not, to any considerable extent, replenish their exhausted supplies.

"The medical supplies sent to meet the emergency on Wednesda, did not begin to arrive on the battle-field until Saturday afternoon, and then in small quantity and entirely inadequate. Many of the same supplies are still here (at Frederick), awaiting transportation, while the Commission has had at least four wagon trains sent to the front that left Washington subsequent to Wednesday afternoon, in addition to two sent before in anticipation of the battle. You can estimate at your office the number of wagons we have sent forward, including Hay's trains, which will be on the battle-field this afternoon. As soon as Brink and Mitchell and Parsons arrived on the battle-field, I sent them over radii, previously ascertained to be within the circle of the late battles. They will be able to state personally the fields of their operations, as I desired them to keep notes. I left Dunning's wagon—in fact all the two-horse wagons and ambulances of our train—constantly going, and carrying relief to thousands of wounded.

The wounded were mainly clustered about barns, occupying the barn-yards, and floors, and stables, having plenty of good straw, well broken by the power threshing machine. I saw fifteen hundred wounded men lying upon the straw about two barns, within sight of each other! Indeed, there is not a barn, or farm-house, or store, or church, or school-house, between Boonesborough, Keedysville, and Sharpsburgh, and the latter and Smoketown, that is not gorged with wounded—rebel and Union. Even the corn-cribs, and in many instances the cow-stable, and in one place the mangers, were filled. Several thousands lie in the open air, upon straw, and all are receiving the kind services of the farmers' families and the surgeons.

"I hope I never shall forget the evidences everywhere manifested of the unselfish and devoted heroism of our surgeons, regular and volunteer, in the care of both Federal and rebel wounded. * * * * * *

"Having studied the field, and the relations of the clusters of wounded to a central point, I took, on Saturday, a store at Sharpsburgh, hiring it of a Union citizen of the name of Cronise. On Saturday evening I brought up the mule teams of Peverley to Sharpsburgh. On Sunday morning, Dunning, Mitchell, Parsons, and myself, unpacked the boxes, and filled the shelves and bins. I took charge of the wagons on Saturday night, because Dunning, Brink, and Mitchell were out with relief, to the right and left, for about three thousand wounded; and Parsons had gone back, under instructions from Medical Director Letterman, and my approval, to Birkettsville, with relief to five hundred and forty wounded.

"To finish the store business, I may say that I have left Parsons and Peverley, and a clerk of Mr. Cronise, in charge of the Sharpsburgh store, taking care to provide, out of our trains, a wagon and a saddle-horse for Dr. Dunning, and the same for Dr. Brink. I have given them written instructions to use the saddle-horses to explore the barn-yards and hamlets of the country, and the wagons to accompany with stores of food, stimulants, bandages, clothing, &c., &c.

"Our plans, so far, are working splendidly, thanks to the vigor with which you at Washington have crowded forward supplies, and the aid given by Dr. Letterman and his medical officers. We have been ahead of every one, and at least two days ahead of the supplies of the Medical Bureou; the latter fact due to its want of independent transportation." * *

* * * * * * *

In the same document [No. 48] the following summary of supplies forwarded to the battle-field, is given officially:

"Our independent means of transportation often enable us to reach the wounded with stores in advance of all Government or other supplies. The first *two* days are more important than the next ten to the saving of life and the relief of misery.

"At the recent battle-ground we were able to be present in advance two days, of all supplies (beyond the small amount in the nearly empty storehouse of the army Medical Purveyor), with twenty-five wagon loads of stimulants, condensed food, medicines, and conveniences. Within a week we dispatched successfully by teams, to the scene of battle, from Washington alone, 28,763 pieces dry-goods, shirts, towels, bed-ticks, pillows, &c., 30 barrels bandages, old linen, &c., 3,188 pounds farina, &c.; 2,620 pounds condensed milk, 5,050 pounds beef stock and canned meats, 3,000 bottles wine and cordials, and several tons of lemons and other fruit, crackers, tea, sugar, rubber cloth, tin-cups, and hospital conveniences.*

"Great and constant, therefore, as the supplies of our Central Auxiliary Associations are, and of the towns and villages on which they depend, they ought not to be surprised to learn that our Washington storehouses are bare of shirts, drawers, slippers, socks, bed-sacks, blankets, and old clothing, and that only the ceaseless and increased activity and humanity of our women can be depended on to meet the new demand."

All this had been done before the smoke of that terrible battle had fairly cleared from the ground where lay nearly ten thousand wounded men of our own army, and several thousands of the rebel forces left to the care of Federal surgeons and the Sanitary Commission, and while the utmost resources of the Commission were being thus applied by means of a system that was more fully adequate to the occasion than similar efforts upon other battle-fields had been, it was at a rate of expenditure that speedily exhausted all reserved supplies of sanitary stores, and sent the last funds of the Treasury into the markets for additional means of succor. It was at that hour of imperative duty and greatest anxiety, on the 21st of September, the fourth day after the battle—that a telegram from California

---

* While the Sanitary Commission was thus sending forward all the means of succor it could then command, it successfully undertook to forward from New York a sufficient supply of hospital clothing. In Dr. STEINER's Report, (published by A. D. F. Randolph, New York,) we find the following allusion to the aid thus rendered:

"In addition to these issues, the Commission succeeded in transporting, from the Medical Purveyor's Office in New York to the depot in Frederick, 83 cases, containing 4,000 sets of hospital clothing and 20 bales of blankets, at a cost of $316 58. Transportation was so embarrassed and crowded at this time that these stores were got through in season only by the energy of the Executive Committee in dispatching special agents to take charge of them, at its own expense. As soon as these stores reached this depot they were turned over to the Medical Department and issued as fast as requisitions were sent in."

brought intelligence of liberal promise of pecuniary aid from the Pacific coast; and with that inspiring promise came the welcome announcement that *a hundred thousand dollars*—the first instalment of the golden treasure—was then on the way to the Sanitary Commission. That hundred thousand dollars at the time seemed to be the means of insuring the successful prosecution of the Commission's greatly expanded methods of aid: and every subsequent passage in the history of its sanitary works, and its relief service, will tell how energizing and how salutary was that early lesson of faith, and how California's gold has strengthened and established the broad plans and humane purposes that might otherwise have fluctuated between necessity and inability.

Though that Providence was scarcely more essential to the Commission's battle-field branch of Relief, than to its other departments of service, the world will justly and most gratefully point to the records of the service rendered at the memorable fields of Antietam, Gettysburg, and Chattanooga, and all the great sieges and battles since the autumn of 1862, as affording never-to-be-forgotten testimony to the great utility and wise bestowment of the golden gifts from the patriotic people of the great mining regions. And the same records will show how timely and how tenderly all the home-gifts and means of succor which the people have turned into the Sanitary Commission's channels, have been administered for the relief and life-saving of the brave men who have fallen in their country's service. All departments of the Commission's work have been equally benefited by the munificent aid from the Pacific States. The records of Sanitary Relief at all the great battles since that of Antietam, show that the enlarged methods of succor that were adopted upon that memorable field have depended in no small degree upon the thoughtful continuance of those golden contributions; and, as we have seen, the commencement of these contributions is forever associated with the memories of humane relief upon one of the most terrible battle-fields of the war.

Battle-field Relief in the Earlier Period of the War.—Let us revert for a moment to the history of the Commission's relief work in the earlier battles. The statements referring to this subject in preceding sections of this narrative, show how impressively the duty and the necessity of rendering such service to the wounded were unfolded upon every successive battle-field. At first the *preparations* on the part of the Medical Department were inadequate, and then it was found that in each successive engagement the armies fought with such unequalled pertinacity and vigor, that the percentage of wounded men greatly exceeded the expectations of the Government, and the preparations for the succor and transportation of the wounded. The Sanitary Commission carefully investigated the facts relating to this subject, and strenously endeavored to procure, through the regular departments, as well as by its own supplementary aid, an adequate supply of personal and material means of succor for the wounded. The wants of wounded men at the battles of Ball's Bluff, Wilson's Creek, Lexington, Springfield, Pea Ridge, Fort Donelson and Shiloh, fully confirmed the opinions which the Sanitary Commission had expressed immediately after the first engagement at the ill-starred battle-ground of Manasses, namely, that unless the Government would actually do all that practically could be done for the succor and benefit of the sick and wounded, the Commission would necessarily be constrained vastly to increase its own resources of supplementary aid. This idea, it will be recollected, had been cautiously expressed by the Preliminary Committee that asked for the organization of a Sanitary Commission; and in December, 1861, the following statement was made by the Commission in its report to the Secretary of War:

"The possibility of an engagement on our own soil at any moment, between two armies of one hundred and fifty or two hundred thousand men each, is so strange a novelty that we naturally fail to appreciate its inevitable consequences, and the immense amount of human suffering which must follow it. The battle of Bull Run has not taught us the lesson, because most of our wounded were then left on the field. Few of the more serious cases reached our hospitals. We must remember that the experience of foreign armies shows that, after a well-contested battle on this scale, we must count on having, at the very least, from twenty to thirty thousand men crying to us for relief from agony."

It is now seen that the necessity and desirableness of such voluntary and supplemental aid has been abundantly confirmed by the testimony of the most experienced military officers and public authorities in Europe,* and the terrible experiences of our successive battle-fields, have shown how vitally important such aid has been in our armies. But the United States Sanitary Commission had no precedents by which to be guided in devising its methods and means of battle-field relief. Government authorities whose practical knowledge of armies and battles extended only to the matters of routine in official service, generally doubted the practicability of rendering supplementary aid to the wounded, and some military officers expressed anxiety in view of the unusual urgency with which the claims of humanity and of popular concern in this war were presented by the Sanitary Commission. But, to the infinite credit of the profession of arms, and to the advancing civilization of the age, the ablest Generals and best officers in all departments of military service, almost without exception, have favored and aided the purpose of the Commission from the first; and the veteran General Scott, like the venerable General Dufour who pre-

* *See Appendix* C.

sided at the recent International Sanitary Conference at Geneva,* was first to express his interest and confidence in such plans for succor to the wounded.

A few great battles during the first year of the war served to illustrate what would be the inevitable wants and woes of our battle-fields, with all the means of succor which the Medical Department possessed, and the Sanitary Commission endeavored to ascertain how far and by what agencies it might be practicable to supplement the insufficiencies and delays of the *regular* methods for meeting the exigencies of great battles. The scenes of suffering that were witnessed after the sanguinary struggles at Fort Donelson, Pittsburg Landing, and some other battles during the first year of the war, cannot be recalled to mind without bringing up ghastly pictures of terror and anguish that

---

* At the opening of the great Conference at Geneva, the President, General Dufour, a military officer of great renown, made the following statements concerning the duty of rendering more adequate succor to the wounded in war:

"You are aware, gentlemen, that the condition of the ambulances in the regular armies affords very inadequate relief to the wounded who are unfortunately left upon the battle-field. There is in this respect a very great defect, which is especially apparent upon those occasions in which promptness and efficient aid would be most desirable. This defect has impressed every one, but it has been especially portrayed, with startling truthfulness, in a work with which you are familiar, published after the battle of Solferino by one of our fellow citizens, M. Dunant. We are convened, gentlemen, for the purpose of discovering some possible method of realizing a philanthropic idea contained in this work. We do not affirm *a priori* that this possibility exists, but we hope that this assemblage of men, essentially qualified to entertain such questions, may be able to arrive at some solution of the difficult problem upon which we are engaged. This is desirable for all, but especially for the unfortunate soldier. We do not sufficiently appreciate the situation of a man serving as a private soldier, who, often, after having for a long time endured privations of every kind (it is sufficient to recollect the sufferings experienced during the severe campaign in the Crimea and the siege of Sebastopol), arrives upon the field of battle, and there, after having fought for his flag with courage and devotion, finds himself, as a reward, suffering the most torturing pains, for which not the least relief is provided, and which are often greatly enhanced by the fearful anguish consequent upon their abandonment.

"Notwithstanding the philanthropic efforts of Peace Congresses—to whose efforts we accord all the respect and sympathy they merit, without being deceived as to the small amount of success which they are likely to attain, as long as human passion exist, and these threaten to continue a long time to come—there will be wars upon this earth; therefore, to be truly useful to the cause of humanity, we must, instead of indulging the vain hope of their suppression, endeavor to render their consequences less terrible if possible, and lend our aid as effectually to those whose

burden the soul like a horrible nightmare. But those scenes, and the realities of insufficient means of succor that lay behind what had been regarded as necessarily and essentially the fate of war, were from the first seriously studied by the Commission; the chief causes of such insufficiency and official neglect were ascertained, and the practicable methods of improvement and of aid were discussed, and as far as possible, the available means of relief were put into operation.

The vital importance of an improved *ambulance system* was faithfully represented to the military authorities, and the duty of organizing and keeping in constant readiness an adequate reserve force to succor the wounded was urged upon the proper authorities. The events that followed the collision of the forces at Bull Run had served to determine the question of the Sanitary

---

duty it is to give assistance to those sufferers by providing the concurrent aid which they need without occasioning any embarrassment to the cause of the armies. Such is the problem to be solved of which we have just been speaking.

"Do we indulge vain fancy in attempting a solution of this problem? Is the end which we wish to attain so high and beyond our powers that the concentration of all our efforts will be inefficient? If that be so, we must submit, but we shall ever have the merit of having made the attempt, which will be a source of satisfaction to those who feel a lively interest in the suffering of the human race. In either case, we shall have sown in the field of our future sun which will hereafter bring forth fruit, when more favorable circumstances shall cause it to germinate, when civilization shall have made more progress, and when nations shall have entered upon broader and more humane paths than those which they have hitherto trodden. It belongs to the future, indeed, to decide this question, but we shall have done what we could. Even if we arrive at no definite result during this conference,—which, on account of its aims and the sympathies which, from its first inception, it has excited throughout Europe, will elicit no inconsiderable degree of attention,—we shall at least have established a starting point for those ameliorations which we may hope to realize in after times. It does not become us, therefore, to be discouraged at the prospect of a temporary want of success. Let us boldly meet the problem; let us do all in our power to solve it; and if success be not within our reach, there will remain to us the consciousness of having done what it became those to do who love their neighbor."

* * "It has been urgd that instead of seeking for expedients whereby war may be rendered less terrible, it would be preferable to attack the evil at its root, and labor to promote the universal and permanent pacification of the world. Our opponents, by their arguments, would seem to insinuate that our efforts have no higher aim than to legalize war, by making it appear as a necessary evil. Is this criticism seriously made? I cannot believe it. Most assuredly we desire as much as any one can that men should cease to slay each other, and repudiate this relic of barbarism which they have inherited from their fathers. With the aid of Christianity, this result will sooner or later be be attained, and we appland the efforts of those who are striving for the amelioration of the human race."—"*Compte Rendu de la Conference Internationale*," Geneva, Oct., 1863.

Commission's duty to accept and disburse supplementary supplies, and also to vastly increase all the resources it could command to meet the exigencies of battle-fields, as well as to extend its first great work of Sanitary Inquiry and Advice. Fully believing that as soon as our armies had become trained to soldierly duties, their valor in combat with the enemy would be equal at least to that of European armies, the Commission urged this consideration upon the Medical Bureau, and at the same time set about its own work of preparation for battle-field succor in combats, when 20 or 30 *per cent.* of all the forces engaged wovld be counted among the wounded. The system and the extent of that work of preparation will appear in the sketch given in subsequent pages relating to the Commission's Branches of supply, and the administration of its system of relief.

In December, 1861, soon after the battle of Belmont, in Missouri, the Commission not only took measures for largely increasing its stock of "Sanitary stores" in the West, but, through its excellent Senior Inspector in that field, Dr. Aigner, the plan of organizing a line of floating hospitals to move with the forces upon the rivers was suggested, and, in a valuable report upon the subject, the practicability and importance of the plan was successfully urged upon the military authorities. Accordingly when General Grant moved up the Cumberland river to capture Fort Henry and Fort Donelson, the first hospital steamer, the *City of Memphis*, was ordered into service by the Medical Director. She was fully furnished with hospital supplies from the Commission's depot at Cairo, and, arriving at that place with a load of patients when news was received of the fight at Donelson, Dr. Aigner instantly ordered all his reserved stores on board, and at once proceeded to the scene of that unconditional contest, where all those supplies and much more were greatly needed. Dr. Warriner was then at Paducah, laboring night and day to supplement wants in the overcrowded hospitals there; and Dr. Douglass, an Associate Secretary, hastened down from St. Louis with all the reserved supplies that the Commission had accummulated at that point, while Dr. Newberry at once steamed down the Ohio and up the Cumberland in the *Collyer*, with a large cargo of supplies, and a corps of volunteer assistants from Cincinnati; while the Branch at Chicago, the Aid Societies of all the large towns in the West, and the people of St. Louis, hurried forward to Cairo vast quantities of valuable and timely supplies. But the woes that were suffered by the wounded during the period that elapsed previous to the arrival of this voluntary aid, can never be adequately described. Hundreds perished before the means of succor reached them. The agents of the Sanitary Commission made great efforts to meet the exigencies of the hour, and what they accomplished, though far short of their desires, because so delayed in reaching the wounded, was so important and so timely, that even the most relentless official routinests confessed the utillity of the work.

The Cumberland river being opened to Nashville, the Commission at once established a depot of supplies in that city, and while the forces under Grant and Buell were moving to the Tennessee to meet the rebel army in Northern Mississippi, Dr. Newberry, the Western Secretary, was massing hospital supplies, etc., at Cairo, Paducah, and such points upon the Tennessee as could be securely occupied until the collission might occur. The vast utility of floating hospitals upon the rivers had been demonstrated by the *City of Memphis*, and other steamboats upon which hospital arrangements had been hastily improvised.

But while the Sanitary Commission was thus massing its "Sanitary stores," at points within convenient reach, the regular supplies of the Medical Department were moved too tardily and in insufficient quantities, and when our forces gave battle at Pittsburg Landing those supplies were far away and utterly insufficient. The Commission's stores were speedily brought up the river, but at first they were inadequate to the terrible exigencies of the occasion. The hospitals at Savannah, a few miles below Pittsburg Landing, had been mainly furnished by the Commission, and the large floating hospital, *Louisiana*, upon which the Associate Secretary, Dr. Douglass, obained transportation for himself and the corps of volunteer surgeons and attendants, about sixty in number, from the Chicago Branch, went up the Tennessee freighted with a cargo of the Commission's stores, which were at once distributed to the wounded upon the transports and in the ambulances; a depot of supplies and a system of destribution were established, and, by the large supplies and aid from Cincinnati and Louisville, directed by Dr. Newberry, that depot, and subsequently the store-boat *Polar Star*, continued to issue every variety of supplementary supplies until the last of the hospitals and the wounded were removed from that place, late in the month of July.

The terrible sufferings and wants of our wounded at Donelson and at Pittsburg Landing were equalled by the valor which now has become historical fame to the armies of the Mississippi valley, and the sympathy and the earnest purpose of the whole population of the West then and continually, became manifest in every town and every household. Contribu'ions of supplies then began to flow, and have ever since kept flowing, in an incessant stream. The Sanitary Commission, instructed by these experiences upon the Cumberland and the Tennessee, as well as upon the Peninsula and elsewhere during that eventful spring of 1862, ordered such improvements in the transportation and massing of "sanitary stores" along the lines of the army as should enable relief agents to succor the wounded with greater promptitude. The terrible earnestness with which the war would be waged was fully illustrated by the first great battles of the year, and the fact had become apparent that the determined purpose and the extended preparations of the Sanitary Commission were not in vain. The generals who led in those battles have continued to be peculiarly friendly to the Commission's purposes and works, and the people at home manifestly learned to appreciate the Commission's service in exact proportion to its sufficiency and promptitude.

Deeply impressed with the importance of rendering its means of succor in active campaigns in the highest degree prompt and effective, the Commission not only took measures to keep up temporary depots of supplies in the immediate vicinity of the forces in the field, but with the Sanitary Inspectors that accompanied the grand expeditions under General Burnside and General Butler during the winter and spring of 1862, the General Secretary ordered large supplies of "sanitary stores" to be shipped in vessels accompanying those expeditions, the noble leaders of which, furnished every facility, and encouraged the undertaking. And it may justly be claimed, that the aid which the Commission thus rendered to the sick and wounded during those perilous but brilliant expeditions, proved very highly satisfactory; and we are warranted in saying that the Commission could not desire stonger friendship for itself and its methods of aid than is entertained by those brave generals and the noble armies they commanded.

In former pages we have referred to the systematic methods by which the Commission early endeavored to be prepared to render prompt and effectual relief when the great occasions of wounds and want arrived. The demands for such reserved supplies followed rapidly, and more and more urgently, from the beginning of the year 1862. The great expeditions down the coast were accompanied by ample and well-chosen "sanitary stores" from the Commission's depot, and each succeeding engagement of our armies in the West, tested the largest resources of those depots and of the boundless liberality and energy of the branches of aid. In short, the correctness of the Sanitary Commission's earliest plans and estimates for meeting the prospective and inevitable wants of our armies in active campaigns, was fully demonstrated even before the opening of the Peninsula campaign. How timely, how great, how enlarged, yet how overdrawn, were the resources which the Commission brought into all the campaigns and to every battle-field during the ensuing months of that year of sanguinary conflicts, a million soldiers and thousands of homes will forever remember with deepest gratitude; and how profoundly the Sanitary Commission shared all the anxieties and patriotic endeavors of the people and the armies during that most momentous period of peril and effort, can never be forgotten. It was *a year of battles*, and of toil, the severest and most incessant of any war in modern times; and, although the Sanitary Commission during all that eventful period did not relinquish its other branches of sanitary work and relief, the history of the development and progress of the present system of battle-field relief, can only be given by recounting the leading facts relating to the campaign work of the Commission during that memorable time.

Progress and Purposes in the work of Battle-field Relief during Dark Days in the Autumn of 1862.—After the appalling exhibition of insufficiency in the means of succor upon the battle-fields at the West and upon the Peninsula, the Commission put forth the most energetic efforts to meet all the deficiencies it could possibly reach. Its humane purposes, its faith, and its utmost resources, were put to the severest test in this undertaking.

In Document 44, published by the Commission July 4th, 1862, the following statement is made respecting the work then in hand, and the rate of expenditure of material and money:

"From May 1st to July 1st, the Commission has expended

$37,585 $\frac{73}{100}$ dollars. About nine-tenths of this sum has been laid out in the purchase of hospital stores and appliances for the relief of the sick and wounded at every important military station, and in the equipment of the flotilla of steamers and sailing vessels now in the service of the Commission as Hospital Transports. Its treasury is now nearly exhausted, at the very moment when the army most needs its aid, and when, *if it had an hundred thousand dollars* at its command, it would still be far too weak for the urgent work before it, and would still be obliged to see hundreds perishing for want of its aid, in the army of the Potomac alone." * * * * * *

And in a statement published on the 11th of September following, the progress of the "battle-field and mobilized relief service," is thus set forth:*

"Since the 1st September (ten days) the Commission has expended six thousand dollars and upwards in the purchase of supplies, which have been distributed by its Inspectors and by members of the Commission on the battle-fields of Virginia."

"They have also thus distributed stores to a vastly larger amount, which have been contributed directly to its depots by their patriotic fellow-citizens in every loyal State. Notwithstanding the generous support that has been rendered the Commission, its present expenses far overrun its receipts. And, although it is daily relieving a fearful amount of suffering, and saving many lives, it is now and long has been obliged to witness a far greater amount of suffering and of death, which it has never had the means to relieve. What it has done, is but little compared with what it could do, had its resources been at

---

* The imperative duty and necessity of such supplementary relief in time of battles, were well stated, in the document above quoted, as follows:

"It may be said that the Government should do all this. Were this true, its default would not justify us in leaving our soldiers to perish. But it is only partially true. While active military operations are in progress, and especially at the close of great battles, the prompt and thorough relief and treatment of the sick and wounded requires an amount of force, in men, material, and transportation which no Government has hitherto been able to keep permanently attached to its medical department. At such times volunteer aid from without is indispensable to prevent the most fearful suffering and waste of life, however faithful and untiring the Medical Staff may be."

all adequate to its work. The more money it commands, the more hospital supplies, restoratives, and beneficent material of every kind, it can apply to the relief of the army."

In a letter published in this statement, a member of the Commission writes to his colleagues, from the battle-field of Manassas, Va., Sept. 7th:

"Everything we brought came into play. From Saturday to Wednesday nearly two thousand of our wounded lay on the battle-field without food or water. Even the surgons were *starving*. One told me that he was glad to pick up a piece of cracker he found lying in the mud, and to eat it. The sufferings of the wounded during this interval were alleviated by a heavy thunder-shower, which gave their lips the only water they tasted. Some of them were taken to farm-houses, some received food from the country people, but *many*, *very many*, died of starvation and exposure." * * * * *

* * * * "A great battle may be soon expected. Urge our loyal people at the North, to send supplies to the Cooper Institute dépôt in New York, and to the Philadelphia dépôt, as fast as possible. Buy as liberally as the state of the treasury will permit. You cannot accumulate too large a stock of clothing, and of hospital supplies of every sort. I should almost advise you to run in debt, if necessary, for I am confident the liberal and patriotic people of New York, Philadelphia, and Boston will carry us through."

The foregoing brief summary of the Commission's first year's experience in efforts to furnish supplementary aid for the succor of the wounded in battle, presents an outline of the origin and progress of this important branch of Relief. The duty and necessity of attempting such voluntary aid were apparent, but the possibility of rendering it in a manner that would be entirely acceptable and successful, was a problem which the Commission's agents must solve, and fortunately that problem was satisfactorily solved, and the largest resources of succor which the Commission could then command were acceptably applied for the relief of wounded men, during the eventful spring and summer of 1862. The decisive work that followed the march of Potomac army into Northern Maryland, and the battle scenes that at the same period demanded like promptitude in the work of succor for the wounded in the Western army,* fully confirmed the enlarged and more energetic method of Battle-field Relief which the Commission had then adopted, and which, by the rich gifts from the Pacific coast, were rendered immediately and permanently successful.

From this point in the history of the Sanitary Commission we shall trace the records of Battle-field Relief in connection with the current narrative of each campaign of the respective armies. But before proceeding further, we must examine the other branches of work which are comprised in the Department of Relief, and which, previous to the opening of the campaigns of 1863, were all working harmoniously and effectively.

The Field Relief Corps and Regular Relief Work in Camps.—The highly gratifying results of the Commission's shipments of "sanitary stores," with the inspectors and relief agents accompanying the respective expeditions of Generals Burnside and Butler, and the incessant requirement for such supplementary aid during the Peninsula campaign, and in all the lines of the Western army, served to demonstrate the importance and the practicability of organizing the present system of a Field Relief Corps and *flying depots* of supply in the several *corps d'armee*. We have already quoted the allusion which was made to this subject by the member of the Commission who successfully attempted the first organization of this nature when our forces were hurrying towards the Antietam. In subsequent pages of this narrative, some of the good results of this

---

* See pages 41 and 42.

admirable method of instant aid in moving columns and distant encampments of the armies will appear; but the reader will obtain a sufficiently distinct idea of the nature and practical operations of this system from the following account given by Dr. L. H. Steiner, chief inspector, concerning field relief work in the army of the Potomac:

* * * * * * * *

"July 17, * * * an effort was made to organize the corps immediately. The army was then resting at or near Berlin, Maryland, and it was thought that our corps could be put in such form as to move with it on its entrance into Virginia. * * * * * After considerable trouble, we succeeded in starting off from Boonsboro' on Sunday, July 18th, four wagons under charge of as many relief agents. * * * In each of six corps of the army, we have a substantial army wagon, which is kept filled with an assortment of such supplies as are likely to be needed by the sick or wounded in the field. This wagon is in charge of a relief agent, who has his tent, and lives in the corps to which he is attached. For convenience, his headquarters and stores are usually with the Ambulance Corps. The agent makes himself acquainted with the wants of the different division, brigade and regimental hospitals, and endeavors to supply their wants from the contents of his wagon. He becomes one of the family, and makes common cause with its interests. It was believed, that, in this way, an agent would become more interested in his work. Sharing the toils and the perils, to a certain extent also, of his corps, he would find himself thoroughly identified with it. Thus there would be superadded to his general desire to aid the army at large, the anxious feeling to aid those who had become his friends through a community of feelings and daily intercouse. This idea has been fully sustained by the results of nearly two months active operations. * * * From the very inception of this work, it has asked only the privilege of working along with the medical officers, supplementing their work and bringing such succor to the needy of our great army as a liberal public is desirous should be extended."

Previous to the adoption of this very complete system of Field Relief, the methods adopted for the same object had worked well, but at times lacked that promptitude in application of the means of succor which this system so effectually insures. The regulations concerning the disbursement of supplies, and the maintenance of temporary or camp dépôts of "sanitary stores," have continued essentially the same since the first autumn of the war, viz., that a dépôt of such supplies be provided in the vicinity of each grand division of the army, and that issues be made upon requisition and receipt of medical officers of the forces, or upon orders from the sanitary inspectors. Before the Commission enjoyed the advantages of independent transportation for its "sanitary stores," the temporary or field dépôts could not always be kept up closely to the forces, yet they have vastly diminished the amount of physical sufferings in the regimental and corps hospitals, and afforded much needed succor to tens of thousands whose lives might otherwise have been sacrificed to the stern necessities of the camp hospitals. Incalculable good was thus accomplished in the armies of the Cumberland and the Mississippi, as well as in those of the East, during the first two years of the war. The present system is simply more prompt and effective in consequence of its independent means of transportation, its more complete organization, and the assignment of a specially trained corps of laymen to the work of Field Relief.

It is not practicable in every army and under all circumstances for the Sanitary Commission to keep up an independent transportation train, as, for example, in the passage of Rosecrans' army over the Cumberland mountains into Georgia, but wherever it is practicable the Commission has an independent wagon-train, or a special detail of army wagons from the Quartermaster, moving the "sanitary stores" with the advancing columns of the forces; and, for sending forward supplies to the temporary or branch dépôts near the field, the Quartermaster and Medical Directors have usually extended to the Commission all the facilities in their power. But, as far as possible, the Field Relief train, or "*flying depots*," have their own wagons and horses, and receive forage, etc., from the Quartermasters when with the other army trains. The nature and amount of disbursements from these "*flying depots*" may be estimated from the following schedule, which we copy from the report of Dr. Steiner, Chief Sanitary Inspector of the army of the Potomac. Reporting the work of his Field Relief Corps from the time it began to move southward with Meade's forces from Boonsboro', July 17th, 1863, until the beginning of January, 1864, that Inspector states, that—

"In addition to the four wagon loads of stores first sent forth —of which no account was made—the following articles have been issued through its agents up to the date of this report:

Extract of Beef	2,792	cans.
Condensed Milk	4,400	"
Corn Starch, &c., &c	4,533	pounds.
Soft Crackers	89¼	barrels.
Pickles	436	gallons.
Jellies	610	jars.
Dried Fruit	21	barrels.
Tea	223	pounds.
Chocolate	1,012	"
Sugar	1,074	"
Chloroform	81	"
Tamarinds	110	gallons.
Tomatoes	156	cans.
Brandy, Rum, and Whiskey	1,936	bottles.
Foreign and Domestic Wine	1,271	"
Jamaica Ginger	840	"
Shirts, wool and cotton	6,301	
Drawers, "	5,513	
Socks, "	4,739	
Bed-ticks	1,522	
Blankets and Quilts	2,310	
Pillow Cases	1,712	
Handkerchiefs	1,414	
Tin Cups	1,204	
Towels	3,547	
Slippers	843	

Pillows	992
Sheets	1,017
Work Bags	200
Tobacco	735 pounds.
Buckets	20

Special Relief.

We have already noticed that the branch of Special Relief naturally grew out of the Commission's *stem* of "Supplementary Supply," and we will now refer to the theory and methods of this branch of Relief, as conceived and put into operation during the first months of the war. The following statements were made concerning the first steps and the first fruits of this work, early in the autumn of 1861:

"The main purpose had in view in this agency has been to lessen the hardships to which the ignorance of the sick volunteers and their officers of the forms and methods of government make them subjeet while in the city of Washington, and to provide for certain wants of the volunteers, when detatched from their regiments, for which the government arrangements had been inadequate, and which the regular inspectors of the Commission, in their visits to camps and hospitals, could not attend to.

"Practically, the chief duty has been—

"First. To supply to the sick men of the regiments arriving here such medicines, food, and care as it was impossible for them to receive, in the midst of the confusion, and with the lack of facilities, from their own officers.

"Second. To furnish suitable food, lodging, care, and assistance to men discharged from the general hospitals, or from their regiments, but who are often delayed for a number of days in the city before they obtain their papers and pay.

"Third. To give assistance and information, and secure transportation to men who arrive at the station house in small numbers, and want to find and oin their regiments. Some of these are men accidently left behind; some are men who have been detained by order for a few days at hospitals in Philadelphia or Baltimore."

*   *   *   *   *   *   *

"When we found men at the reception buildings in need of medical treatment, but not sick enough to be sent to the general hospital, we called in a physician, unless their own surgeon could be obtained."

* * * * * * *

"We fortunately obtained part of a house near the station on Capitol Hill, (the second house from the raiiroad, on the street running from the rear of the station to the Capitol,) and on Saturday night it was furnished with beds and all conveniences for the accommodation of thirty or foriy men; and that night there were twenty-one invalid soldiers resting there." * * * * "The largest number in the house at any one time has been 91, the smallest number 13. On many nights in succession the number has exceeded 50."

Thus wrote the "Special Relief Agent," Rev. F. N. Knapp the presiding genius of the Commission's "Special Relief" Department, at the end of the second month's experiment in this work. He had then given relief and the comforts of the "Home," on North Capitol street, to 1,800 of the way-side sick and needy volunteers about Washington, and, during that period, had determined upon the proper methods of administering sucn aid. Immediately this branch of Relief service was extended to other central poiuts of military rendezvous, and to other sources of distress among invalid or needy soldiers when separated from their regiments.* This expansion of Relief work

---

* In Mr. Knapp's last Report of the Special Relief service, he states that the following additional methods have been in operation during the year:

"To communicate with distant regiments in behalf of discharged men whose certificates of disability or descriptive lists on which to draw their pay prove to be defective—the invalid soldiers meantime being cared for, and not exposed to the fatigue and risk of going in person to their regiments to have their papers corrected.

"To act as the unpaid agent or attorney of discharged soldiers who are too feeble or too utterly disabled to present their own claim at the paymaster's office.

"To look into the condition of discharged men who assume to be without means to pay the expense of going to their homes; and to furnish the necessary means where we find the man is true and the need real.

"To secure to disabled soldiers railroad tickets at reduced rates, and, through

and all its varied and humane interpositions in behalf of the invalid soldier, at all those times and places in which his wants and anxieties are greatest and the Government's care most distant and inapplicable, has proved to be a scheme full of blessing to the thousands of needy men who receive its benefits; and as all its methods and appliances are so managed as to render this service most acceptable to the public authorities, as well as to the persons relieved, there is no doubt that this admirably efficient and humane branch of the Commission's Relief Department will continue in full operation, until permanent peace shall have scattered our armies to their homes and emptied the vast hospitals that have marked the pathway of the war.

This branch of the relief service is not a philanthropic interferance at the expense of the Army Regulations and military discipline, for it is itself as systematic and regular as the regulations themselves, and it manifestly serves the invalid soldier and the National Government with equal faithfulness. Says Mr. Knapp, in his recent report:

* * * * "The authority and importance of military discipline are not set aside or lost sight of; on the contrary, they are always rigidly insisted upon. In this work the Sanitary Commission, as the representatives of the people at home, seeks to do precisely what it believes would gladly be

---

an agent at the railroad station, see that these men are not robbed or imposed upon by sharpers.

"To see that all men who are discharged and paid off do at once leave the city for their homes; or, in cases where they have been induced by evil companions to remain behind, to endeavor to rescue them, and see them started with through-tickets to their own towns.

"To make reasonably clean and comfortable before they leave the city, such discharged men as are deficient in cleanliness and clothes.

"To be prepared to meet at once, with food or other aid, such immediate necessities as arise when sick men arrive in the city in large numbers from battle-fields or distant hospitals.

"To keep a watchful eye upon all soldiers who are out of hospitals, yet not in service; and give information to the proper authorities of such soldiers as seem endeavoring to avoid duty or to desert from the ranks."—*Document 77; Fifth Report concerning Aid and Comfort given by the Sanitary Commission to Sick and Invalid Soldiers.*"

done—were it right or possible to enter into this kind of work—by the Military and Medical authorities themselves, under the administration which the people all so cordially desire to support."

The practical interest which the people have in the details of this branch of relief for the soldier, when he is most friendless, most sorrowful, and needy, warrant our presenting a more particular notice of this work. The details are fortunately before us in recent reports from the two Associate Secretaries, Rev. F. N. Knapp at Washington, and Dr. J. S. Newberry, at Louisville. First,—in Washington and its vicinity the Commission now has the following provisions for its local relief service:

The "Home" and its temporary hospital, on North Capitol street, have 320 beds, and all needed appliances for the care and comfort of the persons received there—nearly 1,000 sick men, many in a dying condition, were received in the "Home hospital" during the past year, and the total "number of different individuals received there from December 15th, 1862, to October 1st, 1863 7,187
Number of nights' lodging furnished............... 26,523
Number of meals furnished........................ 65,621"

"Almost all the men received here have been men discharged from the service on account of disability, wounds, or continued sickness. Of these, one-half at least were delayed in the city on account of imperfections in some of their discharge papers, the final statements, on which to draw their pay, requiring often a number of days for their correction."

"Next in order after the 'Home' is *Lodge No.* 2, in '17th' street: Number of nights' lodging given them from December 15th to March 12th.................................. 1,550
Number of meals.................................. 2,130

"*Lodge No.* 3, in 'F' Street. When this Lodge was built, the office for the payment of discharged soldiers was near by, in 'F' Street; that office having been removed to 'H' Street, this Lodge has been closed; (it now is used as the local storehouse of the Commission, and furnishes excellent accommodations.)

From December 15th until it was closed, this Lodge furnished nights' lodging........................ 3,760
Meals.. 17,950

"*Lodge No.* 4, in 'H' Street. This is the new Lodge with large accommodations, immediately connected with the office of the Paymaster for discharged soldiers. It was opened about the 1st of February.

Number of nights' lodging furnished at Lodge No. 4, from February 1st to October 1st.................. 9,832
Number of meals furnished............................ 50,096

"This relief station consists of six buildings. A dormatory of a hundred beds: a dining-room, seating about one hundred, with a large kitchen attached; a storehouse; quarters for the guard; and a building containing the office of the Free Pension Agency, office of the Medical Examiner for pensions, and ticket office for the Railroad agent, selling through-tickets to soldiers at reduced rates of fare."

"All disabled soldiers discharged directly from this Army of the Potomac or from the Hospitals in this vicinity come to the Paymaster's office, which is within this same inclosure, to be paid off. *Government can no longer hold itself directly responsible for these men, and here is where we take them up.*" * *

"The object of the whole thing at the Lodge is this, viz.: So to supply to the discharged soldier close at his hand and without a cent of cost, all that he needs—food, lodging, assistance in correcting his papers, aid in looking up his claism, help in obtaining his pension and his bounty." * * * *

"Every man who comes to the paymaster with his discharge, at once receives a ticket insuring him care and a helping hand; and by an arrangement with the paymaster, whenever a man appears with defective papers, he is at once referred to the Relief Office for assistance or advice. The work at that office occupies three persons constantly, besides those who go with cases that have to be looked up personally at the hospitals or with the regimental officers in the field, and cannot be arranged by correspondence."

"At this office and Lodge No. 4, from January 1st to October 1st, 1863, the number of discharged soldiers whose accounts against the Government have been settled through our assistance, men who were too feeble to attend to settling their own accounts, or who were unable to obtain their pay, because of some charge against them on the pay-rolls, or some errors in their papers, 2,130."

"Information and directions have been given relative to settling pay accounts, collecting arrears of pay, extra duty pay, commutation money to about 9,000 men."

"The aggregate value of the 2,130 cases amounted to $130,-159.01. This amount was collected and pasd to the soldiers through this office."

* * * * * * * *

"*Lodge No.* 5, near 6th Street Wharf. This was a small building, but it has rendered valuable service, giving food and shelter to sick or wounded men arriving on the boats from Aquia Creek, and furnishing food to be carried into such boats as, loaded with wounded, had no adequate provision for feeding the men on board."

* * * * * * * *

"There was one week, at the time of the breaking up of the Corps Hospitals near Aquia Creek, when we gave coffee and food to over five thousand (5,000) men on board the boats which arrived at the wharf."

At the Lodge on Maryland Avenue (removed from 6th Street Wharf), near Alexandria and Washington R. R. station.

The whole number of nights' lodging furnished at this building from January 1st to October 1st, 1863....	1,620
Meals..	14,590

"Closely connected with the work at the Relief Station in Maryland Avenue, is the Lodge at Alexandria, located within the stockade, near the railway track and junction, where all the cars to and from the Army stop. * * * *
This Relief Station is now the 'Gateway of the Army of the Potomac,' and whenever a train of sick or wounded is coming in, a telegram is sent in advance from the front, and when the train arrives at this point food is ready for them and distributed among them while the train is waiting."

Besides these various lodges, &c., the Commission has established a "Nurses' Home" for the temporary relief of nurses arriving in Washington or returning worn down from service. It also affords daily relief and advice to mothers, wives, and sisters of sick soldiers, when worthily in need of shelter and friendly aid. Then there are special offices connected with the Back Pay and Pension relief agencies of the Commission, where, by much painstaking and gratuitous labor of the relief agents of that branch of service, a vast amount of delay, suffering, waste, and want, are prevented. A detective agent of relief and advice, constantly on duty, rescues wandering and ignorant convalescents, discharged, and furloughed men, from harpies who lie in wait for them and their money; and at Camp Convalescent, with its constant population of nearly 6,000, and an average of arrivals and departures of 2,000 men per week, another agent of "Special Relief" is ever illustrating "what an amount of work can be done, relief afforded, influence exerted by one individual thoroughly in earnest, and with resources at hand." At Annapolis and at Baltimore, the Commission has in operation similar and adequate methods of "special relief;" while at all the great points of military rendezvous in the immediate vicinity of our armies we find the same class of relief agencies in operation, as we shall presently have occasion to notice in the narrative of the Commission's campaign work during the year 1863.

Throughout the lines of our Western armies, in the cities and at all points of rendezvous in the Border States, the Sanitary Commission has heartily united with the people in giving full effect to the same system of relief, so that the methods of such aid are now uniform and equally effective in all places. And it is one of the results of our great Federal struggle, and of the system of humane relief which the Sanitary Commission conducts, that the entire population of the West has become inspired with such universal desire to render its full share in the work,* that the

---

* The reflex influences and national aspects of this fervent sympathy and earnest helping in all the households of the West, is mentioned by Dr. Newberry, the Western Secretary, in the following paragraph, which we quote from his "*Report of the Operations of the Sanitary Commission in the Valley of the Mississippi*," dated September, 1863:

"Before leaving this subject, I cannot refrain from expressing to you my conviction that one of the most important results attained by the Sanitary Commission is

tendency to *individualism* and to incoördinated efforts, that was supposed to be characteristic of Western mind and Western activities, seems already to have become transmuted into a loving and golden bond of co-operative sympathy. Like the people of the sister States at the East, the warm hearts and busy hands of the West are giving outlet and effectiveness to their national and humane sympathies, through the national channels of the United States Sanitary Commission.*

The aggregate statement of the particular branch of the relief service that we have described in connection with the Eastern field, is given as follows by Dr. Newberry, in the Western field:

"*Soldier's Homes.*—From the organization of these Institutions to September 1st, 1863, there have been admitted into

---

to be found in the home field; but one in all our reports to the present time entirely over-looked. I allude to its influence in inspiring the people in every farm-house and cottage, wherever a good grandmother is knitting a pair of socks, or a child making a pin-cushion, with a wider, deeper, higher, and purer patriotism. I need not dwell upon this topic, for I am convinced its truth will be universally acknowledged. And yet it is due that this truth be recognized and put on record. From all parts of the country we have the testimony of our contributors that they are driven by the spirit which pervades their work to open and desperate antagonism with disloyalty in every form; and that unwittingly they are everywhere doing missionary work for the national cause. While our Government has one great army in the field, of those who are pouring out their life-blood in its defense, the Sanitary Commission has, in the home field, another great army, composed of the mothers and sisters, wives and sweethearts of our brave soldiers, workin scarcely less earnestly and efficiently for the same great end."

* Though the State of Missouri might be considered as an exception to this unity and co-ordination of working,—a Special Commission having been appointed, Sept. 5, 1861, by General Fremont, for promoting the "health and comfort of the Volunteer troops in and near the city of St. Louis," and, the subsequent year, authorized to operate in any of the Western forces,—the nationality and completeness of the plans and methods of the United States Sanitary Commission are not the less universal and acceptable because of the labors of the local Commission that was thus called into existence in Missouri. The good works and hearty co-operation of that independent agency at St. Louis, are testified in all the hospitals of Missouri, and upon the hospital transports and the battle-fields of the Mississippi. It undoubtedly will ere long become wholly affiliated to the National Sanitary Commission, as its methods (as a relief agency) are already tolerably in harmony with those of the Relief branch of the Central Commission.

six of the principal ones in the West, 167,090 soldiers. The Home at Cincinnati has furnished food, rest, and other needed assistance to 42,673; that at Cleveland, to 11,704; that at Cairo, to 51,170; that at Louisville, to 50,325; that at Nashville, during five months, to 2,542; and the Lodge at Memphis, during two months, to 3,067 soldiers, who were not otherwise provided for. These figures do not include those passing in companies, regiments, and brigades, whose names are not entered on the books. The data are incomplete in most of the Homes during the earlier months of their existence, so that we can only give approximate numbers; but we can safely say that these Institutions have furnished, since their organization, over 500,000 meals and over 250,000 lodgings, besides all the other services rendered in the correction of pay and discharge papers; procuring half-fare tickets on railroads; collecting pay, and, above all, shielding them from swindlers of every name and degree."*

The Hospital Directory.—Before leaving the subject of Relief, the Hospital Directory must be mentioned as another of the much desired achievements that became practicable under

* The President of the Sanitary Commission has recently referred to this branch of the work, as follows:

"The next large expense is the support of twenty-five Soldier's Homes, or Lodges, scattered over the whole field of war, from New Orleans to Washington, including Vicksburg, Memphis, Cairo, Chattanooga, Nashville, Louisville, Washington, &c., &c. In these Homes and Lodges *twenty-three hundred* soldiers (different ones) *daily* receive shelter, food, medical aid, protection, and care. These soldiers are such as are crowded, by the rigidity of the military system, out of the regular channels; soldiers left behind, astray, who have not their military status, convalescents, discharged men not able to get their pay. Of these, the average length of time they are on our hands is about three days. The priceless value of this supplementary system, no tongue can tell. The abandonment of it would create an amount of suffering which a multiplication of 2300 by 365 days in the year, will but serve to hint at.

"In connection with these homes, at the great military centres, New Orleans, Louisville, Washington, are bureaus, in aid of the discharged soldier's great necessities, growing out of his loss of papers in battle, or during the bewilderment of sickness, or through the ignorance of his superiors, or his own:

"1. A Claim Agency, to secure his bounty.

"2. A Pension Agency.

"3. A Back-pay Agency.

"The mercy of these ministries, by which soldiers and their families, helpless without this aid—the prey of sharpers, runners, and grog-shops—are put in speedy possession of their rights, is inexpressible. We have often $20,000 a day of back pay in our office at Washington alone, which might have been lost forever or delayed until it was no longer needed by the soldier's own family, without this system."—*San. Com. Bulletin, Feb. 15th*, 1864.

the assured support from California's munificence. This special bureau of hospital records was established during the autumn of 1862, and it is designed to furnish recent and accurate information concerning every patient in the military hospitals. It is a complete directory or bureau of information, daily revised and wholly in the interest of military patients and their friends. The extent and nature of this incidental but most gratefully appreciated branch of the Commission's work, may best be estimated from the following brief extracts from its latest published reports, in the year 1863:

"The number of names recorded on the books of the Hospital Directory from June 9th to October 1st, have been as follows:

"At the Washington Office	64,635
" New York "	18,771
" Philadelphia "	12,213
" Louisville, from May 9, ...	96,433
Total	192,052

* * * * * * * *

"The total number of names on record is 513,437.

"The number of applications for information and the number of answers rendered, from the organization of Directory to October 1, 1863, have been as follows:

"Washington Office, ...	No. Inq.	6,712....	No. Ans.	4,524
"New York "	"	656....	"	474
"Philadelphia "	"	547....	"	348
"Louisville "	"	5,852....	"	4,016
	Total No. Inq.	13,767....	Total Ans.	9,362

The following cases illustrate the every day occurrences in the offices of the Hospital Directory: Inquiry is made at the Washington Directory, for information respecting Private ——, Co. C, 64th Regt., N. Y. Volunteers. The reply to the inquiry was as follows: "—— ——, Co. C, 64th Regiment, New York Volunteers, was admitted to U. S. General Hospital, Camp A, Frederick, Md., Nov. 26th, 1862, transferred to Camden Street

Hospital, Baltimore, May 17, 1863, and again transferred to Fort Schuyler Hospital, New York, April 24, 1863. On the 17th July following, he was detached to the 1st Battalion Invalid Corps, and is now on duty at Jamaica, Long Island, New York."

The Superintendent of the Directory at Louisville writes:

"Hardly a day passes when the expense of a useless journey is not saved to some inquirer, who learns from our records that the one sought for is not where he is expected to be found, but is either dead, returned to duty, or transferred to some other hospital nearer home, as it often happens, and near which the inquirer has passed on his journey hither. Not unfrequently the amount saved to the friends of the soldier has exceeded a hundred dollars a day, by means of the information and aid given at this office."

"A father from Pennsylvania presents a letter from the surgeon of a hospital in Nashville, saying that his son will be discharged, and sent to this city in care of the Sanitary Commission, and requests the father to meet him here. He asks, 'Where is he?' We have no note of his arrival. 'He must still be in hospital at Nashville. But stay; here is a report just in.' The name is there, and died August 9, 1863, the very day the father received the letter, and set out to meet him. His son had sent him word not to bring more money than necessary to pay his fare to Louisville, as he was paid off and had enough. What was to be done? We loaned him his passage home; made out the necessary papers to get the effects of his son; wrote to Nashville to Sanitary Commission agents, to forward them, and he left for home that evening.

"An old man enters the office. He has traveled from Northern Ohio to meet his son in this city; he has been told to inquire at the Sanitary Commission rooms for direction to the hospital which contains him. While the clerk turns to the books, he chats of his son and home, of the different articles in his carpet-bag, put in by mother and sisters at home—each had sent some little comfort. He is all animation and hope, as if at the very door which is to admit him to the realization of all his happy anticipations. The *record* says—'died'—that very morning! The *register* says, 'one inquiry, one answer.' It does not speak of the careful preparatory suggestions that sympathy tenderly makes towards the announcement of the saddening fact. It does not show that strong old man convulsed and weeping like a child. * * * * *

He goes slowly and sadly away. One of the clerks accompanies him, who procures a burial-case for the remains of his 'poor boy,' and assists him in all his preparations for his mournful journey home on the same day. The register says—'one inquiry, one answer.'"

Mr. Bowne, the Chief of the Directory Bureau, closes his report for the year 1863, with the following tender allusions to the life-scenes in the work of the Directory Offices:*

---

* The business and methods of the Hospital Directory are described as follows, by a recent visitor at the Washington office:

Each State has a record in one or more of these books. The 69th New York Volunteers, for instance, we find by referring to the index, is on the —th page. Like every other page, it has the following printed headings, each having its proper space, and being appropriately ruled off: "Date of Admission," "Hospital," "Name," "Rank," "Company," "Died," "Discharged," "Returned to Duty," "Furloughed," "Deserted," "Transferred." For instance: Patrick Smith is received at Lincoln Hospital, November 10, The report indicates his admission at that date; so under "date of admission," is written "November 10;" under "hospital" is written "Lincoln;" under "name" is written "Smith, Patrick;" under "rank" is written "P" (for "private") and under "company" is written "F," or whatever it may be. Perhaps, in a short time a morning report from Lincoln Hospital informs the clerks that Patrick has returned to duty. His name is found, and under that heading the date is written—say December 15; or, Patrick may have received a furlough to visit his friends. Then, under "furlough" is written "December 15." Thus it will be seen that the soldier who gets in the hospital, however rarely he may have written home, or however widely his letters may have miscarried, is almost certain to be easily traced out by any anxious friend, or relative, writing or applying to the Sanitary Commission, and answers are given free of all charge. There are, however, exceptions to this easy method of finding the soldier. It sometimes happens that, from some peculiar whim or other, the soldier does not furnish his proper name at the hospital. Others may be deliriously ill when received, and unable to give a reliable name. Some of the Germans, and, indeed Americans, have such peculiar sounding names, that they get sadly misspelled after two or three copyings, but they may be easily identified by the rank and company they were in, and by their "given" name.

We think that many in the country would be greatly astonished at the peculiarity of the names of some of our brave boys. The most remarkable one we ever saw was that of a Western soldier, who was bravely defending the old flag under the appellation of "January Blackbird." The number of names now registered upon the books at Washington alone, is about 200,000! The graater portion of these have been returned to duty or honorably discharged.

The correspondence of the Directory is one of its most interesting features. When inquiries are received asking information of soldiers whose names are not on the books of the office, a letter is addressed, in nearly every instance, to the Surgeon of the soldier's regiment, or to one of the branch offices at Louisville or Philadelphia. The method and detail with which this is done challenge our admiration, as indicating the care taken to secure the most certain information. For instance: a letter is received from Mrs. Jones, a lady in New York City, who has not heard

"The benefit conferred by the Directory has not been merely to friends of the soldier, but also to the soldier himself, becoming, as it has, a medium of communication for wives and mothers searching for husbands and sons—a channel through which has flowed those messages of love, and cheer, and hope grateful to the fevered brain, soothing to the agony of wounds.

* * * * * * * *

"In the nine thousand two hundred and three answers lies hidden a history which no human eye shall ever read. And the gratitude with which they are acknowledged is shown by the letters on file. Mothers write of their 'undying gratitude' for the simple announcement that their boys are doing well in hospital; others 'invoke the blessing of God upon the labors of the Commission,' and sisters 'will cherish the warmest gratitude while memory lasts.' And then the eagerness with which inquiries are made: 'By the love you bear your own mother tell me where my boy is!' 'Only give me some tidings!' 'Is he dead, and how did he die?' 'Is he alive, and how can I get to him?' 'I pray you tell me of these two nephews I am seeking for. I have had fourteen nephews in the service, and these two are the only ones left.'

---

from her son Samuel, a private in the 200th New York Volunteers, Company B, in five months. She feels an intense anxiety. She has heard of the Sanitary Commission, and writes, despondently, for information. The soldier's name does not appear on the books. The Chief Clerk writes to the Surgeon of the regiment. In a book entitled "Applications," he makes the following entry: First, the date of application; next, the name of the soldier inquired for, thus—Jones, Samuel, 200th New York Volunteers, Company B; next, the number of the application, say 2,400; next, the applicant, Mrs. Jane Jones, 274 —— street, New York; next, thus—Wrote Surgeon of regiment, such a date; then, Mrs. Jones' letter of application is endorsed "2,400," and carefully filed away. Then, the clerk takes a blank form, the printed and written matter of which will read substantially as follows: "Information is earnestly desired regarding Samuel Jones, of the 200th New York Volunteers, Company B. When last heard from, he was with his regiment at New Orleans, La., which was five months since. His mother has great anxiety about him. Please reply upon this sheet at your earliest convenience." The sheet is registered at the top "2,400," and addressed to the Surgeon of the 200th New York Volunteers. A stamped envelope, addressed to the Hospital Directory, is enclosed. In the course of a few weeks there arrives one day, among a number of letters, a sheet headed "2,400." It is the same the clerk sent to the Surgeon of the 200th. The Surgeon has written, "Samuel Jones, of Company E, 200th New York Volunteers, of which regiment I am Surgeon in charge, was taken sick about four months since and sent to Barracks' Hospital, New Orleans, and only last week returned to duty, and is now with his regiment. Not getting letters from home, he has neglected to write, but agrees to do so right away." The clerk seeks out application No. 2,400, that was so carefully laid away, and puts with it its duplicate number, the answer, and writes the welcome news to Mrs. Jane Jones. He then endorses the application as answered at such a date, turns to No. 2,400 in the "Application Book," and in a blank space, left for the purpose, writes the date and abstract of his reply to Mrs. Jones. When we say, in addition to this, that the letter to Mrs. Jones is written in copying ink, and afterwards copied into a

"Of the many scenes witnessed in the bureau, I can only mention a few without attempting a description. A mother has not heard anything of her son since the last battle; she hopes he is safe, but would like to be assured—there is no escape—she must be told that he has fallen upon the 'federal altar;' an agony of tears bursts forth which seem as if it would never cease; another less excitable, does not tire of telling 'how good a boy he was.' 'No mother ever had such a son as he,' sobs a third. A father presents himself—a strong man and yet young in years, to receive the same announcement, and sinks with audible grief into a chair; another, with pale face and tremulous voice, anxious to know, yet dreading to hear, is told that his boy is in the hospital a short distance off; he grasps the hand with both of his, while tears run down his cheeks, and without uttering another word leaves the room. 'It is very hard, my friend,' was said to one mute with grief, 'but you are not alone.' 'I know it, sir,' was the prompt reply, 'but he was the *only one* I had.'

"A woman of more than ordinary intelligence and appear-

---

book, the reader will see the vast amount of care and labor bestowed upon this important branch of the Hospital Directory.

* * * * * * * * * * *

It is true that sad news is received sometimes, which it is not pleasant to communicate directly to the anxious relatives; but we feel convinced, from the manifest interest in this department, that sorrowful things would be as gently imparted as possible, and with a sympathetic heart for the mourning mother, or brother, or sister, to whom the letter might be written.

When the Surgeon writes with startling brevity: "John, of whom you inquire, was killed at Chickamauga, September 20, and afterwards buried on the field;" or, "George, of whom you desire information, was severely wounded on the 2d July, at Gettysburg, and died on the 8th of that month in regimental hospital," it is very sad to re-write these facts to the widowed mother, or the only brother and sister, whose hope has been alive at all times, though only upheld by uncertainty.

But there are other letters than these that are painful to write; for example, "Private Jacob ——, of the —th Maine Volunteers, Company K, deserted from this regiment on the 10th of November, and has not since been heard from." The clerk tells us that he had rather write to such a man's friends that he had died of the most lingering and painful disease than to send them *such* a record. Another sad case is such as this, and not unfrequently, we understand: "Henry ——; of the —th Iowa Volunteers, was last seen in the engagement of ———, and, as his body was not found, is supposed to have been taken prisoner by the rebels."

But we were glad to learn that whatever satisfaction there may be in allaying the anxieties and fears of friends with even the worst tidings—giving them gloomy certainties such as we have noted—it is much oftener the pleasing task of the clerk to write such a letter as this: "Your son is well and on duty with his regiment, as late as two weeks since. A letter addressed ———, will be quite certain to reach him;" or this: "It affords me pleasure to inform you that your brother, though severely wounded, as you had heard, at the battle of Chickamauga, is slowly recovering at 11th Corps Hospital." We saw some of the letters received, and were permitted to take a few notes."

* * * * * * * * * * *

—*Washington Chronicle*.

ance, with almost breathless voice, 'I want to find my husband; I have not heard from him for several months. I have written to the officers of his regiment, but do not get any reply; can you tell me where he is?'

"Will you please to give me his name and number of his regiment?" 'O, yes sir.' 'You will find him at Lincoln Hospital; the city cars pass near the building, and the conductor will point it out to you.' A momentary shade of incredulity is perceptible; then turning her full deep eyes, swollen with emotion, she gives one look—a full reward for a month of labor—and in an instant is in the street. * * * * Thus the varied scene goes on. One inquirer leaves the room grateful, buoyant and happy, to be followed by another equally grateful, who will 'tread softly' the remainder of his days, for the 'light of his dwelling has gone out.' As each departs another figure is added to the list of 'inquiries and answers,' and the seemingly monotonous work of the bureau is resumed."

Though this beneficial scheme for the organization of a special bureau of information and correspondence for the benefit of military patients and their home-friends, had been conceived and provisionally ordered previous to the battle of Antietam, the exhausted stock of the Commission's treasury threatened to delay the execution of the thoughtful purpose. But the good providence of California's generous aid at once made the duty practicable and plain, and the ten thousand loyal homes that have already received through this bureau the anxiously sought tidings of their brave ones in distant hospitals, justly regard this as the most loving and far-reaching branch of the Commission's work of special Relief; it is an outgrowth upon the battle-field and hospital branch of the work, and without it the Commission's ministry to the sick and the dying would not be complete; and to the reader who has noted the burden of necessities that was laid upon the Sanitary Commission during the summer and autumn of 1862, the institution of the Hospital Directory at that dark period will afford fresh testimony to the truth that when duty and human necessities demand our labor, "*the Lord will provide.*"

Death and Burial Records.—The history of the Commission's work in the line of aid and thoughtful sympathies for the soldier in his relations to his home and friends, would not be complete if we failed to mention the Memorial and Burial Records of those who fall in the service; for the tens of thousands of brave men whose lives have been sacrificed in our national struggle do not die forgotten and unrecorded. A triplicate registry of the dying soldier's name, military record, home-relations, wounds, or sickness, together with his dying requests, and the designation of his place of burial, is officially ordered and provided by the War Department for every soldier who dies in a military hospital, or in the field, where his body can be recognized. Already tens of thousands of neatly inscribed Memorial Tablets at the soldiers' graves, as directed in Order No. 75 [A. D. 1861] of the War Department, mark the campaign lines and the cemeteries of the hospitals of the army; while in each hospital and at every cemetery office, as well as at the Adjutant-General's office, and in the records of every military post, accurate memorial records of the deceased soldiers are permanently preserved.*

This system of memorial records of the dead was prepared by a committe in the Sanitary Commission, immediately after the the first battles, and was promptly ordered by the Secretary of

* Previously to the introduction of this method of recording and preserving mortuary memorials, the soldier's death-record consisted simply in the entry, "*Died,*" in the Hospital Register, and upon the Military Rolls, and in a quarterly return of the same kind, with the report of "effects," and "final statement of accounts of pay and clothing." But the present system requires not only that immediate report of the death shall be made, but that the following form of a *Death-and-Burial Record* shall be made out on the day of burial; and, that in addition to the copy of such record, which is immediately forwarded to the Adjutant-General's office in Washington, there shall be two other copies of the same record made, and preserved where they will be most accessible by friends of the deceased, viz., one, a permanent copy, in the hospital or kept by the surgeon; and another to be put on file by the person charged with the duty of the burial, either the Sexton or Quartermaster. [*Copy* No. 1, *is kept in the hospital; copy* No. 2, *goes immediately to Washington; copy* No. 3. *is kept on file by sexton or quartermaster.*]

War and provided for by the Medical and Quartermaster's Departments. And whoever will visit the "Soldiers' Cemeteries" in the vicinity of Washington, Baltimore, Louisville, or St. Louis, or inspect the neatly-kept Records of Deaths and Burials in the military hospitals, and at the offices where the duplicates

---

[Abstract of the *forms* of the Death-and-Burial Records.]

No. 1.

"RECORD OF DEATH AND INTERMENT.

Name and number of person interred	....
Number and locality of the grave....	....
Hospital number of the deceased.....	....
Regiment, rank, and company........	....
Residence before enlistment.........	....
Conjugal condition, (and if married the residence of the widow,......	....
Cause of death....................	....
Age of the deceased...............	....
Nativity.........................	....
References and remarks...........	....
Date of death and burial...........	........................186....

"Duplicates sent to the Adjutant-General of the United States Army, and to the Sexton of the..............................Cemetery.

"*Memoranda:* ....

Attached to an official notification which the Surgeon sends to the Quartermaster requesting the interment of the corpse, there goes a certified copy—(*third copy*)—of the foregoing permanent record from the Hospital Book of Burials, with the following order appended, which the Quartermaster forwards to the Sexton, or person having charge of the burial:

"To

The Sexton of...............................

You will receive, and immediately inter, the remains of the person above described, and preserve this record, and also attend to the setting of the head-board at the grave, as provided by the Government and ordered by the Secretary of War."

....

Quartermaster."

["Burial from the....................Hospital.]

"This order for the burial is to remain attached to the Sexton's copy of Record as part of the Record."

of such records are kept on file, will see what practical ends are being served by this system.

Hospital Cars or Railway Ambulances.—It is one of the peculiarities of the present war that the principal military movements and the great strategical points are upon the lines of railroads and the navigable waters. Upon the latter we have seen

---

These new regulations for preserving the death-and-burial records of soldiers, provide, in the words of the order of the Secretary of War, that these records "shall always be accessible to the friends of the deceased, and all are to be kept alphabetically indexed, for reference, and each grave have its number, in the order of interments, distinctly indicated upon a post or plank of cedar, or some other enduring wood. The name of deceased, the date of death, and his company or regimental corps initials, to be engraved upon the said post or plank. This may be effected with an iron letter brand or stamp. These posts or headboards, and the lettering of the name, &c., will be provided by the Quartermaster of the Department or Military Post where the hospital is located, or where the death occurs."

"It is the duty of the senior Surgeon for the Hospital or the Military Company in which a soldier dies, *immediately* after the death, to cause the copies of Record —1, 2, and 3—to be accurately made out, and to forward copy No. 3 to the Quartermaster, or, in the absence of a Quartermaster, to the Commanding Officer of the Division or Company in which the death has occurred.

"Copy No. 2 shall be forwarded, without delay, to the Adjutant-General at Washington, by the Surgeon, or by such other officer as the Commander may designate. Generally, except in the District of Columbia, it will be the Surgeon's duty to forward copy No. 2 to the local Adjutant or Commanding Officer, who, after noting the contents, will place his signature upon the face of the Surgeon's notification attached, and immediately forward it to the Adjutant-General.

"Whenever a Military Hospital is finally broken up or vacated, the hospital records are all to be transmitted to the Surgeon-General's Office at Washington; and they must ever be open to the inspection of the friends of the deceased.

"The sexton is directed to preserve the records and the orders sent to him by the Quartermaster. He must also be required to attend to the planting of the headboard furnished by the Quartermaster for the grave of the deceased.

"In all cemeteries in which deceased soldiers are interred, the burials, if practicable, are to be made in regular series, occupying a separate plot of ground; but if otherwise and promiscuously interred. the number and description of the locality of the grave should be carefully recorded by the sexton."

"The sexton is required to notify the physician of the hospital of the number and locality of the grave before he takes the corpse."

"In the case of a military burial at an encampment, or upon a march, without the aid of a sexton, it shall be the duty of the Commanding Officer of the military corps to which the deceased belonged to cause his remains to be properly interred, and to provide suitable means for marking the grave and erecting a headboard with the proper inscription or stamped record. And, in the absence of a sexton, it shall be the duty of the Adjutant or the Commander of the said military corps to preserve the sexton's copy of record; and it will also be the duty of the Surgeon to said corps to preserve the Hospital copy of said record with the same care, and subject to the same conditions, as similar records in General or Post Hospitals."

what a system of Hospital transports was instituted at an early period of the war. But the positions of our forces and the exigencies of the service have been such as to require that a vastly greater number of sick and wounded soldiers should be removed northward by railways than by steamboats. The painful jar and jolting which the patients suffered in the railway transportation attracted the attention of members of the Commission, who witnessed the removal of sick and wounded from various fields. During the campaigns of 1862, the importance of improving the methods of hospital transportation upon railroads became apparent, and a member of the Commission, at Fair Oaks, soon after the battle there, and "while witnessing the intense agony of these poor fellows, he thought the difficulty might be obviated by mechanical means. Directly and upon the spot he sketched the model of a car, in the contrivance of which the problem was satisfactory solved."*

The importance of having the business of hospital transportation rendered more humane and safe, by means of careful surgical attendance and all necessary appliances for physical comfort, was admitted by all, and the Sanitary Commission has been enabled to contribute very largely to the attainments of this object. Upon the various railroads communicating with the lines of our armies and hospitals, there are now twelve or more hospital-cars in daily use, all of which are fitted up with special reference to the comfort and safety of the patients.† Each of these

---

* See the illustration of Hospital-cars in *Harper's Weekly*, Feb. 27th, 1864.

† In one of Dr. Newberry's reports from the Western Department, it is stated, that—

"To provide for the comfort of the inmates of hospitals in the interior of Kentucky and Tennessee, destined to be removed by rail to Louisville, a train of hospital cars has been fitted up, and is now running, under the supervision of agents of the Commission. These cars are provided with comfortable beds, with food, stimulants, medicines, etc., and are in charge of kind and faithful men. One hundred sick are daily transported in them with as little danger and suffering as though they remained in hospital."

* * * * * * * * *

"Reports have been made of the value of the service rendered by the Hospital

railway ambulances, as they are properly called, are furnished with the comforts and appliances of a good hospital, and the beds are so adjusted as to give entire security and ease by means of stout India-rubber tugs, etc.; there is special ventilation, careful shading of the light, speaking tubes to convey orders from the surgeon to the nurses, and every arrangement has been made for the comfortable posture and support of the patients and their wounded parts, in bed or in invalid chairs; while well-packed stores of warm clothing, ample supplies of concentrated food, coffee, tea and medicines, together with an ingenious culinary apparatus, facilities for the storage and use of water,—in short, the provision of all the apparatus and comforts of a well appointed hospital,—are conveniently arranged and always at hand.

Most of these ambulances are specially adopted for running upon long routes and upon different guages of track. The railway companies and the government have generously seconded the Commission's wishes in the assignment of special cars for such improved transportation of the severely wounded and sick, and already the number of such patients thus transported over long routes far exceeds the total number that were transported by the Commission's *Hospital Transports* from the Peninsula. At the East, the Medical Department has now provided for all the

---

Cars on the Chattanooga and Louisville and Nashville Railroads. Time has only served to increase our estimate of their importance, and as the army has advanced farther and farther from its base of supplies, they have been made more and more useful, until they are now recognized as an indispensable institution."—*Sanitary Reporter.*

Says the Medical Director at Nashville:

"The rapid transportation, the care exercised over the patients in their transit, and the competent attendants that accompany each train, have, I am convinced, been the means of saving many lives.

"I was forced to use steamboat transportation for many wounded immediately after the battle of Stone River; but the length of the voyage, and the necessary exposure to the weather, &c., compelled me to ask your co-operation in order that the men might be transported by railroad. I personally, as well as the sick and wounded soldiers, am under many obligations to the Sanitary Commission, but, in my opinion, the 'sanitary train' does more than anything else for the comfort of the sick." (*See Letter of Dr. Thurston, Medical Director, in the Sanitary Reporter, Vol.* 1, *No.* 1.)

expenses and attendance of the ambulance cars, except the Stewards'; but at the West, the Commission has until recently had the whole responsibility of this important service.*

---

* Dr. Barnum, the faithful Surgeon who has long been engaged in this railway ambulance transportation service, thus mentions some of the facts connected with the Hospital Train at the West:

* * * * * * * * * * *

"At present, there are in use nine hospital cars—seven on the Chattanooga road, under the charge of Dr. Myers, Surgeon U. S. V., and two, under my own immediate supervision, on the Louisville Road.

"The train on the Nashville and Chattanooga Railroad, consists of one passenger, one mail, three box, and three hospital cars. The passenger coach is kept scrupulously neat, for the accommodation of patients alone, and by a special arrangement of seats, can be changed in a few moments to a bed-car, if necessary, which, however, cannot often occur, as every loadof sick will contain some who would prefer to sit."

"The new hospital cars seem to meet the demand exactly, combining all possible freedom of motion, the least jar, good ventilation, a comfortable degree of warmth, and expedition in loading aud unloading."

"These are built on the same plans as those used between Washington and New York, with such modifications as the tunnel and the difference in the width of track rendered necessary. The draw-bar which connects the cars together, is surrounded by a stiff spiral spring, which prevents any sudden jerk. Double springs are under the trucks, and, in addition, the elliptic spring bar on the side to guard against lateral motion. Each car contains twenty-four stretchers, hung by stout rubber bands between two uprights. The stretchers are supplied with hair pillows, and comforts, which can be easily renovated. They can be removed from the car, receive the patients, be re-placed, and again bear them to the hospitals when the journey is completed. The rubber bands prevent all shock and jolting, and communicate a gentle motion, which usually lulls the patient to sleep."

"The stretchers can be removed from the car without disturbing the occupant. There are also seats for those who wish to sit up, and a sofa for the Surgeon or attendant, beneath which is a wardrobe and drawers for books, newspapers, &c. Opposite the sofa, is a kitchen only six feet by three, yet it contains water-tank, wash-basin, sink for washing dishes, cupboarps for stores and dishes, and two large lamps heating copper-boilers, by which soup, coffee, tea, &c., may be quickly and nicely prepared.

"The 'bumper' is surrounded by a stiff spring, which prevents the communication of the jar when the motion is suddenly stopped or applied. The whole interior is fitted up in a style superior to any cars in use in the Northwest.

"Articles of clothing are kept constantly on the train to be given to those needing them, and sanitary stores of every character are liberally supplied.

"Patients speak in the highest terms, and with the deepest feeling, of the kindness and efficiency of Dr. Myers.

"Trips are made tri-weekly from Bridgeport for hospital patients. Large numbers of discharged and furloughed soldiers are carried, but many more of the latter come by passenger and box cars.

"On the Louisville Road, the accommodations are much the same as those just mentioned."

"The food prepared is of good quality; and besides Government rations, many delicacies—such as are comprised in the stores of the Commission—are issued in any amount required.

"Since my connection with the Hospital Train, I have removed **20,472** patients, with the loss of only one man, who was removed contrary to the wish of his Surgeon, and my own judgment, at his earnest desire to 'die at home.'"

Progress in Sanitary Work: Warfare against Scurvy.—The methods of the Commission's branches of labor, as described in preceding pages, have manifestly answered their design, and have worked more and more effectively as the war goes on; and as we follow the Commission's operations through the last summer and autumn, it will be observed that the ever augmenting and ever varying necessities of our campaigns have been wisely anticipated and promptly met, so far as sanitary wants could be anticipated and met by any powers and means which the Sanitary Commission has possessed.

Following up its special inspections of the military hospitals, from the Atlantic to the Mississippi, and urging such improvements as were found wanting, the Commission closed that work early in the summer, assured that the Medical Department was nobly endeavoring to perfect its service and provision for the sick and wounded of the army; and that the department of the Quartermaster-General was generously carrying into effect the improved plans of the Surgeon-General for the better construction and ventilation of military hospitals. Throughout the lines of our armies in the Southwest, the Hospital Inspectors and Surgeons bore testimony to the signal value of the fresh vegetables and fruits which the Western Secretary and agents of the Sanitary Commission, with commendable foresight of perils impending, had steadily supplied to those armies, both in camp and in hospital, and by means of which the demon of *scurvy* had been hunted from our armies.* And this service still con-

---

* The following extracts from official Reports will serve to illustrate the nature of demands for fresh vegetables and other anti-scorbutics, as well as the hygienic importance of the efforts put forth by the Commission to meet such demands, until the regular Commissariat could interpose with adequate supplies.

Early in spring, Lt.-Col. Frank H. Hamilton, a distinguished Medical Inspector, U. S. Army, reported as follows to the Medical Bureau, from the army in Tennessee:

* * * * * * * *

"We find, in the absence of vegetable diet, a cause for a great part of the mor-

tinues, and although it may appear to be simply a gratuitous supplementing of the army Commissariat, it actually is equally a work of inquiry and advice, and of supplementary supply and relief. It is one of the special duties of the Sanitary Inspectors to report and guard against the outbreak of preventable diseases, and, in council with medical officers, to provide the needed prophylactics, and the Commission thus undertakes to furnish large supplies of sueh antiscorbutics as onions, potatoes, and fruits, while the Commissariat is considering and breaking through the difficulties that are found in the way of supplying such sanitary subsistance in its own *regular* channels. In doing this important work the agents of this Commission have sometimes not only

---

tality of our troops, both after the receipt of wounds and from disease. Indirectly it may account for suppuration, gangrene, pyæmia, erysipelas, diarrhœa, dysentery, fever, rheumatism, etc., and we fully believe that one barrel of potatoes per annum is to the Government equal to one man. I have omitted to state that in all of the regimental hospitals, as well as general hospitals, I found the Sanitary Commission had already furnished them with the vegetables they had called for, and which were needed for the sick, so that in the hospitals none were dying from scurvy; on the contrary, in every instance I found them rapidly recovering.

"I would respectfully suggest that for the season of the year when neither fresh potatoes nor onions can be furnished to our armies, they should be supplied with pickled onions and cabbage; also potatoes cut in slices and packed in molasses, as is the practice with sailors, the potatoes to be eaten raw."

In the "*Sanitary Reporter*" we find the following:

"Dr. Read, an Inspector for the Commission, wrote from Nashville, April 13th as follows:

"'Scurvy, to some extent, is appearing in most of the regiments. If called upon to make long marches, many who now appear well will faint by the way. And, if wounded in battle, many wounds, which, in a healthy condition of the system, would be unattended with danger, would, in the present condition of many, prove fatal.'

"Simultaneously with the receipt of the above by mail, the following was received by telegraph:

"Nashville, Tenn., April 14, 1863.

"Dr. J. S. Newberry:

"Sir,—We earnestly indorse Dr. Reed's letter, calling for vegetables, as one upon which the health and efficiency of the Army at this moment depends.

(Signed) "Frank H. Hamilton,
"Medical Inspector, U. S. A.
"Alfred C. Post, M. D.,
"Moses Gunn, M. D.,
"Hospital Inspectors, U. S. San. Com."

swept the markets of such vegetables in the Western cities,* and rapidly pushed forward the needed anti-scorbutics to the distant lines of the army, but it has repeatedly been necessary for the Commission to appeal directly to the farmers to contribute these indispensable supplies from their private stores.

It must not be inferred from this statement that the army has not been liberally supplied with the *regular rations*, for, with but few exceptions, there has been no lack of salt meats and "hard tack;" but with embarrased transportation, and with a remote and almost inaccessible base of supplies, the difficulty of supplying anti-scorbutic rations,—which, it must be remembered, are of a perishable nature,—has been very great; therefore, the Commissariat and the Qurtermaster's Departments have welcomed and aided the Sanitary Commission in its efforts to bring to the camp mess and the field hospital the much needed elements of health. The history of our campaigns in the Southwest will tell how generously and how gratefully Generals Grant, Rosecrans, Sherman, and Thomas, and many others, bade the Sanitary Commission God-speed in this ministry of anti-scorbutics among their forces in the field.† The threatened decimation and utter weakening

---

* A prominent business man in one of the great market cities of the West, has recently informed the writer that during the spring and summer of 1863 the immediate and unheralded purchase and shipment of this class of "sanitary stores" by the Commission's agents, on several occasions so suddenly exhaused the markets, that for days following the prices of such articles were greatly enhanced, until the balance of supply could be restored.

† That the reader may correctly estimate the momentous importance of this incessant watchfulness and warfare against scurvy in our forces, we invite attention to the testimony we have incidentally adduced in previous pages, and also to the following emphatic statements which we quote from the very reliable official and scientific authority, Surgeon J. Janvier Woodward, the Medical Historian of the War, who constantly has before him the official reports of sickness and mortality in all departments of the Federal forces. In his treatise, neatly published, upon "Camp Diseases," Dr. Woodward unhesitatingly declares that "he is well satisfied, from personal observation, that both as a distinct affection in its early

of the armies of the Cumberland and the Tennessee, was effectually prevented by the abundant supplies of potatoes, onions, and fruits that were provided for those forces by the Sanitary Commission. And, as we shall have occasion to notice in future pages, the same homely and substantial method of life-and-health-saving has been very effectively continued in the more distant lines of our armies during the past year, and to the present time.

This portion of our narrative of the Sanitary Commission's work might be indefinitely extended by recounting in detail the history and incidents of daily experience in the various labors of the Relief Department; but the current events in the

---

stages, and as a complicating influence, affecting the other camp diseases of the army, scurvy has hitherto played a large part in the phenomena of disease in the Eastern armies;" and he says he is satisfied that the same has been true of diseases in the armies West and South. And, after showing the part that the "scorbutic taint" has played in the diseases of the Peninsula campaign—"the Chickahominy fever"—and in the prevalent diseases South and West, that well-informed author states that—

"There can be no doubt that the same tendency (the 'scorbutic taint') has complicated diseases generally throughout the army during the past two years, and has even modified the result of wounds and injuries, interfering with the healing process, and increasing the mortality of traumatic cases of every kind."

"The leading causes of scurvy," says Dr. Woodward, "may be designated in a single word as *camp diet.*" And he adds: "There is probably no single instance of scurvy making its appearance among any body of troops who are duly supplied with an abundance of fresh vegetables."

Potatoes and onions—the most available anti-scorbutics—he urges, should be more freely supplied to the men in camp and in hospital, and he says:

"It has more than once happened on a grand scale, during the present war, to see a sudden diminution in the amount of diarrhœa *follow the liberal issue of potatoes* and onions to an army in which the tendency to scurvy was exhibiting itself in a manner too evident to be overlooked."

These conclusions of Surgeon Woodward are undoubtedly correct, and they have been steadily maintained by all the more experienced Inspectors in the Sanitary Commission's service. Well does that excellent Inspector, Dr. Warriner, of the Mississippi field, declare that the Sanitary Commission's achievement in supplying

surpassingly interesting history of that branch of the Sanitary Commission's work, is now being freshly published every two weeks in the pages of the Commission's *Bulletin* and in the *Sanitary Reporter*. Therefore, it is our aim, in this place, to present simply the outlines and a few essential explanations of this important branch of work, which the people so gladly and so abundantly endow with home-gifts and home affections. And, notwithstanding that the pages here devoted to the special history o the Relief service have slightly interrupted the succinctness of the narrative, the reader will not fail to perceive that this branch of the Commission's work has not only interlinked its history with that of the Commission's main design, viz., *the prevention of disease*,—but that the grateful foliage and life-inspiring vigor of this wide spreading *branch*, has naturally tended to quicken, enlarge, and invigorate all other branches of this fruitful tree of loyal and loving sympathies. We think the Sanitary Commission itself would gratefully acknowledge that its well organized Department of Relief, by virtue of the world-wide and munificent sympathies which it has evoked, and to which it has promptly responded, has now become the very best pledge of hearty sup-

---

the troops with fresh vegetables last spring, at Young's Point, "modified history!" All military experience corroborates this view, for scurvy has been the bane of all great armies in campaigns. And to illustrate the true economic and hygienic relation of the Commission's work in sending forward, urging forward, and earnestly recommending supplies of fresh vegetables to our armies in the rebel States, we need only quote the remark of M. Baudens, the distinguished Medical Inspector of the French Army, who, in one of his Crimean reports to the Minister of War, asserts that "100,000 francs, spent in fresh vegetables, is a saving of 500,000 francs in the expense of sending the sick to hospitals."

In a monograph upon scurvy, with special reference to army practice, prepared by Surgeon-General Hammond, and published by the Sanitary Commission [*Document N.*], the vital importance of preventive measures against the ravages of this Protean malady is ably set forth; and Dr. Hammond closes that valuable essay by saying that "scurvy is preëminently a preventable disease," and that those who are charged with the care of our sick soldiers should see to it that the reproach of its presence in camp does not rest with them."

port of the entire scheme of the Commission's work of disease-prevention. That the Relief service has been well and wisely managed, all our armies bear ample testimony. It constitutes the people's share in the Sanitary Commission's work, and until Peace again waves her olive branch over the re-United States, and our triumphant armies shall have dispersed to their homes, the mutual obligations that have thus grown out of golden gifts, and the home contributions of "sanitary stores," will not be forgotten by the men to whom this trust is committed.

Sanitary Work in the Campaigns of 1863.

Anti-scorbutic Supplies to the Armies of the Cumberland and Tennessee during the winter and spring.—With the dawning of the New Year, 1863, the banks of Stone's River, before Murfreesboro', were strewn with nearly 8,000 mutilated heroes of General Rosecran's army. The habit that has become so characteristic of the army of the Great Valley, to "move upon the enemy's works," has unquestionably cost much blood, but it has also given us the inexpressible satisfaction of providing for our own wounded, and of re-possessing entire States of the insurgent district. But there necessarily exists one great source of peril to such vast forces in desolated regions which are far removed from the districts of country from whence fresh vegetable supplies can be obtained. To this subject the Sanitary Commission's Western Secretary, Dr. Newberry, and the Sanitary Inspectors under him, have continually given most watchful attention.*

---

* Major General Rosecrans on the Sanitary Commission and its aid to sick and wounded:

"Headquarters, Department of the Cumberland,
Murfreesboro, February 2, 1863.

"The General Commanding presents his warmest acknowledgements to the

In preceding pages we have had occasion to mention how the camps and hospitals of the Cumberland looked to the Commission for "sanitary supplies." That noble army had campaigned on "scurvy rations" in Northern Mississippi and Southern Tennessee, had marched long distances, and had fought hard battles; and after the terrible engagement upon Stone's River, the causes of scurvy, that long had lurked in the unfreshened rations and crowded camps, threatened all the hospitals and regiments of that army. Gangrene, erysipelas, and obstinate diarrhœal diseases menaced the wounded, and, in almost every regimental camp the scorbutic taint was exhibiting its threatening symptoms. "There were no fresh vegetables furnished to the troops, except what were obtained from the Sanitary Commission for the regimental hospitals," said Lieutenant Colonel Hamilton, the faithful Medical Inspector of the Army of the Cumberland, early in the spring. And in his official report to General Rosecrans, that Inspector goes on to say:

"Nearly all the regiments have been without potatoes and

---

friends of the Soldiers of this army, whose generous sympathy with the suffering of the sick and wounded has induced them to send for their comfort numerous sanitary supplies, which are continually arriving by the hands of individuals and charitable societies. While he highly appreciates and does not undervalue the charities which have been lavished on this Army, experience has demonstrated the importance of system and impartiality, as well as judgment and economy, in the forwarding and distribution of these supplies. In all these respects the United States Sanitary Commission stands unrivalled. Its organization, experience, and large facilities for the work are such that the General does not hesitate to recommend, in the most urgent manner, all those who desire to send sanitary supplies, to confide them to the care of this Commission.

"They will thus insure the supplies reaching their destination without wastage, or expense of agents or transportation, and their being distributed in a judicious manner without disorder or interference with the regulations and usages of the service.

"This Commission acts in full concert with the Medical Department of the Army, and enjoys its confidence. It is thus enabled with a few agents to do a large amount of good at the proper time, and in the proper way. Since the battle of Stone's River, it has distributed a surprisingly large amount of clothing, lint, bandages, and bedding, as well as milk, concentrated beef, fruit, and other sanitary stores, essential to the recovery of the sick and wounded.

"W. S. Rosecrans,

"Major General, Commanding Department."

onions, as a regular issue, and not a few of these regiments have not had more than one or two issues of these vegetables in eight, ten, or twelve months.

"It is not surprising, therefore, that scurvy is beginning to manifest itself throughout the army, a few marked cases of which, perhaps two or three, may be found in most of the regiments."

* * * * * * * * *

"I am very much afraid, however, that in a short period those signs of scorbutic taint will increase and extend, and especially if the men are subjected to any extraordinary hardships in marching, on picket duty, or in the trenches; and that, in the event of a battle, the wounds of those who now appear the most robust would not heal kindly."*

* * * * * * * * *

"The season for vegetables and fruit is approaching, but the army cannot look to the surrounding country for a supply of these articles, since its numbers are vastly disproportioned to the amount of lands which will be cultivated; and fruit trees do not at this time abound within the lines which we command. There is, therefore, in my judgment, a pressing demand for large and immediate supplies of potatoes and onions, and this demand will not cease for some months to come."

* * * * * * * * *

"On my arrival at Nashville on the 11th, I represented these facts to Dr. A. N. Read, Sanitary Inspector of the Department of the Cumberland, whom I found already advised upon these matters by personal inspection, and who had already written upon the subject to Dr. J. S. Newberry, Secretary, and in charge of the Western Department of the Sanitary Commission, with headquarters at Louisville."

---

* And in a letter from the same high authority, which was published May 15th, he says of the Sanitary Commission:

* * * * * * * * * * *

"It is to this Army, what I have found it to be everywhere in the Armies of the United States, one of its most important means of support, and without which its efficiency would be greatly diminished. No one who has watched its working upon the field, in the general hospitals, and on the road towards home of discharged and disabled soldiers, but will agree with me in saying that it is doing a vast deal, both in the cause of our country and in the cause of humanity, and so long as the North continues to send its soldiers to the field, the Sanitary Commission must continue its work.

"The agents, so far as I have seen them, are intelligent, faithful and zealous; and the public has nothing to fear in trusting to them its contributions.

"Would to God that every one at the North could see and understand as well as we do the value and *necessity* of this work.

"(Signed,) FRANK H. HAMILTON,
"Medical Inspector, U. S. A."

Shipments of vegetables now began to be made more freely under his order, on the 13th of April, from Louisville; and on the same date Dr. Newberry writes:

"There will be a succession of large shipments of vegetables for Rosecrans' army by railroad and by boat. The General Superintendent of railroads, Mr. Anderson, has been requested by the Commander-in-Chief to forward promptly all the Commission can send, therefore let them go to the front as fast as possible.

"On the 14th of April, Drs. Post and Gunn, Special Inspectors for the Sanitary Commission, having returned from Murfreesboro', confirmed the statements Dr. Read had already made, and we sent a joint telegram to Dr. Newberry, requesting that the vegetables be sent forward as copiously as possible. On the same day Dr. Newberry replied by telegram to me:

"'Large shipments are being made daily. Yesterday I telegraphed Cincinnati, Chicago, and Pittsburg for vegetables, and have a reply from Cincinnati that large shipments will be at once made from there.'"

Though the Army of the Cumberland had daily communication by railway with the rich markets of the Ohio, by way of Nashville and Louisville, it is evident, from this official testimony, that our camps and hospitals in Tennessee were saved from the ravages of scurvy only by such vigilance and promptitude in watching the points of its appearance, and urging forward the needed supplies of fresh vegetables. The Sanitary Inspectors understood their business, and well did they fulfill their mission. "Vegetables, Humanity, and Patriotism," for the time were synonyms,* in the estimation of those enlightened agents of the

---

* "Vegetables, Humanity, Patriotism.—The things represented by these three nouns are more intimately connected than most people imagine. A supply of vegetables to the army is indispensable to its health, and upon the health of the soldiers depends the integrity of the Union." * * * * *

* * * * "We commend the careful consideration of the following extract from a letter recently received from Dr. Warriner, at Vicksburg:

"'People must be roused forthwith to the importance of sending *vegetables* to the army. We want enough to keep all hands busy distributing them. We want enough to supply whole commands, and not merely the hospitals. We have none now—we can do no better service than feed the army with potatoes and onions.

Sanitary Commission; and the heartiness with which the chief officers of the Medical Staff endorsed and aided the Commission's efforts to eradicate scurvy from camps and hospitals. And when spring opened, the Western Secretary procured official permission for the cultivation of extensive Vegetable Gardens in the vicinity of Murfreesboro' and Nashville. This was an enterprise of great practical importance, for not only were the products of those gardens necessary for the great hospitals in Central Tennessee, but they were soon to be required in hospitals and camps near Chattanooga. The *Sanitary Reporter* thus mentions the organization and purposes of the "*hospital gardens:*"

"While laboring to supply vegetables for the immediate wants of the Army of the Cumberland in the early spring, it was understood that the supply from the North would in a few months fail, and that in the last months of summer the sick in that department would be unsupplied, unless vegetables should be raised in the department for their use. In the whole region occupied by the army, the country was almost a desert, and no dependence could be put upon purchasing supplies of citizens.

There certainly must be a sufficient surplus of these in the North to enable us to do it, if we can once get the subject sufficiently impressed upon the loyal producers of them. It has been only at brief but widely separated intervals that we have had supplies of these in adequate abundance to justify this general disbursement of them. When it has occurred, the results has been in the highest possible degree satisfactory and beneficial. The achievements of the two Commissions in this respect, last spring, at Young's Point, modified history! The effects are not to be weighed or estimated. No one thing has done so much to establish the reputation of the Commission with the army; and yet how very seldom we have been able to supplement commissary stores to this extent. If we could do it continually, we should prevent more sickness than our other efforts are able to relieve. I wish this notion could be preached all through the North, clamorously and with power. Good old brother Chidlaw could do immense good if he could concentrate his whole time and his magnificent good-will-power upon it for a season. I trust you will not neglect to call public attention to this express plan of sanitary labor, and urge the matter in all effective ways. Potatoes and onions for the whole army! Make that the watchword; varying the monotony from time to time by the addition of "*cabbage.*" But don't let people encumber us with other kinds of vegetables, unless, perhaps, tomatoes. Their value is incomparably less than that of those named. I will write again after the arrival of the *Clara Bell.*

(Signed) "'Yours truly,
"'H. A. Warriner.'"

—(*Sanitary Reporter.*)

Vegetables could not be bought, they must be *raised*. Reliance, then, could only be placed upon *hospital gardens*.

*   *   *   *   *   *   *

"The Sanitary Commission has furnished seeds and garden tools, and about 30,000 plants, purchased in Louisville and Cincinnati; and its agents have exercised a general supervision over the work."

*   *   *   *   *   *   *

"A similar work has been accomplished at Nashville, and these two gardens will furnish a *full supply* of vegetables for the hospitals of the department during that part of the season in which they cannot be supplied from the North."

These great gardens, with their teeming products of choice vegetables, anticipated future necessities, and although, in all, about *eighty acres* of fertile land was devoted to this very practically hygienic use, the events of autumn proved how wisely a vastly larger tract of land might have been thus cultivated.* And during the winter and spring months it became necessary to resort to unusual means, and to use the greatest energy to procure and transport anti-scorbutic vegetables to the distant points where the Inspectors found need of such supplies.

Even after the Commissary Department of the Western armies had been aroused by the urgent demand for potatoes and onions, the Sanitary Commission still had more reliable means than those at the command of the Government for supplying that demand. It is stated upon authority, that "recently, when scurvy threatened our army, a Commissary advertised for an adequate quantity of patotoes and onions, and no response was made. Nobody either had, or chose to become responsible for, the de-

---

* In his report to the Commission, September 1st, Dr. Newberry says:

"The Hospital Gardens established in this Department have more than justified all our anticipations. That at Murfreesboro' had, up to August 30th, furnished to the hospitals 248 barrels of assorted vegetables, and the gardener estimates that it will produce during the balance of the season 800 bushels of tomatoes, 1,200 of Irish potatoes, 1,200 of sweet potatoes, 25,000 heads of cabbage, besides large quantities of beans, melons, turnips, &c."

livery of 50,000 bushels of patotoes, and a corresponding quantity of other vegetables, but there were few families in the great West which could not spare from its store a peck, a bushel, or a barrel of vegetables, and so *within a month some thousand barrels were donated*, and an impending disaster was averted, the Commission furnishing a medium of communication between the people at home and their defenders in the field."* But we need not dwell upon further details of the methods and the means by which this warfare against the most dreaded and fatal enemy of the camps and to frontier hospitals was overcome. It was the commencement of a work that must necessarily be continued until the end of the war. And experience has shown that when Commissaries have found the markets exhausted of anti-scorbutic vegetables, the Sanitary Commission, through its branches of supply, never have failed to bring such supplies forward at once.

Late in the spring, when a general movement of the army of the Cumberland was anticipated, the Commission's Inspector at Murfreesboro, Dr. Reed, wrote as follows:

* * * * * * * *

"The supply of vegetables distributed has greatly improved the health and efficiency of this army. No greater amount of good has ever been accomplished in so short a time, and at an expense comparatively so slight. The friends at home who have contributed these supplies should feel that they have done much to strengthen the hands and the hearts of the soldiers for the struggle which all feel is close at hand.

"It will be gratifying to all to know that the most ample and minute preparations have been made for the care of the wounded, should an engagement occur. A special medical purveyor has been appointed for each corps of the army, who has provided himself with a large stock of medicines, hospital stores, clothing and dressings, and all necessary transportation, to enable him to accompany the army and issue his stores upon the field when

* See *Sanitary Reporter*, June 1st, 1863.

and where needed. Also, as I mentioned in my last report, the surgeons of each regiment have very generally furnished themselves each with a box of hospital stores and dressings from our supplies, to be taken with the regiment wherever it moves. And we have in addition furnished to most of the division surgeons a good supply of concentrated beef extract for the same purpose. We hope and expect that all will thus supply themselves from our stores now on hand. Should occasion require it, all our supplies suitable for the purpose will be pushed forward promptly to the temporary field hospitals and distributed whereever they will relieve or alleviate suffering."

* * * * * * * *

"The testimony is uniform by all who know that the great want of the army, after all that has been done, *is fresh vegetables.*

"I hope they will continue to be forwarded as long as they are to be obtained, and that every one who *can* will plant a separate patch of potatoes, onions or cabbage for the soldier."

At the end of the month of May, the same faithful Inspector writes to the Western Secretary of the Commission as follows:

* * * * "In my report to you for April, I had to represent that the great want of the Army of the Cumberland was fresh vegetables; that up to the 10th of that month there had not been more than two issues for eight or nine months; and that in many cases there had not been one issue during that time. As a consequence, scurvy was beginning to appear in almost every regiment, and that this was a sure indication that the soldiers were not in a condition to bear hard marches, or to labor in the trenches; and if wounded in battle, their wounds would not heal kindly, but would be followed by pyæmia, erysipelas, hospital gangrene, and excessive suppuration. The mortality of the Confederate wounded at Murfreesboro' was forty per cent. Dr. Avent, their Medical Director, a surgeon of unusual intelligence, ascribes this large mortality to lack of vegetable diet.

"I have now to report, that from the 1st of April to the 20th of May, there have been about four issues of vegetables by the Commissaries to the troops of Murfreesboro', Franklin, and Nashville. At Gallatin they have not received from Government more than two issues since they entered Kentucky. The police of all the troops is excellent. The external manifestations of scurvy have nearly disappeared; although at Gallatin and Carthage there are several well-marked cases.

"Dr. E. B. Glick, Brigade Surgeon, informs me, May 21st, that all his cases of scurvy have disappeared; that three weeks since he had many cases of ophthalmia, which did not yield to ordinary treatment, but which had rapidly recovered under the use of the vegetables we had supplied him.

"Hospital gangrene has nearly disappeared, and the cases of erysipelas are much less frequent.

* * * * * * *

"During the month, we have received and distributed, from the Nashville depot, 5,897 bushels of vegetables, and 18,730 pounds dried fruit, and, in addition, a considerable amount of canned fruit, pickles, and other sanitary stores.

"These have been distributed as follows:

Sent to	Bbls. Vegetables.	Lbs. Dried Fruit.
Murfreesboro'	1,423	5,955
Franklin	80	1,200
Carthage	23	575
Fort Donelson	127	500
Gallatin	95	
Lavergne	66	750
Brentwood	24	500
Triune	58	165
Clarksville	12	
Nashville	451	9,085
	2,359 bbls..	18,730

Vegetables—equal to 5,897 bushels, at 2½ bushels to the barrel.

"These have been distributed under the rule, that the sick and feeble should be first supplied: the balance to be given to the well men in the regiments."

In another letter from the sanitary dépôt of that army, the following illustration is given of the necessity for such anti-scorbutic supplies, and the faithfulness of medical officers in disbursing them: *

---

* The value and appreciation of this Commission's work in the Army of the Cumberland, is well illustrated by the following spontaneous testimonials of gratitude from Medical and Commanding officers:

* * * * "Among many facts showing, as a rule, the earnest devotion of the surgeons of this army to their work, and their fidelity in the use of sanitary stores, I will mention only the following. At the time when potatoes were exceedingly scarce and valuable, and when the Commission was furnishing the greatest part which were available for the army, the surgeon of ———, who had just returned to his regiment, visited our rooms with his assistant to ask us if we could do anything for him. On exhibiting his person, his legs and body were spotted and purplish, with as little elasticity to the flesh as to a piece of dough; an indentation from pressure would remain for many minutes. The symptoms of scurvy were clear and unmistakeable, and he had been distributing for weeks to the enlisted men under his charge vegetables from our stores—had thus banished scurvy from the tents of the men, and it remained only among

---

"Headquarters 3d Divis., 20th Army Corps,
"Medical Department, May 1st, 1863.

"Sir,—Allow me, through you, to return the sincere thanks of the Medical Officers of this Division to the U. S. Sanitary Commission for their uniform promptness and attention to the wants of the sick and wounded soldiers.

"It has been my lot to be with this Division, as Medical Director, through two hard-fought battles (Perryville and Stone's River), where we had many wounded men, with only limited means of ministering to their comforts; consequently, I have had a good opportunity of judging of the efficiency of your organization, and of the benefits derived from it. Through the promptness of the Commission our wounded were more comfortably situated within forty-eight hours after the battle, than they were eight days after the battle of Shiloh.

"To your organization we are indebted, also, for many valuable suggestions which have added much to the comfort of camp life.

"With the most sincere hope that your organization may receive the continued support it deserves, I am,

"Very respectfully,
"Your ob't servant,
"D. V. Griffith,
"Surgeon 2d Ky. Vols. and Med. Director.

"Insp. U. S. San. Commission."

Endorsed as follows:

"Headquarters 3d Division, 20th A. C.,
"Near Murfreesboro', Tenn., May 4, 1863.

"I take great pleasure in endorsing every word of the within letter, and desire to return, through the Medical Inspector, my sincere thanks to the Sanitary Commission for their almost invaluable services to my wounded men at Perryville and Stone River.

"P. H. Sheridan,
"Major-General."

* * * * * * * * *

"Receive my thanks, my dear sir, for your attention to the health of my command. Your kind issues of vegetables are thankfully received by all the men, and without them our men would soon be victims of scorbutic diseases; they would soon give out on the march, and would not have sufficient physical vigor to with-the officers. When he was directed to use them for the officers also, as far as they needed them medicinally, he expressed surprise and gratitude both; for the supposed they were to be used sacredly for the enlisted men."

That the people of the great West have entered into the na-

---

stand wounds, which good soldiers are apt to receive when faithfully and gallantly performing their duty upon the battle-field.

"I am, sir,
"Your obedient servant,
"A. McD. McCook,
"Maj.-Gen. Com'd'g 20th Army Corps."

* * * * * * * *

* * * * "These vegetables will preserve our men, and advance the interest of our cause.

"The ration of potatoes issued to my entire Division by you yesterday, was thankfully received, and will do much to prevent scurvy and other diseases.

"Young ladies who have lovers in the army are prone to send them handsomely wrought slippers, book-marks, &c., but love will also be unabated if the fair hands will keep those handsome souvenirs until the close of the war, and while we are in the field we promise to love and admire any and all who engage in this good work of supplying us with fresh vegetables.

"Yours very truly,
"R. W. Johnson,
"Brig.-Gen. Vol. Com'd'g."

"Headq'rs, Army of Kentucky,
"Franklin, May 3, 1863.

"Ag't U. S. Sanitary Commission, Nashville, Tenn.:

"I have to acknowledge the receipt of 40 barrels vegetables from your office, which have been issued to the troops in this command.

"The health of the command is steadily improving, largely owing to your kindness and activity in furnishing those important anti-scorbutic remedies.

"Please accept my thanks for this and former invoices.

"Truly yours,
"W. Varian,
"Surgeon U. S. V., Medical Director Army of Ky."

"Headq'rs 2d Division, 21st Army Corps,
"Camp Near Murfreesboro',
"May 3, 1863.

"Inspector U. S. Sanitary Commission:

"Dear Sir,—I can have no more agreeable duty than to acknowledge the value and beneficial services of the Sanitary Commission.

"The army owes a debt of gratitude to the benevolent men and women of the country, who have, through this admirable agency, contributed to relieve the wants of the soldier, supplying those 'small things' so essential to their health and vigor.

"I am, very respectfully,
"John M. Palmer,
"Major-General."

tional struggle with their whole soul, and under the highest inspiration of patriotic duty, is manifested in their effective labors and untiring zeal in suppressing the rebellion. Cheerfully and promptly have they given their sons to the cause, and, in some of the States, even where labor is most in demand, they have exceeded all Federal quotas and calls for troops; and every household, however humble or afflicted, has offered and will continue to offer its loving gifts for the aid and succor of their brave sons in the army. Like the broad rivers of the West, the Sanitary Commission's channels have received and borne southward the tributary streams of the Great Valley; and no person can doubt that the fervent desire and the urgency of the Western people to have their home-offerings go forward undelayed and directly to the places and the men who most needed, though sometimes impatiently overleaping all wise methods and the Commission's authorized channels, have, nevertheless, finally resulted in giving to the Commission itself the very highest practicable degree of energy, largeness of plan, and celerity of execution in its Relief service, and, at the same time, thoroughly imbuing the commanding generals and the whole army of the Valley with their own spirit of earnest co-operation and merciful helpfulness. Indeed, it would appear that from the beginning of the war the great generals of the West have done all in their power to facilitate and give full effect to the works of the Sanitary Commission.*

---

* The following published orders from the two great leaders of our Western Armies, exhibit the spirit in which the war and the men who help in it were regarded by those distinguished Generals:

"HEADQUARTERS DEPARTMENT OF THE TENNESSEE,
Vicksburg, Miss., Sept. 28, 1863.

"Commanding Officer, Cairo, Ill.:

"Sir,—Direct the Post Quartermaster at Cairo to call upon the U. S. Sanitary

With good reason does Dr. Newberry, the Western Secretary, in his report to the Commission of sanitary work accomplished in the forces on the Mississippi, remarks: "Indeed, I may say that our operations in that Department have been, by an irresistible influence, gradually but constantly expanding. The many and great privileges accorded us by the General commanding, and by others in authority, have opened new and wide doors of usefulness, and by accepting the responsibilities thus laid upon us, our duties have necessarily been increased." And not less justly does the Western Secretary yield to the military officers their full share of honors for humane and life-saving work in the army of the Cumberland. He says: "I think I am justified in saying that there is no Department of the whole army where our work is more systematically, thorougly, and well done. The credit of this desirable result is not, however, due wholly to the corps of agents who have represented us so faithfully there, but should be equally shared by the military and medical authorities, all of whom have been at all times most cordially coöperative, not only granting cheerfully every reasonable request we have made, but, even anticipating our wants;

---

agent at your place, and see exactly what buildings they require to be erected for their charitable and humane purposes.

"The Commission has been of such great service to the country, and at Cairo are doing so much for this army at this time, that I am disposed to extend their facilities for doing good in every way in my power. You will therefore cause to be put up, at government expense, suitable buildings for the Sanitary Commission, connecting those they already have, and also put up for them necessary outbuildings. * * * * * * * * *

"(Signed) U. S. Grant,
"Major General."

"Headquarters Department of the Ohio,
Cincinnati, Ohio, Aug. 1st, 1863.

"Special Order, No. 290.

"3. All officers in this Department will extend to the agents of the U. S. Sanitary Commission, every facility consistent with their duties, and will respect and aid them in carrying out their charitable work.

"By order of

"Major General Burnside."

often spontaneously proffering the aid we were about to need. The catalogue of the officers of this army, who have manifested towards the Sanitary Commission cordial and appreciative co-operation, is so long that I have not room to give it, but I may say, in general, that our relations are of the pleasantest character with every one. The evidences of hearty sympathy with us in our work, given by General Rosecrans, General Garfield, his chief of staff, Dr. Perin, the Medical Director, and Dr. Hamilton, Medical Inspector, have been frequently exhibited," . . . .

During the winter and spring of 1863, the forces upon the Mississippi, under General Grant, occupied positions that were exceedingly unfavorable to health, but the ground that had been gained along the course of the great river, during a year of terrible struggles and toil, from Island number Ten, and Memphis, to the Yazoo, was not to be relinquished, and from that perilous base of bayous, swamps, malaria, and difficult transportation, was to be commenced one the grandest campaigns of the war. Late in the month of March, General Grant moved forward strong columns of his forces southward from Young's Point and Milliken's Bend, where the Sanitary Commission was systematically at work by hygienic agencies, that "modified history," and after incredible toil and exposure in marching, bridging, fording and fighting all the way across the peninsula opposite and below Vicksburg, to Grand Gulf, and thence to the bloody contests at Port Gibson and Champion Hill, then quickly followed the triumphant battles and forced marches that scattered the rebel forces from the capital of Mississippi, and drove General Pemberton westward from the Big Black River to the fortifications of Vicksburg.

The masterly Leader of our army had not over-estimated the physical powers and heroism of his forces, but he put them to tests that proved them well, and which most strikingly illustrated the practical value of health and its safe-guards in such a campaign. In the trenches and mines, on picket and in constant skirmishing and fighting, while beleaguring the enemy's stronghold; or upon the morasses of the Yazoo and the Big Black, maintaining our hotly disputed lines, General Grant's powerful army was rendered all the stronger and the braver for the constant presence and influence of sanitary labors and sanitary supplies. General Grant, with his accustomed sagacity, had promptly ordered that ample facilities for the transportation of the Commission's "sanitary stores" should be provided, and as soon as Inspector Warriner and his assistants were able to gain a point of communication with the forces before Vicksburg, large supplies of fresh vegetables and other needed supplies for the health of the forces, and for the succor of the wounded and sick, were poured in from the "sanitary steamers," and other boats on the Mississippi and Yazoo.*

---

* The Commission's Western Secretary, foreseeing the inevitable demand that must continue to be made for anti-scorbutics in the army on the Mississippi, as well as in the army of the Cumberland, endorsed and gave wide publicity to the statements that were sent to him by the Relief agents in the field. The following is an illustration of the view taken by those practical men:

* * * * * * * * * * *

"Let every farmer in the loyal States put in an extra patch of potatoes, cabbages, and onions, for the soldiers; let ever child have his soldier's garden-bed; let the "Onion Leagues" vie with the Union Leagues in number and zeal of membership, and so will the lives of our brave soldiers be preserved, and the country saved. To this same purport is the following appeal of the Rev. B. W. Chidlaw:"

"TO ALL THE BOYS AND GIRLS IN THE NORTH."

"U. S. SANITARY STEAMER 'DUNLEITH,'
"On the Mississippi River, April 27.

"We have just finished the distribution of our precious cargo of good things for our sick and well soldiers in the hospitals and camps, from Cairo, Ill., to Young's Point, La. These things were much needed, and gratefully received.

"Will your kind hearts and willing hands work for the soldier? You may ask what can we do? You can work in your gardens and fields, plant and cultivate potatoes, tomatoes, cabbage, onions, &c. You can gather strawberries, raspberries, currants, and blackberries, and your mothers will *can* them. Your apples, peaches, pears, and plums can be cut and dried, and put up in small bags, then these rich treasures of your gardens, fields, and orchards, the products of your patriotic industry, sent to the Soldiers' Aid Society, and thus to the U. S. Sanitary Commission, will reach the soldier, help him to get well, and cheer his heart.

"*Begin to plan and to work at once.* Keep at it, and thousands of our brave soldiers sharing your gifts will rise and call you blessed."

Under date of May 4th, 1863, Inspector Warriner writes to Dr. Newberry, the Secretary, from Milliken's Bend, La.:

* * * * * * * *

"I have watched with much interest the movement of these troops. It is characterized by most active energy. Most of the tents are left behind, as are also the men who are not strong enough to endure an exhausting and desperate campaign. Supplies in anything approaching sufficient quantity cannot be conveyed to the front by any existing method. Foraging is too precarious, of course, to be relied upon long, and desperate fighting is inevitable. Yesterday the news of a vigorous battle at Grand Gulf, Mississippi, on Saturday, came to hand. I see no escape from a series of such, augmenting in fierceness and intensity, until the question is decided as to who shall hold the river through the ensuing summer. This, with the increase of disease that will keep pace with the advancing season, may, and possibly will, develop a great amount of sickness, and the thought that is pressing most upon me, is how to meet this suffering with some approximation to an equivalent relief. I beg, therefore, that you consider this letter as chiefly a requisition for stores." * * * * * *

From Young's Point, above Vicksburg, Dr. Warriner writes, under date of May 18th 1863:

* * * * * * * *

"We are still unable to get transportation to the Point for hospital stores. The demand for them there is hourly increasing. Several hotly contested battles have already occurred. The one that resulted in the capture of Jackson, Miss., by our forces was especially severe. Not less than 800 were killed. Applying the ordinary rule as to the relative number wounded, there cannot be much less than 2,000 of these, besides a large number from the ranks of the enemy. Previous to this battle I had received reports from Surgeons at Grand Gulf, that 500 wounded had accumulated there. Yesterday firing was heard here all day, artillery and musketry. It was not incessant, but at times was rapid and heavy. The direction seemed to be southeast from Vicksburg; distance not exactly calculable."

* * * * * * * *

"I learned, meantime, that the purpose is to bring the wounded here and ship them North, as rapidly as possible. An installment of several hundred is expected in to-morrow. They will be brought on boats to the lower end of the new road—the road running from this point to the river, twelve miles or so below Vicksburg—thence by wagons and ambulances here. The boats taking them hence will have occasion to make heavy drafts upon us for stores. And I shall make an effort to send to the front by the return teams more or less stores for those who will not be favored with immediate transportation. Persons claiming and, for aught I know, possessing, military sagacity, regard General Grant's chances as in the highest degree promising.

"The convalescents at Milliken's Bend at my last writing have all—excepting those at the Van Buren hospital—been removed to this point. They number nearly 5,000. About ten per cent. are under medical treatment."

From Haines' Bluff, May 27th, Dr. Warriner reports:

* * * * "I have at last reached a point of communication with the main army. Haines' Bluff was abandoned by the enemy when it became certain that Vicksburg would be speedily invested by our enterprising army. Roads have been opened up, and properly guarded, from here to the lines, and supplies of all kinds are pouring along the route with the utmost activity. I had the sanitary wharf-boat moved to this place from Young's Point five days ago. Our ample supplies were already reduced by the convalescents and hospitals, whereof I have already given full reports; but we have enough left to keep all hands busy. I have been out to the front since arriving here, making a hurried inspection of the general condition of the army and of the wounded."

Again, just previous to the capitulation of Vicksburg, that watchful Inspector reports to the Commission as follows:*

---

* The following letters of thanks from officers serve to illustrate to our minds the spirit of thankfulness in which the Sanitary Commission's aid was received at the period of which we are now writing:

"Hospital 14th Div., 13th A. C.,
"Near Vicksburg, June 20, 1863.

"Dr H. A. Warriner,
"Agent U. S. Sanitary Commission:

"Sir,—In behalf of more than four hundred wounded men treated in this hospital since the siege of Vicksburg, and as many sick men pestrated by exposure

"UP THE YAZOO, NEAR VICKSBURG, }
June 23d, 1863. }

"DR. J. S. NEWBERRY,

"Secretary Western Department U. S. Sanitary Commission, Louisville:

"My Dear Doctor,—I send herewith lists of wounded, sick, &c., obtained from several different hospitals in the field and at Milliken's Bend. The *Nashville*, since the list from her was made out, has transferred to the transports nearly all her pa-

---

and fatigue, I hereby express their thanks and gratitude for the indispensable goods with which you have supplied them. When I have told them I have got from you ice, dried and canned fruits, lemons, spirits, shirts, drawers, slippers, sheets, bed ticks, etc., etc., to make them comfortable, some of them have said 'God bless the Commission!'—others would say 'good,' and others would use the very expressive phrase, 'bully!' I have been in the service nearly two years, and am glad to say, our sick were never so well cared for as now, and it is due to, you to say, that we are indebted almost exclusively to the U. S. Sanitary Commission for the means of making them comfortable. I take the liberty of making these observations, because I have been employed by this hospital to procure of you these supplies. May God put it into the hearts of the friends of the soldiers to keep you well supplied.

"Yours respectfully,

"H. J. EDDY,
"Chaplain 33d Ills. Infantry."

"FIELD HOSPITAL, 3D DIV., 17TH A. C., }
"Rear of Vicksburg, June 16, 1863. }

"DR. WARRINER,

"U. S. San. Com. Boat, Chickasaw Bayou, Miss.:

"Doctor,—Many, many thanks, we all send you and through you to the noble ladies of Ohio, God bless them! for the liberal supply of sheets, shirts, drawers, pillow-slips, comforts, fruits, and everything else you have so freely sent us. Without these I know not what we should have done.

"Crossing the Mississippi River as this whole army did, with transportation cut down as ours of necessity was, to just enough to carry rations and ammunition, the prospect was anything but a cheering one to the medical officer looking forward to the time when many of his charge must necessarily become sick from long and wearisome marches, and many more get wounded in battle.

"The battles of Thompson's Hill, Raymond, Jackson and Champion's Hill, more than exhausted the limited supplies of regimental surgeons, so that, had it not been for the Sanitary Commission, who met our victorious army as we arrived at Haines' Bluff, the sufferings of our wounded at the siege of Vicksburg would have been far greater than they have been. The wounded have been cheered and made contented, and many have been saved beyond all question.

"I sincerely hope you have plenty of everything on hand still, for, if I do not mistake the signs of the times, it will not be long before you will again have heavy draughts made upon you.

"Should you have occasion to visit the front, do not fail to call upon us and see for yourself how much good you have done. We think our hospital will compare favorably with any field hospital in the army. I am, Doctor,

"Your sincere friend and well-wisher,

"EDWARD L. HILL,
"Surgeon 20th O. V. Infantry, in charge 3d Div. Field Hospital."

tients. The Van Buren hospital has parted with a large number of its patients. I am not able to give at the present writing the number remaining in either of these hospitals. The number of sick in the field in the rear of Vicksburg, including the wounded not yet removed, is a trifle less than 3,000. Not over one-third of these are grave cases.

"The three corps 'hospitals' are now in operation and fairly furnished with the equipments, conveniences, and supplies appropriate to general hospitals. There are besides eleven division hospitals—all in good condition relatively. In fact, their condition in all respects is unusually good for the field. Regimen-

---

"McPherson Hospital, 17th A. C.
"Department Tennessee, June 18th, 1863.

"Dr. Warriner,
Agt. U. S. San. Com.:

"Dear Sir,—I have just received six loads of Sanitary supplies for the sick and wounded of this hospital. They were much needed and gratefully received. They supplied a want that could not otherwise have been met.

"In behalf of the sick and wounded soldiers, allow me to present to the Commission their heart-felt thanks and high appreciation of their well directed efforts in this noble enterprise. Yours is a noble and patriotic calling. Many a family circle will be made to rejoice and many a poor soldier will be indebted to the care and great labor bestowed on the army, by the Commission, for his life! Many a prayer will be offered in years to come for blessings to descend upon those *now* engaged in this good wotk.

"May God bless and prosper you in your philanthropic enterpriee, and prosper the right, is the wish of those whom you have bountifully supplied,

"I am, very respectfully, your ob'd't servant,

"Geo. R. Weeks,
"Surgeon U. V., in charge."

"Surgeon's Office, Field Hospital,
"3d Div. 15th A. C., near Vicksburg, June 18th, 1863.

"Dr. Warriner,
Agt. U. S. San. Com.:

* * * * * * * * * * *

"You have enabled us to fit up several hundred patients, out in the houseless woods, with many of the comforts and even luxuries of *home*, when with only the allotments of Government procurable here, our hospital regimen of diet and wardrobe would indeed have been meagre. Permit me, for these, our gallant sufferers, to acknowledge the receipt, at your hands, of large supplies of bedding, clothing vegetables, fruits, and a variety of those relishable dainties so opportune to reflush the cheeks made wan by the toils of this herculean campaign.

"I certainly believe that a number of lives have been saved in this hospital from the use of delicacies furnished by your Commission.

"Such tokens as these serve to fix yet firmer in the soldier's breast the jewels he has preserved from the halcyon days of the past—the grateful memories of loved ones far away.

"God bless the Sanitary Commission! * * * * * *

"Very respectfully, your obedient servant,

"Geo. L. Lucas, 47th Ills.,
"Surg. 3d Div., 15th A. C."

tal hospitals are kept up, but the severer cases are chiefly sent to one of the other two classes. The three hospital transports continue active in the removal of patients Northwards.

* * * * * * *

"The steamer *City of Alton* left with me eight half-barrels ale, two casks codfish (1,000 lbs. in all), one barrel butter, and 28 sacks dried apples (130 lbs. to the sack)—all in excellent condition, and very welcome. Since then 500 barrels of potatoes have arrived from Memphis, brought to that point from Cairo by the *Dunleith*. The cause that prevented the *Dunleith* from completing her trip has doubtless been explained to you. The potatoes arrived four days since. They are all issued to-day. I have given them freely to the troops in camp as well as hospital, as I have done by previous lots since being here. It is impossible to preserve large quautities of them for hospital consumption exclusively. Besides, their value to the well is incomputible. No happier hit has been made by the generous North than the sending of a surplus of vegetables to this army. They have done a vast amount of good, and elicited the liveliest expressions of gratitude toward the numerous donors and the organization through whose instrumentality they were procured. The service rendered by the Sanitary Commission and Western Sanitary Commission since the arrival of the army in its present position, in assisting to supply hospitals with needed comforts, has been signally important and more than ordinarily appreciated. I enclose copies of a few of the letters I have received from the recipients of these bounties, acknowledging their value. It would be no ordinary pleasure to me to be able to convey to the givers of these good gifts even a glimpse of the radiantly grateful looks I encounter in the hospitals from day to day, from those whom their gifts have blessed. A thousand times over I hear the expression, "I wonder if they know how much good they are doing." *I* wonder too. Unquestionably, the widespread labors of the Commission through its numerous branches and coadjutors were never so pervasively and thoroughly appreciated as now; and this, it is not to be overlooked, is partly, perhaps largely, due to the proximate success of the efforts to combine and systematize these labors. I may be regarded as an interested witness in this particular, but I certainly have the best possible opportunity to see and judge of the relative value of the two methods of distributing stores; which may be designated the *systematic* and *spasmodic*. And I find it difficult to express my appreciation of the one, and my abhorrence of the other. Not an agent of the spasmodic class has been sent hither but has expressed to me *spontaneously*, after tarrying a few days, and with some enthusiasm, his convictions of the superiority of system. I spend no more time arguing the question. I point to work and results. They are patent and beginning to be known of all men. I must mention in this connection the highest official compliment I have hitherto received at the hands of the military authorities. It consists of 100 tons of Government ice turned over to me for distribution. I asked General Grant, a few days since, for a barge and towage for the same, pledging him that the Sanitary Commission would load the barge with ice. He promptly acceded to my request. On returning to the landing I found the above cargo just arrived. Thinking perhaps that it would be unnecessary expense on the part of the Commission to purchase more ice immediately, I did nothing further about it. Day before yesterday an order came putting the cargo into my hands. This, together with nearly or quite as large a quantity in the hands of the Purveyor, makes the present supply abundant.

"Our issues have been very large for the last month in all articles and items. We are now out of lemons, canned fruit, crackers, potatoes, pickles, crout, drawers and sheets. Nearly out of canned milk (24 cans on hand), running low in shirts, and, in fact, are growing deficient in all things save ice. But the effect for good has been commensurate with the activity of our issues.

"Complaints of the misuse of stores grow less frequent and more mythical. I make it a point to follow up every instance of it reported to me, and generally find accusation and accuser vanishing out of reach before the investigation is concluded. And where I find it otherwise, competent authority is prompt in arresting the evil. I am disposed to think that the amount of waste occurring in this manner is too unimportant to deserve farther consideration.

"I have been occupied for the last week with such inspections as circumstances would permit of the troops engaged in the trenches. They are all clustered in the ravines and on the slopes of the hills descending *from* the city. A portion of the line now rests on the very slopes crested by the rebel works. The air in the ravines is most of the time still, hot and stifling. They live half buried in the ground for protection against the missiles of the enemy. The springs on the slopes and toward the summits of the hills begin to flag, and the principal dependence is now upon the water in the bottoms of the ravines. This naturally grows more and more impure from the drainage of extensive camping grounds, besides growing gradually less in quantity. In short, the surroundings of a large force thus situated and occupied are decidedly unsanitary. No one expects this state of things to continue many days longer, however, and as the regiments are successively relieved from time to time, no considerable mischief has yet resulted from it. On the other hand, sickness is increasing slowly, especially, intermittent fever and its allied ailments. This increase does not confine itself to troops in the trenches. It is doubtless in part but the consummation of effects that have been daily preparing from the commencement of the campaign. The excitement which has held the entire army up to such a key of resistance for these many weeks as to enable it to cope with both visible and invisible foes, is slightly on the decline. The men are sure of their prey. Nobody doubts for a moment the result. No one expresses discontent or discouragement. Add to this the fact that an abnormal tension of brain and nerve must of necessity exhaust itself at length, and one almost wonders that the keen edge held so long. Men obey orders now with a patient rather than exultant courage. An order to storm would change this suddenly enough, but meanwhile malaria and rather unwholesome lodgings and unwholesome water (in many cases), are beginning to show their legitimate effects. I could not but notice that the men in the rifle pits and at work on the entrenchments wore a slightly jaded look, and were stimulated by their momentous and perilous labors barely enough to exercise the necessary caution for thir own protection. All the points now worked by our forces are swept by the bullets of the enemy's sharpshooters. Every step of our advance is along trenches and covered ways. Entire protection is of course impossible. I should judge (although it is partly *guessing*) that fifty men or so are wounded daily. I went into the fort nearest the enemy's works. It is a trifle less than fifty yards distant. A hurricane of bullets swept over our heads incessantly, but no one at that time had been wounded there. The rebels are throwing shell much of the time from two mortars located so far behind their outer works as to baffle all attempts to dismantle or silence them. These shells do relatively little harm, as they appear to be thrown utterly at random. They fly for the most part completely over our line into the neighborhood of hospitals and headquarters. I have heard of but few casualties produced by them, and have witnessed but one. Hospitals that were annoyed by them have been removed to points of safety.

"I have neglected in former communications to speak of the Soldiers' Lodge on the Sanitary wharf-boat. It is not to be overlooked, for it is doing some good in a small way. We have entertained in it since the 1st of May, 156 soldiers, giving an average of two days' entertainment to each. I have an excellent cook for it, and draw rations of the Government, supplementing them with stores of our own.

"Send ample supplies of the following stores for coming emergencies:

Canned milk,	Concent'd beef,
Dried fruit,	Canned fruit,
Sour crout,	Pickles,
Ale,	Bromine,
Green tea,	White sugar,
Lemons,	Potatoes,
Drawers,	Sheets,
Shirts,	Soda crackers.

"I have witnessed the action of bromine in the hospital under Dr. Weeks' care, and am freshly impressed with its value. No one here except him has auy supply of this article, and he has but little left. Gangrene and erysipelas are somewhat prevalent amongst the wounded still left in the field. Most of the cases left, as you are aware, are those that could not bear removal.

* * * * * * * *

"H. A. Warriner,
"Inspector."

On the 11th of July, the Inspector again writes:

* * * * * * * *

"I have received from an Indiana State boat, which arrived here on the ever memorable Fourth, 218 barrels, 45 boxes, 1 sack hospital stores. The barrels contained potatoes, corn meal, and dried apples. The boxes were not invoiced—contents various. The corn meal proves more acceptable than I could have anticipated. Dried apples are always in order. I have also received from the Metropolitan Police of New York city, at I know not whose suggestion, 50 *boxes of lemons*. Forty-one of the boxes are in excellent order. No contribution could have been more welcomed, or more happily timed. We were out of lemons, and had been for some days; and it is unnecessary to speak of their value. In many and many an instance their value has been that of a human life. Combined with ice, they make at this season an organic whole, worth—one may almost say—all other stores united. Ice we are out of. A barge load of it has just arrived, claimed as private property. It is already retailing at ten cents a pound. It is the only ice now in port.

* * * * * * * *

"We are now out of the following articles, in addition to those already named: Canned fruit, canned milk, potatoes, soda crackers, ale, wines, corn starch, codfish, pickles of all kinds, butter, dried beef, eggs, cheese, cinnamon, pepper, allspice, all kinds of liquors; all articles of first rate value and in constant demand. We are also out of sheets, drawers and slippers, also in constant demand. A supply of sheets has accumulated at Memphis, and will be here in a few days, making enough probably for current use. All other articles except those named as lately received, are running rapidly low. No doubt, however, replenishments will arrive before you receive this."

Abundant supplies coutinued to be sent forward every week, yet there never was a surplus of the *staple* articles of "Sanitary stores. The *Dunleith*, and the *Alice Dean*, were exclusively employed as Sanitary steamers.* Ice was sent down the rivers in barges by the hundred tons, and the Sanitary dépôts at Vicksburg, Helena, Young's Point, Memphis, and Cairo, were kept in full operation as places of distribution of every variety of "sanitary stores," as well as deposits for accumulation.

Dr. Newberry thus summed up the amount of "Sanitary stores" distributed in his department during the first five months of the year, (1863):

"Total number of packages to General Grant's Army, 11,926.

"Since the battle of Murfreesboro, the shipments to the Army of the Cumberland have been by rail and steamer 8,300 packages. Of these, 3,000 were barrels of vegetables, sent during the month of May.

"To the preceding sums should be added the stores sent to Western Virginia, Eastern Kentucky, to Bowling-green, Glasgow, Paducah, and Leavenworth, Kansas, altogether forming an aggregate of about 500 cases.

---

*" Abstract of shipments of sanitary stores to the army of the Department of the Tennessee (Gen. Grant's), since January 1st, 1863:

	Pkgs.
" By Sanitary steamer *Dunleith*, 8 trips	9,560
By steamer *Sir William Wallace*	1,402
" *Lebanon*	1,100
" *Alice Dean* and others	1,676
" *Jacob Strader*	1,025
" *Atlantic*, from New Albany	19
"Making a total from January 1st, to July 1st, 1863	14,782

"Combining all these figures, we have a total of 20,726 packages sanitary stores, distributed by the U. S. Sanitary Committee in the Western Department, since January 1st. These packages will average at least a barrel's bulk each, and we shall give hereafter a tabular statement of their contents."

Dr. Newberry, the Western Secretary states that—

"Immediately on receipt of the first news the heroic achievements of General Grant and his noble compatriots, the various branches of the Sanitary Commission sent forward large supplies of stores for the relief of the sick and wounded.

"Pittsburg, whose Commission has from the hour of its establishment, acted with great energy, forwarded five hundred barrels of potatoes, and many other choice stores, stimulants, &c.

"Cleveland, the presence of whose noble Aid Society has been felt through its generous contributions, as a benediction, on almost every field of suffering since the war began, sent four hundred packages,—and Buffalo showed her earnest and patriotic spirit in a very timely donation.

"The Cincinnati Branch fitted out a fine steamer, the *Alice Dean*, with seven hundred packages and a full corps of surgeons and nurses.

"The New Albany Branch sent a liberal supply by the steamer *Atlantic*.

"Davenport, Iowa, Quincy and Alton, Illinois, vied with each other in loading the Sanitary steamer *Dunleith*, which at that time was on the Upper Mississippi, having gone there to obtain a cargo of stores.

"At Louisville, a public meeting was held under the auspices of the Kentucky Branch, and six thousand dollars were contributed by the citizens. The Governor of the State, through an admirable representative, J. T. Temple, Esq., paid a beautiful tribute to the U. S. Sanitary Commission, and expressed his desire and purpose to make it the medium of conveying the State's contribution to the brave soldiers of the Union. The *Jacob Strader*, the largest and finest boat on the river, was chartered by Dr. Newberry, and most generously loaded with ice, vegetables, fruits, garments, and other things adapted to promote the welfare of the sick and wounded. Dr. Andrew is in charge of her, assisted by fifteen surgeons.

"The Chicago Branch acted with its usual promptness, and had a large contribution ready for the *Strader* on her arrival at Cairo."

* * * * * * * *

The total amount of "sanitary stores" which the Commission disbursed at Vicksburg, and in its immediate vicinity, during the months of May and June, was classified by Dr. Newberry, as follows:

Groceries	1,882	pounds.	Spices	2,006	papers.
Wines and liquors	1,979	bottles.	Comforts	1,504	
Butter	3,557	pounds.	Pillows	2,220	
Apple butter	30	gallons.	Sheets	1,840	
Eggs	2,401	dozens.	Drawers	5,376	pairs.
Pickles	2,376	gallons.	Towels, &c.,	7,484	
Molasses	85	gallons.	Farina, &c	266	pounds.
Sour crout	1,532	gallons.	Sago, &c	1,044	pounds.
Potatoes	5,762	bushels.	Bed sacks	758	
Ale and cider	1,031	gallons.	Pillow cases	2,830	
Ice	27,367	pounds.	Shirts	7,909	
Crackers	6,898	pounds.	Dressing goods	422	
Codfish	6,777	pounds.	Socks	2,453	pairs.
Corn meal	2,485	pounds.	Slippers	1,190	pairs.
Tea	532	pounds.	Corn starch	275	pounds.
Relishes	301	bottles.	Cloths and band'gs	50	barrels.
Lemons	13,200		Fruit cans	5,114	
Hosp'l furniture	1,747	articles.	Concent'd b'f cans.	771	
Fans	2,347		Dried fruit	16,430	pounds.
Crutches	65	pairs.	Dried beef	888	pounds.
Cots and matt'ses	199		Cond'sd milk cans	5,631	

These supplies were distributed to the regiments of *fifteen* States, and "all the field and post hospitals, all the hospital boats, and many of the boats of the navy, have been recipients of these benefactions. Here, as heretofore, the question was never asked whether the State represented by the applicant contributed to the stores of the Commission: they were given freely wherever they were needed."*

* Disbursements from the Vicksburg depot of Sanitary Commission during the months of July and August, 1863:

Comforts	925	Sheets	7,189
Bed sacks	363	Drawers, pairs	4,356
Pillows	2,137	Socks, "	1,765
Pillow cases	3,681	Slippers, "	314

The momentous results of the campaigns in the Great Valley during the year 1863, the perils to which the Federal forces were continually exposed, and the practical bearings which the Commission's work has had upon the work achieved by those forces, have imperishably associated the history of that work, and the people's sympathy and aid, with the history, valor, and prowess of those armies. Such physical endurance and heroism as they are exhibiting is one of the direct results of high health and improved sanitary care. We shall again recur to the sanitary service in this field, after we have brought up the narrative of similar work in other fields during the year 1863.

With the transports that conveyed the forces of Major-General Banks' Expedition to the Department of the Gulf, the Sanitary Commissoin sent Inspectors and Relief Agents with many thousand dollars worth of "sanitary stores;" and subsequently, during the spring and summer, frequent and large shipments of supplies

---

Dressing gowns	324	Dried beef, lbs	608
Towels and handkerchiefs	5,746	Tea, lbs	1,045
Farina and Arrowroot, lbs	1,859	Sugar, lbs	4,455
Sago and Pearl Barley	978	Dried Fruit, lbs	28,972
Fans	2,358	Codfish, lbs	6,816
Onions, bushels	150	Butter, lbs	2,282
Corn starch, lbs	547	Other groceries, lbs	478
Wines and Spirits, bottles	854	Eggs, dozen	75
Ale and cider, gallons	2,108	Potatoes, bushels	1,884
Corn meal, lbs	14,556	Relishes, bottles	861
Lemons	12,300	Rags and bandages, pkgs	783
Mosquito bars	125	Pickles and krout, gallons	3,033
Hospital furniture, articles	415	Mustard, lbs	118
Cans, Fruit	2,216	Spices, papers	684
Cond'd beef, lbs	3,755	L. syrup, bottles	965
" milk, "	4,651	Ice, lbs	20,000
Crackers, lbs	19,619	P. cushions	231
"etc.		etc."	

"The above articles were distributed as follows: To 17 Brigade, Division and Corps Hospitals; to 7 Post and General Hospitals; 2 Hospital Steamers; 25 vessels River Fleet; to the Pioneer and Signal Corps; to the Soldier's Home and Christian Commission; and to regiments from the following States: Illinois, 35 regiments; Ohio, 28; Iowa, 20; Missouri, 15; Indiana, 15; Wisconsin, 10; Kentucky, 7; Mississippi, 7; Michigan, 5; Minnesota, 4; U. S. Regulars, 4; New Hampshire, 2; Virginia, Pennsylvania, Massachusetts, Maine, and Kansas, each 1 regiment, besides detachments, &c."—[*Sanitary Reporter*, Nov. 1st, 1863.

were sent to New Orleans;* and before the end of the year, the Commission had established in that city all those systematic methods of *general* and *special* relief, and sanitary service, which have been brought into such complete operation at Washington and Louisville.

The records of the Commission's work in the Department of the Gulf are yet unpublished, but we are informed of the presence and good service of the Inspectors and Relief Agents, and "sanitary stores," wherever the forces of that Department have moved. Whether along the river courses, the Téche, and the bayous of the Attakapas and the Red River districts, or set down to the relentless siege of Port Hudson, the Commission's agencies and "sanitary stores" were always at hand. And during the autumn the means of sanitary aid and special relief were so enlarged as to be adequate to every demand. Some account of the work in that Department will be given in subsequent pages.

With each expeditionary force that has been sent to the Department of the Gulf, and to different regions of the Atlantic coast, the Sanitary Commission sent forward with the fleet of transports a corps of Inspectors and Relief Agents, with ample invoices of "sanitary stores." The first experiments in this way were made in connection with the great expeditions of General Burnside, General Butler, and General Sherman, in 1862; the results were of the most gratifying character, and similar results have followed all such expeditionary relief work since that period. And although it has thus far been an unnoticed and unpublished part of sanitary work, no branch of the Com-

* The Sanitary Commission purchased and sent forward with the first transports of the expedition various supplies to the value of $11,160. Among these were—flannel goods, $6,477 96; beef juice, $1,000; lemonade, concentrated, $250; wines and stimulants, $373 58; chocolate, $150; groceries, $590; medicines, instruments, and vaccine, $95; water beds, $86. The Woman's Central Association at the same time sent 110 packages, containing 15,854 articles.

mission's aid has exceeded it in practical importance. But we must omit in this place the details of sanitary aid to particular expeditions. We proceed to notice the progress of the Commission's work in the several campaigns of 1863. These we must consider separately, for the movements of the several armies were distinct, and, in this third year of the war, the plans and service of the Sanitary Commission had become so methodized, and comparatively independent, in each of the armies, and in each campaign, that we can best continue our examination of the work by following the course of the several campaigns.

Sanitary Work in the Army of the Potomac during the year 1863.—Though the forces in the East have enjoyed the peculiar advantages of nearer observation from the Bureaux of the War Department, and, especially, of convenient bases of supply, there have been during the year 1863, many demands for such services as the Commission has been accustomed to render in that army. A watchful public bears testimony to the faithfulness with which the sanitary wants in the camps and hospitals here have been studied and supplied. The Army of the Potomac has always appeared to receive a full share of the Commission's attention; and until the "*Sanitary Reporter*," and the "*Commission Bulletin*,"—the bi-weekly organs of its chief offices—appeared, recently, there was a prevalent erroneous impression that the Sanitary Commission's labors and disbursements were being mainly expended upon the armies in the East. But, as we have already endeavored to present the true features and proportions of the sanitary work in the West and South, the reader will hold us innocent of any such invidious comparison. The work is *catholic*; it is *Federal*; and any person who will attentively study its methods, its spirit, and the records of its progress, will confess that its limitations or wants, in any field, appear to have been the result of stern necessities or absolute impossibilities.

The Army of the Potomac, after its terrible and fruitless conflict to gain the heights of Fredericksburgh, planted itself for a long winter upon the hill-sides about Falmouth, and, under excellent administration of its Medical and Commissariat Departments, was kept in high health until late in spring, when it marched forth to another most fearful battle with its old enemy, at Chancellorsville. What share the Sanitary Commission had in the care and the supplementary supply for our 25,000 wounded men of the two great battles upon the Rappahannock need not here be dwelt upon in its details. The following facts show what kind of service the Commission undertook, and with what success its work was pursued in that army during the winter and spring of 1863.

Two Sanitary Inspectors and a Corps of Relief Agents were on duty in that army when General Burnside moved against Fredericksburg. The *Elizabeth*, a capacious sanitary supply steamer, of Peninsula fame, was lying in Acquia Creek, at the railway terminus, with its usual cargo of assorted "sanitary stores" and battle-field supplies. Immediately the Inspector in charge ordered forward the requisite supplies to the field, and opened a dépôt near the Phillips House, opposite the scene of action. The Sanitary Relief Corps was largely reinforced from Washington, and the whole business of supplementary aid was effectually systematized. Upon that occasion the organization and working of the Medical Department were more perfect than had been witnessed upon any previous battle-field; yet the Commission had abundant opportunities for its peculiar work. The following extracts from an official report of relief work on that occasion, give a good idea of the manner in which it was performed by the Commission's agents:

* * * * * * * "A propeller was chartered, laden with stores, and with a special relief party, consisting of Dr. H. G. Clark, Dr. S. C. Foster, Dr. Swalm, Dr. Homiston, Mr. Elliott, Mr. Abbott, and Mr. Walter, all connected with the Commission, and, with Rev. Mr. Channing, Mr. Paige, Mr. Hall, and Mr. Webster, volunteers, I started at evening for the front. The regular force of the Commission stationed with the Army of the Potomac at the time of the battle, consisted of Drs. Andrew and Smith, Inspectors of the Commission, with Messrs. Haywood, Peverly, and Clampitt, relief agents; Dr. Smith having accompanied it in its march from Harper's Ferry and Warrenton Junction, and Dr. Andrew, the senior Inspector on the Atlantic Coast, being in general charge. Our floating dépôt, the propeller *Elizabeth*, with an efficient crew and well provided with stores, was at the Acquia landing when the battle commenced.

"The regular party had been reinforced previous to our arrival by our Inspector, Dr. Brink, Mr. H. H. Furness, Mr. W. S. Wood, and Mr. Peck. Mr. W. H. Furness and Mr. Lambdin joined us two days after.

"As soon as the movement for the crossing of the river was made, Dr. Andrew, Mr. Wood, and Mr. Clampitt proceeded to the front from Acquia, visited the field hospitals on the Falmouth side of the river, which had been organized in anticipation of a battle, and distributed several wagon loads of stores.

"After our forces had gained possession of the city, by the successful crossing of the river on the 11th, these hospitals were abandoned and others established in the churches and dwelling-houses of the town, being nearer to the scene of the expected contest. This came on the 13th, and to these hastily prepared hospitals the wounded of that day's fight were removed. On the following Monday these buildings were, in turn, vacated, and the wounded removed to the former field-hospitals on the Falmouth side of the river.

* * * * * * *

"The scene at our field station was a busy one. Could the contributors to the stores and the treasury of the Commission have heard the fervent expressions of grateful relief; could they have seen the comfort which their bounty afforded our brave wounded; could they realize by actual intercourse with the wounded, the suffering from, for instance, cold alleviated by the abundant supply of blankets which their bounty had provided; could they have observed the change produced when the soiled and bloody garments were replaced by clean and warm clothing which they had sent, they would be eager to replenish our storehouses and keep our hands filled with the means to accomplish these purposes.

"Early Tuesday morning, the rain subsided, the sun appeared, and the weather became clear and cold. The wounded were for the most part placed in hospital tents, upon a plentiful supply of hay. Blankets had to repair the absence of stoves, which, by some singular mistake, had arrived in a condition not to be used, the necessary stove-pipe not being included in the shipment. The supply in the hands of the Purveyor soon became exhausted from the unusual demands made upon him on account of the severity of the weather. Fortunately we were enabled to supplement his stores, and to answer his calls upon us from the reserve of 1,800 blankets, and over 900 quilts which we had sent forward. Many of these were employed in covering the wounded during the period of their transportation by car an steamboat from the field hospitals to the general hospitals at Washington.

"It is with a deep feeling of gratitude that I have also to report that the last sad office could be paid to the dead, with an approach to the ceremonies of civil life, through the stores placed by us at the disposal of the surgeons of the hospitals.

"The comfort of the wounded, and the result of the treatment of their wounds, were materially affected by the change of clothing provided by us. We had been able to get up to our field-station 5,642 woolen shirts, 4,439 pairs woolen drawers, 4,269 pairs socks, and over 2,500 towels, among other articles. These were liberally distributed wherever the surgeons of hospitals indicated that there was a need. Certain articles of hospital furniture of which there was a comparatively greater want than of anything else, were freely obtained by all surgeons at our station. * * * *

* * * * * * * *

"In order to meet whatever demands may arise for the proper sustenance of the wounded while on this trying journey, Mr. Knapp, our special relief agent, was despatched from Washington to Acquia Creek to provide suitable accommodations for furnishing food or shelter at that point. A kitchen was improvised upon the landing, and the first night meals were provided for 600 wounded brought down by the cars. Mr. Knapp was cordially assisted in this humane work by several members of the Christian Commission who were present at that place. Through the cordial co-operation of the Quartermaster of the Port, Mr. Knapp had a building erected adjoining our portable storehouse, which affords shelter and a good bed to nearly 100 every night."

So complete had the organization of the Army of the Potomac

become, that disaster failed to demoralize its ranks, and during the long winter which that army spent on the rolling uplands between the Rappahannock and Acquia Creek, the men maintained a high state of health, while being near the great base of supplies at Washington, and also favored with excellent medical care, the demands upon the Commission's relief dépôts were less than in other departments of the army. Still there were great opportunities for the Commission's aid. For example, not long subsequently to the battle of Fredericksburg there was an urgent demand for woolen socks, which the Quartermasters could not at the time meet, whereupon the Commission furnished five thousand (5,000) pairs from the principal Sanitary dépôt at Acquia Landing; these, in due time, were replaced by an equal amount of the same class of goods from the Quartermaster's Department. The Lodge and central office of relief for that army, at Acquia, were also of vast benefit to the thousands of invalids who at that point were transhipped to the steamboats; and during the four months of its continuance there it furnished lodgings to nearly *four thousand* persons, while immense numbers were fed and otherwise attended or aided while *in transitu* from the field to Washington steamboats.

The battle of Chancellorsville, and the military movements that followed, soon compelled the transfer of all the sick and wounded from the vicinity of the Rappahannoek to Washington. This imposed some arduous duties upon the Commission's Relief Agents at Acquia Landing and at Washington; and at one of the wharves in that city those agents fed and otherwise aided, in the course of three days and nights, 8,000 of the sick and wounded, as they were landed fiom the steamboats.

General Hooker having started in his pursuit of the Rebel forces that were marching to invade Pennsylvania, his rapid movement, and the prospect of a terrible collision of the two armies upon the borders of Maryland and Pennsylvania, made it necessary for the Sanitary Commission to anticipate the wants of the prospective battle at several points along the route which our forces were occupying, or hoping to occupy. Large supplies of "sanitary stores" were speedily dispatched with trusty agents to Harrisburg, Baltimore, and Frederick City; and, while the ordinary staff of the Commission hastened forward with our forces, and kept up the "flying dépôts" along the right flank of the moving columns, wagon loads of supplies were dispatched to the troops that had gathered at Harper's Ferry, but the man in charge of that service was captured with his wagon and horses, and was detained in Richmond prison until the subsequent month of February. The "sanitary stores" at Frederick and at Westminster, in Maryland, found timely use, and as soon as our forces had reached the latter place, the Commission sent forward its "battle-field stores" by the car-load daily, until direct communication by railroad had been opened to Gettysburg from Hanover Junction. But previously to this, and while hurrying forward with a Relief Agent and a load of battle-field relief stores, Dr. McDonald, the senior Inspector, was captured, with his personal staff and the goods, by a company of Stuart's cavalry, near Mechanicstown, and was detained in Libby Prison until late in September.

Other Inspectors and Relief Agents reached the field at a later hour, but the loss of valuable men and supplies was severely felt. Soon, however, the Commission's usual battle-field system of relief was in full operation. What that system, and the earnest men and discreet women that worked on that field, accomplished in bringing timely succor to the wounded, we would, if space allowed, record in these pages. But such work, like the patient and unheralded toil and excellent skill of the army Surgeons in the field hospitals after battle, must go mainly unrecorded, except in the hearts and memories of the thousands of bleeding and helpless sufferers who were the immediate recipients of such mercy and such skillful care.

A woman's brief narrative of such work as women did and helped in doing, in "*Three Weeks at Gettysburg*,"* also a report (Document No. 66), published by the Commission, give some idea of the relief and aid rendered by the Sanitary Commission upon that memorable field. We quote the following passages:

"When the enemy was known to have crossed the Potomac in force, responsible and experienced officers of the Commission were stationed at Harrisburg, Philadelphia, Baltimore, and

---

* The following paragraphs from a woman's story of the Relief work at Gettysburg, show how a *few* chosen women in field-hospitals, and *all* women at home, are constantly aiding the Sanitary Commission and the soldier:

* * * * * * * *

* * * * "The railroad bridge broken up by the enemy, Government had not rebuilt as yet, and we stopped two miles from the town, to find that, as usual, just where the Government had left off the Commission had come in. There stood their temporary lodge and kitchen, and here hobbling out of their tents came the wounded men who had made their way down from the Corps hospital, expecting to leave at once in the return cars.

"This is the way the thing was managed at first: The surgeons left in care of the wounded three or four miles out from the town, went up and down among the men in the morning, and said, 'Any of you boys who can make your way to the cars, can go to Baltimore.' So off start all who think they feel well enough, anything being better than the 'hospitals,' so called, for the first few days after a battle. Once the men have the surgeons' permission to go, they are off; and there may be an interval of a day, or two days, should any of them be too weak to reach the train in time, during which these poor fellows belong to no one, the hospital at one end, the railroad at the other, with far more than chance of falling through between the two. The Sanitary Commission knew this would be so of necessity, and coming in, made a connecting link between these two ends.

"For the first few days, the worst cases only came down in ambulances from the hospitals: hundreds of fellows hobbled along as best they could, in heat and dust, for hours, slowly toiling, and many hired farmers' wagons, as hard as the farmers' fists themselves, and were jolted down to the railroad, at three or four dollars the man. Think of the disappointment of a soldier, sick, body and heart, to find, at the end of this miserable journey, that his effort to get away, into which he had put all his remaining stock of strength, was useless; that 'the cars had gone,' or 'the cars were full;' that while he was coming, others had stepped down before him, and that he must return all the weary way back again, or sleep on the roadside till the next train 'to-morrow!' Think what this *would* have been, and you are ready to appreciate the relief and comfort that *was* No men were turned back. You fed and you sheltered them just when no one else could have done so; and out of the boxes and barrels of good and nourishing things, which you people at home have supplied, we took all that was needed. Some of you sent a stove (that is, the money to get it), some of you the beef stock, some of you the milk and fresh bread; and all of you would have been thankful that you had done so, could you have seen the refreshment and comfort received through these things."

Frederick, and a systematic daily communication was established between the agents moving with the different columns of the army and the central office of the Commission. Supplies were accumulated and held ready for movement at different points on the circumference of the seat of war, and care was taken to have ample reserves at the branch offices ready for shipment. With the first news of the battle of Gettysburg, Westminster, the nearest point of railroad communication to the battle-field, was fixed upon as the point of approach, and authority to run a car daily with the government trains to that station was obtained.

"Two wagon-loads of battle-field supplies had been distributed to meet deficiences in the stores of the surgeons, shortly before the battle commenced. These wagons returned to Frederick for loads, and two others, fully loaded, arrived from Frederick at the moment of the assault of Longstreet upon the left wing of the loyal army, and were driven under fire to reach the collections of wounded in its rear. As one of them came to a point where several hundred sufferers had been taken from the ambulances and laid upon the ground behind a barn and in an orchard, less than a thousand yards in the rear of our line of battle, on the left wing, then fiercely engaged, a surgeon was seen to throw up his arms, exclaiming, 'Here is the Sanitary Commission, now we shall be able to do something.' He had exhausted nearly all of his supplies; and the brandy, beef soup, sponges, chloroform, lint and bandages, which were at once furnished him, were undoubtedly the means of saving many lives."

* * * * * * * *

"Supplies having however, arrived at Westminster, *before the close of the battle*, a school-house centrally situated among the corps hospitals, was taken as a field dépôt, to which they were as rapidly as possible brought by the three remaining wagons then on the ground, and from which they were rapidly distributed where most needed. Eleven wagon-loads of special supplies were here distributed to the corps hospitals and to scattering groups of wounded found in the field, before any supplies arrived by railroad. Additional means of transportation were at length procured from the country people, of whom also some stores were obtained, and a station was opened in the town of Gettysburg. On the 6th, the branch railroad to Gettysburg, which had been broken up by the enemy, was so far repaired as to allow a train to approach within a mile of the town. By the first train which came over it after the battle, two car-loads of most valuable goods were sent by the Commission, and two or more went by each succeeding train for a week. The wounded now began to be brought from the field to the railroad for removal to fixed hospitals elsewhere. As they arrived much faster than they could be taken away, they were laid on the ground exposed to the rain, or to the direct rays of the July sun, without food. This having been anticipated and provided for by the Commission's agents, in Baltimore, on the second day the Commission had a complete relief station, on a large scale, in operation, at the temporary terminus of the railroad. It consisted of several tents and awnings, with a kitchen and other conveniences.

"In the meantime, the movements of the army and the prospects of another great battle on the Potomac, demanded the attention of the Commission. Six new wagons, with horses, were procured in Baltimore and Washington, and sent to Frederick, to which point also supplies were forwarded by rail, and thence transferred by wagons to Boonsboro, where a house was taken and a dépôt established on the same day that it was occupied by General Meade. A house for a dépôt was also secured at Hagerstown as soon as the enemy retired from it. Supplies were at the same time sent by rail down the Cumberland Valley, with wagons and horses for their further carriage, procured in Philadelphia."

The Relief agents who accompanied the moving columns to the field at Gettsyburg, reported their first labors as follows:

"Wednesday morning, July 1, and first day of the battle, we were informed, while at General Meade's headquarters, by an orderly just arrived from this place (Gettysburg), than an attack and a battle were expected here that day, as the cavalry with the 1st and 11th corps had already reached this place. I left Mr. Hoag and our wagons in the train of headquarters (to which they had been transferred from that of the 12th army corps), and rode to Littlestown, Pa., thence to this place, arriving at 'Cemetery Hill,' where a portion of our batteries were situated."

* * * * * * * *

"All was quiet until four o'clock P. M., Thursday, when a heavy firing commenced on our left, where the 'rebs' were trying a flank movement. As soon as the wounded began to come in, I started out with the wagons to distribute the stores. We reached five different hospitals, which were all we were able to find that night, and early in the morning three others, which exhausted our stores. We were just in time to do the most good possible, as the government wagons had been sent back ten miles, and many of the hospitals were not supplied with material sufficient for immediate use. (The hospitals supplied were division hospitals of the 1st, 2d, 3d, 5th, 11th and 12th corps.)

"On telling the surgeons that I was on hand with sanitary stores, I was almost invariably greeted with expressions like the following, 'You could never have come at a better time,' and once on mentioning sanitary stores, I received two hearty welcome slaps on the shonlder, one from the medical director of the corps, and the other the surgeon of the division.

"Most of the wounded of this day's fight were carried into the churches and public buildings of the town, under the organization of the first and cavalry corps, and were prisoners at the close of the day.

"The 3d and 12th corps arrived during the afternoon, but too late to enter into battle.

"Thursday, July 2d, and second day of the battle. The 2d corps arrived by the Taneytown road, below Cemetery Hill, at daybreak. The 5th corps arrived two miles from town, on the Baltimore Pike about ten A. M. One division of the 6th corps on the same Pike from Westminster, at two P. M.

"The battle opened about 4 P. M. Found our wagons early in the afternoon. As soon as the surgeons had decided upon the different points where the Corps Hospitals were to be formed, Mr. Hoag moved the wagons to them at once, and commenced to issue our stores, which consisted chiefly of concentrated beef soup, stimulants, crackers, condensed milk, concentrated coffee, corn-starch, farina, shirts, drawers, stockings, towels, blankets, quilts, bandages and lint. We hastened from one hospital to another, as rapidly as possible, issuing to each a proportion of our stores, until the supply was nearly exhausted, when, upon consultation, it was decideded that I should start for the nearest point which a telegram could be sent to Washington, ordering up more supplies."

* * * * * * * *

"A car arrived at Westminster, Saturday, July 4, when Mr. Hovey procured three Government wagons, and that evening started with three full loads of stores, arriving early next morning (Sunday) at the 1st, 2d and 3d Corps Hospitals. By your orders, I left Washington by the 11 A. M. train, July 4, arriving at Relay in time for the 2 P. M. train for Westminster. Owing to a misunderstanding between the two conductors on the road, the trains waited for each other at either end of the road so that we did not get started from the Relay until 8 o'clock, Sunday morning, arriving at Westminster at 10 A. M., where I found Mr. Bacon in charge of the remainder of the car-load of stores. About noon our four-mule team came in from Frederick, in charge of Mr. Gall. It was immediately loaded, and early in the morning I left with it, in company of Mr. Gall, Mr. Bacon still remaining in charge at Westminster.

"A school-house was taken on the Baltimore pike, near the different Corps Hospitals, and about three miles out from Gettysburg, and from it our stores were thereafter issued, until the opening of the railroad permitted our reaching the field by that route, when, on Tuesday morning, July 7, a storehouse was taken in town, and the school-house closed.

"In the meantime, Mr. Hoag had been to Frederick with the two wagons, and had returned with full loads to the school-house, where the stores brought by him were issued.

"Mr. Hovey, after delivering his loads to the three Corps Hospitals, returned to Westminster and took three more loads, and Mr. Gall made a second trip with the four-mule team, which took the remainder of the first car-load sent from Washington."

Rev. Dr. Bellows, the President of the Commission; Mr. Olmsted, the General Secretary, with other members of the Commission, repaired to Gettysburg, and to such points upon the routes connected with the field, as would best enable them to aid the work of sanitary relief. Dr. Agnew, aided by one of the associate secretaries, organized the Commission's work in Gettysburg and the field hospitals, the Chief Inspector, Dr. McDonald, who had previously been charged with that duty, having been captured when hastening to the battle-ground, as has already been mentioned; and notwithstanding the delays in railway connections and transportation, and the interference of the enemy with valuable stores and assistants, a very complete system of succor was soon in full operation. The following account, from Dr. Douglas, the associate secretary, mentioned above, shows how the work went on:

* * * * * * * "The temporary terminus of the railway was then over a mile from the town, and to this terminus crowds of slightly wounded men came, limping, dragging themselves along, silent, weary, worn.

The moment the cars stopped, the crowd of weary and wounded soldiers accumulated there, indicated that point as a place for a Relief Lodge. I immediately had two of our largest tents, together capable of sheltering seventy-five men, pitched, stoves erected, and a lodge established. The wise foresight of Mr. Knapp had included these articles among the first invoice. The two Germans, whose names I have unfortunately lost, volunteered as cooks. That night our tents were full, and we had the great satisfaction of not only affording shelter and attention to the wounded, but also supplying good nutritious food to those within our tents, and those who had taken refuge on the cars."

* * * * * * * *

"Another room, on Baltimore street, was, by permission, taken. The latter place, the store of Messrs. Fahnestock & Co. —the largest in the town—became the centre of the busiest scene which I have ever witnessed in connection with the Commission. Car load after car-load of supplies were brought to this place, till shelves and counter and floor up to the ceiling were filled, till there was barely a passage-way between the piles of boxes and barrels, till the sidewalk was monopolized, and even the street encroached upon. These supplies were the outpourings of a grateful people. This abundant overflow of the generous remembrance of those at home to those in the army, was distributed in the same generous manner as it was contributed. Each morning the supply wagons of the division and corps hospitals were before the door, and each day they went away laden with such articles as were desired to meet their wants. If the articles needed one day were not in our possession at the time, they were immediately telegraphed for, and by the next train of cars thereafter they were ready to be delivered. Thus, tons of ice, mutton, poultry, fish, vegetables, soft bread, eggs, butter, and a variety of other articles of substantial and delicate food, were provided for the wounded, with thousands of suits of clothing of all kinds, and hospital furniture in quantity to meet the emergency. It was a grand sight to see this exhibition of the tender care of the people for the people's braves. It was a bit of home feeling, of home bounty, brought to the tent, put into the hand of the wounded soldier."

* * * * * * * *

"The lodge, which was established at the temporary terminus of the railway, on Tuesday, was continued there until Friday, when the burned bridge which had prevented the cars from running into town, was replaced by a new structure, and the cars resumed their regular runnings to the station. On Thursday, I had a tent and fly erected near the dépôt, in preparation for the change in the terminus of the road, and on Saturday the lodge out of town was discontinued, and the tents used there added to those near the dépôt. This second lodge was in successful operation on Friday, though it was not generally made use of till Saturday.

"Between Tuesday and Saturday noon, we provided at our first lodge, good beef soup, coffee and fresh bread, for over 3,000 slightly wounded soldiers, whose injuries did not prevent them from walking to this point, while we sheltered, each night, about fifty more serious cases, which had been brought down by ambulance, and whose wounds required the attention of a surgeon. We were fortunate in having, during these days, the volunteer aid of Dr. Hooper, from Boston, who devoted himself to this latter work. Mr. Clark, from New Hampshire, Mr. Hawkins, from Media, Pa., and Mr. Shippen, from Pittsburg, also lent their assistance, and all these gentlemen materially aided us at this and at the second lodge, until it was fully organized.

"With the transfer of our material to town, the irregular organization was changed to a permanent working basis. Dr. W. F. Cheney, who arrived on the 10th, was placed in charge of the camp. He brought with him seven assistants, Messrs. Latz, Cooley, McGuinness, Chesebro, Blakeley, Sherwin, Freshoner, from Canandaigua, N. Y. To these were added Messrs. Reisinger and Hall, from Baltimore, and four detailed soldiers. Cooks had arrived, a large shed for a kitchen had been erected, and full preparations were made for feeding any number. Every facility was granted us by the medical officers of the post, and by the commissary. Additional tents were erected, drains made, straw procured, and shelter prepared for 150 men. A store tent was placed near the hospital tents, and given into the charge of two New York ladies, whose long experience on the Commission's transports, during the Peninsular campaign of last summer, had made them familiar with all of the requirements of this camp. The cars stopped immediately in front of our camp, and distant but a few feet from it.

"During the ten days subsequent to the establishment of this lodge, over 5,000 soldiers (Union and Rebel) received food either in our tents or on the cars, and an average of over 100 remained in our tents each night, and had their wounds dressed, and more or less clothing distributed to them.

"This lodge was continued until all the wounded capable of being removed, were transferred from the corps hospitals to the general hospitals of New York, Philadelphia, Baltimore, Harrisburg, and York.

"When the general field hospital was decided upon for the reception of all those whose serious wounds prevented them from being removed, I asked for a place to be assigned us in the plan, and before leaving Gettysburg saw two of our tents erected in the camp, one for our stores, the other for the ladies who would be in charge. This design has been effectually carried out.

"Our plan of operation and our labors were in Gettysburg, as they have been elsewhere, divided into those of inquiry and relief. The latter, from our experience, was subdivided into general and special relief. The first of these was to be extended by issues from our store-house directly to corps hospitals, in bulk, according to the ascertained necessities, and the latter took the direction of attending to those of the wounded—by far the greater number—who, capable of being transported from the field of battle, were daily removed, until only the more serious cases remained. I have already given the history of the store-house and lodge. The tabulated statement of the issues from the former, and the number assisted and relieved at the latter, will tell how well the organization worked. Few left the region of Gettysburg without receiving some material aid from us, either in food or clothing.

"Our trained permanent corps rendered this work easy and immediate. This would not have been possible, in the same time, with a body of men unaccustomed to and ignorant of the work. The large number of volunteers who came to our assistance, under the direction of those already familiar with the work, fell readily into the line of duty, and soon became efficient co-workers."

"The labor of inquiry required the daily visitation of the hospitals, consultation with the medical officers as to the most efficient manner in which we could aid them, the character and quantity of the supplies most needed, the daily movement in the population of the hospitals under their command, with the character and severity of the injuries, and all such information in relation to the disposition of the wounded as would assist us in making our preparations.

"Beside the visits of inquiry to the hospitals, a list of the names and wounds of all the inmates of each hospital was taken and forwarded to the office of the Hospital Directory in Washington, and we held ourselves in readiness to attend to messages of inquiry sent to us from any direction, in regard to any wounded man in these hospitals. This work was performed by Mr. Dooley, from the Directory office. Messrs. Stille, Struthers, Hazlehurst, Dullus, Beitler, and Tracy, from Philadelphia, and Messrs. Hosford, Myers, and Braman, from New York, assisted in this labor as well as at the lodge, and in attending to special cases.

"The duty of visiting the Confederate Hospitals was assigned to Dr. Gordon Winslow, who reported to me soon after I arrived. The following communication, addressed by him to me, will give briefly the result of his inquiries:

"'Gettysburg, July 22, 1863.

"'Sir,—Agreeably to your instructions, I have inspected the several Confederate Hospitals in the vicinity of Gettysburg, and have indicated, on the accompanying map, the locality, division, General who was commanding, surgeon in charge, and number of wounded.

"'It appears that the aggregate of wounded, at the time of my visits, was 5,452, occupying some twenty-four (24) separate camps, over an area of some twelve miles. The wounds, in a large proportion of cases, are severe.'"* ....

"The hospitals are generally in barns, outhouses, and dilapidated tents. Some few cases are in dwellings. I cannot speak favorably of their camp police. Often there is a deplorable

---

* The hospitals visited by Dr. Winslow were situated as below, and contained the number of wounded as indicated in the following table:

Location.	Division.	Surgeon.	No.
Cashtown	Genl. Parine's	Dr. Wilson	171
On Chambersburg Road	" Porcher's	Dr. Ward	700
On Mummasburg "	" Rhode's	Dr. Hayes	800
In Penn. College	" Heath's	Dr. Smiley	700
Hunterstown Road	" Johnson's	Dr. Whitehead	311
Fairfield			50
Fairfield Road	Part of Genl. Johnson's	Dr. Stewart	135
" "	" Early's	Dr. Potts	259
" "	" Anderson's	Dr. Mines	111
" "	" McLaw's	Dr. Patterson	700
" "	" Hood's	Dr. Means	515
Total			5,452

The number of wounded, in addition to those reported by Dr. Winslow, whose wants—beyond those that a beneficent Government cared for—the Sanitary Commission was anxious to supply, can be stated briefly as follows:

		Union		Confederates	
First	Corps (2 portions)	2,519	Union,	260 Confederates	2,779
Second	"	3,500	"	1,000 "	4,500
Third	"	2,300	"	250 "	2,550
Fifth	"	1,325	"	75 "	1,40 0
Sixth	"	300	"		300
Eleventh	"	1,800	"	100 "	1,900
Twelfth	"	1,006	"	125 "	1,131
Cavalry	"	300	"		300
Total		13,050		1,810	14,860

want of cleanliness. Especially in barns and outhouses, vermin and putrid matter are disgustingly offensive. As fast as means of transpertation can be had, those who are capable of being removed will be placed in more comfortable quarters. Some hundreds are being removed daily. Every provision is made by the Sanitary Commission for their comfort during their stay at the Dépôt Lodge, and those who are placed directly in the cars are furnished wholesome food."

* * * * * * * *

"The labor, the anxiety, the responsibility imposed upon the surgeons after the battle of Gettysburg were from the position of affairs, greater than after any other battle of the war. The devotion, the solicitude, the unceasing efforts to remedy the defects of the situation, the untiring attentions to the wounded upon their part, were so marked as to be apparent to all who visited the hospitals. It must be remembered that these same officers had endured the privations and fatigues of the long forced marches with the rest of the army; that they had shared its dangers, for one medical officer from each regiment follows it into battle, and is liable to the accidents of war, as has been repeatedly and fatally the case; that its field hospitals are often from the changes of the line of battle, brought under the fire of the enemy, and that while in this situation, these surgeons are called upon to exercise the calmest judgment, to perform the most critical and serious operations, and this quickly and continuously. The battle ceasing, their labors continue. While other officers are sleeping, renewing their strength for further efforts, the medical are still toiling. They have to improvise hospitals from the rudest materials, are obliged to make "bricks without straw," to surmount seeming impossibilities. The work is unending, both by day and night, the anxiety is constant, the strain upon both the physical and mental faculties, unceasing. Thus, after this battle, operators had to be held up while performing the operations, and fainted from exhaustion, the operation finished. One completed his labors to be seized with partial paralysis, the penalty of his over-exertion."

* * * * * * * *

Upwards of *twenty thousand* wounded men remained upon the field, and as Dr. Douglas has justly remarked, the medical staff was overtasked by the demands of the occasion. Day after day and night after night, the Commission's work of succor and aid was extended to all these wounded men, and to the medical officers such assistance was always welcome. And when all the wounded that could safely be removed, had left the field hospitals by the railway and ambulance trains, and the remaining patients had been gathered to the great field hospitals at Camp Letterman, on the hills east of Gettysburg, the Sanitary Commission established its more permanent and systematic methods of relief at that place, the veteran Inspector, Dr. Winslow, remaining in charge of that service. The amount of "sanitary stores" supplied by the Commission up to the time of that reorganization of the field hospitals was very large, notwithstanding the extraordinary munificence of the Government and the authorities of the various Northern States, that sent agents and material aid to the field. By definite advices from the medical department the Sanitary Commission was enabled to supplement the more urgent wants of hospitals, while by the facilities which its system of labor, and its command of the means of transportation, and of the markets in Baltimore and Philadelphia gave its Relief Agents, sanitary supplies of the most delicate and perishable nature, as well as all ordinary stores, were furnished in unusual abundance.*

---

* The following is a statement of the quantities of the principal articles distributed by the Commission to the wounded upon the field at Gettysburg, the first four weeks after the battle:

Of Articles of Clothing, etc., viz.:

	Estimated Value.
Of Drawers, (woolen) 5,310 pairs	$9,292 50
" " (cotton) 1,833 pairs	1,833 09
" Shirts, (woolen) 7,158	14,316 00
" " (cotton) 3,266	3,266 00
" Pillows, 2,114	1,268 40
" Pillow cases, 264	105 60
" Bed sacks, 1,630	3,463 75
" Blankets, 1,007	3,021 00
" Sheets, 274	274 00
" Wrappers, 508	1,498 00
" Handkerchiefs, 2,659	319 08
" Stockings, (woolen) 3,560 pairs	1,780 00
" " (cotton) 2,253 pairs	451 00
" Bed utensils, 728	182 00
" Towels and napkins, 10,000	1,500 00

The Commission's work at Gettysburg did not cease until the last of the wounded had left "Camp Letterman." On the 17th of November—four and a half months after the battle, the last car-load of mutilated men took its departure for Pittsburg in the railway ambulance.

The army of the Potomac had turned southward, and immediately following the great battle of Gettysburg, the Sanitary Commission set about preparing for any emergencies that might occur from collisions, as the forces pressed on after General Lee; and in expectation of an attack upon Lee at Williamsport, Md., the Commission made large preparations, both in stores and agents, with a fixed dépôt at Boonsboro', and wagon-trains for field-work. Dr. Agnew superintended these

---

Of Sponges, 2.300	$230 00
" Combs, 1,500	60 00
" Buckets, 200	75 00
" Soap (Castile) 250 pounds	50 00
" Oil silk, 300 yards	225 00
" Tin basins, cups, etc., 7,000	700 00
" Old linen, bandages, etc., 110 barrels	1,100 00
" Water tanks, 7	70 00
" Water coolers, 46	230 00
" Bay Rum and Cologne Water, 225 bottles	112 50
" Fans, 3,500	145 00
" Chloride of Lime, 11 barrels	99 00
" Shoes and slippers, 4,000 pairs	2,400 00
" Crutches, 1,200	480 00
" Lanterns, 180	90 00
" Candles, 350 pounds	70 00
" Canvas, 300 square yards	360 00
" Musquito netting, 648 pieces	810 00
" Paper, 237 quires	23 70
" Pants, coats, hats, 189 pieces	96 75
" Plaster, 16 rolls	4 00

Of Articles of Sustenance, viz.:

Of Fresh poultry and mutton, 11,000 pounds	$1,540 00
" " butter, 6,430 pounds	1,286 00
" " eggs, (chiefly collected for the occasion at farm-houses in Pennsylvania and New Jersey,) 8,500 dozens	1,700 00
" " garden vegetables, 675 bushels	337 50
" " berries, 48 bushels	72 00
" " bread, 12,000 loaves	645 00
" Ice, 20,000 ponnds	100 00
" Concentrated beef soup, 3,800 pounds	3,800 00
" " milk, 12,500 pounds	3,125 00

preparations. The promptitude with which the means of sanitary relief were placed within easy reach of the army as it moved, and the improved methods that were adopted before our forces re-crossed the Potomac, have been mentioned in previous pages.

The history of sanitary work in the four or five other Grand Divisions of the Army, during and subsequent to the period that has just passed in review, in reference to the Potomac Army in its campaign that culminated at Gettysburg, is full of instructive interest; therefore, to each of the campaigns South and West we must devote a separate section of this narrative of the Commission's work. But before taking up the line of our narrative of sanitary work in these important campaigns, we must record an event that occurred soon after the Gettys-

---

Of Prepared farinaceous food, 7,000 pounds	$700 00
" Dried fruit, 3,500 pounds	350 00
" Jellies and conserves, 2,000 jars	1,000 00
" Tamarinds, 750 gallons	600 00
" Lemons, 116 boxes	580 00
" Oranges, 6 boxes	230 00
" Coffee, 850 pounds	272 00
" Chocolate, 831 pounds	249 30
" Tea, 426 pounds	383 40
" White sugar, 6,800 pounds	1,156 00
" Syrups, (lemon, etc.) 785 bottles	596 25
" Brandy, 1,250 bottles	1,250 00
" Whiskey, 1,168 bottles	700 80
" Wine, 1,148 bottles	861 00
" Ale, 600 gallons	180 00
" Biscuit, crackers, and rusk, 134 barrels	670 00
" Preserved meats, 500 pounds	125 00
" Preserved fish, 3,600 pounds	720 00
" Pickles, 400 gallons	120 00
" Tobacco, 100 pounds	70 00
" Tobacco pipes, 1,000	5 00
" Indian meal, 1,621 pounds	40 50
" Starch, 1,074 pounds	75 18
" Codfish, 3,848 pounds	269 36
" Canned fruit, 582 cans	436 50
" " oysters, 72 cans	36 00
" Brandy peaches, 303 jars	303 00
" Catsup, 43 jars	11 00
" Vinegar, 24 bottles	3 00
" Jamaica ginger, 43 jars	37 25
Total	$74,838 53

burg battle, and which, in the history of the Commission's work, is associated with that period.

Early in the month of September, Mr. FREDERICK LAW OLMSTED resigned his position as General Secretary of the Commission. From the commencement of the work, in June, 1861, Mr. OLMSTED had devoted himself most assiduously to the duties of organization and superintendence of the plans and the means by which the great purposes of the Sanitary Commission were to be accomplished. While the several members of the Commission gave to the councils of the Board their best efforts, and also accepted such special duties as occasions required, to Mr. OLMSTED, as the General Secretary and representative of the Commission at Washington, was assigned the very responsible duty of methodizing, co-ordinating, and engineering the whole work, so far as the Central Office could determine and guide the Commission's affairs.

For more that two years the first General Secretary had given to this work of organization and superintendence of the Commission's work his greatest energies and all the skill and power of his remarkable genius. How faithfully and successfully he followed out and elaborated those grand designs that had been conceived during the early councils of the Commission, are abundantly testified by the machinery and the working of the various departments of the Sanitary and Relief service witnessed in our armies to-day.

Mr. Olmsted had attentively studied the material and social causes of the Rebellion, and as a tourist he was familiar with the Cotton States and the back country through which the Federal forces must make their way to the ultimate triumphs of our national cause; and, whether judged by his pre-rebellion observations and writings, or by his efforts and influence in the Commission's preventive work and relief-plans in his office as General Secretary, his purposes and his influence have justly been regarded as being most emphatically national, loyal, humane, and ennobling.*

In thus alluding to the invaluable services and extraordinary genius of the first General Secretary of the Sanitary Commission, the labors and qualifications of other members of the Commission

* The following paragraph, from a morning paper, upon the departure of Mr. Olmsted to a new field of labor, renders an appreciative tribute to his character and public labors:

"Mr. F. L. Olmsted sails to day for California, where he is about to assume the position of Manager for the Mining Company which has recently purchased the Mariposa estate from General Fremont. His loss will be felt keenly in the East, not only by troops of warm and admiring personal friends, but by the public, which, for more than seven years, he has served with a fidelity for which, in our day, it has almost ceased to look. It is less than ten years since he wrote the remarkable series of letters, which he afterwards republished in the volume known as the *Seaboard Slave States*, and which, followed by the *Journey Through the Back Country*, and the *Texas Journey*, have, perhaps, done more to influence public opinion touching the social and economical results of slavery than all the rest of the innumerable publications put together, which this absorbing controversy has called forth. In fact, they may be said to have settled at least the economical side of the question in the eyes of all reflecting men here, as well as in England, where the bitterest enemies of the North still quote Mr. Olmsted's statements as conclusive proof." * * * * *

"He left the Park to become General Secretary of the Sanitary Commission at the outbreak or the war. How well he discharged this mission of mercy, thousands on thousands of the victims of this great struggle can testify." * * * * * * * "The war has furnished many noble chapters to history, but in the noblest one of all—that which records the volunteer efforts of the nation to lessen the sum of its misery—Mr. Olmsted's name, and those of his coadjutors of the Commission, will appear in shining letters."—*New York Daily Times*.

The following resolutions, respecting the resignation and the labors of the First General Secretary, were adopted by the Sanitary Commission, at its session in Washington, October, 1863;—we copy from the published Minutes of the Board:

"The President communicated the previously announced resignation of Mr. Olmsted, as General Secretary, and as a member of the Commission, and offered resolutions expressive of the feeling of the Commission, viz.:

"*Resolved*, That this Board accepts the resignation of Fred. Law Olmsted, as General Secretary, with profound regret.

"*Resolved*, That from the beginning of our enterprise, the organizing genius of Mr. Olmsted, trained by rich experience in other large and successful undertakings, has been a chief source of whatever merit has characterized the operations of the Sanitary Commission; and that we find our consolation in the loss of his personal services, in the fact that his plans and ideas are so ineffacably stamped on our work, that we shall continue to enjoy the benefit of his talents and the inspiration of his character, as long as the Commission lasts.

"*Resolved*, That these resolution's be transmitted to Mr. Olmsted, with a letter expressive of our warm personal attachment, and an earnest expression of our wish that he will withdraw his resignation as a member of the Board.

"The resolutions were adopted, and the President was requested to prepare the letter referred to."

are not depreciated or overlooked; nor can the faithful and self-sacrificing services and excellent skill of the Sanitary Inspectors and Relief Agents be the less esteemed because the scheme of their united labors and counsels was committed to the organizing and guiding hands of the General Secretary. The marked success, and the constantly increasing extent of sanitary works in the army and hospitals during the period that has elapsed since Mr. OLMSTED resigned service in the Central Office, prove how intelligently and how devotedly the entire Commission and each subordinate officer have appreciated their individual responsibilities.

To proceed: during the summer and fall the Sanitary steamboats continued their transportation of "sanitary stores" upon the Western rivers; the Hospital Train continued its merciful errands upon the railways of Kentucky and Tennessee; and the Hospital Directory at Louisville, the Homes, Lodges, Supply Dépôts, and Offices for Advice and Aid, at Cairo, Louisville, Nashville, and elsewhere, continued their beneficent operations.*

---

* The following is a condensed statement of *Supplies distributed by the* U. S. SANITARY COMMISSION *in the Western Department, to September* 1st, 1863:

BEDDING AND CLOTHING.

Blankets	13,402	Mosquito Bars,	1,410
Bedticks	25,377	Neck Ties	554
Boots and Shoes, pairs	682	Night Caps	4,817
Comforts and Quilts	40,159	Pillows	84,106
Coats, Pants, and Vests	9,382	Pillow Cases	161,072
Drawers, pairs	113,329	Sheets	92,067
Dressing-gowns	12,610	Shirts	201,603
Havelocks	1,864	Slippers, pairs	16,172
Hats and Caps	591	Socks, "	90,528
Mattresses	716	Straw, bales	181
Mittens, pairs	9,764	Towels and Handkerchiefs	297,960

HOSPITAL FURNITURE AND SURGEONS' SUPPLIES.

Adhesive Plaster, yards	1,298	Bedsteads	385
Arm Rests	1,249	Beds, Feather	9
Bags	1,863	Bed Pans	389
Bathing Tubs	11	Books and Pamphlets	233,000
Bandages, Comp's and Lint, lbs.	239,948	Brooms	358

Sanitary Work at Chickamauga and Chattanooga.—With the forces that moved upon Tullahoma and towards Northern Georgia, at the end of summer, the Sanitary Commission sent forward its agents and supplies. On the first of September, Dr. Newberry reported to the Commission as follows:

* * * * "All of the regiments comprising this army, I believe, without exception, have received careful special inspections, the inspection returns having been forwarded from time to time to the Central Office. I am happy to be able to say, that their sanitary condition is now, and has long been, remarkably good. The percentage of sick is as low, if not lower,

Buckets	539	Lanterns	309
Candles, lbs.	2,306	Lamp Oils, galls.	130
Candlesticks	170	Lumber, feet	118,000
Carpeting, yds.	246	Kettles	20
Chairs	429	Knives and Forks, pairs	1,833
Clocks	6	Matches, gross	18
Combs and Brushes	2,683	Mats, Door	43
Cooking Stoves and Furniture	10	Matting Cocoa, yds.	190
Ranges	2	Mops	153
Coffins	73	Oakum, bales	6
Coffee Pots	118	Paper, reams	380
Cots	442	Pens	5,000
Chambers	765	Pincushions	27,851
Cups and Saucers	791	Pitchers	119
Cushions and Pads	53,142	Spittoons	641
Crutches, prs	3,321	Spit Cups	1,825
Desks	25	Sauce Pans	100
Dippers	81	Scissors	48
Drinking Tubes,	108	Soap, lbs	4,602
Tables	53	Splints	120
Table Cloths	822	Spoons	2,504
Tin Cups	6,352	Sponges, lbs	230
Tumblers	862	Stoves	8
Envelopes,	76,000	Urinals	313
Eye Shades	3,360	Wash Basins	1,100
Fans	12,500	Wash Tubs	10
Furnaces	9	Wash Boards	12
Hatchets	41	Washing Machines	9
Lamps	48	Tin Plates	4,016

ARTICLES OF DIET AND DELICACIES.

Ale and Cider, galls	11,584	Bread, lbs.	10,304
Apples, bush	1,886	Broma, lbs	200
Apple Butter, galls	2,160	Butter, lbs	41,197
Arrowroot, lbs.	3,551	Crackers, lbs	102,016
Barley, lbs.	10,204	Cocoa, lbs.	455
Beef, Dried, lbs	18,710	Chocolate, lbs	96
Beef, Con'd, lbs	33,873	Chickens	4,114
Beans, bush	31½	Chicken, cans	905

than in any other army, and protective measures, such as the policing of camps, &c., are so thoroughly observed that little is left to desire in that respect.

"By reference to the accompanying schedule of disbursements, it will be seen that the amount of supplies furnished to the Army of the Cumberland has been very large (over 10,000 bushels of vegetables alone since Jan. 1st)." * * *

And from Inspectors in the field messages like the following were continually received at the Secretary's office; at the same time that officer was as constantly ordering to the front "sani-

---

Coffee, lbs	2,009	Maccaroni, lbs	160
Coffee, Con'd, lbs	105	Mackerel lbs	50
Corn Meal, lbs	23,119	Oat Meal, lbs	1,878
Cheese, lbs	12,113	Oranges, boxes	98½
Corn Starch, lbs	3,253	Oysters, cans,	1,094
Corn Dried, lbs	644	Onions, bush	3,835
Cakes and Cook's, lbs	4,204	Peas, Split, bbls	2
Cranberries, bush	5½	Pepper, Ground, lbs	768
Catsup, bot	1,339	Pepper Sauce, bot	2,076
Codfish, lbs	52,862	Pie Plant, boxes	61
Eggs, doz	37,638	Porter, bot	1,008
Farina, lbs,	8,344	Potatoes, bush	49,141
Figs, lbs	60	Pickles, gals	28,572
Flour, bbls	37	Rice, lbs	3,872
Fruit, Preserved, cans	103,330	Raisins, lbs	25
Fruit, Dried, lbs	497,365	Sago, lbs	2,608
Gelatine, lbs	31	Salt, lbs	1,170
Groceries, lbs	51,614	Sardines, boxes	44
Grapes, lbs	1,650	Sausages, lbs	427
Hops, lbs	395	Sour-krout, gals	3,780
Herbs, lbs	1,502	Shoulders, lbs	4,160
Herrings, boxes	25	Spice, lbs	68
Halibut, boxes	40	Strawberries, qts	826
Honey, lbs	582	Sugar, lbs	26,066
Hominy, lbs	640	Syrup, gals	688
Horse Radish, bot	574	Tapioca, lbs	1,409
Hams, lbs	9,314	Tea, lbs	8,006
Ice, tons	270	Toast, boxes	76
Lemons, boxes	337	Tobacco, lbs	1,304
Lemon Syrup, bot	2,698	Tongues,	238
Milk, Con'd, lbs	46,807	Vinegar, gals	1,514
Mustard, lbs	1,866	Wines and Spirits, bottles	36,399

[Miscellaneous articles omitted for want of space.]

A careful estimate of the cash value of stores known to have been distributed by our agents in the Western Department during the past two years, fixes it at TWO MILLION TWO HUNDRED AND FIFTY THOUSAND DOLLARS. The expenses attending their distribution have been THIRTY-FIVE THOUSAND DOLLARS, or *one and one-half per cent.* upon their valuation.—*Sanitary Reporter, Dec. 1st*, 1863.

tary stores," and whatever could be pushed forward for the relief and benefit of the soldiers:

"TULLAMOMA, * * * *

* * * * "Having procured transportation on the 11th inst., I came to this place with a car load of assorted stores. Arrived here at two o'clock P. M.; had some difficulty in obtaining storage, and was so much delayed in waiting for detail and transportation from dépôt, that it took me till in the night to get my stores secured under cover. I was worn out.

* * * * * * *

* * * "Having supplied the hospitals (both general and regimental) about Tullahoma as well as my limited supply would permit, I sent this morning, on the telegraphic requests of the Medical Directors, a wagon load each to Thomas' and McCook's corps, and, on the requisition of Dr. Bache, Assistant-Medical Director of the Army, a small load to Hospital No. 1, at Winchester." * * * *

* * * * * * *

* * * "In my walk around the camps, I could not overlook the filthy and unhealthy condition of the town recently evacuated by the rebels. It is the dirtiest, nastiest (no other word will express it) place I have ever been in. I can scarcely imagine any kind of filth, or any combination of vile stench, which is not found here. A small stream, filled with carcasses of mules and horses, washes the town.

"The river Rhine, to all 'tis known,
Washes the city of Cologne.
But who can tell what pow'r Divine
Can ever wash the river Rhine!"

"I have presented the importanee of this subject strongly to the A. A. General, to the Provost Marshal, and to the surgeons."

Thus the Commission kept up its methodical sanitary care in the camps and along the line of march, supplying, until the army of the Cumberland confronted the concentrated rebel forces upon the bloody field of the Chickamauga, on the 19th, 20th, 21st and 22d of September. During all the preceeding weeks of the army's toilsome march over the mountains, the Commission's agents had been massing its battle-field supplies and "Battle-Reserve Stock," at Nashville and at Stevenson, and, the day previous to the commencement of the conflict, the Chief Inspector, Dr. A. N. Read, reports to the Western Secretary as follows:

"CHATTANOOGA, September 18.

"We are expecting a general battle. Dr. Barnum came last night—was very energetic in getting through. Mr. Crary came yesterday morning with seven loads of stores. Mr. Redding and his companion were left at Bridgeport, expecting to come on as soon as possible. They are wanted now at Bridgeport and Stevenson more than here. I shall try to communicate with them to-day by telegraph. Stores designed for this place must be sent to Bridgeport at once, so as to be ready for the trains. They can be stored in tents, which have been furnished to us. We are practically farther from Bridgeport than Bridgeport is from Louisville, and regard ourselves as exceedingly fortuuate to get goods through as we have."

* * * * * * * *

In compliance with orders from the Commission, additional and large supplies were hurried forward from Stevenson, while that temporary dépôt was being daily replenished from the permanent dépôts of Nashville and Louisville.*

---

* Inspector Reed had pressed forward with the moving columns, and from Chattanooga he wrote as follows, on the 10th of September:

* * * * * * * * * * * *

"Between this and Bridgeport we have passed, as all the army trains have, two high mountain ridges over almost impassable roads; so bad, indeed, that we can hardly hope for much transportation for our stores until the railroad is again repaired or a steamboat is put upon the river, and this will not be done for some weeks.

"All things indicate that this must be our headquarters as soon as we can obtain stores. The sick cannot be sent back until that time, and we can send forward but little, I fear.

"The health of the army in the field is so far good, but the men cannot endure long all they have to bear without increasing the sickness.

"There are good hospital accommodations here—good buildings built and vacated by the rebels. The sick must be sent here, and I shall do all I can to bring stores forward. We are liberally supplying with onions, potatoes, milk and beef, and, so far as is needed, with clothing, the general field hospital at Stevenson and two large convalescent camps, one at Bridgeport and one at Cowan, in which there are many sick. After this there will be comparatively few sick at Nashville, and I think that Chattanooga will be to us a center of work as Nashville has been."

* * * * * * * * * * * *

Sanitary Reporter, Vol. 1, No. 10.

The rugged steeps of the Cumberland Mountains, and the obstructed transportation of their over-crowded and rocky roads, did not keep back those sanitary trains. The first train, however, after the battle, comprising seventeen wagon-loads of "sanitary stores" for the wounded, was mercilessly destroyed by rebel raiders in a mountain pass.* Ten loads had previously reached the sufferers at Chattanooga; and thus writes Dr. Andrews, another Sanitary Inspector:

* * * * * * * *

"These stores constituted almost the entire dependence of

---

* The Relief Agent at the temporary dépot of "sanitary stores," at Stevenson, Ala., soon after the battle, thus mentions the wants and the means of succor at that station:

* * * * * * * * * * *

"Large supplies of vegetables were obtained from the garden at Murfreesboro', including potatoes, sweet-potatoes, tomatoes, etc., in abundance, and such other articles as were required from the Sanitary Rooms.

"Receiving word from Dr. Andrew at Chattanooga, who was in temporary charge of the general work in the department, to report at that place, I rode through from Bridgeport on the 3d by the courier route expecting to find our rooms full of stores. But they were entirely empty, our men were living on hard tack, bacon, and coffee which could be purchased only a few rations at a time of the commissary; horses and men all on short rations, and hard tack fast becoming a luxury. A train of about 400 wagons had been destroyed on the second, and with it, our seventeen wagons and all other trains temporarily stopped. About this time, the last of our wounded were sent in from the rebel hands and were in want of all things. Some of them were without shirts, a few without any clothing whatever, the most fortunate with torn clothing, begrimmed with dirt and clotted with blood. I purchased at the only army clothing store in town a few shirts (all I could obtain) and gave them to the most needy. Upon the 6th, I received notice that eight wagon loads of stores were on the way, and on the 7th, procured an order for twenty wagons more to report at our rooms in Stevenson to bring forward stores.

"The work of procuring transportation, I found beset with many and unlooked-for difficulties. The loss of a large train and the interruption of communication had produced some confusion; the army was short of all supplies, and the responsible officers of every department were clamorous for transportation. At the same time, it was evident, that the wounded men left here, numbering about 1,400, must be saved, if at all, by feeding them, and they must have something better than army rations. The sick also, of whom there are many, not an unusual number, stand in almost equal need of better articles of diet. By engaging to ship for the present only articles of diet for the sick and wounded, I have secured a train of forty wagons to be run constantly under our supervision in bringing stores from Stevenson, as long as the necessity shall exist, or until river or railroad communication is opened."

* * * * * * * * * * *

the hospitals at Chattanooga until the Tuesday and Wednesday succeeding the battles. On those days trains containing portions of the Medical Purveyor's stores reached the front; thus furnishing another instance of the necessity of independent medical transportation.

"On Monday the 21st, partly because of the pressing necessities of the hospitals, partly because of possible military contingencies, the order was given to distribute all the Sanitary and medical stores on hand among the hospitals, and by Tuesday evening the Commission's rooms were cleared of their contents, and were occupied by our wounded men. Those who had not fallen into the hands of the enemy were made measurably comfortable.*"

The Chief Relief Agent, Mr. M. C. Reed, under date of September 24th, reported as follows:

* * * * * * * *

"On Saturday, the 19th, the general engagement commenced and continued, suspended at intervals, while changing positions

---

* The following additional extract from the same Inspector's report, presents at once a truthful view of the difficulties and the zealous energy in the work:

* * * * * * * * * * *

"The wounded are generally doing well, and bear with patience the privations which appear unavoidable; but a generous supply of edibles suitable for sick and wounded men is indispensable to their recovery. I trust a supply of these articles will be ready at Stevenson to fill at any time, the twenty (20) wagons and as often as they can make the trip, and if more than that are accumulated there, we will undertake to get them through. There is a demand also for flannel shirts and drawers, sheets, blankets, etc., which, while the present pressure continues, we cannot forward in the "Sanitary train." But let them be accumulated without stint at Stevenson for we hope that communication by the river and by railroad will soon be opened, and I have requested the surgeons here, while waiting for that event, to make requisitions at every opportunity, for articles of the latter description, upon the Agent at Stevenson, and in that way, a very fair supply can be got through by ambulances and hospital wagons.

"As you are aware, the occupation of the railroad for many days in transporting and the subsequent raids upon it between Stevenson and Nashville, stopped for some time, the receipt of stores at Stevenson. The same events caused an unexpected accumulation of sick at the latter place, calling for large issues of sanitary stores there, leaving only enough to fill fifteen of the wagons ordered to report there. These are now on the way, and we look for their arrival to-morrow, the 14th. And as the 20 wagons constituting our train, have probably already reported at Stevenson, where we suppose there are now abundant supplies, we are in a measure relieved of anxiety, and anticipate a constant and tolerably abundant supply.

"I have to-day received a note from Rev. O. Kennedy, who is aiding in our work, that he has reached his post on the west side of the mountain and pitched the tents for the Mountain Lodge."

or falling back, throughout Saturday, Sunday, Monday and Tuesday. During this time, there was no opportunity of making even the briefest memoranda, and the events, of which I am giving you this hurriedly written narrative, may not all be detailed in the order of their occurrence."

* * * * * * * *

"Not a great many wounded were sent back on Saturday, but on Sunday they came in in numbers, far beyond the ability of all of the medical officers to provide even tolerably for their comfort. At the request of the medical director, Dr. Barnum took possession of two large blocks, cleared out the rooms, fitted them up temporarily for the wounded, supplying them with clothing, bandages, and edibles from our rooms, procured and put up stoves, dressed the wounds of those most requiring immediate assistance, and superintended the providing and cooking of rations for the men. All of the rooms were soon filled, and by his untiring efforts from 1,500 to 2,000 were rendered tolerably comfortable. On Sunday, I visited all of the hospitals and temporary resting places for the wounded, notifying the officers in charge of the location of our rooms and the nature of our supplies, asking them to send for everything we had, so far as it was needed. Returning late in the evening, I found a large church on Main street where services had been held during the day, and saw that the steps were crowded with wounded men. Entering the church, it was found filled with a congregation from the battle-field, crippled with every variety of wounds, with no medical or other officer in charge, without food of any kind, without water, and without even a candle to shed a glimmering light over their destitution, silent worshippers in the darkness, patient unmurmuring martyrs in a noble cause, apparently deserted by all except Him in whose sanctuary they had taken refuge. I immediately carried concentrated beef to the residence of Dr. Simms, near the church, a resident physician of rebel sympathies, but a generous, warm hearted man, in whose office we had some days before found quarters, and where my brother superintended the preparation of soup, while I bought candles and a box of hard bread, had them carried to the church, and procuring water, distributed it for the thirsty. Never before had I so high an appreciation of "nature's sweet restorer, balmy sleep."

"Two-thirds of the occupants of the church, some with shattered arms, and some with other ghastly wounds, were sleeping quietly upon the seats and the floor, unconscious of their many wounds. The soup was brought and distributed to the wakeful, and my brother and Dr. Simms commenced dressing the wounds, and continued their labors till sheer exhaustion compelled them to desist. The waking men provided for, the sleeping were allowed to sleep in peace. I reported the condition of these men to the medical director, and medical officers were put in charge of them, and in the morning a chaplain took charge of vegetables and other eatables which I sent from the rooms, and superintended the preparation of food for the men. At this time, Monday, the streets were completely blockaded for their whole length with army wagons, as an order had been issued on Sunday for the whole train to be sent across the river. This was done apparently to avoid confusion, and to save the train if our forces should be compelled to evacuate the place. The only means of crossing was one narrow pontoon bridge, and for two days the trains filled all the streets. Our stores were needed everywhere, but nobody could get to our quarters. After applying to several headquarters, I procured an order for three army wagons to report at our rooms for the distribution of stores. And hastily riding to the different hospitals, obtained approximately the capacity of each, the number of the inmates, and the nature of the articles most needed. The usual answer, however, to the question, 'What do you need most?' was, 'Everything,' a comprehensive, but almost literally a truthful answer. Returning to the rooms, I gave general directions to Messrs. Redding and Larrabee, who superintended the loading of the wagons, and piloted each one when loaded through the dense mass of teams to its destination. At first sight, an apparently hopeless undertaking, but the words, 'This wagon is loaded with stores for your wounded comrades, can you make room for it to pass?' operated like magic everywhere, and in no single instance did I find a driver who did not promptly and cheerfully open a way for the supplies, and that, too, through streets where there were three, four, and five parallel trains, the drivers all eager to reach the pontoon bridge first and secure precedence in crossing. In this way we succeeded in getting a good supply, a full wagon load each to the seminary building and old rebel hospitals on the hill, to the old rebel hospital near the Critchfield Hotel, (now called No. 2), to the Critchfield Hotel, where there were about 1,500 wounded, to two churches west of the Critchfield house, to the Presbyterian Church, and to three blocks of buildings on Main street, and to the officers' hospital in a large brick building, east of Main street.

"This work left no time for gathering statistics, no time to get the names of the hospitals, or the number of the inmates, even had the surgeons had time to give their names or make out registers. Clerks were busy at the latter task, but in no place had they completed their labors. This work consumed the day and my strength, but I felt that my health was good, and with a few hours rest could start afresh. I determined to remain if the place should be evacuated, and if allowed to do so, make out a register of the wounded who were left behind."

* * * * * * * *

"If, when this reaches you, the telegrams from the front advise you that we still hold Chattanooga, my advise would be to send of all supplies as large quantities as possible, for I believe that already this battle is one of the bloodiest of the war. Our loss must already be greater than it was at Stone River, and I do not believe the rebels will fall back before our re enforced army without another desperate struggle.

"Among the stories distributed at Chattanooga, especial mention aught to be made of a box of excellent 'arm-slings' from the Aid Society in Pittsburg. Though not as many as the arms needing such a support, they were valued beyond price by every man who secured one, and were in every respect a valuable article."

* * * * * * * *

Hastening back to Stevenson to push forward the "sanitary stores," of which our men stood in perishing need, about the 1st of October, this energetic Relief Agent reported as follows:

* * * * * * * *

"Every department of the army at Chattanooga is suffering for the want of supplies, and the problem for those in charge of transportation, is how to dispose of it, and apportion it so as to do justice to all. At such a time constant watching, and an importunity which does not offend, is indispensable, in order to secure any transportation for us.

"Under the circumstances, I think we are having good success in getting our stores through. I think a large accumulation here is desirable, as soon as we can secure transportation by rail, that they may be pushed on to Chattanooga by every means possible.

"As soon as our army is sufficiently re-inforced, a battle may be expected, exceeding the recent struggle in the number of wounded. If the rebels fall back and the battle is postponed, Chattanooga will become the base of operations, and of supplies, and the larger supply we can get the better."

* * * * * * * *

The loss of seventeen large wagon loads of most valuable "sanitary stores," at the hands of Wheeler's rebel raiders, immediately after the last of such supplies at Chattanooga had been exhausted, was sorely felt at the time; but that disaster gave additional energy to the Commission's efforts to push forward still larger quantities, and to prepare, if need be, for still greater losses. But the formidable difficulties of transportation from the railway terminus at Bridgeport over sixty miles of steep mountain passes, requiring several days for a single trip, with army trains, miles in length, obstructing all hurried efforts in the forwarding of "sanitary stores," rendered it necessary for the Commission to multiply its resources of relief at or near the field in every possible manner. The situation at Chattanooga was eminently precarious, no less in a sanitary than in a military point of view. For weeks after the battle, the forces subsisted on half rations, and hard ones at that, while the wounded and the sick were in great need of hospital delicacies and an anti-scorbutic diet.

It was no fault of the Medical Directors, that the patients in hospital suffered thus,* and until the enemy could be driven back from the river and the railway between Stevenson and Chattanooga, neither the Sanitary Commission nor the Medical Department could do more than they actually did to succor the men in the hospitals about Chattanooga. As rapidly as possible the wounded men who could bear transportation were removed

---

* The Chief of the Relief Corps, Mr. M. C. Reed, writing from Stevenson, on the river, says:

* * * * "We are able to provide for those who get through to the railroad what is needed in addition to government supplies, but it is essential that large quantities of all the usual articles be shipped through to Chattanoogo as fast as possible. There the destitution and suffering have been, and must for some time be very great. Yet, you must not construe what I write here, or have written above, as an implied censure of the medical officers of the army. I know how persistently the Medical Director of the Army labored to procure transportation for his supplies, and how ready he was to aid us in procuring transportation. I know also that war is and must be cruel, and, situated as our army was before Chattanooga, even mercy to the wounded required that the army, yes, and the horses, should be fed, although the wounded suffered until the battle was over. Over roads, the difficulties of which no one will appreciate until he has tried them, supplies had to be carried for men and horses whose strength and endurance alone could save all of the wounded from the hardships and destitution which the wounded prisoners would encounter at the hands of rebels." * * * *

over the mountains, in ambulances, and on foot, to Bridgeport and Stevenson, and so onward to Nashville. Weary, exhausted, and famishing with hunger, the ceaseless trains of those disabled men, as they wended their way down the ravines of the Sequatchie towards the town of Jasper, halted at a row of tents which the Sanitary Commission erected there and christened as the "Soldiers' Home." That Mountain Lodge was like an *oäsis* in the desert,* and it will live in the life-long remembrance of hundreds whose sufferings were assuaged there.

---

* We append the following from the Cincinnati *Gazette:*

"CINCINNATI, October 31.

"Eds. Gazette,—It is not unfrequently stated that the contributions made by our benevolent citizens to the United States Commission seldom reach those for whom the donations were really intended. Such statements have a tendency to diminish public confidence, and retard the operations of the Commission. I desire, in a public manner, to testify to one act of the Sanitary Commission, done at a time and place to fully testify to the indispensable benefits that institution has done to our suffering men.

"On the 24th inst., I came down the cheerless and horribly muddy road leading down the valley of Sequatchie, from Chattanooga to Stevenson. Major Welsh, of the 18th, was with me, and in an ambulance we had Lieut. D. B. Carlin, a brave and valuable officer of the 18th, who was slowly recovering from a severe wound received at Chickamauga. This officer was yet totally helpless, and had been sent out from the field hospital with less than a day's rations to accomplish a march of *four days.* The country on this route affords nothing for the subsistance of either man or beast. In this emergency I knew not what to do. The officer, as well as the driver of the ambulance, and the officer's attendant, were likely to suffer severely.

"At a point just eight miles above Jasper we espied, on the river bank, three or four hospital tents, and near by a few smaller tents; and riding up to one of these, we discovered a small placard, with the words, 'Soldiers' Home' on it, and we rejoiced to discover the jolly countenance of the kind-hearted chaplain of the 101st Ohio Volunteers, now doing *detached* duty as agent of the Sanitary Commission in this isolated spot, for the benefit of the sick and wounded soldiers being sent to the rear.

"We stated our case, and were liberally supplied with fruit, crackers, tea, &c., &c., with a good bottle of the best of ale (Walker's best), and were kindly urged to remain and partake of a warm supper. This invitation we were reluctantly compelled to decline, on account of the lateness of the hour, and the necessity existing to reach Jasper. This is only one of a thousand similar instances occurring daily everywhere along this line. The fact that this aid, so much needed, reached us when so unexpected, made an impression on my mind.

"Let me urge the people to continue their generous donations. Through this source more aid is rendered us than through all others combined. This conduct of the agents has been such as to improve rather than diminish confidence.

"Yours,

"C. H. GROSVENOR,

"Lieut.-Col. 18th O. V. I."

The severely wounded that had been left in the hands of the enemy on the fields of the Chickamauga were soon permitted to retnrn in the ambulance trains that had been sent out under flag of truce; yet there were but few of them that could endure the journey over the mountains. One of the Relief Agents writes from Chattanooga, the middle of October, as follows:

* * * * * * * *

"The wounded are generally doing well and bear with patience the privations which appear unavoidable; but a generous supply of edibles suitable for sick and wounded men is indispensable to their recovery. I trust a supply of these articles will be ready at Stevenson to fill, at any time, the twenty (20) wagons, and as often as they can make the trip; and if more than that are accumulated there, we will undertake to get them through. There is a demand also for flannel shirts and drawers, sheets, blankets, &c., which, while the present pressure continues, we cannot forwarward in the "sanitary train." But let them be accumulated without stint at Stevenson, for we hope that communication by the river and by railroad will soon be opened, and I have requested the surgeons here, while waiting for that event, to make requisitions at every opportunity, for articles of the latter description, upon the Agent at Stevenson, and in that way, a very fair supply can be got through by ambulances and hospital wagons.

"As you are aware, the occupation of the railroad for many days in transporting, and the subsequent raids upon it between Stephenson and Nashville, stopped for some time the receipt of stores at Stevenson. The same events caused an unexpected accumulation of sick at the latter place, calling for large issues of sanitary stores there, leaving only enough to fill fifteen of the wagons ordered to report there. These are now on the way, and we look for their arrival to-morrow, the 14th. And as the 20 wagons constituting our train, have probably already reported at Stevenson, where we suppose there are now abundant supplies, we are in a measure relieved of anxiety, and anticipate a constant and tolerably abundant supply."

In the *Sanitary Reporter* we find the business of supplies to the wounded at Chickamauga during the first ten days succeeding the battle, summed up as follows:

* * * * * * * *

* * * * "It was for some time impossible to get forward the whole, or even a considerable portion of the 'Battle Reserve Stock,' which had been accumulated at Stevenson and Nashville, especially the latter. Transportation was, under the circumstances, simply impossible, and was acquiesced in as one of those distressing necessities incident to a state of war, particularly where the theatre of operations was at so great a distance from the base of supplies. With provident care the Commission had accumulated a large stock of the articles which long experience has shown to be necessary after a battle, as near the theatre of operations as was consistent with safety. They were pushed forward as rapidly as the other exigencies of the military service would permit. That they have been useful no one can doubt after reading the testimonials of the Surgeons in charge of the various hospitals, which may be found in another part of this number.

"The following table will show what the Commission has attempted since those battles. The 'Reserve Stock,' and much of that which has been shipped since, has gone to Stevenson, and as large a proportion as possible has been forwarded to Chattanooga:

"*Disbursements from the Nashville Dépôt, U. S. Sanitary Commission, to the Wounded of the Battles of Chickamauga, to Oct. 1st, 1863:*

	Battle Reserve.	Additional.
"Blankets	89	12
Bedticks	300	301
Bed Spreads		10
Comforts and Quilts	695	230
Coats, Pants, and Vests	395	175
Drawers, pairs	1,369	5,554
Dressing-gowns	458	107
Mittens, pairs	265	
Night Caps	57	4
Pillows	1,827	683
Pillow Cases	2,881	1,191
Pillow Ticks		102
Sheets	440	661
Shirts	10,163	3,448
Slippers, pairs	468	107
Socks, pairs	3,674	413
Towels and Hankerchiefs	6,252	5,039
Arm Rests	199	59
Bags	75	107

Article		
Bandages, lbs	7,167	315
Bed Pans		20
Books and Pamphlets, &c.	2,545	6,458
Bowls		3
Brooms		48
Buckets		27
Candles, lbs		40
Candlesticks		23
Combs and Brushes		288
Compresses, lbs	4,185	583
Coffee Pots and Tea Pots		15
Chambers		19
Cushions and Pads		1,023
Crutches pairs	55	
Eye Shades	102	18
Fans	2,495	
Envelopes		2,500
Hospital Furniture, articles	105	95
India Rubber Cloth, yds		8
Lanterns		1
Lint, lbs	200	28
Kettles (32 gals. each)		5
Matches, gross		3
Mops		24
Nails, lbs		5
Pincushions	1,344	180
Spittoons		46
Rags, lbs		983
Pans		35
Scissors		30
Soap, lbs.		143
Spoons		122
Sponges		36
Stoves and Furniture		2
Stationary, reams		5
Tin Cups		348
Tin Plates	50	394
Wash Basins		99
Baskets		12
Camp Chests		1
Camp Stools		12
Camp Kettles		27
Coffee Boilers		4
Soup Boilers, large		1
Ale and Cider, galls	500	400
Apple Butter, galls	4	

Arrowroot, lbs		80
Barley, lbs		190
Beef, Dried, lbs		205
Beef, Concentrated, lbs	4,826	1,375
Butter, lbs	150	433
Crackers, lbs		4,597
Cocoa, lbs		140
Citric Acid, lbs		20
Corn Meal, lbs		175
Cheese, lbs	103	281
Corn Starch, lbs		208
Codfish, lbs	344	2,000
Eggs, doz	72	205
Farina, lbs		260
Fruit, Preserved, cans	800	793
Fruit, Dried, lbs	3,800	4,395
Groceries, lbs		34
Herbs, lbs	200	
Jelly and Shrub, qts		91
Bay Rum, galls		16
Lemons, boxes		1
Milk, Concentrated, lbs	2,707	5,712
Mustard, lbs		3
Prunes, boxes		10
Oysters, cans		480
Onions, bush	188	377
Pepper, Ground, lbs		11
Potatoes, bush	397	723
Pickles, galls	26	201
Raisins, lbs		20
Sago, lbs		100
Tamarinds, lbs		25
Spices, lbs		12
Sugar, lbs		1,811
Tea, lbs	46	878
Toast, lbs		14
Tongues,		48
Vinegar, galls	480	40
Whisky, bot		1,425
Wine, bot	692	430
Blackberry Cordial, bot		124

"Since October 1st, eight hundred and sixty boxes, seven hundred and seventy-five barrels, and one hundred and ninety-three kegs, sacks, &c., making 1,834 packages, have been sent to Nashville by railroad, and about nineteen hundred packages by river, in addition to the above.

"P. S. * * * * We are now reaching the wounded of Chickamauga with not less than a car load of valuable stores, per day."

This life-preserving work of incessant supply and careful distribution of "sanitary stores," was continued, in spite of the deficient and obstructed transportation, until General Hooker's forces opened the way up the river to Chattanooga. But during that anxious period of two months when none except the wounded were sure of sufficient daily food, the Sanitary Commission's agents had made ready for the next great battle by ordering forward from Nashville to Bridgeport all the supplies that the Director of Transportation could daily permit to go by railway, viz., one car load of "sanitary stores" each day; and as soon as navigation became practicable as far up as Kelley's Ferry, such stores were hastened forward to that point, ten miles from Chattanooga. Inspector Reed reported the progress of work at that period as follows, under date of Nov. 16th:

* * * * * * * *

"Rev. Mr. Kennedy who had tents and the charge of the Lodge at the foot of the mountain, was informed that he was more needed at the Ferry—both that he might aid in taking care of the goods as they were unloaded from the boats, and also that he might lodge and feed the sick brought to that place by ambulances and who must wait for the boat to return.

"Writing to Mr. F. R. Crary our store-keeper at Stevenson, he says, 'I want you to be here when the goods arrive that you may enjoy with me the pleasure of seeing these hungry men receive their first supply. The want of food here is so pressing that I have often seen the soldiers gathering the grains of corn which had fallen from the feed troughs of the mules, roasting and eating them.'

"The pleasure alluded to they have experienced, and now are sending to Bridgeport, and have been since the 3d of this month, one car load each day—and these stores are sent promptly from Bridgeport to Chattanooga."

* * * * * * * *

"Mr. E. I. Eno sent by the State of Illinois to look after the interests of her soldiers, is with us and of us and ever ready to co-operate in the general work. All stores at his command, and they are many, are turned over to the Commission for general distribution. Mr. Eno also left his office and endured great personal exposure and hardships in organizing our dépôts at Bridgeport and Kelly's Ford—and the removal of the stores from Stevenson. We are under very great obligations to him, for his timely and valuable assistance. His acts all show that he regards the struggle in which we are now engaged as National; and that our sympathy and help should be given alike to all the sufferers. The only question to be asked in the distribution of our stores being: Is he a soldier of the Nation? Is he in want:

"At Murfreesboro' the hospitals are again enlatged; and a larger number of the sick and wounded will be accumulated there, than have been for many months.

"There is one general hospital at Tallahoma in charge of Dr. Woodward, our excellent friend, because he is the true friend of his patients. As usual his hospital is in the best possible condition. At Cowan there is also at this time a large number of sick. The hospital at Stevenson is being removed. At Bridgeport there is a hospital, where those brought from Chattanooga are to remain until taken on by rail. Here we have been feeding them on their arrival. Mr. Pocock tetegraphed me that he fed 100 in one day, which he did with very little material to work with; had a tolerable supply of tin-cups, but had no spoons for his soup. He obtained volunteer help from one of the regiments stationed near.

"Mr. Kennedy is also doing the same work at Kelly's Ferry with better accommodations. Mr. Eno informs me that he saw him feed about 100 as they lay in ambulances, too badly wounded to get out, but compelled to wait for the boat. The passage from that point by boat to Bridgeport is made with little comfort and great exposure; but it is luxurious when compared with the former dreadful ride in ambulances over the mountains, a distance of some sixty miles; climbing the most rugged mountain sides with great difficulty, and then going down the other side as rocky, steep, and rugged; the rocks so large in the path that the patient who had become too exhausted to hold on to the sides of the ambulance, is from the motion dashed from side to side; or if there are two, they are thrown alternately one upon the other.

"Col. Paine of the 124th O. V. I. shot through the thigh, was one of the thousands that took such a ride—and he assured me that he suffered ten thousand deaths—that he would much prefer death to such a ride again; and he had no bones broken.

"The ride now by river occupies about twelve hours, while

by the ambulances over the mountains, the average time I have been informed, was five days, and sometimes much longer."

* * * * * * * *

We introduce this interesting record of the Commission's work after the battle of Chickamauga, much abbreviated, though connected, believing that it cannot fail to present to the reader's mind the best possible *answer* to the question, "whether, after all, there is any sober necessity or fitness in this exertion to sustain an institution which aims to *supplement* Government supplies for the aid or relief of the soldiers."

But the battle of Chickamauga constituted but one act in the grand strategic drama of Generalship and soldierly heroism and sacrifice, that has given to the Federal forces in Tennessee and Virginia the key to the very fastnesses of the rebellion. Just two months after that first terrible conflict, the second great battle before Chattanooga crowned our arms with success, such as hardly finds a parallel in the history of modern wars. What the Inspectors and Relief Agents of the Sanitary Commission found to do on that battle-field, and subsequently in the hospitals and camps of that army, let us here briefly state.

The Western Secretary, Dr. Newberry, as the witness and director of the Commission's work, there reported, under date of Dec. 7, 1863, as follows:

* * * * * * * *

"I have passed the last two weeks, from a tour of inspection through the chain of agencies of the Commission which extend from Louisville to that point. It chanced, luckily enough, that I was at Chattanooga through all the exciting scenes of the recent battles, and was able to contribute something to the success which attended the efforts of the Agents of the Commission to relieve the wants and sufferings of the wounded.

"As you are doubtless impatient to learn more than you know of the recent important events to which I have referred, and more particularly how fully the Commission has sustained its responsibilities, I hasten to make my report as promptly as possible, and shall make it as full as the great pressure of other duties will permit.

"As a pre-requisite to a clear understanding of the military operations, the work of the Commission in and about Chattanooga, and a proper appreciation of the difficulties overcome, it is quite necessary that anyone should have gone over the ground himself."

* * * * * * * *

"Until I had been myself to Chattanooga, I had no just appreciation, even with description after description, of the daring and energy which had led General Rosecrans to follow to the very heart of its mountain fastnesses, the retreating army of General Bragg; and after overcoming obstacles at first sight insurmonntable, to seize and hold the key to all the lines of communication through this great mountain-labyrinth.

"From near Tallahoma to Chattanooga, the whole interval is occupied with mountains of formidable height, terminating laterally in precipitous escapments, separated by deep and narrow valleys, over which even a footman finds his way painful and perilous. In justice to those who planned and executed the military movements prior and preparatory to the late victories, I must say that our people of the Northern States have no just conception of what our army has done and suffered in reaching and holding Chattanooga; and I am sure if all could see what I have seen, of difficulties overcome, hardships endured, and privations so cheerfully suffered, there would be much less than there has been of flippant criticism of the soldiers and the Generals of the Army of the Cumberland."

* * * * * * * *

"Chattanooga itself must have been, before cursed and blasted by rebellion, one of the most charming places on the continent. It stands in the valley of the Tennessee, shut in on all sides by picturesque mountains, from a thousand to two thousand feet in height, while the town itself is in part perched on eminences of two or three hundred feet, from which the lowlands, reaching to the base of the mountains, are all clearly visible. When, therefore, I tell you that the last battles were fought in a semi-circle around the points of view in the plain or on the mountain side, never more than three miles distant, you will concede that those of us who were present enjoyed an opportunity of witnessing military evolutions—all the varied phases of attack and defence by artillery and infantry, of assault and repulse, of victory and defeat—such as has fallen to the lot of few since Priam watched the struggle between the Greeks and Trojans from the walls of Troy.

"Of the battles themselves, I do not now propose to say much, as it will be foreign to my purpose, and they have already been described to you in the letters of Army Correspondents and the admirable telegraphic summary of General Meigs—so fully that it would scarcely be desirable, if possible. I, however, enclose a topographical map, which was made at Chattanooga, more full and accurate than any yet published. With this and the descriptions you have at command, you will be able clearly to comprehend the successive steps by which our army secured its final victory, and appreciate, in some measure, the daring bravery of our troops in scaling the heights of Lookout Mountain and Mission Ridge.

"My business, however, is with the noble spirits who *fell* in these glorious charges, and it is with no ordinary satisfaction that I can say that, thanks to the proximity of the battle-fields to suitable receptacles for the wounded, and to the wisdom and energy displayed by the Medical Officers, and last, not least, the prompt and potent aid that the Sanitary Commission with its abundant stores was able to render, none of those cases of neglect or protracted suffering which have been considered as inseparable attendants upon the carnage and confusion of battle-fields, so far as I know, were permitted to occur. I am quite sure that I do not exaggerate when I say that the wounded in no considerable battle since the war began have been so well and promptly cared for; and I can say also with equal confidence, that the aid rendered by the Sanitary Commission has never been more prompt and efficient, more heartily welcomed, or more highly appreciated.

"Owing to the difficulties of transportation—difficulties which had prevented the issue of full rations to the army since the battle of Chattanooga—our stock on hand previous to the battle was not as large as I could have wished; but we were accorded even more than our full share of such facilities for transport as were at command of the Quartermaster's Department, and fresh supplies of the most needed articles, including all the staple battle stores, continued to arrive, so that our warehouse was constantly replenished, and every requisition was promptly filled. Of concentrated beef, milk, stimulants of various kinds, compresses, bandages, dried fruit, vegetables, shirts and drawers, we had a sufficient supply to meet every demand.

"In order that you may see precisely how our work was done, permit me to take up, in the order of their succession, the principal events connected with it during my stay at Chattanooga.

"Toward midnight of Saturday, the 29th of November, in company with Dr. Soule, I arrived at Kelly's Ferry, ten miles below Chattanooga. Here we were hospitably entertained by our agent, Mr. Sutliffe. As I shall have occasion to return to this point in the course of my narrative, I will for the present defer reference to the great good which he has been doing here. On Sunday morning we started for Chattanooga on foot. Kelly's Ferry was at this time the head of navigation—the river being blockaded above by the rebels—and all supplies were transported from this point in wagons. As a consequence, we found the road blocked up for miles by trains going and returning, all hurrying to accomplish their almost impossible duty of preventing the army above from perishing by actual starvation. Crossing Raccoon Mountain, we came into Will's Valley, where we found Hooker's forces occupying the vantage ground gained by their night descent of the river, and came into full view of the rebel encampments on the side, and rebel batteries on the summit of Lookout Mountain. From the latter, from time to time, came a puff of white smoke, and the sullen boom of the forty-pound Parrots, which had continued day after day to throw shells, fortunately without practical result, sometimes into Chattanooga above, sometimes into Will's Valley below their commanding position. Descending the valley, we crossed the river at Brown's Ferry, and traversing an isthmus some two miles in width, recrossed the river to the town. At this time large detachments of Sherman's forces were leaving their encampment in Will's Valley and moving up the river, nobody knew whither.

"In Chattanooga I found our Agency in charge of Mr. C. Read, occupying fine rooms which, with characteristic partiality, the authorities had assigned to our use by displacing the Chief of Police who had previously occupied them. Soon after my arrival I ealled on the Medical Director, Dr. Perin, by whom I was most cordially received, and was gratified to hear him express not only a high respect and appreciation for the Commission, but bear strong testimony to the value of our Agency at this point, to him and to the army, as well as to the energy and discretion of our chief representative, Mr. Read. The corps of agents on dnty here were as follows: M. C. Read, in charge; Rev. W. F. Loomis, hospital visitor; F. R. Crarey, store-keeper, with two detailed men as assistants; M. D. Bartlett, agent of hospital directory; A. H. Sill, transportation clerk. With Mr. Read, I called at several of the headquarters, and from all the officials heard only kind words for the Commission, and assurances of their readinees to co-operate with it by all means in their power."

* * * * * * * *

"On Sunday evening a large part of the 11th Army Corps came up from below, passed through the town, with three days' rations in their haversacks, and took their position, without tents or baggage, in front of the fortifications. On Monday our forces moved out, formed in double line of battle, with a front several miles in length, posted reserves in the rear, threw out skirmishers, and made a general advance, taking possession of the first line of the enemy's entrenchments, and occupied Orchard Knob in the centre of the valley, on which batteries were planted. This advance was made in excellent order, and the ambulances following close in the rear and through the skirmishing, extended along the whole line. The number of wounded was comparatively small, and they were immediately picked up and carried to the hospitals in time. On Tuesday, General Sher man having crossed the river three miles above, advanced, and without serious opposition took possession of the north end of Mission Ridge.

On the morning of the same day General Hooker moved up from Will's Valley and attacked the rebel forces occupying Lookout Mountain, and by a most daring assault gained possession of all the northern portion, with the capture of many prisoners and the loss of 250 killed and wounded. The latter were immediately carried to the hospital established near his headquarters, where they were well cared for by their own officers, supplies being sent to them from our dépôt at Kelly's Ferry near by. Early the next morning Mr. Read and Mr. Sill went down and saw that all the aid which the Commission could render was furnished them.

"On Tuesday night the north ends of Lookout Mountain and Mission Ridge were aglow with the camp-fires of our forces, and we had the satisfaction of knowing that by the brilliant achievements of the morning the blockade of the river was raised, and advantages had been gained which promised important results in the impending struggle of the morrow.

"Wednesday morning our flag floated from the summit of Lookout, and our forces advanced on the rebel stronghold of Mission Ridge, from our right, left, and front. After much severe fighting on our left, in which Sherman's forces suffered very heavy loss, the rebel entrenchments along the base of Mission Ridge were stormed by our advancing lines, and then began that perilous but glorious ascent of its slope of 1,000 feet at six different points, which so surprised and appalled the rebel garrison, and has covered with glory the brave men who dared attempt it. After an hour of suspense, inexpressibly painful to the thousands who were merely powerless spectators, the summit was gained and held, the roar of the forty pieces of artillery which crowned it was suddenly silenced, and we knew that a great victory had been won.

"Two wagons had been secured before hand, with which to transport stores to any point where they might be required; but no part of the battle-field being more than three miles distant from headquarters, and ample provision having been made by the Medical Director for the immediate removal of the wounded to hospital, they were held in readiness to use, if needed, while Mr. C. Read and myself, with a small supply of stores, went over to the battle-field along the middle line of Mission Ridge, and Mr. Loomis went toward the northern end, to see if any help were required by the wounded of Sherman's Corps. By midnight all the Union wounded men on that part of the field which we visited had been transferred to hospital, and such of the rebels as remained in the houses to which they had been carried had received all the aid we could give them; and so, at 1 o'clock, we returned to the town. Just as we arrived, Mr. Loomis came in and reported that the wounded of the 15th Army Corps had all been gathered into the Division Hospitals, but that their expected supplies had not arrived, and they were greatly in need of our assistance. A wagon load of milk, beef, crackers, tea, sugar, stimulants, dressings, &c., was immediately dispatched to them, and was, as may be imagined, of priceless value.

"Early the next morning, Thanksgiving Day, Mr. Read and myself visited the hospitals of the 2d, 3d, and 4th Divisions of the 15th Army Corps, situated three miles up the river. The 4th, containing the largest number of wounded (399), we found pretty well supplied, for the time being, with the stores we had sent up the night before; but these were rapidly disappearing, and, at our suggestion, another load was sent for and received during the day. The 2d and 3d Division hospitals, situated on the bank of the river, containing respectively 75 and 230 patients, had received, up to this time, no other supplies than such as had been carried in their medicine wagons, sufficient to meet the first wants of the wounded, but by this time almost entirely exhausted. Just as I was offering to Dr. Rogers, the Surgeon in charge of the 3d Division hospital, the resources of the Sanitary Commission, one of the assistant surgeons approached and said to him, 'Doctor, what shall we do? Our supplies have not arrived; our men are lying on the ground, with not blankets enough to make them comfortable. We've no stimulants, or dressings, or proper food. Now, if the Sanitary Commission only had an agent here, we should be all right.' I was happy to inform him that the spirit he invoked had come at his call, and when I promised that in an hour's time he should have concentrated beef, milk, stimulants, dressings, fruit, vegetables, clothing, bedding, and some ticks stuffed with cotton, his satisfaction shone from every feature, and both he and the surgeon in charge spontaneously ejaculated, 'Bless the Sanitary Commission'—an institution of which they had abundant experience on the Mississippi, where the kind and efficient ministrations of Dr. Warriner were remembered with pleasure and gratitude. At the 2d Division hospital I met two old professional friends, Dr. Potter, the Division Surgeon, one of the most efficient medical men the service, and Dr. Messinger, formerly from Cleveland, Ohio. The meeting, I think, was mutually pleasant, and Dr. Potter, who was just mounting his horse to follow his Division, expressed great satisfaction in leaving his men with some other resources than the light stock of supplies which they had brought in their wagons all the way from the Mississippi, and most of which must be immediately hurried to the advance, for other battles were impending. All these hospitals continued to be supplied from day to day with such things as were needed.

* * * * * * * *

"On Thanksgiving afternoon occurred the bloody fight at Ringgold, in which we lost, in killed and wounded, 500 men. Most of those wounded were soon brought into Chattanooga, but our stores, which were promptly sent, and in abundancy, reached them in good time, and became of great value to them.

"During the week succeeding these battles, through which I remained at Chattanooga, large quantities of stores were daily issued from our rooms to all the hospitals in the vicinity; timely arrivals of the more important articles compensating for the heavy drafts made on our stock. Of the kind and quantity of goods thus issued, you will in due time, get a full account from the storekeeper, Mr. Crary.

The subsequent advance of our forces towards Knoxville was accompanied by two of the three steamers plying on the river, both loaded with supplies. By this means our transportation was again reduced to its minimum, and for a few days, in common with all departments of the army, we shall be able to get forward a smaller quantity of supplies than could be advantageously used. We can calculate, however, upon a continuance of the cordial co-operation of Gen. Meigs, Dr. Perin, and the other military and medical authorities, and the good work which we have been doing will not be allowed to languish.

* * * * * * * * *

"I am sure that after the battle of Chattanooga there was neither the opportunity nor inclination, on the part of surgeons or nurses, to misappropriate stores furnished by the Sanitary Commission; and the Metropolitan Police, who enabled us to distribute to the sufferers the rare and much prized gifts of sound, fresh lemons; the loyal women who stitched the shirts and drawers, who rolled the bandages and made the arm-slings; the Aid Societies and Branch Commissions who have sent us so liberally of dried and canned fruits, of milk and beef, wine, spirits, ale, butter, tea, sugar, farina, codfish, and other precious articles, which we were able to distribute in abundance—may rest assured that here, at least, they have accomplished all the great good which they had hoped of them."

* * * * * * * * *

While these means of relief were being thus widely and prudently administered to the wounded at Chattanooga and along the line of dépôts and hospitals between that place and Nashville, agents from the Commission's Central Dépôt at Louisville were pressing forward with wagon trains of "sanitary stores" to Knoxville, and at the same time a reserved stock of choice hospital supplies was in readiness to be moved up the Tennessee River by the first boat or train that should go towards General Burnside's beleagured forces. December 6th, a Relief Agent, Mr. Strong, who had reached Knoxville by way of the river, reported as follows to Dr. Newberry:

* * * * * * * *

"You have little idea how badly the sick here need sanitary supplies. While there are about 1,800 patients, a third of whom are wounded, the present supply is scarcely sufficient for one-half. The sick have nothing to eat but such as the common soldier in health receives. Stimulants, dried fruit, delicacies, &c., are above all very much needed. I will not specify in detail further, as the requisitions of surgeons enclosed are explicit.

"Sanitary stores should come with all possible despatch. What will be done until your supplies arrive, I cannot say. I hope to get the ladies here interested in the matter of furnishing what bedding and clothes they can spare, while I may induce some from the country to send in chickens, fruits, &c. But every thing is very scarce. The two armies have exhausted this country. Your agents can appreciate the condition of affairs and send such articles and such amount as they see fit. But by all means let them *come soon*."

* * * * * * *

Another Agent, Mr. Butler, who had gone forward from Louisville with supplies early in November, and from Camp Nelson, Ky., Dec. 3d, succeeded in entering Knoxville, Dec.

26th. An extract from his first report will serve to illustrate what such *relief* work is, and what obstacles have to be encountered in it:

* * * * * * *

"Leaving Camp Nelson on the 3d, we reached the foot of 'Big Hill' at noon on the 7th, without trouble or adventure, notwithstanding that the guerrillas had appeared in Mount Sterling, Ky., and were frequently reported in the vicinity of our train, *we did not see them.* We had been so far favored with a good road that we made moderate progress, but now the *Big Hill* was before us. The ascent, though only one mile, occupied two of the hardest days' work that we had yet known, and involved considerable destruction of mules, harness, and teams.

"From the foot of *Big Hill*, we look in vain for anything but rocks and ruts, consequently a few miles—from three to fifteen, suffice for a days' travel."

* * * * * * *

"In nearly every house from the top of *Big Hill* I found that soldiers in every degree of disease had been left upon the hospitality and care of the people. In one house I found six soldiers occupying beds, and the constant attention of a widow lady, and her two daughters. The poor sick and weary men were unable to proceed any further, and these patriotic Samaritans, whose brothers were among our soldiers in the field, were, out of their scanty means, administering to their relief and comfort.

"Having received information of such necessities before leaving Camp Nelson, I had provided a quantity of beef extract, milk, crackers, an assortment of woolen under-wear, and sundry other things, which I found were actually required by men sick, hungry and naked.

"I found Dr. Burd collecting these poor fellows and affording all aid possible within his power. He had procured a building, which he had made as comfortable as his resources would allow, and he strove arduously to make his miscellaneous Hospital as effective as the emergency demanded. I was gratified in being able to furnish him with a variety of stores for his sick patients, for I know him to be one of the kindest and most faithful of men.

"During the forenoon of the 16th inst., I reached a house on Lincamps Creek, and saw two men working at a coffin.

"After some inquiries, I learned that twelve days previously a soldier had stopped at the house, complaining of chronic diarrhea and rheumatism. The people shared their morsel with him, and employed their limited knowledge of Medicine for his relief.

"The poor fellow also suffered with colic, which finally set in as an adjunct to his complicated disorders and tortured him until he threw his armor down for his long rest in a mountain grave. I desired the sergeant of the guard to ascertain his effects, and finding only ninety cents, I threw the sum over to the poor family as a very small remuneration for their attention to the soldier.

"Turning one day, a mile from the road, I found a grave, which, I was informed, contained six soldiers who had died in the neighborhood; but no human scribe was found to register their names ere death made them oblivious to all but God. And so it has been with many others, how many God only knows. But in the case of him whose rude coffin was being made before my eyes, I especially realized my duty to the soldier, although dead, and also to his parents.

"I gleaned from the family all the particulars necessary to advise his parents of his disease and death, and also the locality of his grave. I wrote at Barboursville to his father, &c."

* * * * * * * *

"Before leaving Camp Pitman we obtained a new supply of mules, harness and wagon tongues, also a large amount of forage. No event, except such as have become of common occurrence, transpired until we passed through Cumberland Gap, on the 20th inst., when a rumor was afloat that no train would be allowed to pass on the direct road to Knoxville, as the rebels were infesting that portion of the country. By the advice of the Post Commandant we took the Jacksboro' road, though twenty miles further, as it was considered safe.

"Leaving Cumberland Gap on the evening of 21st, we made better progress, while the forty guards, who had heretofore been employed in assisting the teams, were ordered by the officer in command, to march in advance of the train *under arms*."

* * * * * * * *

"Several encounters had taken place in our vicinity, between General Wilcox and Longstreet, only a few days previously, and others were pending, while the cannonading was distinctly audible in our train.

"There was marked anxiety among the guard to protect the train to Knoxville, as they knew the great need which existed in the hospital there."

* * * * * * * *

"On Monday, the 28th instant, Mr. Crary arrived from Chattanooga with three hundred packages of select stores. Other shipments have been arranged from and by way of Chattanooga."

At this period the ever faithful Inspector, Dr. Reed, was with the army at Chattanooga, superintending the Commission's work there. December 25th, he forwarded by steamboat to Knoxville, 200 boxes of "sanitary stores," and before New Year, the Commission's supplies were coming forward from Bridgeport and Nashville with less delay, the Hospital train having resumed its full trips, and returning from Nashville with its cars loaded with stores from the Sanitary dépôts. Quartermaster-General Meigs, who was then in that field, had rendered all the aid in his power to facilitate the work and purposes of the Commission, but until the bridges had been rebuilt upon the river, and the railway trains were run directly to Chattanooga, *sufficiency* of transportation was an impossibility.*

During the tedious months that had elapsed before supplies could be adequately provided at Chattanooga and Knoxville, scurvy, the inveterate pest of camps in such campaigns, had begun to manifest its various symptoms. At the beginning of winter Dr. Read writes to Dr. Newberry:

* * * * * * *

"Now that the railroad is open to Chattanooga, I trust that

---

* In a communication to the Central Office of the Commission, Dr. Newberry wrote, at this period:

* * * * * * * * *

"We had the entire and hearty co-operation of the military and medical authorities, and yet were, of course, compelled to share with them the inevitable necessities by which they were controlled. *More than our share* of transportation was granted at once, and when our first train of seventeen loaded wagons were included in the destruction of the three hundred loaded with Government stores, another train of twenty wagons was ordered for us, and from that time to the opening of the river we fully shared all the resources of the military and medical authorities. On the first trip of the steamboat, by the authority of General Meigs himself, who was there, we were allowed to make up a liberal share of its load, and from that time to this, by special and comprehensive orders, we have been furnished with a regular allotment of transportation of a car-load a day from Nashville to Chattanooga. *From here we forwarded all and more than could by any possibility reach the scene of suffering.* In addition to the very liberal stock held in reserve at Nashville and below previous to the battle, we have since forwarded there over 5,000 packages."

soon the more pressing wants of the sick will be relieved. Then will come the question of furnishing a supply of fresh vegetables, which must be done, or scurvy in all its Protean forms will come; *it is already upon us.* The hardships and privations endured by the Army of the Cumberland, since the battle of Chickamauga, have produced such changes in the constitution, that the wounds of the battle of Chattanooga have been far more fatal than those of Chickamauga.

"Scarcely one case of amputation of the thigh has recovered, and all wounds, while they have had more care, have been more serious; comparatively slight wounds have been fatal. To obviate this in part, the Medical Director is desirous that hospital gardens be made at Chattanooga, Tullahoma, and Murfreesboro'. He has given me a list of the garden implements and staple garden seeds which he desires the Commission to purchase, and forward to Chattanooga as soon as possible. Onions and peas can be advantageously planted as soon as the middle of February.

"I have promised him that the Commission will aid him in procuring all that may be wanted in either place. And while writing this, I have received a similar request from Dr. J. Moses, Medical Director in Murfreesboro'. He says: 'We *are now* commencing our arrangements for a garden at this post. May I ask if we can obtain seed, &c., &c., from your Commission."

* * * * * * *

Immediately the Inspector set about the duty of extensive official inquiry concerning the demand for anti-scorbutic supplies, and also to what extent the scorbutic taint was receiving the attention of Surgeons and Commissaries. Good results could not fail to flow from such inquiries, for they not only helped to keep alive the vigilant attention of military officers in reference to the importance of the subject, but the aid of the Sanitary Commission was invoked on every hand. General Hooker sent to the Sanitary dépôt at Bridgeport for eighty barrels of the Murfreesboro' potatoes, and Medical Officers urged the enlargement and continuance of the Commision's supplies of anti-scorbutics. The following extract from a letter which was addressed to Inspector Read, by a distinguished Medical Inspector of the army, Dr. R. H. Coolidge, proves the justice of the estimate which is placed upon the work in which he found the Commission's Agents engaged in Eastern Tennessee:

"Doctor,—I am on my return to Washington, from an inspection of the hospitals and troops at and near Knoxville, and would represent to you that, in my opinion, the Sanitary Commission can do a great deal of good, by sending to that point *anti-scorbutics* and *garden seeds*.

"The troops are comparatively healthy, but they have been deprived of vegetables so long, that there is danger of scurvy; indeed some of the premonitory signs of that disease are now apparent.

"In reply to your note of inquiry, I have to state, that raw potatoes, sliced and pickled, or preserved in molasses, are an excellent anti-scorbutic. Indeed, when I have the fresh potatoe and can have it cooked, I prefer using it raw, sliced and dressed as salad, for my scorbutic patients.

"I have advised the Medical Director at Knoxville to have one garden made for the hospitals in that city, which now accommodates 2,500 patients. I have also advised that gardens be made for the troops now in winter quarters in the vicinity of Knoxville, even though there be no possibility of the troops remaining long enough to reap the fruit of their labor further than relates to early greens, such as lettuce, turnip-tops, spinach, radishes, mustard, &c.

"The seeds most needed are lettuce, beets, turnips, tomatoes, radishes, spinach, mustard, pea, early cabbage, onion sets, corn, potatoes, and a general supply are wanted."

* * * * * * *

Testimony and urgent requests upon this subject are being continually received by the Sanitary Commission,* and help to give

---

* The following extracts give further illustrations of the practical value and necessity of the Sanitary supplies furnished by the Commission:

"HEADQ'RS 1ST BRIG. 3D DIV. 14TH A. C.,
"CHATTANOOGA, January 4, 1864.

"Dear Sir,—The accompanying document of Dr. Whitford, my Brigade Surgeon, induced me to address myself to you, asking for vegetables.

"It is important to heal the sick, but it is just as important, and more so, to preserve the healthy from sickness. We have not seen vegetables since the battle of Chickamauga, September 20th, 1863, and although the health of my brigade was excellent at that time, it is now shattered to such an extent, that Scurvy commences—and once that plague breaks out, its ravages will be tremendous if not stayed in time.

shape and energy to its well-formed purposes of Sanitary care. It was not alone the twenty thousand men in hospitals after the

---

"We have now fifteen cases of scurvy in camp, and about fifty cases showing signs of it. But this is nothing compared with the fact that hundreds are predisposed to it, and liable at any moment to be covered with sores, and be unfit for duty. It is a sad state of things, produced by dire military necessity.

"Next spring will be telling on our numbers, if the troops are without vegetables till then. A good many men, whose limbs were amputated after the last battle, died from exhaustion, they being too weak to withstand the shock. We hope tht our communication will be bettered, and that before long we will be generously supplied with vegetables. But before that time comes, your supply of vegetables for this command will be gratefully appreciated.

"Very respectfully, I remain yours, &c.

"F. B. Turchin.
"Brig.-Gen. Commanding.

"To Dr. A. N. Read,
"Sanitary Commission, Chattanooga."

"Chattanooga, Tenn., Jan. 4, 1864.

"General,—In compliance with your request to be furnished with a statement of the sanitary condition of the 1st Brigade, I beg leave to submit the following:

"From the reports furnished by the regiments composing this Brigade, I find that the general health of the men is as good as at any time since the organization, but owing to the total exclusion of vegetables, from the short supply of rations furnished the men for the past three months, and insufficient supply of wood to make them comfortable, I find that twelve or fifteen marked cases of scurvy have already been reported, and a large number who are beginning to show symptoms of that disease, and, in fact, nearly all the camp diarrhœa we are now having throughout the different regiments, partakes more or less of the scorbutic character. This is plainly shown by marked improvement in their condtion, by having a few day's supply of vegetables furnished by the U. S. Sanitary Commission, and could there be a liberal supply of vegetables furnished for all the men, scurvy would soon disappear, and all other diseases which originate in an impoverished condition of the blood. I would, therefore, urgently request that means be taken to procure the kind of diet so much needed to make our men efficient, and able to render good service by the opening of the spring campaign.

"J. H. Whitford,
"Senior Surgeon 1st Brigade.

"To J. B. Turchin, Brig.-Gen."

"General Field Hospital,
"Chattanooga, January 7th, 1864.

"Doctor,—I have to state, in answer to your inquiry, that the chief necessity for sick and wounded men at this point is a supply of vegetable food, milk, butter, and similar articles, and that the principal cause of the mortality from gangrene, Pyæmia, and allied diseases, is due to impoverished blood, the consequence of defective nutrition.

"I am, Doctor, very truly,
"Your obedient servant,

"Roberts Bartholow,
"Ass't Surgeon U. S. A., in charge.

"Dr. Read, Sanitary Commission."

battles of Chickamauga and Chattanooga who needed sanitary supplies from the Commission; a few weeks elapsed, and then the occasion for battle-field relief and special aid to the wounded became far less important than the supplying of antiscorbutics to the camps. Upon evidence like that furnished in the following official statements, the Western Agents of the Commission have set about their work at the beginning of the year 1864:

"OFFICE MEDICAL DIRECTOR, 11TH CORPS,
"Lookout Valley, Tenn., Jan. 11, 1864.

"Sir,—In accordance with your desire expressed during your visit on the 6th ult., I take pleasure in laying before the Sanitary Commission through you, the following statement of the hygienic condition of the 11th Army Corps, and earnestly solicit any assistance that the Commission may be able to furnish.

"Reports from regimental medical officers show an alarming increase of sickness during the last month, the number daily excused from duty on this account, varying from five to fifteen per cent. of the effective force, while the number prescribed for, of course much exceeds this. The principal disease, that indeed

---

"OFFICERS' HOSPITAL,
"CHATTANOOGA, Oct. 26, 1863.

"In the midst of the confusion and suffering immediately after the battle of Chickamauga, the Sanitary Commission came nobly to the rescue; nourished the wounded and famished soldier, pillowed his weary head, and by their timely aid saved many valuable lives.

"C. C. BYRNE,
"Ass't Surgeon U. S. A., in charge."

"HOSPITAL No. 2.
"CHATTANOOGA, Oct. 26, 1863.

"It is with feelings of the deepest gratitude and admiration that I recall to mind the donations from the Sanitary Commission to this Hopital immediately after its opening.

"After the battles of the 19th and 20th ult., outside this city, the wounded were brought in in thousands, and this Hospital, in common with the rest, was filled to overflowing. Here was a state of affairs suddenly brought about, and to be immediately provided for—and here was the Sanitary Commission—here the hour of need—it was an oasis in the desert. Here we received from it dressings for our wounded men, wines, clothing, and several luxuries and necessaries. No one who at this time witnessed the *timely and material* aid of the U. S. Sanitary Commission, but must say, 'It is truly a heavenly institution—may heaven bless and preserve its supporters.'

"PETER H. CLEARY,
"Surgeon U. S. V., in charge."

which, in its prevalence, its obstinacy under treatment, and its frequent fatal termination, becomes our most dangerous adversary, is chronic diarrhea. Within the last three months, the 141st N. Y. V., has lost from this cause six per cent. of its aggregate strength present, while the mortality in the 143d N. Y. V. is even greater than this, amounting to twenty-five deaths since the 1st of November, 1863, to an average strength of 450 men. Of those remaining, 174 are reported sick by Assistant-Surgeon Craft. Some of these have died in corps hospital, some in camps; and it has been observed as a strange and enigmatical feature of the disease, that its victims have been the sturdiest and ruggedest men in the regiment. No effect whatever has resulted from the various plans of treatment tried. Some of the men did duty up to the hour of death, and several surgeons have expressed their astonishment, that so near their end, men could display the muscular force they do. Such is not the character nor course of ordinary camp diarrhea, and it leads one to seek some complication which may explain it."

* * * * * * * *

"Though few cases of positively marked scurvy were reported, the symptoms of the scorbutic blood-poison, the peculiar gums, the hemorrhagic cachexia, the want of union in new, and the re-opening of old wounds, listlessness and hebetude, the purpural discoloration of the skin, etc., were noted in very many of the regiments present.

* * * * * * * *

"The type of disease is low, the fevers of malarial and sporadic character rapidly assuming a typhoid aspect, and the general appearance of the men, especially in the regiments comparatively lately enlisted, is depressed. They are in need of clothing and blankets. Many have no change of clothing, nor have had for many weeks; consequently they are filthy in the extreme. This is especially the case with the 33d New Jersey.

"All the hospital stores of this regiment—and it came out excellently provided by State authorities—were lost in the Tennessee river by the capsizing of the boat in which they were. Shoes, blankets and pants have not yet been furnished in sufficient quantity by the Quartermaster's department, and changes of stockings, shirts and drawers are generally wanted. The Commissary Department is tasked to its utmost to furnish the absolute necessaries of life, and there have been no issues of potatoes or onions since our return from the fall campaign. A limited supply of beans and rice has as, far as I am aware, been the only issue of dry vegetables, and *one* three-fourths ration of wkiskey partially distributed, the only issue of spirits in the same time. The amount of fresh meat furnished has also been limited.

"The following extracts from the reports of different regimental surgeons, will illustrate our present condition.

"'Not over one-third of our men have a change of under clothing, and not one-half have sufficient clothing to keep them warm while on duty; nearly or quite all are compelled to do their cooking in parts of old worn-out canteens.'—(Surgeon Spooner, 61st O. V. I.)

"'Diarrhœa prevails to an alarming extent and of a character not to be controlled, to any great extent, by medicines. About two-thirds of the whole command are more or less affected by it. The rations are scanty and ill-cooked, scarcely any vegetables being furnished.' (Report of Asst. Surgeon Matthews, 143d N. Y. V.)

"'For nearly a year no full rations of vegetables have been issued to the 141st N. Y. V. During this time vegetables have not been issued in one-tenth the quantities allowed by army regulations to men in the field. The men have lost their relish for hard-bread and bacon. Their blood is impoverished and symptoms of scorbutus appear. When they get sick, it is impossible to treat them with desirable success, from this cause.' (Report of Surgeon Blake, 141st N. Y. V.)

"'The prevailing disease is diarrhea and other affections of the alimentary canal, which can be traced directly to the insufficiency and irregularity of rations and cooking and particularly to having been without vegetables.' (Report of Surgeon Hubschman, 26th Wis. Volunteers.)

"'An unusually large number of our men are suffering from diarrhea, and of that character over which medicine seems to have but little control.

"'We can attribute this condition only, I think, to an impoverished condition of blood, caused by an improper and scanty diet.' (Report of Asst. Surgeon Hoag, 134th N. Y. V.)

"I would not have you think that this is owing to any lack of efficiency in the officers managing Quartermaster and Commissary departments, for I am convinced, that as far as those in this corps are concerned, no exertion has been spared and no trouble avoided to remedy it, but such are the facts, and I state them plainly, in order to explain the present sanitary condition of the corps, and to lay its claims fairly before the Sanitary Commission.

"The articles that are imperatively needed both as prophylactics, with the well, and remedies with the ill, are potatoes, onions, vinegar, soft-bread, dried and subacid fruits, fermented cabbage, pickles, soup, and spirits, in diet; and shoes and under-clothing of all kinds; in quantities sufficient to restore a normal functional action, and furnish healthy blood for several thousand men.

"Until this change is effected, the surgeen must continue to witness his most approved remedies fail, and all his cases one by one approach an inevitably fatal termination. It is the unanimous opinion of all the medical officers, that no symptoms of improvement are manifesting themselves, and that on the contrary, the hygienic condition of the corps is deteriorating day by day. We need help and we need it soon, and I cannot refrain from repeating my earnest solicitations to the Sanitary Commission through you, that early efforts be made to provide, at least to some extent, for these our urgent necessities. I am aware how many appeals for aid the Commission receives, but I am also aware how nobly it responds to them, and this it is that emboldens me to state our wants plainly, and perhaps with some importunity.

"I have the honor to remain, with great respect, your obedient servant,

"D. G. Brinton, Surgeon U. S. V.,
"Medical Director 11th Army Corps

"A. N. Read, Sanitary Commission,
"Nashville, Tennessee."

Scattered and wasted by the continued presence or transit of vast armies the entire region of the Tennessee and the Cumberland Rivers, as well as the regions southward from them, no longer supplies the means of healthful subsistence to the armed forces, nor even to the fixed population of these districts. All the able-bodied male population, even to the boys, appear to have gone into the ranks of the army. And now, with numbers vastly augmented, our forces are pressing onward to finish up the business for which they left their homes. But another year of toil is before them, and while some must inevitably fall in stern conflict with the enemy in battle. the Medical Officers and the Sanitary Commission see and prepare against perils more certain and more dreaded than rebel sabres and cannon. The latest intelligence from the great field in Tennessee, Northern Georgia, and Alabama, received just as this volume is going to press, reads as follows:

"U. S. SANITARY COMMISSION,
"CHATTANOOGA, February 24.

"DR. J. S. NEWBERRY:

"My Dear Sir,—I am able to report some progress in garden arrangements, but it is after great tribulation, for all efforts of officials, Medical Director, and others, failed. But to-night eight good men are encamped on the grounds selected for the garden, with twelve horses and harness, one wagon, ploughs, a tent and necessary fixtures for camp-keeping, and now the ploughs are to start in the morning surely. I have work which will keep me busy to-morrow, in receiving additional material and orders, and the next day I shall endeavor to go out through the lines with a wagon and guard, and procure half a dozen more ploughs, for the time is slipping away so fast that it is indispensable that a large force be put to work.

"The seed I have sent for will be needed as soon as it can be got through, and I hope that you will not be frightened at my large estimate, but send it all. I will see that it brings forth, some forty, some sixty, and some a hundred fold.

"I believe I wrote you in regard to that large vineyard. There are in it 14,400 bearing vines (Catawba), and our gardener says it can be made to yield about 130,000 pounds of grapes this year, if it is a fair bearing season. I told him that he must raise this year's and next year's crops this season, and I see by his talk he knows how to do it. Of course, it will spoil the vineyard for a couple of years, but the crop is needed now.

"I have had to make myself personally responsible to the Quartermaster for all the Government property turned over to us—horses, harness, wagons, tents, spades, shovels, axes, &c.—so you see that I am dipping in pretty freely."

* * * * * * * *

"M. C. READ."

"U. S. SANITARY COMMISSION,
"CHATTANOOGA, February 29, 1864.

"DR. J. S. NEWBERRY:

"Dear Sir,—Yours of the 25th was received to-day, and shall have as prompt attention as possible. * * *

* * * * * * *

"To-day it rained too much to plough. To-morrow, I think, if pleasant, we shall have nine ploughs running. I have twelve horses in the camp, and shall take out ten to-morrow. To obtain teams seems the great difficulty. General Thomas' Adjutant and Chief Quartermaster both said it was not possible to spare a single horse or mule for ploughing, and to avoid a failure, I have culled the best from the convalescent corralls, and as I work them with convalescent soldiers, everything corresponds.

"M. C. Read."

"U. S. Sanitary Commission,
"Knoxville, Tenn. March 1, 1864.

"Dr. J. S. Newberry, Sec'y West. Dep't:

"Dear Sir,—The bearer, Mr. Wm. M. Culbertson, who is in the employ of the Commission, I have sent to you for the purpose of procuring a supply of seeds and implements for a garden at this place. He is a practical gardener, and will be able to give you all the necessary information respecting our plans. We propose to have put under cultivation from 50 to 75 acres, and if it meets your approbation, to have him superintend it. I think it very important to have a garden at this place. All the potatoes, onions, and other vegetables we can raise here, will save a vast amount of transportation and expense.

"Enclosed I send you a request of the Medical Director, with the proper endorsements.

"I should have moved in this matter earlier had we not been in so unsettled a state in military affairs. Now that Longstreet has retired, and our army advanced, we can go on with the work without molestation.

"Mr. Culbertson will confer with you respecting some ploughs that are here belonging to parties in Louisville.

* * * * * * * *

"Vegetables and all eatables are very much needed here. You cannot send too many potatoes and onions, also krout. Good ale is much wanted in hospitals. We want all the socks you can send. The Government are wholly destitute of them. Should like some shoes, hats, and pants. It may soon be necessary to establish a post in front.

* * * * * * * *

"M. M. Seymour, M. D."

The soldier, the surgeons, and our best Generals, acknowledge that the Sanitary Commission is in earnest, and there is every reason to believe that there will be but little rest either to the Army of the Great Valley, or to the Sanitary officers in it, until the war is ended.

Sanitary Work on the Mississippi and Westward.—Immediately after the fall of Vicksburg and Port Hudson, General

Grant's forces were sent in various directions, both eastward and westward, but they were everywhere exposed to the malarious influences of the districts they traversed, as well as to occasional want of fresh vegetables in their subsistence stores. The sick and wounded were mostly ordered to Northern hospitals, yet there remained within the Department then commanded by General Grant, from 6,000 to 8,000 patients at the beginning of September. The "*Clara Bell*," the "*Dunleath*," and the "*Imperial*," were in service as "Sanitary steamers," conveying supplies from the Commission's dépôts at Louisville, Cairo, and Memphis, down the river. The Western Secretary, himself a veteran campaigner, anticipated the perils of malarious exposures to which the patients along the Mississippi, as well as the military forces there, were exposed, and sent forward timely shipments of quinine bitters, for prophylactic use under direction of the medical officers. By advice from General Grant, immediately after the capitulation of Port Hudson, the agent of the Commission sent down to General Banks' forces a cargo of fresh vegetables, &c., and when the expeditions were ordered up the Arkansas and the White Rivers, the military authorities provided a steam-transport for the Commission's "sanitary stores." Dr. Warriner, the Inspector, writing from Vicksburg, under date of September 9th, 1863, says:

"I have secured an order for a boat to take the place of the *Dunleith*. The boat is here and will be turned over to me in the morning. I wrote you, three days ago, the difficulties in the way of such an order growing out of the necessity of sending troops to reinforce General Steele. And the order has this proviso, that the boat shall be used, in the present emergency, for the transportation of troops up the river to some point not divulged. I shall, nevertheless, put aboard such stores as we can spare from this point and accompany the expedition. I have invited Mr. Plattenberg, agent of the Western Sanitary Commission, to add what he can and go with me. He accepts. Should the troops be disembarked this side of Helena, we shall run the boat at once up the White River. Otherwise we may go on to Memphis and complete a load there first. We shall not have much in quantity and but a small variety of stores to spare from here. This brings me to mention the stores that are exhausted here, and which form a great part of what we are accustomed to issue. They are in constant demand—many of them of first-rate importance, as follows:

"Farina, corn starch, canned milk, arrow root, canned fruits, liquors, spices, pickles, soda, butter, raspberry vinegar, pillow cases, socks, comforts, slippers and bed sacks.

"The quinine bitters, as I anticipated, was a great hit. I should deem it a capital investment to purchase as much more at once, and prepare in the same manner. Not a surgeon here was using the article as a prophylactic, and not one but highly appreciates its importance as such. The Government supply remains, and will continue, *inadequate*."

* * * * * * *

Sept. 12th:

"The expedition to Arkansas, including the Sanitary steamer *Clara Bell*, has just moved from here. Dr. Fithian arrived just in time to take charge of the stores and relieve me for more important work here. I put on the boat 24 barrels crackers, 22 barrels dried fruit, 10 barrels quinine bitters, 20 boxes concentrated beef, 5 boxes codfish, 1 box fans, 1 box coffee, 6 boxes lemon syrup, 5 caddies tea, 144 sheets, 375 pairs drawers, 500 shirts, 200 towels, 500 handkerchiefs, 3 kegs crushed sugar, 1 box pepper, 1,100 pillows, 36 quilts, 130 pads, and 235 pillow cases.

* * * * * * *

* * * "Dr. Fithian has full instructions to carry out the programme mentioned in my last respecting the movement of the boat. 'U. S. Sanitary Commission' is already nailed to the vessel.

"I shall proceed to set the Hospital Directory going here. Reports of disbursements for July and August are nearly finished Tone is sick again, and the other boys nearly so. So we go.

* * * * * * *

"Dr. Fithian brings a good report of affairs from Natchez. He also brings Hospital Directory report and report of disbursements there for August. The agency commenced operations there on the 6th." * * * * * * * *

Before the end of September, the Inspector who went with these stores for General Steele's expedition, wrote to the Commission:

"I am happy to report to you the successful and expeditious accomplishment of our trip up White River, to the Arkansas expedition under General Steele. We were not of the sunk, burned, or captured, as reported in newspapers. We left Memphis on the 17th, and returned yesterday. It was a trip of 800 miles, half of which was in the difficult and dangerous stream of White River. Our stores consisted of 153 barrels, 227 boxes, 3 kegs, in all 390 packages, being all that could be spared, and gathered on board at Vicksburg, Memphis and Helena. The troops and sick of the expedition are found to be at Helena, Duvall's Bluff and Little Rock."

* * * * * * * *

"I found that our advanced Sanitary supplies, taken from Helena by Dr. Casselberry, medical director, were well disbursed and appreciated. and that the lot of stores subsequently brought there from the Western Commission were opportune, yet but partially disbursed. The gunboats then had received no supplies, and many articles were still wanted in the General Hospital. Our stores on the *Clara Bell* supplied what was needed there and at Little Rock. We left on the morning of the 23d, safely reached Memphis on the 25th, and are now duly proceeding up the river to Cairo for another and full load of stores for the lower Mississippi, as instructed by Dr. Warriner.

"The Sanitary boat *Imperial* had left Memphis before we arrived, and passed the mouth of White River the night before we came out. She left no supplies at Memphis or Helena, and will discharge all her load, I suppose, at Vicksburg."

* * * * * * * *

At the end of the year 1863, another Agent reports:

* * * * * * * *

"The Sanitary steamer *Clara Bell* left Cairo on the evening of November 20th, with orders from Dr. Warriner to proceed to Vicksburg and Natchez, supplying intermediate points. and, if there still remained a stock sufficient to justify such a course, to go on to New Orleans.

"The cargo consisted of 939 barrels, 672 sacks, 215 boxes and 33 kegs, mostly vegetables and in very bad order; nearly one-half the packages being broken before finally stored.

"The boxes especially were many of them large and unwieldy. containing from six to twelve bushels of vegetables, and after the amount of rough handling to which they were necessarily subjected in the process of transportation from Chicago to some point on the Mississippi below Cairo, were generally shattered and broken.

"The practice of putting vegetables in old dry goods boxes, is always attended with considerable loss, to say nothing of inconvience in handling.

"At Memphis I left about one hundred and fifty packages, this being thought sufficient to last until more would be received from Cairo.

"The demand for sanitary stores at Memphis is slowly decreasing, one hospital (church) having been discontinued, another (Union) having received orders for breaking up, and four more (Webster, Washington, Jefferson and Officers') being expected soon to follow. There will still remain to be supplied four large general hospitals (Overton, Adams, Gayoso and Jackson), besides the post and regimental hospitals of the 16th Army Corps. The supply was very limited, and I regretted that I could only assist them in the matter of vegetables.

"At Helena I left thirty sacks of vegetables, Dr. Weeks, Medical Director thinking that quantity sufficient for present use.

"At Skipwith's landing and Milliken's Bend are several regiments of colored troops, but these places being in direct and regular communication with Vicksburg, from which point they were in the habit of drawing supplies, none were left there.

"At Vicksburg I found a large supply of vegetables. * * * * Mr. Benson was issuing onions to regiments for general use, at the rate of one bbl. to fifty men."

* * * * * * * *

"Between Natchez and New Orleans supplies were furnished to the gunboats *Osage*, *Chilicothe*, *Choctaw*, *Lafayette* and *Champion*. Receipts for the articles thus issued were left at Vicksburg, and will appear among the distributions of that dépôt.

"The remainder of the cargo (about 1,500 packages) was delivered to Dr. Blake in New Orleans. The vegetables were considered a Godsend, this being the first adequate supply he had received. Dr. Blake informs me that vegetables for the Department of the Gulf will have to be brought down the Mississippi, the loss in transporting them by sea being too great to justify that method of shipment. Other articles can be better supplied from the East. While the *Clara Bell* was in port, he received a large shipment from New York."

* * * * * * * *

Thus the work went on in that department during the beginning of winter, and, on the 17th of February, the Inspector at Memphis wrote to the Commission: "Our boat, the *Mississippi*, has just arrived here. She left Cairo at 7 P. M., yesterday." * * * * "Our shipment to Vicksburg will be most timely. Already over two thousand sick and wounded have accumulated there, and wounded are arriving all the while from the advance, skirmishes being of daily occurrence. At this place there are two thousand five hundred sick in hospitals. Our rooms are quite bare of bed-clothing. Bed-ticks, sheets, drawers, and pillows, are the only dry goods on hand. These are in fair abundance for the present. I leave some 150 packages, mostly barrels of vegetables. Vicksburg promises to become once more, for a season, a main base of supplies. I shall probably leave the larger part of my cargo there. The residue will go on to New Orleans. The demand for vegetables there is very pressing."

The people in the State of Maine had contributed large quantities of potatoes and other vegetables to the Commission, which were shipped by the cargo to New Orleans, but similar supplies that were sent down the Mississippi from the Western Department were most timely. At the same time the Chief Inspector of the Sanitary Commission, in General Banks' Department, having fitted up the steamer *Laurel Hill* as a Hospital Transport, to ply upon the Mississippi, was enabled to receive by that vessel return cargoes of "sanitary stores," from Cairo and the Northwest. Thus the labors and the "sanitary stores" of the Western Department, over which Dr. Newberry presides, harmoniously meet and commingle upon the lower Mississippi with those of the Eastern Department, over which Mr. Knapp presides. The work is one, the purpose one, and the results one, harmoneous and national. And these characteristics have become so apparent as to disarm and dispel the petty jealousies and the tendency to "State exclusiveness," that for a year or two had been seriously threatening to diminish the utility of the popular sympathies and spontaneous contributions of the people. State Agents, for relief of State troops, have found the National Sanitary Commission already disbursing equal and impartial aid and means of succor to the soldiers from every State, as Federal troops, and into the common dépôts and channels of this Commission, the several States and their special Agents now most gladly pour their gifts; and the special Commission that was organized at St. Louis, under General Fremont, while it has brought into the work of humane succor and sanitary aid vast resources and the long continued and energetic personal labors of such noble philanthropists as Mr. Yeatman and Rev. Mr. Eliot, has earnestly and often co-operated most opportunely with the Agents of the Central Commission. The loyal forces, and refugees in Kansas and Arkansas have not been overlooked a permanent agency of the Commission, under the care of Mr. Brown and Dr. Slocum being long established at Leavenworth, and, through Medical Officers and otherwise, the troops at Little Rock and along the Arkansas and White Rivers, "sanitary stores" from the Sanitary Commission are being continually received and disbursed.

The great central channel of our national commerce is again open to the use of the long line of States which before the rebellion proudly claimed it as the grand avenue of mutual wealth and a trusted material bond of Federal unity. Rescued from disloyal rule by military valor in battles that live in history, that great channel of the Mississippi will be guarded by forces that will never yield any portion of its course to insurgent obstruction, though for more than a thousand miles our most trusty troops must, for this purpose, continue to brave the perils of its malarious flanks of bayous and bottom lands. The Commission has thoughtfully foreseen this, and is now preparing for such sanitary service and aid as may be required. The

Medical Department and the Government at Washington are preparing for the better care of the Colored troops in that region, and the Commission has appointed a special Inspector to investigate and report the wants of that important class of the National forces in the Great Valley.

State of the Sanitary Commission's work in the Department of the Gulf.—The large cargo of "sanitary stores" that was sent forward with General Banks' expedition, was advantageously applied by the Commission's Agents, as our forces moved across the Teche, and subsequently against Port Hudson. A special dépôt of supplies having been established at Baton Rouge, a Field Relief Corps, with ample stores went forward with the forces that were sent into the Red River country, and the aid then rendered was most timely. One of the Sanitary Inspectors, who had been officially requested to aid in providing for the wounded who were to be sent to the rear, from the vicinity of Franklin, writes, under date of April 22d, 1863:

* * * * * * * *

"Orders having been given to the captain of the *Laurel Hill* to proceed with his boat up the Teche, and receive on board the wounded lying at Grover's division hospital. At the special request of Dr. Reed, the Medical Director of General Grover's division, I took charge of this boat, saw that two days' rations of beef, pork, tea, sugar, etc., for three hundred men were placed on board, and that the boat was prepared to receive the wounded. Having left Mr. Mitchell to go on with the army, I reached the hospital with the *Laurel Hill* about two o'clock in the afternoon, and immediately reported to Dr. Pease, of the 6th New York Regiment, the surgeon in charge. The work of placing the wounded on board was at once commenced, but the hospital was at some little distance from the river, and our corps of assistance small; we succeeded, hewever, after impressing into service a few negroes and mule teams, which we found on the plantation, in getting all our wounded comfortably on board the transports, by two o'clock the following evening; about one hundred of the wounded lay on the floor of the main saloon, as many more on the main deck, partially protected by the upper deck and some canvass awnings; most had either a blanket or an overcoat, many had both—many had neither. As the night was quite cool, there was probably more suffering from a want of clothing than from any other cause which it might have been possible for us to remedy.

"I saw that all were furnished with a supper of beef broth, made from beef which we had shot and dressed the same afternoon, and with which we were abundantly supplied. The boat started down the river about sunrise, when we all recommenced our labors adjusting, dressing and serving to all beef broth, tea and bread. Late in the morning we had a quantity of most excellent milk punch, made from the milk which I had brought on board, which was administered to those who needed it.

About one o'clock, P. M., we reached Brashier City, and within two hours fifteen cars were ready to receive the wounded, all of which, with the exception of about thirty of the severest cases, it was proposed to move to New Orleans. The work of transferring from boat to the cars was now commenced, and continued until about nine o'clock in evening. In the meantime I brought on board another supply of milk,, by means of which we were able to prepare a large quantity of very nice coffee, several canteens of which were given to each nurse to be issued on the way down. I also purchased all the soft bread which I could find in the town—seven or eight dollars' worth—had it cut into slices and buttered, and distributed it myself through the train before it started for New Orleans.

"Two facts are noteworthy in the whole of this expedition. First, the wounded had plenty to eat and drink. Second, there were no tedious and wearisome delays in our transportation. Indeed, I think I may say, with truth, that nowhere within the range of my experience have wounded men been transported so great a distance with less discomfort; and it affords me the greater pleasure to make this statement as I am representing what has occurred in the far Southwest, in a department so remote as to be almost beyond the reach of criticism, as well as inaccessible to that kindly succor which has so often come to the relief of the armies of Virginia and the West."*

---

* We find the following statement respecting the Commission's work in the Department of the Gulf, in a communication from a well known Surgeon, published in the Stamford (*Ct.*) *Advocate:*

* * * * * * * * * * * *

"My first acquaintance with the Sanitary Commission came through a small pamphlet, sent me by its agent, soon after our arrival at Camp Parapet. Following up the invitation contained in it, I made the acquaintance of its agent, and

With the army investing Port Hudson the Sanitary Commission had sent up such means of supplementary relief as it was able at the time to command, but there began to be experienced a great want of fresh vegetables, and at the time the enemy capitulated, the most important sanitary aid that could be rendered was the supplying of that want; and this, as we have

---

found that through him I could obtain, without circumlocution, the essentials for the housekeeping department of a military hospital, whether in active campaign, or guard duty, or the more settled condition af post, or city hospital, and whether the patients were suffering from disease incident to the locality in which they were situated, or from wounds received in battle. And, Mr. Editor, I wish to bear testimony to the fact that, in all these various conditions, the Sanitary Commission furnishes to the suffering soldier just that kind of delicacy or substantial which a judicious mother or wife would furnish if they had opportunity. I have seen empty old buildings, as by magic, assume in a day the air of comfort and order of arrangement of long-established city hospitals. Not soon shall I cease to warm over the recollection of some of these transformations. For example, men to the number of several hundreds, after the fight at Bisland, were brought to Berwick City in flat-boats, skiffs, and little steamers, wounded in every conceivable manner. They had received all the attention that good medical skill could afford amid the din and smoke of actual conflict, but were so dirty, black, and uncomfortable, as not to be recognized by their most intimate friends, until the renovating hands of tender nurses had washed away their blood and dust, and put on them and their beds clean clothes; all which, not excepting a piece of soap or a row of pins, were furnished by the *model department* of the Gulf, and the Sanitary Commission, sent thence eighty miles over a slow railroad, but in time to do all I have intimated. And I must say, that he who had looked, on the morning of April 18, at the interior of that deserted building in Berwick City, store below and tenements above, its large and small rooms, dusty, cobwebbed, gloomy, and also at the large hall of an adjoining building in the same condition, making in all a floor area of about 1,500 yards, had seen on the following morning every available yard of this space covered with wounded men, *our country's braves*, suffering anguish such as a wounded soldier only knows, without the shadow of comfort; on the same evening again seen all these sufferers arranged in trim rows, on iron bedsteads and good mattresses, clean wounds, clean bandages, clean lint, dressings, &c., clean shirts, clean drawers, clean sheets and pillow-cases, clean wards, with towels, and bowls, and brushes, and rows of pins in their places, tables supplied with vases of flowers, pitchers of ice-water, tumblers, bowls, vials, packages, all in their places, and the poor sufferers sleeping quietly under their musquito nets, all order, all cleanliness, all beautiful, at Post Hospital No. 2. Anybody, I say, that saw, as I saw, all this, and was not moved with deep gratitude towards the institution that furnished the means for all this magic change, is a character for a cage in a menagerie. The Post Hospital, No. 2, is but an illustration of Nos. 1, 3, 4, at Berwick City, at the same time, also at Brashear City at different times; also at Lafourche Crossing. In short, it but illustrates what may be at every hospital, extemporized or appointed, in the field or in the city, all over the Department of the Gulf, as no doubt is the case in every department; and if all or any of this is wanting in any case, it is due to negligence on the part of officers in charge of hospitals, not to want of means furnished by Medical Department and Sanitary Commission.

* * * * * * * * *

"W. H. Trowbridge,
"Ex Surgeon, 23d Regt. C. V."

already noticed, was being done through the thoughtful co-operation of Dr. Newberry, the Western Secretary, and at the earnest suggestion of General Grant. At the same time the Commission was sending forward to New Orleans, from New York and Boston, large invoices of anti-scorbutic supplies, and it may justly be inferred that the excellent results of surgical and hospital treatment generally in General Banks' command, and the remarkably small sickness-rate of his forces have not been uninfluenced by the co-operation of the Sanitary Commission with the intelligent Medical Officers of the Department.

During the autumn and winter, the Commission has shipped immense quantities of potatoes, onions, cabbage, and other anti-scorbutic supplies to its dépôts in that Department. At the same time, all the Commission's methods of Special Relief have been put into successful operation at New Orleans,* and at other points in the Department, Lodges and Supply Dépôts have been established. A remarkably high state of health has for many months prevailed among all the forces of the Department. At the close of the year Dr. E. A. Crane, one of the Commission's Inspectors, reported from New Iberia, La., as follows: "The sanitary condition of the army is remarkable. I have never seen in any of our armies so little disease. But little over *four per cent.* (4.3) of the present force is on sick list. Only 5.4 per cent. have been

---

* The following notice is to be seen in all parts of New Orleans, and in the hospitals and places of military rendezvous in the Department of the Gulf:

DISCHARGED SOLDIERS

Can obtain all needed ASSISTANCE and INFORMATION in regard to their *Papers, Claims for Arrears of Pay, Bounty, and Pension,* without charge, at the Special Relief Office of the United States Sanitary Commission,
No. 96 JULIA STREET,
between Camp and Magazine Streets.

O. C. BULLARD,
Special Relief Agent.

New Orleans, La., Nov. 20th, 1863.

reported sick, including those sent to General Hospital since Oct. 1st. The highest rate obtains in the cavalry division, as most of the picketing now falls upon it. One division of the army reports only 1.4 *per cent. sick.*"

The Inspector attributes this remarkable freedom from sickness to "light duties, *fair rations, including sweet potatoes, and an abundance of fresh meat, and a healthy climate.*"

The work of the Relief Agents in that Department is occasionally varied by opportunities for rendering aid to returning prisoners, as in the following instance, which was recently reported by Mr. J. Stevens, Jr., in the Téche and Red River districts:

"I have given out the larger portion of my stock, and am now packed up ready to leave for Franklin to-morrow, if possible. I have determined to make this move after consultation with those who know best here. There will be no need of me for a few days at least, and I can easily return if necessary. Nearly all the sick have already been sent from the General Hospital. When the vegetables and pickles arrive I wish you would advise me, for they are needed here, although there is plenty of fresh meat.

"On Christmas, at the invitation of Dr. Sanger and Col. Molyneux, I went out with a flag of truce for the exchange of prisoners, taking supplies for the sick. An ambulance for chests and a horse was placed at my disposal. There was quite a large party of officers, making it very agreeable. We took out some two hundred and fifty rebels, and received seven hundred of our own men. They were a most forlorn looking set of men. Covered with rags and dirt; many of them foot-sore and worn out by the long march, hardly one with a whole pair of shoes, they had not even their nakedness covered. I had punch, coffee, and beef stock made for the sick, who took it greedily, and seemed refreshed. The rebel officers thought the Sanitary Commission was 'quite an institution;' said they had heard of it before."

Sanitary watchfulness and work in the Department of the Gulf, will continne to be of the utmost importance until the end of the war. In that climate—especially in camp life—*the price of health is eternal vigilance!* And the fact should here be stated that the unceasing thoughtfulness and official attention of the successive Military Commanders in that Department, respecting all matters affecting the health of New Orleans and of the military posts of that region, are to be mentioned as among the most essential causes of the high state of health in the large towns and the military commands of the Department.

Sanitary Work in North Carolina.—Malaria and scurvy have continued to be the chief sources of peril to the Federal troops along the coast of North Carolina, and the Sanitary Commission has always instructed its Inspectors to render all necessary aid in providing the great prophylactic or preventive means against the prevalence of those important causes of sickness. This preventive work has been of priceless value to the soldier. The same is true of vaccination, which, as in almost every other division of the army, has been continually urged and practically aided by the Sanitary Inspectors. Particularly has this been important wherever colored troops are recruited, for, as a general fact, they come into the ranks unvaccinated. The various hospitals of our forces in that district have continually received such aid as occasion required, and whenever the troops are in active service, the Commission's Agents go with them and render such service as they can.

Dr. Page, who is the Commission's Inspector in that district, is a gentleman of great intelligence, and was for several years a resident at Newberne. He has urged the necessity of making adequate preparations for the protection of the troops against scurvy, which from time to time manifests itself among them. Potatoes, onions, and the cruciferous vegetables are now being largely cultivated under his direction and advice, seeds and implements having been furnished by the Commission. He writes in March:

* * * * * * * *

"By the interest of General Peck, we have secured the disposal of fifty acres of good land, of proper exposure; some of the coarser implements, such as ploughs, hoes, &c.. have been obtained from the service. Any amount of manure is at hand, and the transportation furnished; and the labor is secured partly by volunteers from the soldiery, and partly from detailed contrabands. An intelligent Lieutenant of the 19th Wisconsin has charge of the practical working of the farm, and there is much of emulation and intelligent zeal among the volunteer yoemen-soldiers engaged. It will teach them a lesson of the yield of this soil, and of its capabilities under our warm sun and long season, which will surprise and delight them.

"I am encouraging, in every way, the disposition of our hospital surgeons, stewards, and others to establish gardens, large and small, My own little *patch* of last year and this winter seems to act as a strong stimulant. The movement will be a God-send, literally, to our troops."

* * * * * * * *

At an earlier date, Dr. Parrish, who visited the district, reports:

* * * * * * * *

"The district allotted to the doctor covers a wide range, embracing in all sixteen general and post hospitals, including a convalescent camp. To all of these stores have been supplied upon the requisitions of the surgeons, and I am happy to know that the most cordial relations exist between the surgeons and the Commission, and that they co operate most earnestly to promote the well-being of our troops. During my visit it was my privilege to accompany Dr. Samuel McCormick, the Medical Director of the Department, whose inquiries into the condition of the hospitals were through and accurate. It was equally pleasing to notice the readiness with which the Medical Director of the post and his associates not only responded to the investigations of their superior officers, but were anxious to make a full exhibit of all the affairs intrusted to them. Dr. Page accompanied the Medical Corps, and the occasion presented a cheering evidence of the unity and fellowship existing between the surgeons and the Commission, and their joint efforts to aid each other in the great work of promoting the comfort of our soldiers.

"The Stanley Hospital, at Newbern, the Mansfield, at Morehead City, and the Hammond, at Beaufort, are the chief in size and importance. The two first are erected on the pavilion plan;

and are well ordered in all respects. Dr. DeCormick directed the use of china table furniture where tin was used, because of its wholesome moral influence upon the troops. It is more home-like, and promotes the reflection that the Government is careful for the comfort and well-being of its defenders.

"During the seige at Washington, N. C., the agents of the Commission were on hand with their varied stores, and their usefulness is a matter of record. All the hospital transports were well supplied with the means for 'aid and comfort' from the dépôt at Newbern. About forty regiments have been under inspection, and I judge, from an examination of many of their camps, that they are well policed in most regards. I was particularly impressed with the substantial and comfortable appearance of many of the camps. Log houses, with *glazed windows* and open fire-places, are common. The regimental hospitals are generally comfortable and well supplied.

"In the marshy district between Newbern and Morehead City, and on the line of the railroad between these two places, there are several encampments, in which there has been much sickness. At Newport barracks, especially, the men have suffered from intermittent fevers. It is unsafe to allow the same troops to remain long at a time at this point. *The quinine ration has been used freely, and in some localities with marked advantage.* If company officers were held to strict account as to the care of their men, and were required to inspect each one daily, with reference to under-clothing especially, cleanliness, the use of prescribed prophylactic means, the temperature and ventilation of quarters, &c., I am satisfied much sickness would be prevented. It is not unfrequently remarked that some companies in the same camp are more sickly than others, and the difference is doubtless owing to the difference in the attention and care given to the men by their officers.

"The prisoners of war, confined by rebel authorities, have also been the recipients of aid from our agents in this department; and the cases of individual relief afforded refugees and to soldiers needing transportation, &c., are not a few. Mr. Geo. B. Page acts as the relief agent, and is an earnest worker in the cause."

From these statements it is manifest that although attracting but little public notice, the Sanitary Commission's work in North Carolina is too important to be overlooked.

The Sanitary Commission in the Department of the South.— The statistics of the sickness and mortality in General Gilmore's army present conclusive evidence that at the date of the occupation of Jacksonville, and the battle of Olustee, the sickness-rate of the forces in that Department had become reduced to a minimum almost unprecedented in the history of armies in any latitude. Yet at that period it appears that the Sanitary Commission's *preventive* methods of labor there were continued in full activity, and, as we shall presently have occasion to notice, the means of battle-field relief were in perfect readiness for every exigency. The present Sanitary Inspecter and Superintendent of the Commission's work in that department, Dr. M. M. Marsh, had at that period, just completed his first year of service there. The following extracts from his annual report will satisfactorily present the record of Sanitary work accomplished. Better results could not be desired by the Sanitary Commission and the people:

Dr. Marsh commenced his labors in the Department in the month of February, 1863. At that time the forces then under General Hunter were stationed at eleven different localities, and extended a distance of 250 miles along the coast. He says:

"The larger portion of this command, mostly from New England and New York, had been here from the occupancy of these islands in November, 1861. They were innured to toil, obedient to discipline, observant of sanitary laws, in person and quarters, and were an efficient contented body of men. By the side of these were regiments from the —— army corps, who were discontented, and occasionally accused of a tendency to insubordination, neglectful of conditions essential to health. Among these there was a much greater percentage of sickness than in other portions of the army similarly situated. The first business of the Inspector was to advise officers and privates of the necessity of strictor compliance with sanitary laws, to secure an increased standard of health. And with this compliance came not health, simply, but a marked improvement in efficiency and discipline. This fact was subsequently acknowledged by those in command. We are justified in ascribing the approved *morale* to attention to sanitary rules, hitherto neglected, by the fact that in this —— corps were regiments subjected to all the conditions of locality, &c., which produced in contiguous regiments a disorderly spirit, but which were efficient, contented, and happy; and that these were the regiments most remarkable for personal neatness, and for the cleanliness of their camps and quarters. Your Inspector believes that not the least of the benefits in this war rendered to officers by the Sanitary Commission, has been its indirect influence in promoting discipline by increased attention to sanitary precautions, among the men of their respective commands.

"Among the first efforts to mitigate suffering in this department, was the attempt to alleviate the condition of the soldier going North, discharged from the service in consequence of sickness. Up to this time, the man who had served his country faultlessly, and sickened in her service, was discharged; and without any provision for his enfeebled condition, in clothing or care, was shipped upon any Government transport, as a thing no longer useful. The consequences can be readily seen—much suffering and many deaths in transit. The Inspector immediately supplied all that could contribute to the personal comfort of these unfortunate men; and, in some instances, sent attendants to minister to their wants upon the voyage. This, however, could not meet the exigency entirely. Upon these transports was no accommodations, nor proper medical care. After consultation by your Inspector with members of the Commission, and subsequently with Gen. Hunter, the *Cosmopolitan*, a spacious steamer, with capacity for three hundred and twenty-five beds, was set apart by the General as a hospital ship, for the purpose of conveying the sick or wounded to their destination, and consigned to the Medical Director of the Department.

"The Commission immediately issued to this steamer two hundred and fifty beds, and other requisites; and has since continued to contribute supplies. This provision has been crowned with success; and under the able management of the surgeons assigned it by the Medical Director, many lives have been saved that must by ordinary modes of transportation have been sacrificed.

"The last two weeks in March, and first two in April, were devoted to preparation for the first Charleston expedition. Abundant preparations were made by us for any exigency; but happily no casualty occurred, nor was there any call upon our stores.

"A schooner of ample dimensions had been assigned us by General Hunter, giving, as was his wont, timely notice for preparation. And here it is but simple justice to this officer to remark, that there has been no reticence in his communications to the Commission of whatever would contribute to an early preparation for any emergency. Immediately after this unsuccessful movement, preliminary steps were taken towards a repetition of the advance upon Charleston, by way of Morris Island, &c. General Gilmore has since secured Morris Island as the base for further advances.

"The months of May and June were devoted by your Inspector and his assistant to the wants of the troops conducting offensive operations against Morris Island, and of those stationed at Hilton Head, Beaufort, Fernandina, and other posts in the Department.

"Very early in July active operations commenced on Folly Island. A large brig (and a tow) had been assigned us by the General commanding to transfer all necessary stores. On the 8th and 9th we took in cargo from the dépôt at Beaufort; on the 9th left Port Royal harbor; and early on the morning of the 10th, in the waters of Stono, threw out to the breeze, from the mast-head, the flag of the Sanitary Commission. The successful assault was made on that morning, with trifling loss on our part. The circumstances connected with it have been already communicated, and I will not repeat them. It is proper, however, to remark, in this connection, that the *Cosmopolitan*, which was returning from a trip north with disabled men, was at 8 A. M. passing off Stono, and noticing what was transpiring, ran to Hilton Head, fifty-two miles distant, reported, and returned to the scene of operations before 4 P. M.; thus making one hundred and four miles in less than eight hours. I mention this to show the zeal of the Medical Department in the discharge of its obligations. And if at any point in this article I speak of seeming deficiencies in that department, I wish it distinctly understood that these arose from circumstances beyond control, and not from any lack of sympathy, activity, or intelligence on the part of the medical staff.

"If the history of this war is ever properly written, its brightest page will be that which recounts (imperfectly even) the untiring assiduity and self-denial of the Medical Staff in the discharge of its immense responsibilities.

"Dr. Crane, Medical Director, and Dr. Dibble, Chief Medical Officer of the island, with ambulances, immediately proceeded to the upper end of the island, where, early in the day, hospitals had been improvised for the wounded, principally Confederates, few of our men having suffered. These wounded were consigned to your Inspector, who transferred them to the *Cosmopolitan*, in charge of Dr. Bontacue, for which position there are few so well qualified by professional ability and energy.

"The wounded, comfortably placed in berths, were the same night removed to Hilton Head; and the next morning at eight o'clock, the *Cosmopolitan* entered the harbor. During the morning it was ascertained that the boat could ascend Folly River, on the opposite side of the island, within a half mile of the hospitals. At 11 A. M. the boat was anchored there At 12 M., of the same day, (July 11), an unsuccessful assault, in which we lost one hundred and thirty-one men, was made upon Fort Wagner, to which the enemy had retired the morning previous. These wounded were first cared for at the hospitals, and thence transferred to the boat. And here I ought to pay a tribute to the untiring energy and tact of Messrs· Hoadley and Day, of the Commission, who, with their assistants, met the necessities of every wounded man on the preceding, on this, and on subsequent days; administering to their wants in the temporary hospitals, supplying clothing, accompanying the ambulances to the boat, furnishing extra clothing and stores upon it, if needed, on its passage to the general hospitals at the Head and Beaufort; cheerful under exhausting labors, and inspiring the sufferer with hope. From the 11th to the 18th the willing strength of the whole command was taxed continuously in preparation for the coming assault. Every particle of transportation was necessarily devoted to the munitions of war, which accounts, in part, for any deficiencies that may have been experienced in the medical and commissariat departments. In this interim the Commission added in large quantities to the stores it already had on Morris Island; conveyed thither by a circuitous route, not less than seven miles, in rowboats, furnished, and in part manned, by the obliging quartermaster, Captain Dunton. The men detailed for this unusual and somewhat hazardous employment (the enemy holding one bank of the stream), worked night and day with a will; and many a poor fellow who subsequently received the benefit of the supplies of the Commission, may thank these soldiers for the sole and laborious method by which these abundant supplies were placed within available distance. On the evening of the 15th our tents were arranged and flag floating. After consulting Brig. General Seymour, commanding the advanced force, it was resolved to supply every man in the front, and ultimately all who should participate in the assault, with tea, Boston crackers, and concentrated beef for soup. This provision was absolutely essential, from circumstances already given; and many a poor fellow, on the night of the 18th, fought with great bravery, aided by the encouragement and strength afforded by this food, continuously bestowed by the Commission for nearly seventy-two hours previous.

"The manner of the attack, (on Saturday night, the 18th July), incidents connected with it, disposition of the respective forces, numbers, &c., being purely military matters, I shall pass over. The participation of your employees in the scenes which transpired I will briefly describe.

"On the afternoon of the 18th each individual attached to the Commission had his work assigned, and the means with which to accomplish it put within his reach; and greater praise cannot be given than the statement of the simple truth, that the next morning witnessed that each man (with one or two exceptions, and for a few moments only, and in circumstances of great peril) had faithfully discharged the duty appointed him.

"The Sanitary corps were distributed as follows: A portion to act as auxiliary to the medical force in the front and in the hospitals; another to assist the wounded at the hospital, and conduct them thence to the boats, (two besides the *Cosmopolitan* had been secured), which were to convey them to the general hospitals at Beaufort; and a third to render any additional assistance which might become necessary in their transit. This terrible repulse illustrated the benefits and defined the position of the Sanitary Commission. For on this fatal night, to the extent of my knowledge, not a blanket nor change of apparel, nor bedsack nor pillow, to save torn limbs or fractured heads from the crowded decks, but was furnished by the Commission. As previous to the assault the Commission fed, so now it supplied whatever could mitigate the sufferings of the unfortunate soldier. Abundant changes of clothing were placed upon each boat, to use if necessary during the voyage. In anticipation of casualties, the Commission, previous to the expedition, had supplied the five hospitals in Beaufort to the extent of their capacity. On the arrival of the wounded six more hospitals were opened, and fully furnished from our stores.

"We will pass over the interim of ten days on the field. Nature, meanwhile, is not forgetful of her dues. For weeks previous to the assault, in the enthusiasm of toil and confidence of triumph, she had given the soldier credit for her expenditures; but now in the despondency which ever follows defeat, the exhaustion of vital force, the scantily furnished and unsuitable diet, with depressing climate and continuous labor, she prosecutes her claim. Decisive evidence of a tendency to scurvy becomes quite general throughout the command. And although inspired by the unwavering hope of ultimately reducing Charleston, the vital forces were compelled to succumb, and soon, in many instances, one half the regiment answered to the sick call. Here again the untrammeled capacity of the Commission for immediate action demonstrated its utility. Your inspector made at once immense requisitions on the Commission, which were honored with a liberality that will forever endear them to these suffering patriots. The abundance of fresh vegetables and acid fruits which they furnished, soon produced a decided and happy change. And here it may be remarked that the ordinary diarrhœas and even dysentery of this region are most successfully treated by the exhibition of acids. Pickles, onions, vinegar, lime juice, the mineral acids, particularly nitric, and the 'Liquor

Ferri Nitratis,' proved the most certain remedies. At this point was introduced a new feature by the agents of the Commission in this department, and ultimately sanctioned by their superiors. This was to supply with vegetables not only the sick and wounded, but all on duty; which seemed the only way to check the prevailing malady. The malady was thus not only checked, but eradicated; for at the present time not one well-marked case of scurvy—the scourge of crowded, ill-nourished troops—is reported in the entire command. The appreciation of this act of the Commission in furnishing these absolutely essential supplies, cannot be better illustrated than by the congratulatory order of the Major-General Commanding, which was read at the head of every regiment throughout the department; unless, indeed, the voluntary honor paid the flag of the Commission by the passing salute of various regiments be so considered.

"Another feature peculiar to this department has been a liberal supply of ice, furnished by the Commission to all privates in the command. The frozen streams of Maine have been made to cool, not only the burning lips of fever, but to assuage the thirst of exhausting toil in South Carolina. It is believed a far greater amount of labor and a higher standard of health have been secured by these daily issues of ice to every soldier.

"There are two points in connection with this campaign that deserve special notice. One the constant and still continued aid rendered your employees by the military authorities. Not a wish could be suggested but it was complied with, and not unfrequently requests were anticipated. Fines and goods confiscated for infraction of laws of trade have been turned over to the Commission for distribution to the soldier. And especially has the nurturing care of the head of the department Maj.-Gen. Q. A. Gilmore, been extended to the Commission.

"The other point to which I would call attention is, the fraternal welcome and assistance in the discharge of duty extended by the entire medical corps in the department. Their systematic aid has rendered unnecessary the employment of numerous agents, lightened the personal labors of your inspector, and conferred upon him obligations that he will ever remember. And here it is proper to state that the devotion of many of these medical men to their regiments has awakened everlasting gratitude in the hearts of the recipients, and called forth the admiration of every beholder. Though not so directly exposed to the bullets of the enemy, yet to a danger even greater, by constant contact with disease, no class of men in the army deserves so well of their country as the regimental surgeons.

"The enthusiasm that fired the soldier in the earlier period of the siege may have somewhat abated, but his determination to do remains unchanged. Many instances of chivalrous daring could be given. but these belong to military history, The health of the command is good; the total of sickness and casualities at present not exceeding 6¾ per cent.

"The amount of expenditures during the first eight weeks of the siege was exceedingly liberal, and has secured for the Commission a character for acute discernment and active sympathy with the suffering soldier that will ever be remembered by the army in this department."*

---

* Receipts and Issues in the Department of South Carolina for the Current Year, 1863.

		Received.	*Issued.*	*In Store.*
Cotton shirts		4,900	4,544	356
Woolen "		5,758	3,534	2,224
Cotton drawers		3,163	3,013	150
Cotton flannel drawers		568	406	162
Woolen "		2,676	1,552	1,124
Cotton soaks		2,107	1,890	217
Woolen "		3,532	1,271	2,261
Slippers		2,736	2,499	237
Wrappers		1,089	789	300
Handkerchiefs		9,154	6,814	2,340
Outside clothing	boxes	6	5	1
Bed-sacks		1,472	1,350	122
Pillow ticks		1,888	1,517	371
Pillows		1,263	1,118	145
Pillow cases		3,206	2,396	610
Sheets		2,859	2,531	328
Blankets		701	435	266
Quilts		712	682	30
Towels		9,776	7,106	2,670
Cushions		2,213	2,023	190
Lint	bbls.	39	32	7
Bandages	"	34	31	3
Old cotton		112	91	21
Groceries, miscellaneous	lbs.	104	104	..
Beef stock	"	3,629	2,885	744
Dried fruit	bbls.	70	63	7
" apples	"	87	82	5
Green "	"	209	209	..
Ale	"	5	5	..
Crackers	"	392	330½	61½
Sugar, white	"	34½	32½	2
Vinegar	"	36	30	6
Cabbage in currie	"	255	253	2
Onions	"	219	217	2
Pickles	"	119	107	2
Jellies and preserves	boxes	65	63	2
Domestic wines	"	70	63	7
Foreign "	botts.	619	583	36
Brandy	"	612	545	70
Whiskey	"	638	566	72
Berry, Cordial	"	582	526	56
" Shrub	"	324	300	24
Cherry brandy	"	484	472	12
Blackberry "	"	184	184	..

Probably there could not be found in the history of armies a better example of the utility of sanitary works and the ap-

		Received.	*Issued.*	*In Store.*
Lemons	boxes	40	40	..
Conct. Lemon	"	6	6	..
Cider	cases	16	15	1
Syrups	boxes	4	3	1
Ext. Ginger		15	13	2
" "	bbls.	2	2	..
Arrow Root	lbs.	225	182	43
Apple Butter	galls.	60	57	3
Beef-stock	lbs.	3,629	2,885	744
Butter	"	375	355	20
Broma	"	216	192	24
Candles	"	108	81	27
Cheese	"	135	115	20
Cocoa	"	400	359	41
Chocolate	"	1,400	920	480
Coffee	"	1,452	1,071	381
Conds. Milk	"	4,002	3,170	833
Corn Starch	"	2,150	1,366	784
Tapioca	"	100	100	..
Farina	"	2,300	1,436	864
Ext. Ginger	boxes	15	13	2
" "	bbls.	2	2	..
Cider	cases	16	15	1
Gelatine	boxes	10	8	2
Nutmegs	lbs.	2	2	..
Oat Meal	"	150	150	..
Tea	"	560	510	50
Tomatoes	boxes	107	101	6
" fresh	bushels	50	50	..
Fish, preserved	lbs.	5,000	5,000	..
Mustard	"	25	22	3
Tamarinds	bbls.	10	10	..
Lemons	boxes	40	40	..
" Concent.	"	6	6	..
Oranges	bbls.	70	70	..
Hospital utensils	doz.	12	12	..
Alcohol	galls.	10	7	3
Bay Rum and Cologne	botts.	200	180	20
Fans		2,000	2,000	..
Combs	gross	10	6	4
Lanterns		26	22	4
Sponges	lbs.	8	5	3
Tin Cups		1,705	1,693	12
" Pans or basins		804	792	12
" Plates		925	920	5
" Spoons		1,000	978	22
Flannel bandages		2,236	1,911	325
Lime and Disf. Agents	bbls.	8	4	4
Pipes	box.	1	1	..
Tobacco, papers	doz.	205	205	..
Reading matter	boxes	6	6	..
Ice	tons	390	300	90

plication of the plainest principles of hygiene, than has been presented in General Gilmore's army these many months past. A large army of volunteer troops, occupying the marshy islets in front of Charleston and southward along that malarious coast, after maintaining continued and laborious seige operations and keeping up an unremitting line of pickets, and guarded defences upon that perilous coast from Morris Island and Beaufort to St. Augustine, instead of being annihilated or even weakened by the peculiar insalubrity of climate and the exposures of camp-life in that region, at the end of a year's service is reported to be suffering a percentage of sickness not greater than the same classes of men usually suffer while pursuing their ordinary avocations in civil life. And that this result is largely owing to the unceasing vigilance and faithful service of Sanitary and Medical officers, those who are best informed entertain no doubt.

The energy and constant watchfulness that have characterized the management of the Commission's work, have won the confidence and admiration of military officers of every rank,* while

---

		Received.	*Issued.*	*In Store.*
Quinine	ozs.	62	29	33
Morphine	"	3	319	52
Chloroforom	lbs.	25	22	3
Tannin	ozs.	6	6	..
Liq. Ferri Nitratis	lbs.	55	44	11
Mosquito Netting	pieces	60	60	..
Eggs	doz.	79	79	..
" Nog	boxes	2	2	..
Oil Silk		70	36	34
Rubber Cloth		68	35	28
Miscellaneous	boxes	70	69	1
Hops	barrels	2	1	1
Fresh garden vegetables		15	15	..
Potatoes		354	354	..

["*Sanitary Commission Bulletin,*" No. 8.]

* The following General Order which was issued by the General in command of the Department, shows how sanitary work is regarded by that distinguished officer:

"DEP'T OF THE SOUTH, HEADQ'RS IN THE FIELD,
"MORRIS ISLAND, S. C., Sept. 9.

"*General Orders, No.* 73.

"The Brigadier-General commanding desires to make this public acknowledgment of the benefits for which his command has been indebted to the United States

the soldiers in the camps and trenches, as well as in the hospitals, express their gratitude by voluntary offerings to the Sanitary Treasury. They keep in grateful remembrance the watchful care that brought ice and wholesome beverages to them when sweltering and fainting on Morris Island, in the approaches to Fort Wagner, and in the planting of their morter batteries against Sumpter and Charleston, and they never forget the thoughtfulness and heroism that were displayed by the Sanitary Relief Corps in the trenches and moat before Fort Wagner, on the 18th of July;* nor can the sick be unmindful of the aid which the hospitals have been continually receiving

---

Sanitary Commission, and to express his thanks to the gentlemen whose humane efforts in procuring and distributing much needed articles of comfort have so materially alleviated the sufferings of the soldiers.

"Especial gratitude is due to Dr. M. M. Marsh, Medical Inspector of the Commission, through whose efficiency, energy, and zeal, the wants of the troops have been promptly ascertained, and the resources of the Commission made available for every portion of the army.

"By order of,

"Brig.-Gen. Q. A. GILLMORE.

"ED. W. SMITH, A. A. G."

* A writer in the *North American Review*, in illustrating the Sanitary Commission's methods of *Preventive* and *Relief* work, makes the following allusion to the *battle-relief* at Fort Wagner:

* * * * * "The reader cannot fail to notice that, in a great variety of labors upon which the Commission has entered, these two grand divisions of its work and purposes are necessarily and happily conjoined and co-ordinate. It would be difficult to say whether the one or the other element, in this theoretical division of the work, predominates in such labors as we have been describing. And when, for nearly seventy-two hours previous to the terrific assault upon Fort Wagner, upon the night of July 18th, the Commission's Inspector, Dr. Marsh, with the cordial approval of the leader of the assault, held his brave detail of aids unflinchingly to the duty of supplying the storming party in front with nourishing food and beverages until they reached the fatal moat, and then himself led his heroic helpers in the humane and perilous work of rescuing the wounded, and at the same time supplying almost all the means of succor and comfort which those mangled soldiers received until they were brought to the general hospitals, sixty miles away, that succor and *relief* was the best, the only, *sanative* care those brave men could receive. By such beautiful illustrations, which have continually marked the war-work of our army, often upon a grand scale, yet ever regarding the individual wants of the sufferers as well as the general results to be reached, has the Sanitary Commission's first postulate been proved both true and practicable,—namely, that 'this war ought to be waged in the spirit of highest intelligence, humanity, and tenderness for the health, comfort, and safety of our brave troops.'" —*North American Review, April,* 1864.

in the line of special comforts and home-like delicacies, together with an abundance of fresh supplies for each hospital by every steamer from New York.*

While the reader cannot fail to notice the vast quantities in which certain articles were supplied to the troops before Charleston during the summer and autumn,—for example, ice to the amount of 390 tons, cabbage in currie [a very nicely prepared anti-scorbutic] to the amount of 255 barrels, &c., &c.,—it should be remembered that the example and influenee of the Sanitary Commission, while furnishing such special sanitary supplies were even more important than the supplies themselves, for the Sanitary Inspector made it an object of chief concern to advise and aid the proper authorities to procure and regularly furnish all the staple articles for an anti-scorbutic diet, and also to improve by every possible means the essential conditions of personal and camp hygiene.

Just previous to the movement of General Seymour upon Olustee, in Florida, Dr. Marsh reported that a "critical reinspection of most of the troops (in the vicinity of Charleston) has been made within the last four weeks, their wants ascertained and supplied, and their sanitary condition closely scrutinized. *The percentage of sickness in the force is very low.* It would not be proper to state here how low. Almost the only malady is chronic diarrhœa."

He also states that he "has endeavored, by a free issue of vegetables, to supplement the Government rations, and thus diminish the tendency to diseases arising from a want of variety in the food of the men." And while thus engaged near Charleston, the Inspector was also ordering "sanitary stores" forward to Jacksonville, Fla., so that the first men who sickened or were

---

* These fresh supplies for the extra diet of the hospitals, were requested by the Medical Director, and are not included in the list given on pages 237 and 238.

wounded after the occupation of that place, received all needed aid. Then came the sudden order from General Seymour to move forward some fifty miles, where, in the swamps of Olustee, a large number of his brave men suddenly encountered a tragical fate. The Commission's Relief Agent, Mr. Day, with a select corps of assistants, had pressed forward from Jacksonville, taking with him all the battle-field stores he could transport. What duties occupied the hands of those fearless and thoughtful Relief Agents, and what necessities there were for the means of succor which they had so hurriedly brought with them, let the following statements from eye-witnesses of that murderous battle explain. A correspondent of the *New York Daily Times* says:

* * * "On the anticipation of an immediate action, the Chief Medical Officer, who, by previous experience, knows upon what source to rely, telegraphed to the Post Surgeon at Jacksonville, who informed the Commission of the emergency, and also the fact of his utter inability to furnish any supplies of any nature. The Commission immediately forwarded its stores, with a corps of efficient workers, under the direction of one to whom such scenes were not unfamiliar. The first ten miles of this rolling road was a foot-race, and quickly performed. The services of the Commission on this field are represented by all as inestimable. Indeed, no other supplies were on the field. This fact is universally acknowledged. Thus your readers, whose hands are toiling to furnish means to alleviate suffering, can know that the efficiency of their agents accomplished all that human effort could to lighten suffering and strengthen the ebbing current of life. The Commission first met the wounded and saw the last placed on the cars to leave for the hospital in Jacksonville. This brief notice is but a faint expression of remarks spontaneously given, from the private to the highest in command."

All this occurred as a matter of course in the regular way of the Commission's method of operation in that department of the army. The Chief Inspector had promptly sent forward an ample supply of "sanitary stores" and competent Relief Agents to Jacksonville. He was ready to render *aid* to the Medical

Officers and to the wounded; and when the Medical Director summoned that aid at Baldwin and Sanderson, it was promptly rendered. Whatever were the causes of delay and insufficiency of the regular medical supplies, the Sanitary Agents had prudently avoided the necessity of any explanations and apologies to the Commission. Such an illustration of the method and utility of the Commission's work in the most distant fields and upon the most sudden and trying emergencies, will never be forgotten by the men and officers who witnessed the service.* The people at home will never forget it.

But while praises are awarded on every hand to the Agents of such *Battle-field Relief*, the *Preventive* or strictly sanitary work of the Commission goes on noiselessly and unseen, producing results equally as humane and far greater in their importance to the health and strength of the army than any means of succor that could be brought to the men who fall in battle. To aid occasionally in giving needed succor to hundreds of wounded soldiers upon the field, and for weeks subsequently in the hospitals, is a work worthy of all the care and cost of the Commission's sanitary establishment in any Department; but the saving of thousands of troops every month from disease, by means of

---

* The following Order was promulgated by the General in command, on his return to Jacksonville:

"HEADQUARTERS, DISTRICT OF FLORIDA,
"DEPARTMENT OF THE SOUTH,
"JACKSONVILLE, FLORIDA, March 8, 1864.

"*General Orders No.* 10.

"The Brigadier-General commanding gratefully recalls to the recollection of the troops of this command, the debt incurred by them during the recent movements, to the Sanitary Commission and its Agent, Mr. A. B. Day. Much suffering has been alleviated and many inconveniencies removed by the energy and promptness with which the supplies of the Commission have been placed at the control of our medical officers; and for those who have been so benefited, officers and men, the Brigadier-General offers his own and their most sincere thanks.

"By order of,

"Brig.-Gen. T. SEYMOUR.

(Signed) "R. M. HALL,
"First Lieutenant First U. S. Artillery,
"Acting Assistant Adjutant-General."

well-directed preventive labors and "sanitary stores," adds to the humane character of such labors the attributes of military strategy and patriotic aid in sustaining our country's cause. The perfect cordiality that characterizes the official relations of the military authorities and the Sanitary Commission's Agents in the Department of the South, and the earnestness with which they co-operate, prove that the sanitary work and "sanitary stores" are regarded as faithful allies to the heroic work and engineering in which our army there is engaged.

Latest aspects of the work of Special Relief.—The Sanitary Commission's Homes, Lodges, Hospital Directory, and the various offices and methods for relieving special distress, may justly be regarded as permanent institutions, which the Commission must maintain until the end of the war. There are now [March, 1863], twenty-five Homes and Lodges scattered along the lines of our armies; and, "in these Homes and Lodges," says the President of the Commission, in a letter to Rev. H. W. Beecher,* "*twenty-three hundred* soldiers (different ones) *daily* receive shelter, food, medical aid, protection, and care. These soldiers are such as are crowded by the rigidity of the military system out of the regular channels; soldiers left behind, astray, who have lost their military status, convalescents, discharged men, not able to get their pay. Of these, the average length of time they are on our hands is about three days. The priceless value of this supplementary system no tongue can tell. The abandonment of it would create an amount of suffering which a multiplication of 2,300 by 365 days in the year, will but serve to hint at.

"In connection with these homes, at the great military centres, New Orleans, Louisville, Washington, are bureaus in aid of the discharged soldier's great necessities, growing out of his

---

See Rev. Dr. Bellows' letter in Sanitary Commission Bulletin, Feb. 15, 1864.

loss of papers in battle, or during the bewilderment of sickness, or through the ignorance of his superiors, or his own: 1. A Claim Agency, to secure his bounty. 2. A Pension Agency. 3. A Back-pay Agency. The mercy of these ministries, by which soldiers and their families, helpless without this aid—the prey of sharpers, runners, and grog-shops—are put in speedy possession of their rights, is inexpressible. We have often $20,-000 a day of back-pay in our office at Washington alone, which might have been lost forever, or delayed until it was no longer needed by the soldier's own family, without this system."

This is a kind of service for the soldier that will necessarily tend to increase rather than diminish, while the war continues; and, experience is showing the Commission, daily, the necessity of still farther enlarging its agencies and means of Special Relief as our armies move forward still further from the basis of operation and points of rendezvous, recently near the front. Meanwhile, invalids and claimants for pension increase, while freshly recruited forces are hurrying to the field.

For our famished and sickly prisoners in the hands of the enemy the Commission has exerted itself to the utmost to convey the means of relief, and whenever the door has been opened its supplies have been quickly sent forward. And it may here be remarked, that the means for meeting such opportunities for conveying succor to Federal soldiers in prison, must be kept constantly in hand by the Commission. Both the treasury and the dépôts must be abundantly supplied.

To the Confederate prisoners in our keeping, the Sanitary Commission has extended all the succor that has been allowed by the military authorities. To their sick and wounded, when accessible to the Agents of the Commission, such means of succor and humane care have been extended as the claims of a common humanity have required. In its regard for the woes of the enemy's wounded and sick, when they have fallen into the hands of our forces, the Sanitary Commission has practically established the principle and usages of *neutrality* in respect to the treatment of such persons.

The Commission's concern for our disabled soldiers, wherever they may be found in need of sanitary care or friendly aid, cannot be essentially diminished at any point during the war; and several questions are now assuming great importance respecting the more permanent wants of the disabled classes. To these questions the Commission must give increasing attention.

At an early period of the war the Commission's methods of Special Relief brought to light important facts relating to the present system of *invaliding and pensions.* Indeed, the whole subject of the sanitary and social welfare of the permanently *invalid* class pressed itself upon the attention of the Commission, and in the month of August, 1862, the special inquiries upon this subject took shape, and have been pursued with increasing interest until the present time. An associate member of distinguished ability, then undertook, without cost to the Board, the work of personal inspection and inquiry respecting the *military invalid systems* of Europe, and he has since reported very fully upon the subject. Other associate members have been giving continued attention to the study of the subject in its various aspects at home, until conclusions well based and highly important to the welfare of the *invalid class*, as well as to the economical and social interests of the nation, have been reached.

That these inquiries were originally undertaken in the full belief that the *absorbing capacity and tendencies* of our social state and the patriotic spirit of each community, would render great national Asylums or "*Hôtels des Invalides*" unnecessary and unsuited to our wants, is evident from the following passage which we quote from a Document of the Commission, published in the autumn of 1862:*

---

* *Document No.* 49, Sanitary Commission.

"The Sanitary Commission are much exercised with the subject of the future of the disabled soldiers of this war. They calculate that, if it continue a year longer, not less than a hundred thousand men, of impaired vigor, maimed, or broken in body, and spirit, will be thrown on the country. Add to this a tide of another hundred thousand men, demoralized for civil life by military habits, and it is easy to see what a trial to the order, industry, and security of society, and what burden to its already strained resources, there is in store for us. It is, in our judgment to the last degree important, to begin now, to create a public opinion which shall conduce to, or compel the adoption of, the wisest policy on the part of our municipal and town governments, in respect of disabled soldiers—so as to discourage all favor to mendicity. * * * *

* * * * * * *

* * * * "We don't want a vast network of soldiers' poor-houses scattered through the land, in which these brave fellows will languish away dull and wretched lives. Nor do we want petty State asylums, to be quarrelled about and made the subject of party politics. We want to economize our battered heroes, and take care of them in such a way as to maintain the military spirit and the national pride; to nurse the memories of the war, and to keep in the eye of the Nation *the* price of its liberties." * * * * *

After much experience and observation in connection with the Special Relief work—in the matter of discharged soldiers, invalids partial and permanent, back-pay, pensions, &c., as provided for by that branch of the Commission's service—it was finally resolved, at a recent session of the Commission, to give authority to a sub-committee of the Board to establish *experimental Sanitaria* for certain classes of disabled soldiers.*

---

* The following were the resolutions adopted at that meeting, [March 10th, 1864], upon the subject of the *Invalid Class:*

"*Resolved*, That a Committee of four be appointed by the Chair, to consider the subject of the organization, location, and final establishment of National Sanitaria for disabled soldiers, to report at their earliest convenience.

"That said Committee have power to employ any necessary number of skilled agents to collect all available information in regard to the number of persons destined to be thrown on the public care by the war; to inquire what portion of these are likely to fall under the protection of the States, and what of the Federal Government; to learn what State enterprises are already a-foot, or in operation, and

Meanwhile the great struggle for subduing the rebellion goes on with increasing vigor, and the number of soldiers who must receive Sanitary care and Special Relief in various ways at the hands of the Commission, is continually increasing.

A brief statement must be made in this place respecting the present plan of Sanitary aid in the Convalescent Camp near Alexandria, Va.; and likewise respecting Fresh Supplies to the great Hospitals in the Department of Washington.

"Camp Convalescent," near Alexandria, will long live in the memory of the thousands of soldiers who have tarried there as convalescents, preparing for their return to their regiments after leaving the hospitals. It is now known as the "Rendezvous of Distribution," and about the period that the Sanitary Commission commenced its labors there, it was popularly known among soldiers as "*Camp Misery.*" The frequent inspections and reports for the benefit of *Camp Misery* had failed to reform its sanitary and social condition. Several thousand feeble and needy men from the hospitals were every week added to its population, and as many thousands departed thence for the field, or again to hospital. Under the direction of the military authorities and Surgeon-General Hammond, a radical improvement of the administration and medical care of the Camp and its vast population was commenced, and for the Sanitary Commission's share in the work of reform there a lady was selected as the Agent. A recent number of the "*Bulletin*" refers to the history of her labors as follows:

"At the late quarterly meeting of the Commission, a very full and interesting report was presented by Miss A. M. Bradley, the

---

their character and prospects; and what Federal provisions are under consideration. Also, to tabulate and systematize the results of the inquiries pursued by Mr. Olmsted, Mr. Perkins, and Dr. Ordronaux, in relation to this subject.

"*Resolved*, That under the advice of the Standing Committee, this Committee have power to establish such experimental Sanitaria as they may think necessary, to settle questions that cannot be reasonably determined on theoretical grounds."

agent of the Commission at the Convalescent Camy, Alexandria, Va. It covered the operations of Relief from January 17th to December 31st, 1863.

"During this period of twelve months 111,825 soldiers entered the camp, in passing from the military hospitals to their respective regiments, or to their homes, on certificates of permanent disability. To these soldiers, including the inmates of the Camp Hospital, Miss Bradley distributed the following 'Sanitary Stores' among others: 64 blankets, 67 quilts, 355 pairs of slippers, 10,096 towels, 100 woolen vests, 850 woolen mittens, 1,263 woolen shirts, 200 woolen drawers, 500 cotton drawers, 24,200 envelopes, 1,272 cotton shirts, 803 coarse combs, 178 fine combs, besides corn starch, cocoa, beef-stock, brandy, rice, sugar, tamarind vinegar, &c., &c., &c."

* * * * * * * *

"I arrived on the 17th December. On the 21st, when the soldiers were all assembled in line for inspection, I passed around with the officers and supplied seventy-five men with woolen shirts; I worked on the principle of supplying only the very needy. The same day I visited the tents, and finding many sick men, induced the commanding officer to place at my disposal some hospital tents. I soon had a hospital, and commenced to nurse such poor fellows as I gathered from among the well men of the camp. I found others whose discharge papers had been lying in the office for some time; these men being too feeble to stand in the cold and wet and wait their turn. I carried them to my hospital and warmed and clothed them, applied for their papers, and then sent them into Washington on the way to their homes."

* * * * * * * *

"In order to guard against misapplication of the stores, Miss Bradley prepased cards to be used as requisitions upon her Store-house, and placed them in the hands of a selected soldier in each division in the camp. This soldier or wardmaster examined the knapsacks of the men in his division, and thus acquired a knowledge of the real wants of all. Having ascertained the actual wants of the men, he sent them to the quartermaster to ascertain whether he would issue clothing on Government account. If not, they were then sent to Miss Bradley to obtain clothing or other necessaries from the Commission storehouse. By constant daily personal inspection, Miss Bradley rendered herself familiar with the wants of the soldiers, and supplied them quickly and fully. She says that from May 1st, 1863, to December 31st, 1863, with few exceptions, all the soldiers discharged from service in this camp were conveyed by her to the Commission Lodges at Washington. The number of such beneficiaries was over two thousand. When it is remembered that the vast majority of these men were suffering from incurable disease, prostrated in strength, and rendered excessively sensitive to all the trials and exposures of transportation, the value of Miss Bradley's services may be in some sense appreciated. They were conveyed to Washington in ambulances, and transferred to the comfortable Lodges of the Commission to await, in comparative ease and comfort, the completion, through Commission agents, of their discharge papers. Many lives were thus saved and incalculable suffering prevented."

Similar labors are being carried on, upon a smaller scale, in connection with other places of rendezvous and at the various great centres where convalescents are gathered, but it is seldom that a woman has found such a field of labor as that which is occupied by Miss Bradley. Her peculiar fitness for the duties of "lady superintendent" of hospital nursing and administration were proved in the Hospital Transports during the Peninsular campaign, and in her place at the Rendezvous of Distribution her labors have been above all praise. Recently, she has started a weekly paper entitled "*The Soldiers' Journal*," of which she is the Editress, and which is published for the moral benefit of the convalescents and for the pecuniary benefit of the children of deceased and disabled soldiers.

Fresh supplies for the General Hospitals.—The exhausted and barren market of Washington being really incapable of furnishing suitable supplies daily for the extra diet of the great hospitals in that district, the proper method of meeting so great a want was regarded as a sanitary question, and it was settled by establishing, in Philadelphia, a purchasing and forwarding agency for the needed fresh supplies for those hospitals. The business was commenced in June, 1863, by an official order from the Medical Director to the officers of all the hospitals, directing them to accept this voluntary channel of the Sanitary

Commission as the regular source of supply, and that as far as practicable the *hospital fund* should be applied to the payment of the *cost* of the articles thus furnished, thereby re-imbursing the Commission as far as possible.

Thus the best of all the fresh supplies of vegetables, meats, dairy products, fruits and delicacies that can be fonnd in the markets of Philadelphia, are furnished in the most perfect condition every morning, by *refrigerating cars*, at the Dépôt in Washington.* Of course, the results of this system of supplies are eminently satisfactory to the Medical Officers and patients in the hospitals. This self-supporting branch of Sanitary aid to the hospitals is still continued with entire satisfaction. The total weight of the fresh supplies that have thus been furnished by this agency to the hospitals in the vicinity of Washington, from June 24th, 1863, to April 1st, 1864, amounts to *more than*

---

* * * * * * * * * * *

* "The object of the Commission, in undertaking this work, was to secure to the soldiers in the hospitals a greater amount, with larger variety, and better quality of food than could otherwise be purchased by the hospital fund; for previously all supplies had to be bought at the Washington markets, which are extravagantly high, and limited in variety. Most of the purchases had to be made on credit instead of at cash prices; for the hospital fund by which supplies are bought is not credited to the hospital until the end of the month, when it is known how many of the rations due to that hospital have not been drawn from the Commissary."

* * * * * * * * * * *

"These ends were secured first by purchasing all supplies at wholesale prices at Philadelphia, where the whole State is a garden, by means of our agents, who had no single interest but to obtain the very best materials possible at the most reasonable cost, at cash prices; for the Commission advances the money day by day, and at the end of the month receives it from the Commissary, upon orders from the several hospitals.

"These supplies are brought to Washington by Adams' Express Company, in arctic cars, which run daily. These cars are refrigerators, lined with zinc, and carry ice.

"The supplies for the day, bought the afternoon previous in Philadelphia, are ready for delivery at five o'clock in the morning, when the wagons are sent from the hospitals, each for its invoice, as ordered, leaving the order for the day following. Thus, with perfect system, all wants are met and every article in its season which the best market in the country affords, is furnished to the soldiers in hospital.

"The hospitals say that their men were never before so well fed, with so good a variety, and at such reasonable cost. The average money-saving to the hospitals by this agency is estimated at about fifteen or eighteen per cent., with a corresponding increase of food for the soldiers."—*Sanitary Commission Bulletin.*

a thousand and thirty tons (exactly 1,030 tons, 1,174 lbs.); and the total cost of this vast amount of material has been $139,-271 44.

Practically this system of supplies is in operation in all the great centres of military hospitals remote from Northern markets, as at Nashville, Murfreesboro', Chattanooga, Vicksburg and Beaufort, although at those places the accumulations of the "hospital found" are not expected to re-imburse the Commission as the Washington hospitals do.

The Sanitary Commission's Aid to the Sick and Wounded in the Navy.—The opportunities for rendering assistance to the Sanitary service of our Navy have been comparatively infrequent, but whenever any wants of the sick and wounded upon gunboats and ships of war have come to the knowledge of the Commission, its agents have rendered all the relief in their power. The gunboats upon the Mississippi and other rivers have received from the Sanitary dépôts and Sanitary steamers considerable quantities of hospital supplies, delicacies for the sick, &c. The facts relating to this subject are so well stated by Dr. JENKINS, the General Secretary, in the following correspondence, that his letter is here introduced entire:

"U. S. SANITARY COMMISSION,
"823 Broadway,
"NEW YORK, February 9th, 1864.

"Madam,—I have received from Mr. Strong your note of yesterday, drawing attention to a statement that alleged neglect by the U. S. Sanitary Commission of the claims of the Navy on its regard, is alienating friends who are not informed as to the facts of the Commission's past and present relations to that arm of the public service.

"Though you do not need to be again told what you know so well, that the Commission has, from the first, sought to exercise its functions impartially, as a 'Commission of Inquiry and Advice in respect to the Sanitary Interests of the *United States*

Forces,' whether afloat or ashore, you will perhaps allow me to present to you such facts pertinent to the matter as now occur to me, for the information of any of your correspondents who may be less familiar with our work than you are.

"Soon after the organization of the Commission in 1861, its good offices were officially tendered to the Hon. the Secretary of the Navy, and its practice has ever since been to renew to the Chief of the Medical Bureau of the Navy and to commanders of squadrons, as occasion has arisen, its offers of service and assistance. At its last quarterly meeting in January, the Commission appointed a committee to confer with Dr. Whelan, the Chief of the Naval Medical Bureau, concerning the present sanitary condition and wants of the Navy. That its opportunities have been vastly fewer to serve the navy than the sister service in the field, detract not from its disposition to minister equitably to all the national forces, whenever it may be privileged to serve them. The Commission's view of equity, in assisting the two branches of the service, is to give aid in proportion to the *need* of each.

"The Navy, from its compact organization, its adequate system of supply vessels, which, besides the ordinary stores of food, clothing, and medicine, regularly take to each of the blockading squadrons, ice, fresh meat, and vegetables, and bring home its sick men to its well-provided Marine Hospitals; and its small percentage of casualties in its peculiar blockade duty, has much less frequently than the army afforded to the Commission the opportunity of supplying any lack of Governmental service. The fact, too, that every sailor is at home on shipboard, receives regularly his food and clothing, and generally secures his sleep, insures for the Navy an average sanitary condition far higher than the army often attains.

"And yet the occasions are, though relatively, not really few, in which the Commission has been able to supplement for the the navy the provision which the best-orded bureaux cannot in time of extended operations secure against occasional deficiences.

"Without referring to our records, I may mention some of the facts of which I am personally cognizant, which illustrate the above statement.

"During the early summer of 1862, the gunboats in the Pamunkey River guarding the supply dépôt of the Army of the Potomac, at White House, Va., received not unfrequently ice, and wine, and delicate food, for the comfort of their sick. So in the James River, for a month after the memorable "seven days," the naval flotilla shared to the extent of its needs the attention of the Commission, required fortunately far less by it than by the land forces.

"In July the Commission communicated to Commodore Wilkes its willingness to send semi-weekly a steamboat from Hampton Roads to the uppermost station of the James River Flotilla, which should visit each gunboat and naval vessel, receive its sick, and care for them while in transit to the hospital at Portsmouth, or elsewhere, at the pleasure of the Commodore.

"The Blockading Squadron before Charleston, and the commands of Admirals Farragut and Porter on the Mississippi, have, on many an occasion, had reason to bless the kind hearts at home who projected and sustain the U. S. Sanitary Commission, whose open hand is never withheld from the sufferers of either service, when once their wants are known.

"You recollect the occasion when, during the bombardment of Forts Jackson and St. Philip, below New Orleans, the Medical Officers of the navy were enabled, by the assistance of Dr. Blake, the Commission's Inspector, to establish at Pilot Town, in the Southwest Passage, a hospital for the fleet, and to furnish it liberally with sponges, chloroform, oiled silk, adhesive plasters, bandages, lint, sheets, &c., &c., at a time when the destitution of the fleet as regards these articles, were most complete.

"I pick up the '*Sanitary Reporter*' of January 1st, and read that on a recent trip of the Sanitary steamer *Clara Bell* down the Mississippi, the Commission's agent made provision of fresh vegetables to supply the wants of the U. S. gunboats about Vicksburg; and between Natchez and New Orleans furnished similar supplies to five others, the *Osage*, *Chilicothe*, *Choctaw*, *Lafayette*, and *Champion*.

"While I am writing this letter a report comes in from a Relief Agent of the Commission, who has recently visited the naval stations at and about Key West, Florida.

"I make a brief extract: 'We also found at Tortugas the gunboat ——, Capt. ——, commander, no surgeon on board, number of men sixty-five. Capt. —— stated that there has been no vegetables on board during the past six weeks. Consequently, I thought it proper to issue to the men a limited supply, which was very gratefully received.'

"I have frequent reason to know that the officers of the navy themselves do not share the opinions of those who think that the Commission neglects the navy. That some of them at least feel differently, is shown by the fact that on the first day of National Thanksgiving the officers of the sloop-of-war *Saratoga* made a generous offering in aid of the Treasury of the Commission, of whose impartial beneficence they had been witnesses; and by the other fact that at the late Fair in aid of the Cincinnati Branch of the

Commission, both officers and crews of the Northern Mississippi flotilla, from the Admiral to the powder boys, cheerfully gave a day's pay to swell the funds, which were to return in part to them converted into the material of relief for their future necessities.

"Desiring to enable you to set right your correspondents, I have not waited to seek evidence from our archives, but hope that I have been able to show that the U. S. Sanitary Commission has ever desired to lend its helping hand to any portion of the national forces, East, West, or South, afloat or ashore, that requires its ministry.

"I am, Madam, very truly yours,

"J. Foster Jenkins,

"General Sec'y of the U. S. Sanitary Com.

"Miss Louisa Lee Schuyler, New York."

The Treasury and Financial Resources of the Sanitary Commission.—The financial history of the Sanitary Commission yet remains unwritten, but we are enabled to present the following brief sketch of the resources and administration of the Central Treasury, upon which the life and progress of the Commission's plans have depended.

Immediately upon the organization of the Board, in the month of June, 1861, the Commissioners took counsel with a few discreet and patriotic gentlemen connected with Life Insurance and with other great corporate interests in our cities, and having received assurances of approval and necessary aid, sufficient funds for immediate requirements were soon forwarded to the Treasury, in response to a single appeal, in which the Commission said: "We look to the Life Insurance Companies, whose intelligent acquaintance with vital statistics constitutes them the proper and the readiest judges of the necessities of such a Commission, to give the first endorsement to our enterprise by generous donations—the best proof they can afford the public of the solid claim we have on the liberality of the rich, the patriotic, and the humane."

The promptitude, heartiness, and the encouraging words, with which the leading Life Insurance Companies responded helped the Commission at once to inaugurate its plans of practical labors in camps and hospitals. The leading merchants of New York had, immediately upon the organization of the Commission, started its Treasury, and their preliminary aid was followed by contributions from the New England Life Insurance Company amounting to $1,000; from the New York Life Insurance Company, $5,000; the Mutual Benefit Company $2,000; and the Mutual Life Insurance Company of New York, $3,000, which has since been swelled to $9,000.* Other classes of business men offered their counsel and aid at the beginning of the Commission's work, and having, in July, 1861, organized a Central Finance Committee, they bade the Comissioners go on vigorously with their plans.†

---

* Various corporations have at times made very liberal contributions to the Sanitary Treasury. The Banks in the city of New York made a contribution of $16,900 in the summer of 1863; the Pacific Mail Steamship Company has given $4,500, the Erie R. R. Company has given $5,000, and the Hudson River R. R. Company has contributed $5,000, to the Metropolitan Fair. These are worthy examples.

† The following extract from that Financial Committee's first appeal, illustrates the spirit of its spontaneous offer of aid and co-operation:

* * * * "Never before, in the history of human benevolence, did a gracious Providence vouchsafe an opportunity for doing good on such a scale; to so great a number; in so short a time; and with comparatively so little money. Of the immense array of three hundred thousand men now in arms in our defence—to be swelled, if necessary, to five hundred thousand—the experienced military and medical members of the Sanitary Commission declare that *one-fifth*, if not one-fourth, who must otherwise perish, may be saved by proper care.

* * * * * * * *

"Men and Women of New York! We beg you to awake to instant action. Death is already in the breeze. Disease, insidious and inevitable, is now stealing through the camps, on scorching plain, in midnight damp, menacing our dearest treasure—the very flower of our nation's youth. You surely will not permit them thus ingloriously to perish. In the name of humanity and patriotism—in the name alike of justice and manly generosity, bidding us save them who stake their lives in saving us—in the name of the honored ancestors, who fought for the land we live in—in the name of the Blessed Being, the friend on earth of the sick and the suffering, we now commit this holy cause to your willing hearts, your helping

The financial embarrassments of the times, during the first year of the war, rendered it necessary for the Commission to arrange its methods of operation and the rate of expenditures upon a very guarded and economical scale; and that circumstance, as well as the large experience and business habits of several members of the Commission, led to the introduction of a most rigid system of accountability and economy in the use of the funds of the Central Treasury. The Treasurer, George T. Strong, Esq., was unanimously elected to his position in the Board, no less on account of special experience and fitness for such a trust, than for his acknowledged ability in counsel and philanthropic labors, and it is known that the financial concerns and prospective wants of the Commission have received his unremitting care. The popular support and success of the Sanitary Treasury, upon which such vast interests have continually depended, have been worthy of the faithful care and effort that have been bestowed upon the Commission's financial affairs by the Treasurer, and by those associates whose business habits have justly constituted them the trusted advisers of the Board in all matters pertaining to the safe and economical management of funds.

Though the immense quantities of material supplies that are received and disbursed through the sanitary Commission's chan-

---

hands; with our earnest assurance that whatever you do will be doubly welcome if done at once.

"Samuel B. Ruggles,
"Christopher R. Robert,
"Robert B. Minturn,
"George Opdyke,
"Jonathan Sturges,
"Morris Ketchum,
"William A. Booth,
"David Hoadley,
"J. P. Giraud Foster,
"Charles E. Strong,
"Members of the Executive Committee of the Central Financial
"Committee U. S. Sanitary Association.

"New York, July 13, 1861."

nels are mainly the home offerings of the people and the products of accumulation or purchase by the Branches of aid, the maintainance of a Central Treasury, always adequate to the demands for systematic efforts in every field, by Prevention and Relief, has from the first been a paramount necessity. To its funds California and the gold-mining districts have contributed most naturally and liberally, as it has been almost the only way in which the people of those regions could directly render aid to the national cause.* The spirit, the manner, and the amount of their giving, are golden ties that add new strength to the Federal unity and fraternal sympathies of all the loyal States, from the Atlantic to the Pacific.

Perhaps it would be invidious to designate the amount which each State and city has contributed to the Central Treasury, for in a particular State or city all, or nearly all, the contributions may have flowed into the local treasury of a Branch of Supply, to be employed by it in purchase of "sanitary stores," as has been the case in the States of Ohio, Illinois, and Pennsylvania, and in the cities of Buffalo and Philadelphia. The Branch of Supply in the latter city received, in cash, during the two years ending the first of January, 1864, the sum of $119,682 04, nearly all of which have been expended by the excellent Managers of that Branch in purchase of supplies at Philadelphia, and directly in the Relief service of the Commission in that city and elsewhere.

The total amount of money that has been received into the Central Treasury of the Commission, to March 4th, 1864, is—

At the Treasurer's Office in New York..........	$1,112,877 61
" " " " " Washington........	12,321 05
" " " " " Louisville..........	8,487 62
Total receipts of Central Treasury..........	$1,133,628 28

* For some particulars respecting the rich contributions from California and the Mining regions, see pages 73, 74 and 104.

The total amount of disbursements by the Treasurer up to the date of the above footings is nine hundred and eighty-five thousand four hundred and fifty-seven and $\frac{41}{100}$ dollars [$985,457.41]. The aggregate of the sums which have been expended by the numerous Branches and Aid Societies in the purchase of "sanitary stores," &c., would amount to a much larger sum than the total receipts of the Central Treasury. Over such expenditures the Sanitary Commission exercises but little authority, but acts as the accredited adviser. Yet the more successful Branches, like those of Philadelphia,* Boston, Cleaveland, and elsewhere, practically hold their funds, as well as their stock of supplies, subject to official orders from the Commission. This is manifestly the true theory of effective and economical administration of such auxiliary aid. The Women's Central Association of Relief, which was established in New York as a model for such Branches of supply, furnishes a perfect example in this respect.†

The management of all details in the current expenditures of the Commission, is conducted with the same rigid exactness and rules of accountability that prevail in commercial life, and in

---

* The following statement, which we copy from a recent report of the "Philadelphia Branch," very clearly sets forth the facts relating to the practical relations of that flourishing auxiliary to the Sanitary Commission:

* * * * * "It will be observed that the large sum of $82,000 has been expended by the Philadelphia Agency, mainly for supplies. It is proper to remark, in explanation, that the supplies purchased with this money, have been bought by order of the Officers of the Commission at Washington, and have been forwarded to points designated by them. The Philadelphia Branch has always been regarded by its Officers as an Agency of the Central Commission, in the strictest sense of the term. With the exeption of certain comparatively small sums expended for local relief, they have considered all the funds collected by them as subject to the order and control of the Central Office, for the general purposes of the Commission.

* * * * * * * *

* * * * * "From the beginning, the Philadelphia Agency has maintained the policy he holding all its funds, except those required for local purposes, at the disposal of those Officers of the Commission whose duty it is to ascertain where the greatest need exists."

† *See Appendix A.*

the legal care of financial concerns. Proper vouchers and specifications show precisely how all funds have been expended, and these, after having been critically examined, are audited at each stated session of the Board, while the requisitions, estimates, and daily record of the various agents and employès of the Commission are under constant revision by the Standing Committee and other responsible officers. The rate of remuneration in the several branches of active service under the Commission is considerably below the average cost of similar work in ordinary avocations; and, as has been recently stated by the President of the Board,* "these two hnndred men receive, on an average, $2 per day for labor, which is, say half of it, highly skilled, sometimes of professional eminence, and worth from five to ten times that amount. Few of these men could be had for the money, but they work for love and patriotism, and are content with a bare support. The Board (all included, twenty-one in number)—President, Vice-President, Treasurer, Medical Committee, Standing Committee—*give* their services and their time gratuitously. *They receive nothing. Their traveling expenses alone are partly refunded them, and these are trifling, excepting the case of one or two who go frequently on tours of observation.*"

The Sanitary Commission's Relations with the "Christian Commission" in the Army.—During the Peninsula campaign and subsequently in the field hospitals at Antietam, the officers and agents of the Sanitary Commission found "Christian delegates" laboring with much zeal and self-sacrifice for moral welfare of the wounded and the sick. Consequently, after proper counsel upon the subject of fraternal relations, and opportunities for co-operation with such "Delegates," the General

---

* See Dr. Bellows' Letter to Rev. H. W. Beecher, in *Sanitary Commission Bulletin*, Feb. 15th, 1864.

Secretary of the Commission issued the following official circular of instructions to the Sanitary Inspectors:

"Central Office, Sanitary Commission,
"Washington, Dec. 16th, 1862.

"To each Inspector of the Sanitary Commission:

* * * * * * *

"You are instructed, whenever the delegates of the Christian Commission offer to give you their aid for battle-field relief operations, or in other emergencies, to accept it gratefully; and, for the time being, you will deal with them, as far as possible, in the same manner as you would if each individual had been sent to you for special battle-field duty by officers of the Commission.

"You are also instructed at all times to give special attention to the representations of the accredited agents of the Christian Commission with regard to the wants of the hospitals, and will meet those wants to the extent of the means at your control as far as possible, consistently with a just prospective regard for the wants of others.

(Signed) "Fred. Law Olmsted,
"General Secretary."

The respective objects and methods of the two organizations are and should be so distinct as well as harmonious, as to permit only the most effective co-working in the same camps and hospitals. The following statements from an esteemed "delegate of the Christian Commission," illustrates the happy result of such cordial co-working:

"U. S. Christian Commission, Branch Office,
"Nashville, July 23, 1863.

"Dr. J. S. Newberry,
Sec'y West'n Dep't U. S. Sanitary Commission, Louisvillle:

"My Dear Sir,—I desire, on behalf of the Christian Commission, to render grateful acknowledgment for the uniform, generous and cordial co-operation of yourself and the agents of your Commission in our work of bringing spiritual comforts and blessings to the soldiers. But for your assistance at the first, and its continuance all along, our wôrk would have been greatly impeded in the army of the Cumberland.

"Also in my recent trip to Vicksburg, in the service of the Christian Commission, I was at all points kindly received and materially aided by the Sanitary Commission. My own feelings—that the work of both Commissions, though wrought in different departments, should be entirely co-operative—were fully reciprocated by your agents at Cairo, Memphis, and on the Barge on Yazoo River.

"My observations of your work on that Barge were very pleasant. I saw stores dispensed to needy applicants most freely, and in surprising quantity and variety; and when I got back to the Bluffs, where the sick and wounded were coming into the division hospitals, I found bedding with your mark, dried and canned fruit, and lemons and chickens, which could have been furnished from no other source. I knew that, without the timely help of the Sanitary Commission, there would have been destitution, and consequent suffering, in many of those hospitals.

"I want to bear testimony to the noble Christian philanthropy of the men in charge of your Commission in that department. I am persuaded they could not do that work from unworthy motives. Money could not procure such services as you are receiving, for instance, from Dr. Warriner at Vicksburg.

"Every week's experience in my army work, bringing me among the camps and through the hospitals, and giving an opportunity, which I always improve, to look in at the different quarters of your Commission, leads me to a continually higher estimate of the work you have on hand. I am satisfied that your system of distributing hospital supplies is the correct one. Such large contributions as the people are making cannot be handed over to the army on any volunteer system, unless it be for a few days amid the emergencies of a severe battle. A business involving such expenditure would be intrusted by a business man only to permanent and responsible agents.

"That among all your employés there should be no unworthy man, is more than a reasonable mind can ask. The Christian Commission and the Christian Church would go down under that test.

"Let me close this letter of thanks, my dear brother, with my daily prayer—a prayer which I learned in your Soldiers' Home in Louisville, and have often repeated since in the Soldiers' Rest at Memphis, on the Barge in Yazoo River, in the Division Hospitals under the guns of Vicksburg, in the Nashville Home and Storeroom, and in the camps and hospitals at Murfreesborough; a prayer fresh on my lips, as I have just come from seeing wounded and typhoid patients at Tullahoma and Winchester lifted from rough blankets and undressed from the soiled clothes of march and battle, and laid, in your clean sheets and shirts, upon your comfortable quilts and pillows—a prayer in which every Christian heart in the land will yet join—God bless the Sanitary Commission.

"Most cordially yours,

(Signed) "EDW. P. SMITH,

"Field Agent, U. S. Christian Commission."

Most of the supporters of the "Christian Commission" are also friends of the Sanitary Commission, and it is manifestly desirable that there should never be any misconception of the fact that the Sanitary Commission has officially instructed its agents to offer to the delegates of the Christian Commission such fraternal and material aid as would tend to facilitate their work and benefit the patients in hospital. A scheme of philanthropy that, like the Sanitary Commission, has undertaken to diminish the sickness and mortality in our armies to a fraction of that which would occur without such interposition, should be aided by labors that judiciously bring religious instruction and consolation to the patients in the hospitals, and to the wounded in the field, and such philanthropic co-operation continues to be a rule of the Sanitary Commission.

The International aspects and influence of the United States Sanitary Commission's work and purposes.—In responding to the claims of our common humanity, however humble or however imposing the demand for aid, we influence in greater or less degree the welfare of our fellow-men throughout the world. In our day is not every word and every effort that is deliberately and earnestly put forth in behalf of human welfare, sure to take root wherever the progress of Christian civilization has prepared the mind of men for sympathy in such humane purposes and efforts?

During the autumn of 1863, a spontaneous movement was made in Paris in aid of the work of the United States Sanitary

Commission, and already the work of the European Branch has become well organized, and its agent has shipped most valuable supplies to the Commission from the vineyards and storehouses of Europe.* It has opened correspondence with the prominent American residents in the various cities of the continent, and also with the leading philanthropists of Europe, who, in becoming interested in the progress of such an enterprise for humanity, also become interested in the great results of our national struggle.

American residents in Great Britain have likewise given similar expression to their sympathy and aid for their fellow-countrymen, and noble minded Englishmen have already sent some munficient contributions to the Sanitary Treasury for our sick and wounded soldiers. A British Branch of Supply in aid of the United States, Sanitary Commission, has been organized upon a most promising basis; and, like the Continental or European Branch, this movement has been at once spontaneous and business-like.† And while these foreign Branches correspond in many respects with those that have sprung into existence in our loyal States at home, they cannot fail, while directly aiding to succor the sick and wounded of the Federal army, at the same time also to awaken increased regard for the welfare of our country, and likewise engage the fraternal interests of the philanthropic minds in all nations. Indeed there is good reason to believe that the spirit and purposes of the United States Sanitary Commission as well as its intelligence and example in the practical applications of sanitary science and humane succor in armies, are already widely felt in Europe.

The proceedings and spirit of the *International* Sanitary Conference which was recently convened at Geneva, prove how readily the progressive civilization and Christianity of our day

---

* See Appendix B. † See Appendix B.

accepts and puts in practice the grand problems upon which the Sanitary Commission is working, and there is gratifying evidence that the spirit and purposes of this American work are already largely shared by many leading minds in Europe.*

Influence of the Commission's labors upon Sanitary Science, and upon the popular estimation of the Sacredness of Human Life.—The art of *preserving* health depends upon a definite knowledge of the laws of health. It is a branch of medical art, and is properly termed "*preventive medicine.*" In armies it has not been customary to give any other attention to Sanitary Regulations than that which is connected simply with military discipline. The Army Regulations, as such, do not make any provisions for the preservation and care of the health of the soldier, nor is the subject so much as mentioned even in the Revised Regulations of our Army. But there are many points connected with the order, regularity, and discipline of soldier-life, which incidentally promote and protect the health of men in camp, in quarters, or on the march. To collate and explain all such passages contained in our Army Regulations was one of the very first duties performed by the Sanitary Commission.† A medical member of the Commission, long familiar with army life, prepared this little manual, and very large editions have continued to be published and gratuitously distributed among officers and soldiers.

A highly practical "*Report upon Military Hygiene and Therapeutics,*" as prepared and authorized by a competent committee of the New York Academy of Medicine, immediately followed the little manual of *Rules*, etc.; and of that valuable report many editions have been printed and furnished to military surgeons.

---

* See Appendix C.

† See Medical "Document C," "*Rules for preserving the health of soldiers.*"

A great number of specially prepared essays or *monographs* upon the most important subjects in army hygiene and medicine have been put forth by the Commission, with the design to aid the Medical Officers of the army in a way that would be at once the most acceptable and most effective.* The interest and active inquiry that have been awakened by these twenty monographs have helped powerfully to keep up a constant watchfulness against the causes of preventible disease and mortality. This is one of the unseen agencies of which the Sanitary Commission has been enabled to increase and perpetuate Sanitary information, together with the most practical and advanced knowledge in the art of medical care and healing. No other army has ever enjoyed the influence of such an agency.

But aside from the influence thus exerted by means of published monographs on hygiene and the care of sickness and wounds, the general effect of many of the Commission's ordinary reports and circulars has been to awaken thoughtful attention to the great priñciples and means of *preserving health;* while every branch of sanitary work for the soldiers, has strongly tended to keep alive a proper estimation and consciousness of the value of life and health, and of the skill and care required by those who suffer wounds and sickness. In this way the popular appreciation of HEALTH and the means of preserving it has been rapidly increasing among all classes; and while the carnage of our terrible war has naturally been weakening the common estimate of life's value and sacredness—an effect inseparable from the bloody strife of continued battles—the varied appliances and earnest purposes of the Sanitary Commission and its branches of aid, have been continually and everywhere taught in an impressive manner that *life is sacred*, and that human

---

* See Appendix D.

suffering and human sympathies are insignia of human brotherhood which command universal regard and affectionate care.

Sanitary science and its more common precepts are rapidly becoming household words. The vital importance of fresh air, cleanliness, cheerfulness, proper food, and self-care, are daily becoming understood, both in our armies and in our homes; and the imperative duty of intelligent care and provision for suffering fellow beings is more universally and more deeply felt among us than when the war began. And, says a leading critical review, "it will yet be seen in the history of our republic, and in the records of human progress, that the United States Sanitary Commission's works and purposes of relief and mercy have had an important mission in hastening the day when

"'Man to man the world o'er
Shall brothers be, and a' that.'"

The woes of wounds and sickness, and the deepest griefs that follow in the bloody pathway of our great war, have served to hasten the practical development of a higher civilization and a broader application of the Golden Rule of Christianity. Unlike all previous wars, the present relentless contest of arms in the struggle for our national birth-right has given new life to the spirit of philanthropy. The soldier is no longer regarded merely as a mechanical agent in the war, but as a brother; while to our foe when fallen and in need, our sympathies and care are spontaneous and unstinted. Not only has the Sanitary Commission endeavored practically to establish the doctrine of *neutrality* for the enemy's wounded and sick, and for their attendants, but the progress of Federal forces in the insurgent States, is providentially opening a vast field for the extension of sanitary aid and succor to multitudes of the enemy's invalids that are now languishing and dying for want of such relief as the sick and wounded in our own hospitals receive. To aid in the sanitary protection and care of our loyal forces, while they are pressing forward upon the rebellion, through malarious and wasted regions to the Gulf; to aid our conquered enemy in the relief of his destitute and wounded; and to follow up the sanitary care of our invalid soldiers until all practicable means of recovery and comfort are fully enjoyed by all of them, must continue to be the duty of the Sanitary Commission acting as the aid to the Medical Department of the army, and as the agent of the people's humane and patriotic desires.

Sanitary condition of the Federal Army; present rate of Sickness and Mortality.—Military considerations that must be respected in the time of active campaigns debar the full publication of recent statistics of sickness and mortality in the forces. The few statistics we have given in the first sections of this narrative, relate wholly to periods and events that are past. The vast aggregates of patients reported in military hospitals, and of losses by death, as occasionally published in our daily newspapers, sometimes may awaken deep anxieties in philanthrophic minds; but the Sanitary Commission has its own watchful Bureau of Statistics, and is faithfully informed of the sanitary condition of every division of the forces, and its principal mission is to to aid in *preventing disease*, and to have and supply beforehand all needed supplementary means of succor for the men who fall by wounds and sickness.* It is true that more than a

---

* The following extracts from a recently published letter from the Medical Director of the 15th *corps d'armée*, illustrates the view that is taken of the Sanitary Commission's work. The statements here given of the rates of sickness and mortality are similar to the reports that have been coming in from all departments of the army during the period here mentioned:

"Headquarters 15th Army Corps,
Medical Director's Office,
Huntsville, Ala., Feb. 22, 1864.

"My Dear Sir:

* * * * * * * * *

* * * "I cannot refrain from expressing my thanks and obliga-

hundred thousand graves of our soldiers who have died in hospital or on battle-fields, tell what sacrifices have sealed

---

tions to the United States Sanitary Commission, the immediate and active agencies, which have been, under Providence, largely instrumental in preserving the health of the troops, and thus maintaining a state of efficiency rarely equalled, and perhaps never surpassed.

"Coming to the present location from the long march of nearly eight hundred miles from Memphis to Knoxville, and so far back, and fighting at Colliersville, Cherokee, Tuscumbia, Lookout Mountain, Missionary Ridge, and Ringgold, and losing throughout in killed, wounded, and missing, nearly two thousand men, the gratification of the gallant corps could hardly shape itself into words, when, on reaching at last a resting place, weary, worn, ragged, foot-sore, and hungry, it found the inevitable Sanitary Commission with its supplies of vegetables, delicacies, hospital supplies of food and clothing, and experienced once more the benefits of that active and loving sympathy, which, in its organization and results, challenges history for a parallel, and which, in its never-varying love, labor, sacrifice, hopefulness, broad catholic charity and courage—inspiring words of cheer, corresponds fittingly with, and is a glorious pendant to the patriotism, valor, endurance, and high-heartedness of the noble army, braving disease and death, enduring all things in the present, and hoping all things in the future, fighting for those altars and fires at and around which they are daily made to feel they are perpetually remembered. * * * * * * *

* * * * * * * * *

"I am satisfied from this long and familiar intercourse with the army in active service, that men are brave and fearless, both because of the knowledge that they are watched by loving eyes that fill with proud and happy tears when they do nobly, and because they are 'sustained and soothed by an unfaltering trust,' that happen what may, preparation and provision have been made for the emergency, even against their hour and manner of suffering.

"The soldiers look with confidence to the Commission for prophylactics also, and the liberal distribution of vegetables has been productive of incalculable good, by preventing that deterioration and deprivation of the system, which is the precursor of Typhus, Scurvy, and all those formidable evils which arise in the army from derangement of the nutritive function. The Medical Department of the army supplies bountifully now what is needed in the way of medicines and hospital stores; those medical officers whose ideas of service and administration were found incompatible with the needs of the emergency and the spirit of the times, having been forced to yield their notions or be pushed aside altogether.

"So far, then, as this portion of the army is concerned, it seems to me that the greatest amount of good may be done in the way of prevention, and I would respectfully urge, as my opinion of the method of bringing the greatest good to the greatest number, that the Commission should direct the large-hearted liberality of the soldiers' friends towards gathering and forwarding to the army those vegetables which are the most difficult to procure on the part of the Commissary Department, or which are not in the army ration, and which have proved so valuable hitherto in the prevention of disease arising from the derangement of the function of nutrition and the depraved condition of system, which is nearly certain to follow confinement to one class of food. The occupancy for a long time past of this part of the country by both armies has stripped it of supplies, and many of the inhabitants are forced to apply to the Army Commissary for subsistence.

"The health of our troops is now so excellent, that the greatest expectations may be based upon their efficiency in the coming campaign, and if the articles mentioned can be furnished, I have no fear that the number of sick will exceed the four per cent. now reported, although the months of February and March are

the faith and loyalty of our people. Every town and neighborhood in the land has borne a share in this sacrifice, and the voice of mourning for the fallen brave and loved ones has mingled with new vows of devotion to the national cause in every community at the North. This has occurred in an army whose death-rate from disease has been less than was ever before known in the annals of great campaigns,* and actually less than one-third the percentage of mortality from sickness in our volunteer forces in the Mexican war. And it may safely be stated that had the rates of sickness and mortality which prevailed in our Mexican campaign, and that have characterized all great wars, been experienced in this protracted struggle of our nation, the present catalogue of the dead for whom we mourn, would have contained more than thrice its present number of names; the voice of wailing would have ascended from almost every family in the land, and the number of invalids languishing in

---

most trying to troops who are allowed to deteriorate during the change from winter to spring.

"I should remark that only four per cent. are excused from duty, and only two per cent. are really so ill as to need medical attendance. In many regiments there is not an inmate of a regimental hospital. We have not sent a man to the General Hospital since leaving Bridgeport, on Christmas, and have at this place a Post Hospital, mainly for the care of sick belonging to the Provost Guard, on duty in town, Quartermaster and citizen employees, &c., less than twenty in all, being reported as "remaining sick." I know that this information will be gratifying to those who bear in remembrance the patriotic citizen who has become a soldier, and to you, the representatives of those Sanitary Commissions, whose bounties I have witnessed during so long a period, and under so many trying and desperate circumstances, and it is with a warm and grateful feeling at my heart that I declare that in a service of nearly three years, performed in the States of Maryland, Tennessee, Virginia, Arkansas, Louisiana, Mississippi, Alabama, and Georgia, I have never been in circumstances, however trying, in positions, however desperate and hopeless, or in places of danger, however great and imminent, but either preceding us, close by our side, or following in our very footsteps, were to be found the active, self-sacrificing, ubiquitous agents of the Sanitary Commission, braving disease, and danger, and death, in the pursuit and exercise of a noble philanthropy. * * * * * * *

"I am, sincerely and truly, your friend,
CHAS. McMILLAN,
Surg. U. S. Vols., Med. Director 15th A. C.

Dr. A. N. READ, Inspector, U. S. San. Com.

* See Appendix E.

hospitals or in our homes incapable of service, would have been very far greater than that which now exists.

The unprecedented success of medical and surgical treatment in our military hospitals has brought lasting honor to the Medical Department of the army, and it is a proper subject for gratitude and devout thanksgiving; while throughout the lines of our armies in the field, there is such health and manly vigor as never before was enjoyed by volunteer soldiers in long campaigns. Under the good Providence that holds the destiny of our national cause, these unspeakably great blessings are due to the skillful care, the timely succor, and the sanitary service which a liberal Government, and a patriotic, loving, and intelligent people have provided for their armies.

APPENDIX.

APPENDIX A.

THE BRANCHES OF SUPPLY.

THE origin and objects of the first two "Branches" of Supply to the Sanitary Commission, are mentioned upon pages 59 and 60 in this volume. A summary statement of the aid rendered by those and other leading "Branches" of the Commission will here be given, so far as the facts relating to their respective operations are at present in hand.*

---

* *The First Soldiers' Aid Society.*—At one of the meetings of the U. S. Sanitary Commission, soon after its organization, one of the Commissioners presented as a *souvenir* of Revolutionary days, an *autograph copy of a letter from General Washington to Mrs. Bache (Daughter of Benj. Franklin)*:

"HEAD-QUARTERS IN BERGEN, N. J.,
"14th of July, 1780.

"MADAM: I have received with much pleasure—but not till last night—your favor of the 4th, specifying the amount of the subscriptions already collected for the use of the American soldiery.

"This fresh mark of the patriotism of the Ladies entitles them to the highest applause of the country. It is impossible for the army not to feel a superior gratitude on such an instance of goodness. If I am happy in having the concurrence of the Ladies, I would propose the purchasing of coarse linen, to be made into shirts, with the whole amount of their subscription. A shirt extraordinary to the soldier will be of more service to him than any other thing that could be procured him; while it is not intended to, nor shall exclude him from the usual supply which he draws from the public.

"This appears to me to be the best mode for its application, provided it is approved by the Ladies. I am happy to find you have been good enough to give us a claim on your endeavors to complete the execution of the design. An example so laudable will certainly be nurtured, and must be productive of a favorable issue in the bosoms of the fair, in the sister States.

"Let me congratulate our benefactors on the arrival of the French fleet off the harbor of Newport, on the afternoon of the 10th. It is this moment announced, but without any particulars, as an interchange of signals had only taken place.

"I pray the Ladies of your family to receive, with my compliments, my liveliest thanks for the interest they take in my favor.

"With the most perfect respect and esteem, I have the honor to be, madam,
"Your obedient and humble servant,
"GEO. WASHINGTON."

"*The Woman's Central Association of Relief*," NEW YORK.—This Association was organized April 29, 1861, at a meeting of nearly three thousand ladies. Its officers at the present time [March, 1864] are—

President.................VALENTINE MOTT, M. D.
Secretary.................SAMUEL W. BRIDGHAM.
Treasurer.................HOWARD POTTER,
of the firm of Brown, Brothers & Co.,
59 Wall street.

Executive Committee.

Miss L. L. SCHUYLER, Mrs. GEORGE CURTIS, Miss A. POST, Mr. GEORGE WM. CURTIS, Mr. E. L. GODKIN, H. W. BELLOWS, D. D.,	Sub. Com. on Correspondence and Diffusion of Information.
Miss ELLEN COLLINS, Mrs. T. d'OREMIEULX, Miss GERTRUDE STEVENS, Mrs. C. R. LOWELL, Mr. SAMUEL W. BRIDGHAM, Mr. JOHN CROSBY BROWN,	Sub. Com. on Receiving and Forwarding Supplies.

Special Relief Committee.

Mrs. W. P. GRIFFIN,
Mrs. H. BAYLIS,
Mrs. CYRUS W. FIELD,
Miss A. H. NEVINS,
Mr. HOWARD POTTER,
WM. H. DRAPER, M. D.,
ELISHA HARRIS, M. D.,
R. D. HITCHCOCK, D. D.

Purchasing Committee.

Mrs. J. A. SWETT,
Mrs. HAMILTON FISH.

ASSOCIATE MANAGERS.

CONNECTICUT.

Miss LYDIA R. WARD.......................Bridgeport, Fairfield Co.
Mrs. C. E. BACON ....Danbury, Fairfield Co.
Mrs. JOHN OLMSTED.......................Hartford, Hartford Co.
Mrs. T. G. TALCOTT.......................Hartford, Hartford Co.
Mrs. BENJAMIN DOUGLAS.................Middletown, Middlesex Co.
Mrs. THOMAS B. BUTLER...................Norfolk, Fairfield Co.
Miss HELEN EVERTSON SMITH.................Sharon, Litchfield Co.

NEW JERSEY.

Mrs. Eliza Howard Powers....................Paterson, Passaic Co.

NEW YORK.

Mrs. Emily W. Barnes........................Albany, Albany Co.
Mrs. George Letchworth......................Auburn, Cayuga Co.
Mrs. Henry Mather...........................Binghampton, Broome Co.
Mrs. Henry S. Randall.......................Cortlandvillage, Cortland Co.
Miss G. B. Schuyler.........................Dobbs' Ferry, Westchester Co.
Mrs. Charles B. Stuart......................Elmira, Chemung Co.
Mrs. Harriet N. Wing........................Glen's Falls, Warren Co.
Mrs. Eliza A. Redfield......................Goshen, Orange Co.
Miss Jane L. Hardy..........................Ithaca, Tompkins Co.
Mrs. Elizabeth Saunders.....................Newburgh, Orange Co.
Mrs. A. B. James............................Ogdensburgh, St. Lawrence Co.
Miss C. M. Brooks...........................Owego, Tioga Co.
Mrs. Morris Brown...........................Penn Yan, Yates Co.
Mrs. W. B. Williams.........................Rochester, Monroe Co.
Miss R. B. Long.............................Rochester, Monroe Co.
Mrs. Edward Huntington......................Rome, Oneida Co.
Miss E. Washington..........................Schenectady, Schenectady Co.
Mrs. Pierre Van Cortlandt...................Sing Sing, Westchester Co.
Mrs. Lydia Wallace..........................Syracuse, Onondaga Co.
Mrs. W. D. Hamlin...........................Utica, Oneida Co.
Mrs. W. V. V. Rosa..........................Watertown, Jefferson Co.

RHODE ISLAND.

Mrs. G. H. Thorndike........................Newport.
Miss Fanny M. Green.........................Providence.

Total Receipts of the Woman's Central Association of Relief, from May 1, 1861, to Feb. 1, 1864.

Articles of Hospital Clothing, &c.

Flannel shirts	58,969	Quilts	21,429
Cotton "	121,739	Blankets	7,043
Flannel drawers	42,234	Sheets	45,593
Cotton "	52,350	Bedsacks	13,045
Socks	99,400	Pillows	28,850
Slippers	22,389	" cases	59,425
Dressing gowns	13,644	" sacks	7,592
Coats	3,169	Cushions	16,884
Pantaloons	4,203	Towels	99,891
Handkerchiefs	88,468	Musquito nets	3,100

Articles of Hospital Clothing, &c.

Lint, bbls...............	563	Jelly, jars...............	17,937
Bandages, bbls..........	1,053	Wine, bottles...........	13,247
Old cotton, "	476	Condensed milk, lbs.......	11,491
Dried fruit, "	1,245	Beef-stock, lbs............	7,15
Vegetables, "	446	Groceries................	17,676
Fresh fruit, boxes.........	233	Pickles, gals.............	7,781
Fans....................	10,088	Lemonade, lbs............	3,072

The total estimated value [at wholesale and cost prices] is $655,337 00.

The amount of money received has been $36,805 71, all of which has been expended in purchasing hospital supplies, and in "*special relief.*"

These articles were received from more than twelve hundred towns and villages with whose Aid Societies the Central Association had established correspondence. At page 59 in this volume, the origin and purpose of this Association have been mentioned, and no higher praise could be awarded to its management than to state the fact that the original purpose of aiding in the organization, methodizing, and most effectual application of woman's help in this war, has been steadily pursued and successfully carried out in every particular. The abstract of receipts and shipments and the catalogue of auxiliary Aid Societies, on the preceding page, present but an imperfect idea of the arduous labor that has been performed in this Association. The correspondence, and the hard work of re-packing, assorting and forwarding, which constitute the daily duties of its lady managers, at their central office, have for nearly three years past presented scenes of cheerful industry, intelligent care, and rigidly business-like system that have won universal admiration and respect.

The Association has made but little effort to contribute pecuniary aid, as the Sanitary Commission treasury is kept in New York. It has chosen rather to become a direct and reliable channel and main artery to the Commission's department of Relief. Its services have been of untold value to that department. The spirit in which its labors are pursued may be judged by the following extract from the last published report of its Executive Committee:

"When the time comes that we may rightfully lay aside the needle and the pen, we shall be told it, and not until then bring this work to a close, which it is our privilege as well as our duty to be engaged in.

"There is one result of the work of the Commission, not to be found in any of the reports, not to be counted, nor weighed, nor measured, nor seen. For two and a half years, while we have been filling the boxes and forwarding them, enrolling ourselves as workers of the order of the "brown-linen apron," and busy with the needle, the hammer, and the pen, this mighty work has been silently gaining strength and gaining ground. Before resuming our work, let us clear our eyes for a moment from the dust of these welcome bales and boxes; let us free our ears from the whirr of the sewing machine, and consider what part our work is taking in a national, in a patriotic point of view. A wounded rebel, from South Carolina, not along ago, asked our inspector, "What is the meaning of this stamp, 'U. S. Sanitary Commission,' on my shirt?" It was explained to him. "What," said he, "do you have *women* in your army?" "The women are the back-bone of our army," was the reply; "we have ten thousand of them working for it all the time." I never mean to fight against those women again," was the rejoinder. It was a low estimate—ten thousand women—only one division of the grand army scattered throughout the loyal States, representatives merely of the many hundred thousands banded together in one common sympathy, united in one national cause. In the spring of '61 every village was busy fitting off its own dearly loved soldier boys—the best, the bravest, the flower of the flock. How gladly would we have followed these sons and brothers to the field to shield them from danger, to nurse them when sick or wounded—but it might not be. They voluntarily gave up their own identity, as soldiers of village, or county, or State, and enrolled themselves as soldiers of the Union. They had given their lives to their country, and to the principles which that country represents—they had sworn to support the Government; and turning to those at home, anxiously endeavoring to follow the loved ones with home comforts to the field, they say: "The Government is our best friend, you can only help us by helping it, by working with it and through it—it cares for all alike, it does for us the best it can, but it cannot do everything,—help us by helping it." And so we are no longer working alone for our own sons and brothers, but for the sons and brothers of the Union. The spirit of rivalry and jealousy, the false pride, the taunt of "Our company so much better taken care of than yours," has given place to something far higher and holier. What are these but the germs of that spirit which rankles at the root of secession? When we think that this state of things might have existed all through our country, does this ideal work of the Commission, this 'merging of the domestic interests of the people in the army,' seem so unimportant because it is not to be estimated in figures?

"Friends, sisters, let us think seriously of the responsibility of rightly using this mighty influence which rests with us. Shall it be brought to bear upon nothing higher than the alleviation of present suffering—is there nothing nobler in our work than this? While we bind up the wounds may we not also strengthen the hands and the hearts of those who are fighting for principles on the battle field, by fighting for those principles at home? Is not this consecration of ourselves to *the right* as much our duty—more so—than anything else? Let us, then, in the security and happiness of our own homes, as "Soldiers of Christ," fight the good fight of humanity, of patriotism, of Christianity—fight it through all reverses, knowing no discouragements, nor compromises, nor defeats, but believing and knowing that the right must triumph in the end. Henceforth may our watchword be Union and Liberty, and then shall the bond which has bound us so closely together, as lovers of the soldiers of the Union, shine out in its true light of a loyal, national league—a league of no written articles, requiring no signatures, but none the less known and felt to be binding."

In the report from which we quote, it is stated, after reviewing the progress of the battle and siege work of the army, that—

"In looking back at our own work during the same time, it will be noticed, that no appeals have been made in behalf of our sick and wounded soldiers for any of these special occasions.

"They were unnecessary. Our friends know that it is too late to prepare for a battle after it is over, and wounded men cannot wait a fortnight for clothing and bedding to be made and forwarded to them. In Mr. Olmsted's last circular, written just after the battle of Gettysburg, he says: 'Hundreds will owe their lives this week to those who did not hold their hand when there was no special public excitement, by which the Commission had stores ready at Frederick, Baltimore, and Washington, and reserves at Philadelphia, New York, and Boston. Those who wish to cordially co-operate with the Commission will now go to work as if we were just entering upon a long war, and with no thought of its ending. A momentary enthusiasm is not desired, but the Commission offers its agency to all who wish to *steadily* contribute to the relief of the sick and wounded, and to the comfort of the army. * * * * * Let those who have not begun to work systematically for the army begin now. Let those who have been working steadily become more steadfast and orderly in their work.'

"And to those steady workers—women who have made the weekly meeting at the Soldier's Aid Society as much a part of their business as any other duty in life—to those steady workers, uniting with our Government, is due the fact that in no country in the world, in time of war, have the sick and wounded received such tender care, such loving-kindness, as to-day with us."

"*The New England Women's Auxiliary Association*:" BOSTON BRANCH.

OFFICERS FOR 1864.

HENRY B. ROGERS, ... *President.*
S. G. HOWE, ... *Vice-President.*
RUFUS ELLIS, ... *Secretary.*
GEORGE HIGGINSON, ... *Treasurer.*

Executive Committee.—Mrs. D. Buck, Mrs. G. S. Curtis, Mrs. Otto Dresel, Miss Isa E. Gray, Miss Grace Heath, Miss Mary G. Loring, Miss Abby W. May, Miss Annette P. Rogers, Miss Martha C. Stevenson, Miss Sarah C. Williams.

Industrial Committee.—Mrs. F. W. Andrews, Miss Caroline A. Brewer, Miss Isabella P. Curtis, Mrs. Wm. Glidden, Mrs. Sarah S. Hunt, Miss Anna P. Loring.

Financial Committee.—Mrs. C. B. F. Adams, Frank W. Andrews, James M. Beebe, J. Ingersoll Bowditch, John C. Dalton, Mrs. Wm. Endicott, Jun., Edward Jackson, Mrs. J. C. Johnson, Arthur T. Lyman, Mrs. Lyman Nichols, Mrs. G. H. Shaw, Geo. W. Wales.

Associate Managers.

Maine.—*Augusta*, Miss Burton. *Bangor*, Mrs. H. Bowman. *Belfast*, Mrs. J. G. Dickerson. *Calais*, Miss M. I. Cooper. *Castine*, Mrs. Dr. Stevens. *Dover*, Miss L. M. Johnson. *Eastport*, Mrs. Aaron Hayden. *Ellsworth*, Mrs. Lucy T. Phelps. *Farmington*, Mrs. Charles Alexander. *Gardiner*, Miss E. H. Gardiner. *Hallowell*, Miss L. M. Emmons. *Houlton*, Mrs. J. Donnell. *Kennebunk*, Mrs. J. A. Swan. *Lewiston*, Mrs. E. S. Davis. *Machias*, Miss U. M. Penniman. *Orono*, Mrs. Israel Washburn. *Rockland*, Mrs. C. N. Germaine. *Saco*, Mrs. J. T. G. Nichols. *South Berwick*, Miss M. O. Hayes. *Waterford*, Miss C. M. Douglass. *Wiscassett*, Mrs. Alex. Johnston.

New Hampshire.—*Amherst*, Mrs. H. Eaton. *Charlestown*, Mrs. Richd. Hubbard. *Claremont*, Mrs. E. L. Goddard. *Concord*, Mrs. Ira Perley. *Derry*, Mrs. L. T. Morris. *Dover*, Mrs. A. S. Whidden. *Exeter*, Mrs. E. S. Cobbs. *Fitzwilliam*, Mrs. W. L. Gaylord. *Hanover*, Mrs. C. A. Aikin, Mrs. W. P. Abbott. *Keene*, Mrs. T. K. Leverett. *Lancaster*, Miss E. M. Weeks. *Manchester*, Mrs. M. Currier, Mrs. E. H. Hawkes, Miss M. O. A. Hunt. *Meredith*, Mrs. E. Stevens. *Nashua*, Mrs. J. A. Baldwin. *Plymouth*, Miss M. E. Mc-Questin. *Portsmouth*, Mrs. Eliz. C. Tilton. *Winchester*, Mrs. S. W. Buffum.

Vermont.—*Brattleboro'*, Mrs. Hampden Cutts, Mrs. M. G. Davenport. *Burlington*, Mrs. J. M. Pomeroy. *Chelsea*, Miss L. H. Dickenson. *Coventry*, Mrs. E. D. White. *Johnson*, Mrs. R. M. Forrest. *Manchester*, Mrs. D. S. Boudinott. *Middlebury*, Mrs. A. F. Bascom. *Newbury*, Miss H. M. Hazen. *Rutland*, Mrs. Wm. Y. Ripley. *St. Albans*, Mrs. Emily B. Safford. *St. Johnsbury*, Miss A. M. W. Lee. *South Hero*, Miss Landon. *Waterbury*, Miss Jenny Griswold. *West Concord*, Mrs. L. H. Tabor. *Windsor*, Miss M. A. Phelps. *Woodstock*, Mrs. N. Williams.

Massachusetts.—*Abington*, Mrs. Mary T. Powers. *Andover*, Miss H. K. Webb. *Attleboro*, Mrs. G. W. Shephardson. *Barnstable*, Mrs. S. B. Phinney. *Barre*, Mrs. J. H. Goddard. *Beverly*, Miss H. L. Rantoul. *Brookline*, Miss Griggs, Miss Winsor. *Cambridge*, Mrs. Lewis Stackpole, Miss M. G. Washburn. *Charlestown*, Mrs. Henry Lyon. *Chelsea*, Mrs. F. B. Fay, Mrs. James Hovey. *Concord*, Mrs. G. Reynolds. *Danvers*, Mrs. Lydia M. Fletcher. *Dedham*, Miss H. B. Chickering. *Deerfield*, Mrs. Mary W. Fogg. *Dorchester*, Mrs. Walter Baker. *Dorchester*, Mrs. N. Hall. *E. Bridgewater*, Miss M. E. Sheldon. *Fall River*, Mrs. R. Borden. *Fitchbnrg*, Mrs. E. Torrey. *Framingham*, Mrs. C. Upham. *Gloucester*, Mrs. R. P. Rogers. *Great Barrington*, Mrs. I. Sumner. *Greenfield*, Mrs. J. F. Moors, Mrs. W. D. Osgood.

Hingham, Mrs. R. T. P. Fiske. *Ipswich*, Mrs. Robert Southgate. *Lancaster*, Miss E. P. Russell. *Lawrence*, Mrs. G. A. Walton. *Lexington*, Mrs. L. J. Livermore. *Lowell*, Mrs. G Herrick. *Lynn*, Miss M. L. Newhall. *Malden*, Mrs. G. Wilson. *Medford*, Mrs. Eliza H. Carret. *Milton*, Mrs. F. Cunningham. *Nantucket*, Miss A. W. Gardner. *New Bedford*, Mrs. Matt. Howland. *Newburyport*, Mrs. J. C. Marsh, Mrs A. W. Miltimore, Mrs. Eben F. Stone. *Newton*, Mrs. Dr. Bigelow. *Northampton*, Miss M. Cochran, Mrs. E. M. Daniels, Miss E. Lyman. *N. Bridgewater*, Mrs G. Wilbour. *Northfield*, Mrs. John Mattoon. *Pepperell*, Mrs. Hannah F. Wallace, Mrs. John Buckingham. *Plymouth*, Mrs. C. G. Davis. *Quincy*, Mrs. Wm. Whitney. *Roxbury*, Mrs. A. D. Hodges, Miss A. C. Lowell. *Salem*, Mrs. A. Huntington, Miss H. R. Lee. *Sheffield*, Miss J. O. Ensign. *Somerville*, Mrs. Charles Lowe. *Taunton*, Mrs. S. Southgate. *Wareham*, Mrs. A. C. Fish. *Watertown*, Mrs. L. W. Titcomb. *W Brookfield*, Mrs. H. Barnes. *Westfield*, Mrs. James Fowler. *West Tisbury*, Miss Julia A. Coffin. *Winchester*, Mrs. O. P. Curtis, jun. *Woburn*, Mrs. S. E. Davis. *Worcester*, Mrs. T. K. Earle, Mrs. G. W. Richardson.

RHODE ISLAND.—*Newport*, Miss K. P. Wormley.

CONNECTICUT.—*Hartford*, Mrs. S. J. Cowen.

This great Association was founded upon the basis which had been laid "by the Boston Branch," early in the history of the war, and like that "Branch" this larger body has proved to be a most munificent and faithful auxiliary to the Commission's department of Relief. The following statement exhibits the amount and nature of supplies contributed during the year 1863:

	Total of Distributions.
Cotton shirts	31,761
Cotton drawers	19,904
Flannel shirts	17,709
Flannel drawers	10,624
Cotton-flannel shirts	2,551
Cotton flannel drawers	8,560
Stockings	31,887
Slippers	14,946
Handkerchiefs	28,276
Mittens	1,564
Wrappers	3,650
Caps	2,197
Slings	2,294
Body-bandages	869
Ration and work-bags	649
Towels	20,141
Cushions	5,128
Sheets	12,105

Quilts	5,459
Blankets	3,003
Bed-sacks	4,680
Pillow sacks	757
Pillow cases	14,493
Pillows	2,134
Fans	2,231
Crutches, &c	144
Old clothing, cases	18
Lint bandages, cases	175
Books and pamphlets, cases	66
Cologne, baywater, &c., "	91
Medicines, "	6
Wines and spirits, "	580
Syrups, shrubs, &c., "	386
Jellies and preserves, "	230
Farinaceous, "	415
Pickles, "	310
Tea, coffee, chocolate, &c., cases	329
Beef-stock, &c, lbs	1,820
Condensed milk, cases	229
Dried fruits, "	396
Tamarinds, "	230
Salt fish, "	124
Sugar, "	63
Crackers, "	217
Fresh and canned fruits, and vegetables, bbls	212
Herbs, cases	10
Ale and cider, "	37
Extract of ginger, "	10
Chloroform, "	2
Soap and tallow, "	15
Hospital furniture, "	13
Miscellaneous, viz., " Games, Stationery, Spices, Combs, Cravats, Netting, Splints, Sponges, Cheese, Pipes, and Tobacco.	39
Special cases to various addresses	170

The "Industrial Committee" of this auxiliary reported that during their first year they "spent for materials, $22,081 71, as follows: For flannel, $14,906 27; for buttons, tape, thread, &c., $559 47; for silecia, $524 63; for paper for patterns, $28 22; for cotton, $2,564 04; and for ticking for bed and pillow-sacks, $3,498 18." Also, that they had cut and prepared, "during the year, 34,142 articles, consisting of 5,709 flannel drawers; 8,787 flannel shirts; 227 pairs slippers; 5,353 bed-sacks; 167 pillow-sacks; 65 woolen caps; 1,176 cotton shirts; 425 cotton-flannel drawers; 9,504 cotton drawers, etc., etc."

During the last year (1863) the Society expended upwards of $67,000;

and during the two years, the total amount of expenditures for materials, etc., was upwards of $98,000. The spirit of this excellent auxiliary is well illustrated by their very complete system of effort throughout the towns and villages of New England, and the sacred spirit of patriotism and humanity that animates these mothers and daughters is beautifully expressed in the concluding paragraph of the Society's last Annual Report:

* * * * "Has not God given it to us, as a solemn and a daily duty, to take care of His 'sick and in prison,' 'hungry,' 'thirsty,' and 'poor?' There is but one answer. The responsibility is plain. A large portion of our daily lives belongs to our country, in this time of war. Let us freely offer such amount of physical power, working for the common weal, as we deeply owe. Let us add to this our wisest thought, our moral strength, and our tenderest sympathies, all consecrated and harmonized by a deep religious purpose. Let us remember that every one can do a share, larger or smaller, towards bringing the war to an end, as well as in the immediate work of carrying it on."

The Sanitary Fair that was held by this New England Auxiliary brought into its treasury $156,000, and nearly a third part of that sum was generously made over to the Central Treasury. Its office at Boston has become the centre of a very complete and extended scheme of Special Relief for the benefit of invalid and destitute soldiers in that city, or *in transitu*. It also maintains the daily service for attendance upon the railway ambulances between New York and Boston.

"*Women's Relief Association of the City of Brooklyn.*"—This excellent association was organized during the autumn of 1862, and was regarded as auxiliary to the Sanitary Committee of the Brooklyn War Fund Committee, and practically it has proved to be one of the most valuable branches of supply to the Sanitary Commission. Its contributions have been made through the depots of the Woman's Central Association in New York; consequently, its abundant gifts have been included in the aggregate statements of receipts by the latter. During the first five months of its operations, viz., to May 1st, 1863, the Brooklyn Association expended $10,637 53 for materials for hospital clothing alone.

In no other city has greater harmony and success marked the history of an association of this kind. At the date of its organization thirty churches were represented by lady delegates, and soon nearly every religious congregation in that city was thus represented. The fruits of such hearty and intelligent co-operation have been beautiful and surpassingly rich. The Brooklyn Sanitary Fair was a marvel of success, and after sending to the Sanitary Commission's Treasury *three hundred thousand dollars*, the Association had a reserved fund of a hundred thousand dollars for the purchase of materials to be worked into hospital supplies.

The soft flannel garments and the superior delicacies which this Association has contributed for the use of the sick and wounded will never be forgotten by them, nor by the medical officers who have witnessed the beneficial effects of such aid.

OFFICERS OF THE WOMAN'S RELIEF ASSOCIATION OF BROOKLYN.

Mrs. J. S. T. STRANAHAN, *President.*
Miss KATE WATERBURY, *Secretary.*

Executive Committee.—Mrs. W. I. Buddington, Mrs. E. Shapter, Mrs. J. W. Harper, Mrs. J. D. Sparkman, Mrs. James Eells, Mrs. Henry Sheldon, Mrs. Jeremiah Johnson, Jr., Mrs. J. L. Duffin, Mrs. Henry E. Pierrepont, Mrs. Luke Harrington, Mrs. H. Waters.

Sanitary Committee of Brooklyn.—Dwight Johnson, Henry E. Pierrepont, Samuel B. Caldwell, James H. Frothingham, James D. Sparkman.

The Philadelphia Branch, U. S. Sanitary Commission.—The noble part that the city of Philadelphia has borne in the philanthropic labors which the events of the war have called forth is worthy of her ancient reputation, and her high social culture. The men who wept as they read the bulletin announcing the rebel attack upon Fort Sumpter, and the women who then dedicated their sons and brothers to the defense of the nation, have ever since been active in works of aid and succor for the soldier. Immediately after the organization of the Sanitary Commission a supply depot was spontaneously established in that city by the gentlemen who had become Associate Members. This continued in good service in connection with a branch office for aiding the work and purposes of the Commission. Horace Binney, Jr., a member of the Commission, was President, and Wm. Platt. Jr., was the General Agent of the Branch.

During the winter of 1863 the Branch became more effectively organized, and its methods of operation were greatly enlarged. Mr. Platt, whose labors had been of unspeakable value to the work, had been called from his works of love and mercy on earth. He died from the effects of excessive labors and exposure he took upon himself in the Commission's service after the battle of Antietam.* His associates have carried out the

---

* In St. Thomas' Church, Philadelphia, a tablet, erected by the members of the Philadelphia Branch of the Commission, commemorates the deceased laborer, and the cause in which he sacrificed his life. A report of that branch says:

"All the services of Mr. Platt were rendered gratuitously. When the battles in Maryland were impending in September, 1862, Mr. Platt hastened to Washington, and volunteered to take charge of a wagon train of hospital stores, for use in the field. Visiting and supplying the hospitals at Rockville, Frederick and Middletown, and reinforced with other supplies forwarded by the Commission, he left

labors and spirit in which he so nobly worked. A system of special relief adapted to the wants of soldiers *in transitu*, or in the great military hospitals at Philadelphia, was put in operation; a Hospital Directory established, a Pension Agency and War Claim Office established, and a very complete system of auxiliary organizations carried into effect throughout a vast district of which that city is the centre.

With all its methods and purposes perfectly harmonious with those of the Sanitary Commission, it aids all departments of sanitary work with peculiar effectiveness and economy. The Branch is composed of the Associate Members of the Commission, and comprises many of the leading physicians and philanthropic citizens, not a few of whom have rendered signal aid as *infirmiers volontaires* at the battle fields. The names of Platt, Furness, Stillé, Johnson, and Clement Barclay, will forever be remembered in connection with such labors.

The women of Philadelphia have organized very effectively, under the general system proposed by the Branch, and have adopted the title of "The Women's Pennsylvania Branch of the U. S. Sanitary Commission." This branch reports that it now has auxiliaries as follows:

Constantly contributing Societies	209
Occasionally do. do.	22
Organized Aid do.	63
Corresponding Associations	93
In all	394

The "sanitary stores" supplied through the agency of these co-operative associations, have been immense—exceeding $200,000 in value.

Officers of the Women's Branch: Mr. Caleb Cope, President and Treasurer; Mr. R. M. Lewis, Secretary.

Middletown at eleven o'clock at night, on the 17th of September, and proceeded with his train of wagons to Boonsborough, and thence to Keedysville, and arrived at the headquarters of the army at nine o'clock the next morning. His own modest official report of his services omits mention of the fact that, as he came within sound of the cannon, he quickened his speed, driving the leading wagon himself, and when darkness threatened to delay the train, he left it and walked in advance, carrying a lantern, and compelling the reluctant drivers to follow.

* * * * * * * * * * *

"But Mr. Platt's earnestness was not satisfied with mere direction and supervision. On the 20th of September, as the ambulances appeared bringing the sufferers from the bloody field of Antietam, but unaccompanied by competent assistance for their removal, Mr. Platt gave himself up for a long time to this arduous service, carrying the wounded in his arms to places of shelter, and there rendering them the tenderest offices of a nurse. Thus engrossed, he overtasked himself, and through fatigue and exposure contracted the disease which, on the 22d November, brought to a close, in his 37th year, his short but well-spent life."

Executive Committee.—Mrs. M. B. Grier, Chairman; Mrs. Bloomfield H. Moore, Corresponding Secretary; Mrs. George Plitt, Recording Secretary; Mrs. B. Griffith, Mrs. Wm. H. Furness, Mrs. D. Samuel, Mrs. J. Edgar Thomson, Mrs. Joseph R. Chandler, Miss S. Dunlap, Mrs. Lathrop, Mrs. C. J. Stillé, Mrs. T. A. Budd, Mrs. R. M. Lewis, Miss M. M. Duane, Mr. Philip P. Randolph.

Sub-Committee on Correspondence.—Mrs. M. B. Grier, Chairman, Mrs. B. H. Moore, Corresponding Secretary, Mrs. George Plitt, Recording Secretary, Mrs. S. H. Clapp, Assistant Corresponding Secretary, Ex-officio; Miss M. M. Duane, Mrs. Lathrop, Mrs. Furness.

Officers of the Branch of Associate Members of the U. S. Sanitary Commission in Philadelphia:

Executive Committee.—Horace Binney, Jr., Chairman; M. W. Baldwin, Rev. H. A. Boardman, D. D., John C. Cresson, J. I. Clark Hare, John F. Meigs, M. D., Samuel Powel, Thomas T. Tasker, Edward Hartshorne, M. D., Secretary; Caleb Cope, Treasurer.

The Pittsburg Branch of the U. S. Sanitary Commission.—After nearly two years of continual effort to render effective aid to the sick, the wounded, and the way-worn, by means of Relief Societies and a local "Subsistence Committee," the people of the "Iron City" organized a branch for aid to the U. S. Sanitary Commission.

The energy and liberality that had, during the early period of the war given food and comfort to 100,000 soldiers passing through their city, besides contributing large supplies for relief, &c., at the battle of Shiloh, furnishing at once two steam-boat loads of such supplies and returning them with precious loads of the wounded, have been exhibited in their work as a Branch of the Commission. Dr. Newberry says, "Nowhere, indeed, so far as I know, since the war commenced, has any similar society accomplished so much in so short a time after its organization."

Officers of the Pittsburg Branch:

Mr. Thomas Bakewell, President, and Mr. J. R. Hunter, Secretary of the Gentlemen's Committee; Miss Rachel McFadden, President, and Miss Mary Bissell, Secretary of the Committee of Ladies.

The General Aid Society of Buffalo.—This hard-working Branch, is a most efficient and successfully managed tribuary to the Commission's Western Department of Relief. The amount of its contributions of supplies during the first two years of its operations reached nearly 140,000 articles. During the year 1863, the number of articles forwarded to the supply dépôts was 72,601, and these were appraised at $50,000. In its "cutting department," upwards of 25,500 yards of material have been cut and worked up.

This model Society, after having instituted a *Bazaar* during the summer of 1863, which brought nearly $8,000 to the treasury, established a Fair during the subsequent winter, and by that means added about $40,000 more to its means.

Officers of the Buffalo Branch:

Mrs. Horatio Seymour, President; Mrs. Henry R. Seymour, Vice-President; Mrs. J. R. Lothrop, Vice-President; Mrs. James P. White, Treasurer; Miss Grace E. Bird, Secretary; Miss Emily W. Babcock, Assistant Secretary; Miss Josephine L. Saltar, Directress of Cutting Department.

Executive Committee.—Mrs. Cyrus Ahearn, Mrs. D. B. Waterman, Mrs. Chas. A. Hopkins, Mrs. James Brayley, Mrs. Isaac A. Jones, Mrs. F. A. McKnight, Miss Susan E. Kimberly.

The Cleveland Branch: "Soldiers' Aid Society of Northern Ohio."—Organized the 20th of April, 1861, for immediate aid and relief to volunteers that were hurrying to the first places of military rendezvous, the history of this Society has continued to be that of a pioneer among its kindred associations. Its system, efficiency, and harmony of operation, have from the beginning been the subject of admiration, and of very extensive imitation and influence throughout the West. It became a Branch of Supply to the Sanitary Commission in October, 1861. Its officers then were—

President, Mrs. B. Rouse; Vice-Presidents, Mrs. John Shelley, Mrs. Wm. Melhinch; Secretary, Mary Clark Brayton; Treasurer, Ellen F. Terry.

The great intelligence and ardent patriotism of the people of Northern Ohio everywhere responded to the suggestion and plan of this model Aid Society for the institution of minor auxiliaries in every town and village. And in the Society's first report they offer their "grateful tribute to the energy and devotion of Dr. J. S. Newberry, the well-known and most worthy representative of the Western Department of the U. S. Sanitary Commission." And it is stated that "to his exertions are owing the enterprise that has marked the action of the Commission in the Southwest, in following closely upon the track of our advancing army, establishing agencies in every Southern city, almost simultaneously with the raising of the Stars and Strips, and thus opening wide the door for the influx of the stores that are poured in exhaustless streams from the loyal North."

Previous to September, 1863, this Branch had furnished 10,000 packages of "sanitary stores," and had given local aid to nearly 12,000 needy soldiers *in transitu* at the Cleveland "Home." During the month of February, 1864, this Branch held a Fair for the purpose of replenishing its means for the purchase of "sanitary stores." Over $100,000 in cash was realized, thus enabling its excellent Managers to carry out their cherished purposes of greater aid to the Sanitary Commission. And, says the Western Secretary: "We cannot but think that the good results of such Fairs as have been held in Chicago, Cincinnati, Cleveland, and other cities, are not to rest with the contributions to the soldiers' comfort alone; are not to be estimated in so many dollars for socks, sour-krout, onions, and potatoes. To promote their comfort, to be able to buy these essentials for the army, is an incalculable good. But this charity is 'twice blessed.' A rich and subtle blessing must lie in the wide sympathies called out, the new relations of acquaintance, friendship, and intimacy formed, and in the surprising revelation of talent and worth in remote and unexplored localities. Neighbors and neighborhoods must come to respect each other more, to depend upon each other more, and wonder that they have missed finding each other out so long. Prejudice must be softened; artificial barriers must give way to a freer intercourse, and tenderness of feeling and judgment must take the place of sour suspicion. After so complete a flooding of all the field of life with the resistless tide of a sweet and noble enthusiasm, we cannot but look for a new bloom and unexampled harvests."

Cincinnati Branch of the U. S. Sanitary Commission.—In the autumn of 1861, Dr. Newberry reported to the Commission the organization and promising labors of the Branch at Cincinnati, with R. W. Burnett, Esq., as its President. The history of relief work and sanitary aid, through the agency of this Branch, has been worthy the Queen City of the West. And, previously to the organization of the Branch, there had been an immense and spontaneous stream of aid poured forth from every church and soldiers' aid society. That stream had been wisely guided in its applications at Camp Dennison, at the wayside stations for soldiers in the city, and particularly at the "Marine Hospital," which the Secretary of the Treasury had given up to the purposes of hospital care for soldiers. This work was directed by Dr. Mussey and Messrs. Burnett, Anderson, Geoffrey, B. P. Baker, C. J. Wright, Pearce, Burton, and others.

The matchless energy and munificence of the Cincinnati Branch in its offerings of whole steamboat-loads of "sanitary stores," and corps of *infirmiers voluntaires* and surgeons, at the battle-fields of Fort Donelson, Pittsburg Landing, and elsewhere, can never be forgotten.

As we have not at hand the requisite material for a complete sketch of the work performed by this Branch, the reader will gain some idea of its nature and extent from the following extracts from the Commission's publications. In document No. 75, the Western Secretary states that this Branch had distributed, previously to September, 1863, "over twelve thousand packages of stores, and is still as active and prosperous as at any former period of its history. In addition to the contribution of materials to which I have referred, the Cincinnati Commission has expended large sums of money, and a vast amount of labor, of thought, of sympathy and kindness, in the care of the sick in the hospitals of that city; in the equipment and management of hospital steamers; in the care of troops passing through or quartered in the city; and in sustaining its admirable 'Home,' which has now accommodated forty thousand soldiers. So great and varied are the charities which it has dispensed, that I can do no more here than allude, in a general way, to that which it would take volumes to describe—that which has served to make the Cincinnati Branch of the Sanitary Commission known and blessed in every department and division of our Western armies."

This Branch issues a monthly *Bulletin* to its tributaries of aid, acknowledging supplies received, and publishing advice, extracts from letters received from the armies, etc. The following is a specimen of such information given in the *Bulletin* of March 1st, 1864.

"CHATTANOOGA, February 16, 1864.

"EXECUTIVE COMMITTEE AND GENTLEMEN:

* * * * "*Every one* we meet—officers in the army, from staff down, as well as men, and the surgeons—concur in saying that scurvy, in its incipient stages, is manifest in the Army of the Cumberland; and think an effort should be made to send anti-scorbutics to the regiments in front. One man, well qualified to judge, made the remark, *that one barrel of potatoes to the army now is equal to one man for the spring campaign.*"—(*Letter from Messrs. Bailey and Butler.*)

* * * * * * * *

"But little change seems to have taken place in the hygienic condition of the Western Army since the publication of our last *Bulletin*, the most pressing demands being still for warm under clothing and healthful diet, vegetables, and such other articles as will aid the surgeons in combatting those dangerous foes, diarrhoea and scurvy. * * .

CHAS. F. WILSTACH,
THOS. G. ODIORNE,
E. C. BALDWIN,
L. B. HARRISON,
CHAS. E. CIST,
} *Executive Committee, Cincinnati Branch U. S. San. Com.*

JOHN B. HEICH, *General Secretary.*

The Sanitary Fair which was held in Cincinnati, during the winter (1864), brought into the Treasury of this Branch upwards of $220,000.

The Kentucky Branch, Louisville.—Under the inspiring examples of devotedly loyal men and women in Louisville and its vicinity, the work of sanitary and humane relief became organized in that city early in the war. Rev. J. H. Heywood and others led in this service, and although they treated friend and foe with equal charity in the hospitals, their work received no sympathy from the disloyal families. Says the western Secretary of the Commission:

"I look back with a kind of horror to those dark days in the history of this rebellion, when the theatre of war was at the very doors of the citizens of Louisville; when camps were in her suburbs and troops thronged her streets; when the hastily improvized hospitals, including all the public school edifices, were crowded with sick, so imperfectly supplied with care and comforts, that every loyal family felt impelled to contribute a tithe of its domestic treasures, and send its delicately-reared ladies to minister, by their own personal efforts, to the suffering and destitute in the hospitals of the wards in which they lived. No similar scenes had been witnessed in our previous history, unless in the epidemics of yellow fever at Norfolk and Philadelphia, in which the same paralyzing gloom pervaded these cities, on which dark back-ground were illuminated similar bright examples of christian charity. In the works of love and mercy of those days, our Louisville associates bore a conspicuous part; and from that period to the present, they have never ceased to devote a large part of their time and thought to the great number of objects of pity and charity which merciless war has thrown upon their hands. When the armies were further removed, and the central office was transferred to this point, all the general business of the Sanitary Commission was relinquished to this office, while the members of the Kentucky Branch, by a division of labor, assumed the responsibility of all the local work, the care of the city hospitals, twenty-two in number, and addressed themselves to devise new measures of relief for soldiers passing through the city, who were the proper objects of our charity. The "Home," with all its cares, was entrusted to their management; was largely extended, at an expense of several thousand dollars, paid from the local treasury, and was made capable of accommodating one thousand men at a time. It is now the most extensive and complete establishment of the kind which exists in the country."

Previous to September, 1863, the Kentucky Branch had issued upwards of 6,000 large packages of sanitary supplies.

The Northwestern Branch of the Sanitary Commission.—The headquarters of this Branch are in the city of Chicago, and its tributaries are scattered throughout the States of Illinois, Wisconsin, Iowa, and Minnesota. This happy co-ordination of auxiliary work in aid of the Sanitary Commission throughout the Northwest, was one of the incidental results of the great Fair that was held at Chicago during the autumn of 1863.

Previous to that period the Chicago Branch had nobly represented the spirit and resources of aid in Northern Illinois. The steadiness and intrinsic value of its stream of supplies have not been exceeded by aid received from any similar population.

During the three months of summer the Branch purchased and sent forward to the Commission's agents in the field over $100,000 worth of supplies, a large portion of which consisted of anti-scorbutics. The "Soldiers' Fair" brought into the treasury of the Northwestern Branch, $80,000. This money is being judiciously expended by its own officers, for such supplies as the Commission requires in camp and hospital. During the last three months of the year 1863, this Branch "sent to Western Hospitals, 7,450 boxes and barrels, including 8,000 pounds codfish, 11,595 pounds butter, 317 pounds tea, 5,000 bushels onions, 5,000 bushels potatoes, 500 pounds condensed beef, 347 barrels and 80 boxes pickles, 3,620 shirts, 1,683 pairs drawers, 8,000 pounds crushed sugar, 2,688 pounds condensed milk, 783 comfortables. Average these boxes at $10,00 each, and the amount will be $74,500. Average them at $8,00 and they will amount to $59,000."

This Branch has also been very successful in works of local relief to the needy families of volunteers. Soldiers in the hospitals have besought their attention and charity for their poor families, and it is a notorious fact that many a poor fellow's illness in the hospitals proceeds as much from anxiety for the helpless ones left behind, as from bodily disease. Consequently, the ladies connected with the Commission organized a "Ladies' Association for the Relief of Soldiers' Families," which was wisely made auxiliary to the "Young Men's Christian Association," which is organized for general charitable work. "The city has been divided into districts by this Association, each one of which is under the personal visitation of one or more ladies, who relieve the suffering of the needy, and solicit donations to the Association of those whose circumstances allow them to give it."

The people of the Northwest have acquired most practical ideas respecting sanitary measures and life-saving. Their "Onion Circulars" and "Potato Circulars" have produced practical results, which, as Inspector Warriner has said, have modified history. The following extract from the last [April, 1863,] report of the Branch illustrates the spirit of their appeals:

"An urgent appeal is again made to the people of the Northwest for vegetables, pickles, dried and canned fruit, and other anti-scorbutics, for the army of Gen. Grant. Already scurvy has extensively manifested itself among those war-worn veterans, who only know defeat when attacked by the fearful diseases of army life, and speedy and abundant shipments of vegetables can alone save them from alarming sickness and mortality.

They are encamped hundreds of miles from their base of supplies—the country around them is literally laid waste, and furnishes no vegetable diet, and no variety even to their daily rations, so that the dreaded appearance of scurvy has been almost inevitable.

"The Sanitary Commission has moved immediately to remedy this evil. From Louisville, Cincinnati, and Chicago, large shipments of vegetables have already been forwarded, and these are to be followed by others, as fast as circumstances will allow. We have sent Circulars to our auxiliaries throughout the Northwest, calling earnestly for large donations of anti-scorbutics, to which we hope generous responses will be given. Wisconsin has promptly answered the appeal by large shipments of pickles, sour-krout, vegetables, and dried fruit, sent through the Milwaukee Aid Society, and we are notified that larger quantities are forthcoming. We hear also of shipments on the way from Michigan, Illinois, and Iowa, while in Chicago, the ever-generous Board of Trade has moved in the matter by a subscription to be exclusively applied to the purchase of anti-scorbutics."

"The success of our arms depends largely on the way in which this appeal is answered. We stand listening for the distant clash of arms, and shiver with dread as tidings of battles, with their hundreds slain, are flashed over the wires, but we forget that the diseases of camp and army life are more fatal to our brave fellows than the bullets of their Southern foes. They are now called to cope with one of the most formidable of these diseases, and it is for the people of the Northwest to reinforce them, largely and speedily, that they may not suffer overwhelming defeat in the unequal contest. Let not this appeal be unheeded, but send forward without delay, in quantities commensurate with the fearful need, every variety of vegetable that can be collected, and every species of pickle that can be manufactured, as remedies for the sick, and preventives to illness for the well."

This appeal is accompanied by, and seems to be based upon, a very practical report of a Medical Director in the Army of the Mississippi.

Officers of the Northwestern Branch.—E. B. McCagg, President; Rev. Wm. W. Patton, Vice President; H. E. Seelye, Recording Secretary; Cyrus Bentley, Corresponding Secretary; E. W. Blatchford, Treasurer; Wesley Munger, B. F. Raymond, J. K. Botsford.

Associate Managers.—Mrs. A. H. Hoge, Mrs. D. P. Livermore, Chicago; Mrs. E. C. Henshaw, Ottawa, Ill.; Mrs. J. S. Colt, Milwaukee, Wis.

This history of the good works of this fruitful Branch of the Commission would fill a volume by itself. But a brief notice of its great Fair is all we will add to this notice of those works of patriotism and love.

On the 1st of September last (1863), a preliminary meeting of delegates from Soldiers' Aid Societies and Union Leagues of the four Northwestern States convened at Chicago, to consider plans for a great Fair that had been proposed by the Governors of those States, and the chief officers of twenty-two of the leading Societies and Leagues. It was immediately decided by the delegates in convention, that the Sanitary Fair be opened on the 27th of October, and that, if possible, $25,000 should be realized from its sales. It was a novel experiment, but the hearts of the people were quickly aroused with sympathy for its humane objects, so that when the Fair had closed it was found that not $25,000, but nearly $90,000, had been received in cash, besides much valuable property remaining unsold!

The history of that marvellous and significant union of the hearts of the Northwest in the *pioneer* of the Sanitary Fairs, cannot be given in these pages, but the following simple incidents will well illustrate how deeply the spirit of the Fair and of home-love for the soldier and the flag, permeated the popular mind:

"The contributions to the Fair, to be sold for the benefit of our sick and wounded soldiers, were large, were munificent, but it was this tone of deep-seated earnestness which was largest. It was not merely what men and women said and did, but the *way* the the thing was done, which carried with it this impression of wholesale generosity of spirit. Delicately wrought articles, such as usually adorn the tables of Fairs, the work of ladies' hands, were not wanting; but then the farmers from miles and miles around, kept coming in with their wagons by twenties, and fifties, and hundreds, loaded down with their bulky farm produce; others came leading horses, or driving before them cows, or oxen, or mules, which they contributed instead of money, of which, perhaps, they had none; others brought live poultry which had been fed for months by the poor man's door; they brought this because they must bring something, and this was all they had. Some wagons were loaded from rich dairies, with butter and cheese by the ton. Then came great loads of hay from some distant farm, followed by others just as large from farms farther off. The mechanics brought their machines, and gave them in, one after another;—mowing machines, reapers, threshing machines, planters, pumps, fanning-mills—until a new building, a great storehouse, had to be erected to receive them; and here were ploughs, and stoves, and furnaces, and mill-stones, and nails by the hundred kegs, and wagons, and carriage springs,—and axes, and plate glass, and huge plates of wrought iron, (one the largest that was ever rolled from any rolling-mill in the world,) block tin and enameled leather, hides, boxes of stationery, and cases of boots, cologne by the barrel, native wine in casks, purified coal-oil by the thousand gallons—a mountain howitzer, a steel breech-loading cannon, a steam-engine made by the working men in one of manufactories of engines in Chicago.

"Then loaded wagons came in long processions, toiling into the city from far-off country places, bearing marks of frontier service, and the horses or mules, together with the drivers themselves, most of them told of wear. Many of them were sun-burnt men, with hard hands and rigid features; and a careless observer would have said that there was surely nothing in those wagons, as they passed, to awaken any sentiment. Yet something there was about it all, which brought tears to the eyes of hundreds, as the old farmers with their heavy loads toiled by. Among the crowd of spectators there was noticed a broad-shouldered Dutchman, with a face expressive of anything but thought or feeling; he gazed at this singular procession as it passed,—the sun-burnt farmers, and the long, narrow wagons, and the endless variety of vegetables and farm produce,—he gazed there as these men, with their sober faces and their homely gifts, passed one by one, until when, finally, the last wagon had moved by, this stolid, lethargic-looking man "broke down" with a flood of tears, and could say nothing and do nothing but seize upon the little child whom he held by the hand, and hug her to his heart, trying to hide his manly tears behind her floating curls."

The sons of such a people will triumph, or die in the battles they fight. Such earnestness and unity of purpose in their homes, gives strength to the soldiers in the field.

Other Auxilary Associations.—In New Haven, Hartford, Albany, Troy, Utica, Syracuse, Elmira, Rochester, Newark, N. J., Columbus, Ohio; Baltimore, Md.; Washington; New Orleans, and other central places, active aid is rendered to the Sanitary Commission's Supply Department by means of well organized Auxiliary Societies of Aid. Indeed, the network of these Auxiliaries and their primary tributaries now extends to almost every town and neighborhood in all the loyal States.*

---

* *The "Western Sanitary Commission," St. Louis.*—This organization, though independent of the National Commission, has continued to be an important auxiliary in the great work of relief. It sprang into existence under the philanthropic and loyal leadership of Rev. Wm. G. Eliot, Mr. J. E. Yeatman, and other patriotic citizens of St. Louis, during dark days in the autumn of 1861, when, as a popular writer has said, "one-half the cannon planted on the forts for defence of the city were pointed *at* the city, to keep in awe the enemies within, and when the Ladies' Union Aid Society was almost a secret movement."

The noble-hearted men and women who braved the obloquy of the hour, and when the wounded arrived from Springfield and Rolla, famished, and in their gore, fed, nursed, and provided hospitals and care for them, at once became the trusted friends of the military authorities, and received a special commission from Gen. Fremont to continue and systematize such work.

The Commission consists of the following persons: James E. Yeatman, President; C. S. Greely, Treasurer; J. B. Johnson, George Partridge, Rev. W. G. Eliot, J. G. Foreman, Secretary.

At present it is devoting much attention to the relief of freedmen and refugees. It also continues its general work of relief in the hospitals of Missouri, and at Vicksburg, Helena, Memphis, and elsewhere. Up to July, 1863, it had expended in cash, $146,464 30, and had distributed "Sanitary Stores" valued at $395,-

Though the brief sketches that have here been presented are designed particularly to illustrate the *plan* by which the Commission's Department of *Relief* is sustained, the record of the works of any one of the principal branches that have been mentioned present something more. They illustrate the affections, thoughtfulness, patriotism, and undenying sympathies of the mothers, wives, and daughters of the Republic. By these things are our homes sanctified in the war that is raging, and by these the battle-worn veteran finds his home made doubly endearing.

The *prevention* of sickness, and of all causes of unnecessary suffering, has been from the first the chief design of the Sanitary Commission's efforts but the requisite means for succor and aid to the sick and wounded have flown in so abundantly and so systematically from the branches and Auxiliaries of Supply, that the Commission has been enabled to carry out plans of Relief which otherwise would have been impossible. The whole system of this co-operative yet spontaneous aid is so simple that school girls readily comprehend it when they form their "busy-bee circles." Is it not a work in which the hand of Providence marks the way of duty?*

---

335 96. Its expenses for distribution are estimated in the last *Report* at 1¼ *per cent*, which corresponds with the estimates of the U. S. San. Com. [See p. 167.]

This humane labor of the St. Louis Commission has truly been "loyal work," and, as has recently been said by a prominent leader in that work, "as things now stand, we can see no reason why the two commissions should not harmonize into one." The work of the St. Louis Commission is spontaneous and fervent, and its advantages to the army and to the world may be increased by the unity that has now become practicable and highly desirable.

---

* The cause of humanity needs no defence, yet its claims are not well understood by those persons who fail to see and commend the object and necessity of voluntary assistance and even of woman's aid in the care of the sick and wounded in the war. Let the simple eloquence of the following statements defend such work.

At the opening of the Sanitary Fair in Washington, President Lincoln, in a brief speech, said:

"The extraordinary war in which we are engaged falls heavily upon all classes of people, but the most heavily upon the soldier. For it has been said, all that a man hath will he give for his life; and while all contribute of their substance, the soldier puts his life at stake, and often yields it up in his country's cause. The highest merit, then, is due the soldier.

"In this extraordinary war, extraordinary developments have manifested themselves, such as have not been seen in former wars, and among these manifestations nothing has been more remarkable than these Fairs, for the relief of suffering soldiers and their families. And the chief agents in these Fairs are the women of America.

"I am not accustomed to the use of language of eulogy; I have never studied the art of paying compliments to women; but I must say that if all that has been said by orators and poets since the creation of the world in praise of women, were applied to the women of America, it would not do them justice for their conduct during this war. I will close by saying, God bless the women of America!"

The system of Aid throughout the land is now essentially one; and the more harmoniously and steadily it is kept in operation the more good will be done by the spontaneous offerings from our homes. The great SANITARY FAIRS—the marvel of the hour—have not only supplied means to meet the great demands for succor when the impending battles are fought, but they have proved how easy it is for warm hearts and ready hands to work in harmony.

"HEADQUARTERS, ARMY OF THE POTOMAC,
"Friday, April 8, 1864.

"L. MONTGOMERY BOND, Esq.:

"Dear Sir,—I have the honor to acknowledge the receipt of your communication of the 6th instant enclosing circulars of the 'Committee on Labor, Incomes, and Revenues' of the Great Central Fair for the United States Sanitary Commission.

"It is hardly necessary for me to assure you that I am with you heart and soul in the great work of benevolence and charity which you have entered on.

"It has been my duty to make inquiry as to the practical working and benefit of the United States Sanitary Commission, and it affords me great pleasure to be able to bear testimony, so far as this army is concerned, to the inestimable benefits and blessings conferred by this noble association on the suffering, sick, and wounded soldiers.

"A few facts in connection with this point may be of use to you.

"At the battle of Gettysburg the number of wounded of our own army alone amounted, by official reports, to thirteen thousand seven hundred and thirteen (13,713); those of the enemy left on the field were estimated by our medical officers as amounting to eight thousand. This would make in all nearly twenty-two thousand suffering beings requiring immediate attention to save life.

"Few people can realize such large numbers, but if you tell them that should they fill and pack your Academy of Music in Philadelphia (which holds, I believe, some thirty-five hundred people) *six times*, and then imagine every soul in this immense crowd wounded, they will have a chance idea of the great work for humanity on the field of Gettysburg.

"Now, although the Government is most liberal and generous in all its provisions for the sick and wounded, yet it is impossible to keep *constantly on hand* either the *personnel* or supplies required in an emergency of this kind.

"In addition to this difficulty at Gettysburg, I was compelled to pursue the retreating foe, and as I expected in a few days to have another battle at some distant point, it was absolutely necessary I should carry away the greater portion of our surgeons and medical supplies, so that the wounded at Gettysburg were in a measure dependant upon such extra assistance as the Government could hastily collect, and upon the generous aid so cheerfully and promptly afforded by the Sanitary and Christian Commissions and the various State and Soldiers' Aid Societies. All the additional aid from every source was here most urgently needed, and it gives me great pleasure to say that, from the reports of my medical officers, I am satisfied the United States Sanitary Commission, as well as the others above mentioned, were fully up to the work before them.

"What has occurred in the past may occur in the future. There is no nobler or holier work of Christian love or charity, and if the voices of the brave soldiers are of any influence, you may rest assured you have their hearty wishes and earnest prayers.

"Most respectfully and truly yours,

"GEORGE G. MEADE,
"Major-General, Commanding Army of the Potomac."

APPENDIX B.

The European Branch of the U. S. Sanitary Commission.

A meeting of American gentlemen was held at the American Consulate, Paris, November 30th, 1863, for the purpose of organizing a Paris Branch of the United States Sanitary Commission.

The Rev. John McClintock, D. D., was duly appointed President, and Mr. James W. Brooks, Vice-Consul of the United States, Secretary *pro tem.*

An Executive Committee was appointed, consisting of the following named gentlemen:

Rev. John McClintock, D. D., (Pastor of the American Chapel, Paris); Mr. John Bigelow, U. S. Consul; Mr. Chas. S. P. Bowles, Boston; Mr. Edward Brooks, Boston; Dr. T. W. Evans, Paris; Mr. Robt. M. Mason, Boston, Mr. Geo. T. Richards, Paris; Mr. J. Phalen, New York; Mr. Wm. H. Thomson, New York; Mr. Henry Wood, Boston.

Such Committee to have general supervision of the action of the Paris Branch, subject to the approval of the Central Board of the Commission, with power to fill its own vacancies.

At a subsequent meeting Dr. McClintock was, on motion, duly elected Chairman of the Committee, and Mr. Wm. B. Bowles Secretary.

It was resolved that the Secretary open a correspondence with American Consuls, and with prominent American citizens residing in Europe, with a view to the extension and increased efficiency of this Branch of the Commission.

Resolved,—That the title of the Branch be "The European Branch of the United States Sanitary Commission."

Mr. Wm. S. Thompson offered his name as one of ten to subscribe five thousand francs each for the objects of the European Branch.

The European Branch has established its headquarters at No. 2 Rue Martel, Paris, and has raised a considerable amount of funds, and shipped to the Sanitary Commission large quantities of hospital supplies.

AUXILIARY SOCIETY ORGANIZED IN LONDON.

(*From the London Star, March* 4, 1864.)

A meeting of Americans was held at the London Tavern yesterday for the furtherance of the interests of the United States Sanitary Commission. The Hon. William M. Evarts, of New York, occupied the chair.

The Chairman said he had great pleasure in taking any part in aid of the organization now to be commenced. He hoped it would be the means of materially assisting the great Sanitary Commission of the United States, and that it would take an important share in its benevolent and charitable labors. The object of the meeting, as they no doubt were made aware through the notice that had been circulated, was the establishment of an auxiliary amongst the Americans of the United Kingdom, so that by concentrated efforts they might take part in the charitable work of alleviating the wants and sufferings of their wounded, sick and dying brethren in America. There was no other claim to its bounty and to its services than the misfortune of the recipients, making no distinction between friend and foe in the administration of its aids. It was natural that the Americans of the United Kingdom should feel a deep interest in such a movement, and that they should not alone continue the assistance they had heretofore given as private individuals, but that they should also desire to make a combined effort to swell the contributions in aid of this important and continued need. To establish an organization for the effecting of that combined effort was the object of the meeting.

Mr. Stevens moved than an organization of Americans in the United Kingdom, as an auxiliary to the United States Sanitary Commission be established, and that an executive committee be appointed with power to fill vacancies and add to their number; with power also to elect officers, appoint sub-committees, and to transact all business in aid of of the Sanitary Commission.

An Executive Committee, consisting of between sixty and seventy well-known American residents in England was appointed; and at a meeting of the Executive Committee of the Organization of Americans in the United Kingdom as an Auxiliary to the United States Sanitary Commission, held at the Palace Hotel, in London, on Saturday, the 5th of March, 1864, the following Officers and Standing Committee were chosen:

President.—Mr. Joshua Bates, 21 Arlington street, W.

Vice-Presidents.—Mr. George Peabody, 22 Old Broad street, E. C.; Mr. C. M. Lampson, 64 Queen street, E. C.; Mr. Alexander Duncan, 7 Prince's Gate, S. W.

Standing Committee.—Mr. C. M. Lampson, 64 Queen street, E. C.; Mr. Russell Sturgis, 8 Bishopsgate street, E. C.; Mr. J. S. Morgan, 22 Old Broad street, E. C.; Mr. E. L. S. Benzon, 32 Nicholas Lane, E. C.; Mr. Henry Stevens, 4 Trafalgar Square, W. C.

Treasurer.—Mr. Henry Starr, 150 Cheapside.

Secretary, pro tem.—Mr. E. C. Fisher, 150 Cheapside.

Bankers.—Messrs. Baring, Bros. & Co., 8 Bishopsgate street; Messrs. George Peabody & Co., 22 Old Broad street; Messrs. Brown, Shipley & Co., Liverpool.

APPENDIX C.

The International Sanitary Conference, and Voluntary Aid in the Sanitary Service of European Armies.—On the 1st of September, 1863, the "Society of Public Usefulness, of Geneva," in Switzerland, issued a circular to the several Governments of Europe, and to leading philanthropists, as well as to chief military authorities, inviting their co-operation at an International Conference, and particularly requesting the representation of the different Governments by delegates, to convene at Geneva the 26th of October. The object of the Conference was, "*to consider the means of providing for the insufficiency of the Sanitary Service of Armies in the Field.*"

The "Geneva Society of Public Usefulness" some time ago appointed a Committee, consisting of General Dufour, M. Moynier, Doctors Appia and Mallnoir, and M. Henri Dunant, to consider the subject, and to prepare the way for such a Conference. Accordingly, the principal governments sent delegates in response of the Committee's invitation, and the last week of October was spent by them in discussing the subject that had so appropriately been brought forward in the leading philanthropic association of central Europe.

The nations of Europe were represented as follows:

M. le Docteur Unger, from Austria (Surgeon-in-Chief of the Austrian Army); Surgeon in-Chief Steiner, from Baden; Surgeon-in-Chief Theodore Dompierre, from Bavaria; Surgeon-in-Chief Dr. Lœffler, from Prussia; Surgeon-in-Chief Dr. Basting, from Holland; Surgeon-in-Chief Don N. A. C. Landa, from Spain; Surgeon-in-Chief Boudier, from France; M. de Preval, from France; M. Chevalier (Consul), from France; Dr. Rutherford (Inspector-General of Hospitals), from England; Mr. Mackenzie, from England; Dr. Oelker, from Hanover; Major Brodruck, from Hesse; M. Capello, from Italy; Prince Henry XIII., from Prussia; Dr. G. Housselle, from Prussia; Capt. Van de Velde, from Holland; Dr. Gunther, from Saxony; Capt. Alex. Kirriew, from Russia; M. E. Essakoff, from Russia; Dr. Schœldberg, from Sweden; Dr. Edling, from Sweden; Dr. Hahn, from Wurtemberg; Dr. Wagner, from Wurtemberg; M. F. De Montmollin, from Switzerland; Dr. Lehmann, from Switzerland; Dr. Briere, from Switzerland; M. F. De G. Montmollin, from Switzerland; Professor Landoz, from Switzerland; M. Moratel, from Switzerland; Dr. Engelhardt, from Switzerland; M. M. General Dufour, President; Henri Dunant, Secretary.

The questions submitted to the Conference had reference mainly *to battle-field relief*, by means of Voluntary Aid, and notwithstanding the full presentation of military considerations, that have until now prevented the recognition of such supplementary assistance, the Conference unanimously very strongly sustained all the claims which had been put forward by the philanthropic men who invited the meeting.

The two leading questions discussed were:

1st. *Is Voluntary Aid for the succor of the wounded in battles practicable, and is it desirable ?*

2d. *Shall neutrality and full military protection be asked from all nations, in time of war, for the wounded, their surgeons, and all persons and things employed for their succor ?*

These questions were not new, but they were put forth and discussed by men familiar with war and battle-scenes; and all the subordinate and most practical questions relating to the required improvements of ambulance systems, and the more immediate means for relieving the wounded, were discussed under the influence of truly humane and patriotic sentiments. Said General Dufour: "Noble and generous is the purpose of those Governments which have not hesitated to respond to the appeals which have been addressed to them in the name of suffering humanity. Too long have the shouts of triumph stifled the groans of those who had purchased it with their blood; the roaring of the cannon which announced the victory has drowned the plaintive cry of those who, after having fought for it, ask as their only reward a litter to bear them from the scene of carnage, and the joyous ringing of the bells has deadened the heroes' funeral knell of agony. The Surgeon and the Sister of Charity were the only witnesses of their suffering. Such scenes possess but few attractions for amateurs, and the multitude pursue with their applauses those who return with their brows crowned with laurels, without giving one thought or regret to those unfortunate ones whose casualties are summed up in a brief announcement appended to the last line of the bulletin of the battle."

All the propositions which the Committee of the Geneva Society had submitted having been fully discussed by the Conference, the following conclusions were reached and adopted, on the fourth day of the session:

"The International Conference, desirous to render aid to the wounded in those cases where the army sanitary service is insufficient, adopted the following resolutions:

"1. That in each country there be a committee whose mission is to assist in time of war, if it is required, in providing, by all means in its power, for the sanitary wants of the armies. The committee will organize itself in such manner as shall seem most useful and convenient.

"2. Sections, without limit in number, may be formed for the purpose of aiding this committee, and which shall act under its general direction.

"3. It shall be the duty of the committee to place itself *en rapport* with the government of its own country, in order that its service may be received, if there is need.

"4. In time of peace, the committees and the sections shall look for the best means for rendering themselves really useful in time of war, especially in preparing material help of all kinds (*secours materiels de tout genre*), and in endeavoring to organize and instruct volunteer nurses (*infirmiers volontaires*).

"5. In the event of war, the committees of the belligerent nations shall furnish, according to their means, relief (*secours*) to the respective armies; their particular duty is to organize and set at work the volunteer nurses (*infirmiers volontaires*), and to prepare, in accordance with the military authority, the places in which the wounded shall be attended.

"They may solicit the co-operation of the committee of neutral nations.

"6. Upon application and with consent of the military authorities, the committees shall send the *infirmiers volontaires* upon the battle-field; they shall, at such times, be under the direction of the chief military commander.

"7. The *infirmiers volontaires* who follow the army must be provided by their respective committees with all necessary means for their sustenance.

"8. That, in every country, they wear, as uniform, a white band upon the arm, with a red cross.

"9. The committees and sections of the various countries may assemble an International Congress to communicate the results of their experience, and to consult upon the measures to be pursued in the interest of the work.

"10. The exchange of communications between the committees of the several nations shall be provisionally made through the committee at Geneva.

"*Besides the above resolutions, the Conference promulgates the following recommendations:*

"A. Let the governments grant their highest protection to the committees of relief which shall be formed, and facilitate, as much as possible, the fulfillment of their mission.

"B. Let *neutrality* be proclaimed in time of war, by belligerent nations, for the ambulances and the hospitals, and let it be equally admitted, in the most complete manner, for the *personnel* of the sanitary staff (*personnel sanitaire officiel*), for the *infirmiers volontaires*, for the country people who may go to assist the wounded, and for the wounded themselves.

"C. Let a uniform distinctive badge (*signe*) be recognized for the sanitary corps of all armies, or at least for the persons of the same army who are attached to that service. Let a uniform flag (*un drapeau identique*) be also adopted for ambulances and hospitals in all countries."

These conclusions, and the debates that preceded them in the Conference, have awakened profound interest throughout Europe.

It appears that it was no part of the design of the Geneva Conference to take up any of the great questions relating to the sanitary care of armies excepting those leading points that relate to the succor of the men who fall in battle—the humane and sanitary provision for the ambulance and field-hospital service; and upon the questions that were raised respecting the necessity or duty of great improvements in that service, the delegates expressed most decided and harmonious sentiments. The presence of such veteran campaigners and military surgeons as MM. Boudier, Unger, Basting, and Lœffler, enabled the most experienced class of delegates to present in a strong, but true, light all the essential difficulties that stand in the way of successfully utilizing the offering—*personal and material*—of voluntary aid for the relief and care of the wounded in active armies. The positions taken by the ablest and most experienced members of the Geneva Conference, strongly corroborate and sustain the established policy and works of the United States Sanitary Commission.

Henri Dunant, a citizen of Geneva, who was travelling as a tourist in the regions occupied by the vast armies that met at Solferino and Magenta, had his soul so stirred by the scenes of carnage and woe that he witnessed there immediately upon the cessation of the conflict, that he deemed it a duty to humanity to offer such volunteered aid as he was able to organize and put into operation upon the spur of the occasion. The record of that timely and merciful work is in the hearts of the multitude of mutilated sufferers who, but for the succor which that noble man and his obedient helpers rendered, would not now be able to recount the scenes of the terrible battle-field of Solferino.

Thus, naturally, this noble-hearted and earnest man, M. Dunant, was led, by his brief and thrilling experience, to reflect upon the practicability of calling into existence an organized national and *international* scheme for applying the services of trained corps of voluntary nurses, so as to secure a uniform system, rendered by study and experience superior, if possible, to the hastily extemporized band of voluntary attendants, organized and led by him at Solferino. The unanimous approval was given, in the deliberations of the Conference, to the proposed plan for encouraging the timely preparation of *materiel* for the succor of the wounded, and especially for effectually *organizing* the humane endeavors and charities of the people. Said the distinguished representative of the Government and Army of Prussia: "Behold, gentlemen, the great field of activity for permanent 'Societies of Relief,' organized in time of peace, and prepared beforehand with all suitable means to supply the work of official authorities, and to satisfy the wishes of a truly religious philanthropy."

The medical delegates at the Geneva Conference joined heartily with the non-medical delegates in all the debates and purposes of the Conferences. Their sentiments in reference to such works of live-saving are happily expressed by a French physician, Dr. Henri Favre, who, as a public journalist, has earnestly advocated the objects of the Conference. He writes: "The physician has science; let him confer with the benevolent and sympathetic; let him encourage them with his approbation, and enlighten them with his counsels. *Knowledge will thus heighten the value of benevolence, and the result will be beautiful.*" And justly does that eloquent physician ask: "Is it not the highest mission of the true physician to aid with his professional knowledge the endeavors of the benevolent and self sacrificing?" Such appears to have been the spirit not only of the medical delegates at the International Conference, but of the various Sovereigns and Ministers of War who sent messages of counsel and encouragement.

The effort to secure absolute neutrality and a fraternal recognition for the wounded and for all who are legitimately engaged in providing for them among belligerents, will lead to most important results. Some of the arguments presented on this point in the Conference the reader will peruse with interest. Dr. Landa, Surgeon-Major, and delegate from the sanitary corps of the Spanish army, said:

"I congratulate the Conference that they have included *the wounded* among those for whom *neutrality* is demanded. As a sanitary officer of a permanent army," Dr. Landa, as far as he was concerned, "could never have accepted this exemption of the person of military surgeons from risks, by neutrality, if the wounded were not also allowed the same exemption, for it is their duty to share the fate of those under their care. It is undoubtedly a principle which has been generally admitted in time of war, that everything remaining upon the ground occupied by the conqueror, belongs to the conqueror, still, as a wounded man is properly committed to the care of the surgeon alone, hostile generals have not unfrequently mutually agreed to restore the wounded to liberty. During the session of this Conference, the diplomatic treaty made during the last century between Prussia and France, for the neutrality of sanitary service, has been cited upon this point. This treaty is not an isolated case, since examples may be found in the history of more remote times. In the '*order of St. John of Jerusalem*,' there exist analogous souvenirs of the Sultan Saladin, and may we not reasonably expect that in this civilized age, the sovereigns of Europe would not willingly appear less humane and generous, than many centuries ago was a Saracen Sultan of the desert."

An experienced surgeon of the Austrian army, said he would call attention to the fact that—

"Those persons who comprise the sanitary corps in the field, are military persons and bear arms, which they only lay aside during the execution of their mission to the sick and wounded. They may be taken prisoners wherever they are found, since this is the right of war, and as injury is inflicted upon a hostile army by depriving it of its stores of supplies and provisions, so also it may be made to suffer if deprived of the whole or a part of its sanitary corps. Upon the field of battle, however, those places where they deposit their arms to take care of the wounded, should be considered by the enemy as sacred; and to effect this, an international flag of a particular color should be raised; and since this Conference has proposed a white badge with a red cross to designate the voluntary nurses, let all places where the wounded and their attendant surgeons are found be also indicated by a flag of this color. All nations have now adopted a flag for their ambulances, but each has a flag of a different color. It is white in Austria, red in France, yellow in Spain, in other countries it is black, and the soldiers composing the armies are only familiar with the color of their own ambulances. This difficulty would be remedied if a white flag with a red cross should float over the ambulances of all the armies of Europe. In his [Dr. Unger's] opinion, the enemy must retain the right *to make prisoners of military surgeons*; but he must respect their persons, and the places of asylum and succor upon the field of battle, the ambulance, and the hospital in the rear, indicated by the national flag, shall be considered neutral.

Dr. Mannoir said he could not appreciate the motive which induces Dr. Unger to suppose that the neutrality of sanitary corps cannot be accepted. The history of war has never demonstrated that an army has been destroyed, or a sovereign compelled to make peace, because such army or sovereign had lost its sanitary corps. The only result of the loss of the sanitary staff and supplies is, that the wounded cannot receive proper care. It is the soldier who suffers, and this is of no advantage to the hostile army, as no general has ever hesitated to engage in battle from such a motive. Moreover, *Dr. Mannoir* objected to what can only be considered a mere hypothesis on the part of Dr. Unger, for unfortunately neither this Conference nor military surgeons possess the authority to decide this question, and M. Mannoir affirms, as his personal opinion, the entire innocence of the neutrality of the sanitary service. He would, therefore, propose the following amendment;

"Conference, before adjourning, unanimously recommends:

"That the several States of Europe co-operate in urging the *neutrality* of persons who compose the sanitary staff of armies in the field, including in this neutrality not only the staff actually in service, but the corps of voluntary nurses, civilians who may go to assist in the care of the wounded, and the wounded themselves. Conference believes that this decision, while it does not modify the results of war, would be worthy of this age of progress and humanity."

The humane labors of the Order of "St. John of Jerusalem," the example of M. Dunant's hastily improvised corps of *infirmiers volontaires*, and the beautiful illustration of woman's sympathies and timely methods of succor under the guidance of Lady Helena Paulowna, during the Russian campaign in the Crimea, and more recently in Poland, were happily quoted as examples of the nature and practicability of the voluntary aid which should be given to the sick and wounded in time of war.* And the Russian Minister of War, Lieut.-General Milutin, in an official communication to the Conference when in Session, states that special committees or "Commissions are now organized and at work in St. Petersburg, for the introduction into the Sanitary service of the army, of all the improvements (*ameliorations*) that modern science can seek out in time of peace against the time of War."

The Sovereigns of Europe are becoming aware of the economical value of the life and health of their people, and particularly in their armies, and while the war-clouds have been gathering on the Continent, the people

---

* The ancient order of St. John, here mentioned, is at present doing much for the mitigation of human suffering. During the month of March, 1864, it has established and fully furnished a large military hospital at Altonia, for the wounded of all classes of the belligerents in the Danish war. The order also has the entire care of eight hospitals in Prussia, seven in Germany, and one in Beirout.

The system of Field and Hospital succor that was founded by the Grand Duchess Helena Paulowna during the Crimean campaign, has done immense service for humanity, and has been everywhere favored by the Russian military authorities. More than two hundred of its trained women-nurses were on duty in the Crimea, where, says an eminent surgeon in that war, "They were indefatigable in nursing the wounded, not only in the hospitals of Sebastopol and Simpheropol and in the ambulances, but also close to the batteries in the midst of most appaling scenes, actually exposed to shot and shell." They also attended the wounded and sick in the land transports to the rear, and back to Moscow and St. Petersburg. The distinguished Professor Perigoff describes the services of those devoted women as being above all praise, their heroism, and endurance, and discretion, as marvellous, and their assistance to the medical officers of priceless value. The "Letter of Instructions" under which these women enter this service of Relief opens as follows: "In the name of Jesus Christ our Lord, in perfect charity and self-devotion, zealously to assist the medical authorities in the care of the sick and wounded, and also to strengthen the patients under their sufferings by Christian consolation."

In this spirit these persons have continued their labors since their organization, and, after large numbers of them had died from fevers and hardships in the Crimea and the Russian hospitals, they entered upon a similar field of labors in St. Petersburg, among the needy classes; and more recently their aid has been successfully given to the sick and wounded belligerents of both parties in the Polish war.

have humanely undertaken to mitigate the woes they fear. And while it has fallen to the lot of the UNITED STATES SANITARY COMMISSION to present the first complete example of voluntary means applied "to provide for the insufficiency of the Sanitary service in armies," the development and progress of similar work in Europe is a subject in which all philanthrophic minds feel mutually interested. The present state of this good work in other nations will be best stated in this place by quoting the following brief extracts from recent European journals:

In "*La Nation Suisse*," a daily journal in Geneva, of February 7th, (1864,) it is stated that "the recommendations of the International Conference have already been *officially adopted* by many European governments, the Federal Council of the Swiss Confederacy being first on the list."

"Prussia treats the question of neutrality diplomatically, and Denmark is disposed to favor an international convention for the consideration of this subject. In Germany the suggestions of M. Dunant have everywhere enlisted the warmest sympathies of the people, and the same is true in Sweden, where committees of ladies have been formed to prepare, collect and forward woolen socks and other warm garments for the Danish soldiers.

"In anticipation of the war which threatens so many portions of Europe, it becomes the duty of everyone to disseminate as widely as possible the humane suggestions contained in the work entitled, *souvenir de Soferino.*

"Let us still, however, indulge the hope that the time will come when the blood of the soldier shall no longer moisten the earth which the sweat from the brow of the laborer should alone moisten."

In "*Le Moniteur de l'Armée*," a leading military journal in France, of February 11th, 1864, we find the following statement, including the copy of a letter from the French Emperor to M. Dunant:

"Sir,—The EMPEROR has acquainted himself with the resolutions adopted by the International Conference recently convened at Geneva, under the presidency of GENERAL DUFOUR, for the purpose of considering the question of international efforts for the relief of soldiers wounded upon the field of battle.

"*His Majesty heartily approves of the object of the Conference and the resolutions adopted for its accomplishment.* He desires to co-operate with you in your work by authorizing the formation of the relief committee which you propose to appoint at Paris, and wishes you to be assured of all the sympathy with which he regards this effort.

"The EMPEROR has, moreover, commissioned me to communicate to the Marshal Minister of War his desire that he should authorize the appointment of some officers of high rank to a place upon the committee that you propose to organize.

"I pray you to accept my assurances of devotion,

"The Colonel Aid-de-Camp,

FAVRE."

"His Majesty, the Emperor of Russia, has authorized His Imperial Highness the Grand Duke Constantine to assume the direction of the committee under the patronage of their Imperial Majesties.

"In Saxony, His Majesty the King and his Ministers, and many influencial citizens, have enlisted heartily in the work.

"In Wurtemburg the committee which has been organized at Stuttgart, under the patronage of the royal family, has succeeding in forming auxiliary committees of ladies throughout the country.

"In Spain, His Royal Highness, the Most Serene Infant Don Sebastian of Bourbon and Braganza, Grand Prior of the Order of Saint John of Jerusalem, in the language of Castile, enthusiastically favors the idea, and has solicited authority from Her Majesty the Queen to accomplish for Spain (out of respect for the resolutions of the Conference of Geneva) what His Royal Highness Prince Charles of Prussia has done for this work at Berlin, for the Bailiwick of Brandenburg. The Spanish Marshals and Generals heartily approve of this proposal.

"The Minister of War of the Kingdom of Denmark has officially informed the committee at Geneva that his government cordially approved the resolutions adopted at the International Conference of October.

"On the other hand, His Majesty the King of Prussia, who takes the liveliest interest in everything relating to this subject, has, by his Ministers, recently put to a practical use the question of neutrality. The Knights of Saint John of Jerusalem have already erected at Altona a large hospital for the soldiers who may be wounded during the war with Denmark."

The Danish Ministers and the King of Prussia having officially approved the resolutions of the Conference at Geneva, M. Henri Dunant as secretary of the International Committee, has solicited Denmark and the German Powers to conclude a mutual agreement upon this important question of humanity.

In the "*Cologne Gazette*," in January, 1864, we find the following statement:

"It is very desirable that without delay voluntary associations should be made by the public to furnish the German troops, now in arms against Denmark, with clothing suited to the cold weather. Their supply is not enough to protect them against this enemy. The subjoined letter from the Prussian Minister of War is a confession, and a very significant one too, although not nearly broad enough in its statements. The association in Halle to supply the Prussian troops sent to Holstein with warm winter clothing, asked the Minister of War whether he thought their purpose commendable and useful. He answered: 'It is true that it is the duty of this department to give our troops clothing suited for winter; but it is equally true that owing to the suddenness with which we have been obliged to move our army, it will be difficult to give the men a full supply of proper clothing, unless we receive the patriotic help of all good citizens. For these reasons I shall be very grateful to your association for a full and prompt supply of woolen socks, gloves, under-shirts and drawers, and for articles for hospital use; and those who have money to give, can direct it in no way better than through your society.' "

The following is a copy of the official call, here alluded to, for such aid by the Prussian Government:

"Our columns are now moving towards Lubeck, to be ready to enter Holstein. In consequence of excessive cold weather the men suffer terribly for want of warm clothing. Many of the soldiers have no woolen socks, and only a little straw or a few rags with which to fill their shoes, and are in great danger of having their toes frost-bitten. Very few of them have shirts of any kind, or nearly enough under-clothing to protect them from the cold. I propose collecting articles of this kind, and money to purchase and have made others as fast as possible, to be forwarded to the army. I therefore appeal to all who are friends of our soldiers.

"BREITENBACH, ROYAL COMMISSIONER."

These events are just now transpiring in one of the richest and most complete military Governments in the world. Who, then, will doubt that the UNITED STATES SANITARY COMMISSION is an essential Aid to our National Cause as a beneficient agency, which, under Divine Providence, is a saver of precious lives?

APPENDIX D.

THE SANITARY COMMISSION'S PUBLICATIONS.

Three classes of publications are comprised in the Commission's printed documents:

I. *Reports and Essays relating to Military Hygiene, Medicine, and Surgery.*

II. *Special Reports upon the regular labors of the Commission relating to Sanitary work, and to the business of Relief.*

III. *Circulars, and various Public Statements; also two semi monthly periodicals.*

1. The Sanitary and Medical Publications.—Medical *Monographs.*—This series now numbers twenty monographs upon the most important subjects in military hygiene, medicine, and surgery. Several of them have passed through many editions, and they all possess permanent and acknowledged value, as being among the most practical and reliable contributions to the literature of the medical profession; and to the ever-changing, ever-enlarging, medical staff of the volunteer forces, they are of inestimable value. The following catalogue of the titles of this class of the Sanitary Papers will best explain their purpose. These Medical Essays are designated by letters, and have been published with the following titles:

Medical Monographs.

An Introductory Paper on Employment of Anæsthetics in Military Surgery.

A. Report on Military Hygiene and Therapeutics.

B. Directions to Army Surgeons on Field of Battle.

C. Rules for Preserving the Health of the Soldier.

D. Report on the Use of Quinine as a Prophylactic.

E. Report on Vaccination in Armies.

F. Report on Amputations.

G. Report on Amputations through the Foot and at the Ankle-joint.

H. Report on Venereal Diseases, with special reference to Practice in the Army and Navy.

J. Report on Pneumonia.

K. Report on Continued Fevers.

L. Excision of Joints for Traumatic Causes.

M. Report on Dysentery.

N. Report on Scurvy.

O. Report on Nature and Treatment of Fractures in Military Surgery.

P. Report on Nature and Treatment of Miasmatic Fevers.

Q. Report on Nature and Treatment of Yellow Fever.

R. Hemorrhage from Wounds.

S. Control and Prevention of Infectious Diseases in Camps, Transports, and Hospitals.

To the great number of medical officers who have entered upon service in the field, this well-considered gift of a portable professional *Library* has been of inestimable benefit; and there can be no doubt that it has been the means of greatly improving the medical and hygienic service in our armies. The fact should here be mentioned, that the Medical Bureau has adopted a liberal plan for supplying to every military surgeon a larger and better assortment of standard medical books than was formerly allowed. But the Sanitary Commission's *Monographs* are indispensable to the inexperienced and to the overtasked medical officer, and their intrinsic merits have already won very high encomiums from the medical press at home, and in foreign countries.

We have not space in this place for the catalogue of the current publications which the Commission has continued to issue, upon the ordinary business, results, and plans of the various branches of the work, as it progresses. These publications are numbered, usually, according to the dates of issue, and may be regarded as constituting a kind of record in outline of the progress of the Commission's work. The publications of the 2*d Class* are numbered as *permanent* documents, and several of them have passed through large editions. These now number between 70 and 80.

The 3*d Class* of publications comprises all the ordinary and transient printing that is found necessary in management of the affairs of the Commission. Under this head may also be included the publication of the "*Sanitary Reporter*" and the *Sanitary Commission Bulletin.*

APPENDIX E.

A complete Example of Sanitary Science practically applied in Camps and Hospitals.—" That the prevention of disease is possible, but its suppression difficult and uncertain,"* was the very first postulate laid down by the United States Sanitary Commission at the commencement of its labors. Acting upon this principle by most practical methods, and with an unflinching determination not to be thwarted in the purpose to insure for the soldier in camp and in hospital all the means of Sanitary protection which the combined intelligence and liberality of the government and the people could apply, the results are such as will forever be remembered with gratitude by our people and by the philanthropic minds of every country.

The *first complete example* of practical application of *sanitary science* in camps and hospitals during a long war, is now being wrought out in our Federal army. But Great Britain, in the recent campaign of its army in China, has furnished a very instructive illustration of the life-saving power of the improved sanitary system that has been established in the British forces since the Crimean campaign, and we cannot more forcibly illustrate the practical value of that improved system than by quoting the following statements from Miss Nightengale's tribute to Sir Silney Herbert's administration and the reform that he officially ordered. She presents

---

General Instructions for Camp Inspectors; Sanitary Commission, Document

A writer in the *North American Review* states that, "In the Mexican war, our volunteer forces lost, from disease alone, at the rate of 152 per 1,000 per annum, and the regulars at the rate of 81, from the same cause. In Wellington's entire campaign in the Peninsula, his losses from disease were 113 per 1,000 strength. In times of peace, our regular army lost annually at the rate of 26 per 1,000 strength; and the British infantry, serving at home, annually lost about 18 per 1,000 from disease, until Lord Herbert's great reforms were instituted; but by those reforms, which mainly consist in supplying fresh air and an improved diet, the annual loss is reduced to about 8½ per 1,000 strength; and the entire loss in the British army during the past four years, from *all* diseases, is less than the annual loss previously from disease of the *lungs only*."—(See *North American Review*, April, 1864.)

the statistical evidence that even during the *first three years* experience of that reform, viz., 1859, 1860 and 1861, the mortality among the "infantry of the line serving at home" was diminished from 17.90 deaths to 1,000 living, to 8.56 to the 1,000, which is less than half the standard death-rate previous to the reform.* Truly does MISS NIGHTINGALE remark that the "faithful records of all wars are records of preventable suffering, disease and death. It is needless to illustrate this truth, for we all know it. But it is only from our latest sorrow, the Crimean catastrophe, that dates the rise of any sanitary administration in this country," (Great Britain.)

The latest returns of sickness and mortality in the British forces at those permanent stations abroad where the losses have always been quite uniform, present to us the most remarkable results, confirming all that Lord Herbert, Miss Nightingale, and the advocates of Sanitary reform ever claimed, and proving that the work and purpose of the Sanitary Commission of our own army are based upon soundest reasoning and the most philanthropic designs. We quote the following illustration of the latest results of life-saving in the British army by means of simple sanitary improvements in camps, barracks, hospitals, and the care of troops.

> "The last official returns of sickness and mortality among the British forces present the best argument upon this subject. In Jamaica, the death rate from disease has fallen, since the recent reform was carried into effect, from 260 per 1,000 to 20; in Trinidad, from 106 to 0 (in 1860); in Barbadoes, from 58 to 6; in St. Lucia, from 122 to 1; in British Guiana, from 74 to 6; in Canada, from 16 to 10; in Nova Scotia, from 15 to 7; in Newfoundland, from 11 to 4; in Bermuda, from 28 to 8; in Gibraltar, from 11 to 7; in Malta, from 15 to 10; in Ionia, from 15 to 7."*

Here we see the mortality reduced at ten military stations from 70.5 to the 1,000 living, to 6.9. Let us now look at a summary of the results of the British Sanitary Commission's work in the Crimea during the years 1855–6.

For the following brief synopsis of the results of the operations of the British Sanitary Commission in the Crimea, we are indebted to a member of the U. S. Sanitary Commission.

The following tables exhibit the total and comparative statistics of sickness and mortality in the British Army in the Crimean campaign, and the rate per cent. of the diseases and deaths of all the forces, for, 1st. A period of six months just previous to and at the commencement of the works of

---

* See *North American Review*, April, 1864.

the Sanitary Commission, viz.: from January to June, 1855; and, 2d. A period of six months, from January to June, 1856, after those works for Sanitary improvement had produced their legitimate results. [All sickness and deaths in the Medical Staff, among Commissioned Officers, the Land Transport, and the Mounted Corps, *as well as all martial wounds or deaths in battle,* are excluded from these tables; also nearly 5,000 cases of sickness that failed to be properly registered during the early period of the campaign.]

Return showing total sickness and mortality from Disease in the British army in the East, from April 10th, 1854, to July 1st, 1856.

NUMBER OF CASES OF SICKNESS.		DEATHS.
From Fevers....................	31,230	3,452
" Diseases of the Lungs.....	12,382	644
" " " Bowels....	55,765	5,950
" Cholera....................	7,574	4,502
" Scurvy....................	2,096	178
" Ophthalmia	3,301	....
" Ulcers and Boils..........	12,542	37
" All other diseases.........	37,583	3,295
Total number of cases......	162,473	18,058

The rate per cent. of the entire Army—sick and dying from disease—during two periods of six months each, as above stated.

	1855.		1856.	
	Rate p. ct. sick.	Rate p. ct. of deaths	Rate p. ct. sick.	Rate p. ct. of deaths
January.....	34.8	9.78	9.3	—.18
February	23.0	8.16	7.7	—.08
March.......	19.3	4.68	8.1	—.09
April.........	14.3	1.86	7.-	—.07
May..........	16.2	1.69	6.-	—.06
June	28.3	2.65	3.6	—.03
Total.......	135.9	28.82	41.7	—.5 *

* This (—.5) shows that the mortality during those last six months was only half of *one per cent.*, or, at the rate of exactly *one per cent. per annum*,—which would give ten deaths to every 1,000 men in service.

Thus the fact is demonstrated, by the most unerring statistics, that during the period beginning eight months after the commencement of reforms by the Sanitary Commission in the Crimea, the rate of sickness in the army was reduced to *less* than *one-third* of that which prevailed until those reforms were inaugurated, the exact ratio of that decrease being as 1359 to 417, or $\frac{139}{453}$! While the mortality—which is the more significant test of the utility of Sanitary improvements—presents the marvelous contrast of 28.82 to —.5, or 5764 to 100!! *i. e.*, the rate of mortality from *disease* in the army, after the work of Sanitary reform had been fully inaugurated, was *less than one fifty-seventh* of the rate of mortality that prevailed during the same length of time preceding the reform.

It is worthy of remark that, while the statistics show that considerable sickness continued to prevail during the latter or improved period, the records of the Army Hospitals exhibit the fact that the particular diseases that were *most remarkably diminished* were those which Sanitary measures are known to prevent or greatly diminish, viz., the Zymotic diseases, such as fevers, and those maladies that are so largely represented in the list given in the foregoing table.

That this wonderful improvement in health, which was the salvation of the British forces in the Crimea, was directly and positively dependent upon *Sanitary works and preventive hygienic measures*, is a fact confessed alike by the military and medical officers of those forces.

And in further corroboration of that fact, it should be stated that while the British troops were thus being rescued from the fatal diseases that had threatened to make their encampment a Golgotha, the French camps, though located more favorably, and within a rifle's range of the British, continued to grow more and more sickly during all the time of the grand improvement in the camps of their allies. In the latter, the best Sanitary regulations were introduced and rigidly enforced by a Sanitary Board, while in the former (the French camps) such regulations were utterly neglected, "until," as a distinguished historian of the war has said, "with the French army, *peace become a military necessity.*"

The Crimean Sanitary Commission consisted of three gentlemen, viz., Dr. Sutherland, Dr. Milroy, and Mr. Rawlenson, a civil enginneer. *Each of these Commissioners had, for several years, made Sanitary Science and its applications, a special study.* They proceeded to the Crimea in April, 1855, taking with them upwards of thirty skilled assistants and laborers, together with such implements and apparatus as they knew would be required in the ventilation and sewerage of hospitals and barracks, the cleansing and drainage of encampments, and the purification or disinfection of transports and ships. Among these means were pipe tubing, drainage-pipes, filters, ten thousand square feet of perforated zinc plates for ventilation, hinges, pulleys, window fixtures, a ship load of peat charcoal, etc., etc. Immediately upon arrival on the Bosphorus and in the Crimea, the Sanitary works were commenced; first by thorough cleansing, both within and without, the hospitals, barracks, and tents, and in these works nearly one hundred men were employed for many months; old sewers were cleaned and flushed; new drains were made; surface filth, refuse, and decaying materials, by *thousands of cartloads*, were removed, and such sources of offence as could not be *removed* were deeply covered with dry earth and peat charcoal. Water courses, springs, and the water supply were cleansed and controlled; the tents and camping grounds were rigidly inspected and purified, and an abundant supply of fresh air and pure water was everywhere secured in hospital and in camp, and, so far as practicable the diet and general comfort of the soldiers were improved.

The results of this simple and inexpensive labor astonished the world, though Sanitary science has always promised, and its advocates prophesied, just such results.

Says Miss Nightingale, "It is the whole experiment of Sanitary improvement upon a colossal scale. * * * We had, in the first seven months of the Crimean campaign, a mortality of 60 per cent. per annum among the tıoops *from disease alone*; * * * we had in the last six months a mortality not much greater than among our healthy Guards at home."

APPENDIX F.

THE PLAN AND DISTRIBUTION OF PERSONAL SERVICE

IN THE

SANITARY COMMISSION'S WORK.

Explanation of the Diagram.

The *larger circles* represent Departments and Branches of labor.

The *lines* represent lines of Responsibility; each centre from which lines diverge is responsible for the right management of the several Departments and Branches radiating from it.

The duties that are distinctly Medical and Sanitary are associated with the work of Inspectors; but it will be observed that the lines of such duty finally meet the lines of Relief, &c., that flow from other centres of responsibility.

N. B.—The *smaller circles*, as well as the lines, represent Branches and Subdivisions,—not individuals,—and, in most instances, several individual officers and assistants are thus represented on a single line, or at a single ultimate circle of duty.

The Number of Sanitary Officers, Relief Agents, and Assistants.

The average numerical force of the several corps of Inspectors, Relief Agents, and Assistants, under pay by the Commission, has, during the second and third years of the war, been about *two hundred*. But in addition to these men, there is a considerable number of volunteer helpers in the various branches of labor. Men, from the ranks of the army, are also *detailed* occasionally, by their commanding officers, to aid the officers of the Commission in the field. Without such voluntary and military aid the expenditure for labor would be considerably greater than it has been hitherto.

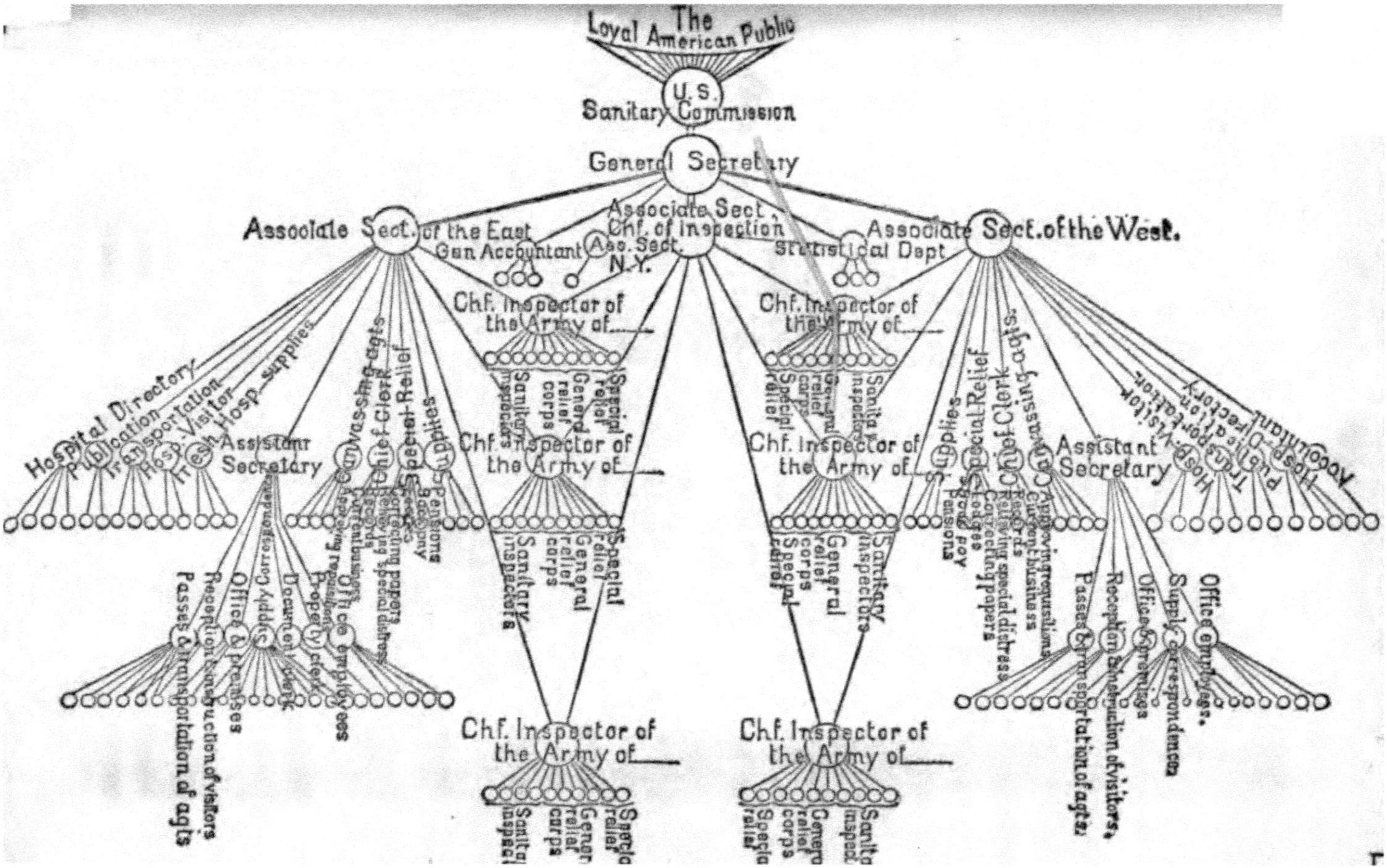

The Loyal American Public
U.S. Sanitary Commission
General Secretary
Associate Sect. of the East
Associate Sect. Chf. of Inspection
Associate Sect. of the West.
Gen Accountant
Ass. Sect. N.Y.
Statistical Dept
Chf. Inspector of the Army of
Special relief
General relief corps
Sanitary inspectors
Hospital Directory
Publication
Transportation
Hosp. Visitor
Fresh Hosp. supplies
Assistant Secretary
Canvassing agts
Chief Clerk
Special Relief
Supplies
Pensions
Back pay
Lodges
Correcting papers
Relieving special distress
Records
Current business
Approving requisitions
Office employees
Property clerk
Document clerk
Supply Correspondence
Office & premises
Reception & instruction of visitors
Passes & transportation of agts

CONTENTS.

INDEX.

CPSIA information can be obtained
at www.ICGtesting.com
Printed in the USA
LVHW022010120422
716028LV00006B/244

9 783752 591644